Other books by Fred Patten

Best in Show: Fifteen Years of Outstanding Furry Fiction (2003)
reprinted as: Furry! The World's Best Anthropomorphic Fiction! (2006)
Watching Anime, Reading Manga:
25 Years of Essays and Reviews (2004)
Already Among Us: An Anthropomorphic Anthology (2012)
The Ursa Major Awards Anthology:
A Tenth Anniversary Celebration (2012)
What Happens Next: An Anthology of Sequels (2013)
Five Fortunes (2014)
Funny Animals and More: From Anime to Zoomorphics (2014)
Anthropomorphic Aliens: An Interstellar Anthology (2014)
The Furry Future: 19 Possible Prognostications (2015)
An Anthropomorphic Century: Stories from 1909 to 2008 (2015)
Cats and More Cats: Feline Fantasy Fiction (2016)
Gods with Fur: And Feathers, Scales (2016)
Furry Fandom Conventions, 1989-2015 (2017)
Dogs of War (2017)
Symbol of a Nation (2017)
Dogs of War II: Aftermath (2017)
What the Fox?! (2018)

Exploring New Places

Edited by Fred Patten

Exploring New Places

Production copyright FurPlanet Productions © 2018
Cover artwork copyright © 2018 by Demicoeur

Published by FurPlanet Productions
Dallas, Texas
www.FurPlanet.com

ISBN 978-1-61450-421-4

First Edition Trade Paperback July 2018

To

Brigadier Sir Hywel Catterwaul, Scratch Sharp, and the four other cats of the Great Cat Expedition, to climb the H.K.P. (Highest Known Peak) in the Kingdom of Catdom

In *Scratch & Co.; the Great Cat Expedition* by Molly Lefebure (Victor Gollancz, September 1968), the oldest novel I know with anthro animal explorers. A British pastiche of Himalayan mountaineering expeditions, with cat Pukka Sahib British explorer Sir Hywel leading (at first) and young Scratch Sharp, Oliver Simpkin, Tybault Brightstone, Dr. Thomas Black, and Felix Mouser; sponsored by the Royal Feline Geographical Society; Manx Scoop and Whiskey Bylines, rival reporters for *The Cat Times* and *Cat's Courier*; rabbit lowland native bearers, terrier upland Sherpa guides, fox hill bandits, and Ranjit Singh, Manx Scoop's mongoose Hindu servant. Jolly good fun.

If you want real animal explorers, the champions are the rats (*Rattus rattus*, the black rat, and *Rattus norvegicus*, the brown rat). Other animals such as sled dogs, and dogs, monkeys, and mice sent into space have been used by man for exploration, but the rats are the most avid explorers on their own for pure curiosity. Other rodent pets such as dormice, gerbils, guinea pigs, hamsters, lemmings, and mice tend to stay in their cages and squeak to be fed. Rats will escape their cages if they can, to explore.

Table of Contents

Introduction

by Fred Patten

Who were the earliest explorers?

When did humanity begin? Apparently somewhere in what is today northeast and east Africa, about three to one million years ago.

Man spread to Europe, Asia, and Oceania from 500,000 to 40,000 years ago, going by the archaeological evidence of fire sites and stone tools. Man crossed over from east Asia to North America via the Bering land bridge which was then above water, about 16,500 years ago.

Why did humanity expand to fill the planet? Population pressure, or curiosity? We may not know.

But the span of recorded history is full of the feats of exploration. The earliest-known semi-legendary ship was the *Argo*, captained by Jason with a crew of fifty to a hundred "heroes". It sailed from Thessaly in Greece to Colchis in Georgia on the Black Sea and back, to fetch the Golden Fleece. The legend dates from about 1300 BCE. A complete myth, or based upon one of the first trading expeditions? Byzantium, which later became Constantinople and still later Istanbul, started as an organized colony from the Greek city-state of Megara around 660 to 650 BCE.

According to Norse records, Vinland was settled in 1000 AD by the Viking Leif Erikson after he was blown off-course while sailing from Norway to Greenland. Leif recognized Vinland from the descriptions of Bjarni Herjólfsson, who had himself been blown off-course there a year or two earlier, but he had not stayed. Leif organized a group of 35 settlers and returned in the first attempt to create a permanent European settlement in North America.

Columbus' "discovery" of America was an accident; he was exploring to find a trade route from Europe to India. The 16th-century Spanish explorations in North and South America are well-known. Juan Ponce de León was looking for the legendary Fountain of Youth in Florida. Francisco Vásquez de Coronado was looking for Cibola, the "Seven Cities of Gold", somewhere in New Mexico or further north. Legends of El Dorado, the native kingdom somewhere in Colombia or Venezuela or some area of the upper Amazon, whose ruler covered himself with gold dust, brought several Spanish expeditions and two English expeditions led by Sir Walter Raleigh (he was executed by King James I after complaints from the Spanish).

So it is human nature to go exploring. What about anthropomorphic animals? Some of the best works of furry fiction have been tales of exploration. The quest of the Sandalford breakaway rabbits in *Watership Down* to find a new home. Rat's seven-year walkabout from Ottersgate around the world, in *Rat's Reputation*. The decades-long trip of twelve light-years of the *ahsin bey*, the catlike space explorers in *The Alien Dark*, to the Chai-te stellar system to explore it for colonization. The last unicorn's search for the Red Bull of King Haggard, and, ultimately, for other unicorns.

If humans ever bioengineer animals in their image, can the urge to explore be left out of them? Here are 19 stories about individuals or groups of anthro animals who find themselves Exploring New Places, and what they discover there.

Music is an ethereal magic that is supposed to mystically transport the listener to another world. From the lyre-playing of Orpheus (before the 6th-century BCE) to the 1943 jazz-trumpeter's "I'm gonna send you right outta dis world!" (Leon Schlesinger/Warner Bros. "Tin Pan Alley Cats"; direction by Bob Clampett, story by Warren Foster), music has sent listeners to strange dimensions.

Where will Taymer and Snow end up?

To Drive the Cold Winter Away

by Michael H. Payne

Inside Stone Creek's main barn, the air simmered like the height of summer. Taymer kept having to flick sweat from the tips of his whiskers, and he hadn't moved a paw from his perch on one of the elderberry crates separating the hay-covered dance floor from the rest of the room.

The band was *just that good.*

Ranging in size from robin to otter and in instrumentation from fiddle to conga drums, the septet had been swinging away all evening with hornpipes and cha-chas, mazurkas and reels, tongue-twisting calypso numbers and jigs that practically set the walls to bulging and swaying. Taymer leaned into the music and marveled at how the tacky Harvest Festival bunting seemed to glow where it stretched from beam to beam across the barn's ceiling. Even the scents of the casseroles, fish perloos, and cobblers mixed with the chattering of his fellow mice and the other townsfolk filling the barn—rats, sparrows, foxes, squirrels, rabbits, hawks—tickled Taymer's senses rather than assaulting them.

Well, except for the hooting and hollering of his classmates—his *former* classmates, he meant, after graduation at the beginning of the summer. As always, they'd gathered shouting at the front of the barn, but this year, rather than congregating around the food tables, they were thronging the beer and cider kegs.

Taymer pursed his lips. Not that reaching his own eighteenth birthday had proven to be any more of a milestone. Sure, he had an apartment now, one room in a converted beehive tucked among the branches of an old hornbeam down the way. But he was still working at Doc Ristoli's tree surgery and spending the rest of his waking hours at his harp, trying in vain to get it to sound like the music surging through his head.

So, yeah. Nothing had really changed.

The polka the band had been pounding through spun to an ending with a breath-taking run of notes from the badger's accordion. The dancers went wild, stomping and clapping, and Taymer fanned himself, already hungry for the next tune.

But instead of another raucous number, the bobcat guitarist set up a slow, waltzing rhythm with a pattern of major and minor chords that shivered through Taymer's fur. The rat strummed his mandolin gently on the first beat of each measure, and when the slim white mouse out front tucked her flute to her side and began singing in a low, dusky voice, everything else in the whole place vanished as far as Taymer was concerned.

> *"I revel in rain, for I saw as a youth*
> *How waterfalls, massive, expansive, and free,*
> *Cascading and shattering stone, were in truth,*
> *Collections of drops even smaller than me."*

The robin came in with an instrumental break, her wings spread out behind her like a skirt and holding her up as her claws caressed a liquid flow of notes from the fiddle tucked to her chest. The badger, her eyes closed, summoned a low humming note from her accordion, the otter tapping the same note on his double bass.

A slight smile rustled the mouse's whiskers, and when the top of the verse came around again, she continued:

> *"The frostiest mist in the morning extends*
> *Through forest and meadow, replacing the air.*
> *But melting to steam, it's the warmest of friends,*
> *Alive and embracing, enveloping care."*

With a quick tattoo of his wings across the conga drums and a spatter of sharply plucked notes from the banjo in his talons, the crow at the back of the stage led a modulation into a section dominated by minor chords. Taymer's neck fur prickled, the mouse clenching a forepaw as she sang:

> *"It's snow that disturbs me, that troubles my mind,*
> *A stranger on silent, unstoppable paws*
> *Inviting me, urging me, 'Leave it behind.*
> *Relax and accept them: the teeth and the claws.'"*

Another modulation brought the major chords into ascension, and when the rat, the robin, and the bobcat raised their voices in quiet but soaring harmony above and below the mouse, Taymer never wanted the moment to end.

"Inevitability! Push it away!
Together, we're stronger than instinct or time!
United, we struggle each night and each day
To spend our existence in reason and rhyme!"

Every hair on his body prickling, Taymer almost fell over backwards when the crow gave four piercing caws and the band burst into a two-step so lively, it swept through the barn like a swarm of butterflies. Everyone cheered, the stillness of the previous song shattering, and the party kicked back into gear as if the suspension of the last few seconds or minutes—Taymer wasn't sure which it had been—had never happened.

The next couple hours flew by, but folks did eventually start leaving, the barn's warmth dimming, the crowd on the dance floor thinning, the food tables behind Taymer emptier every time he glanced at them with the thought that he really ought to grab some supper. So when the mouse announced, "One more, perhaps," and the band launched into as crisp a rendition of "Campbell's Farewell to Red Gap" as he'd ever heard, Taymer couldn't decide if he felt exhausted or refreshed. And while he wasn't the only one left in the barn when the group wrapped the tune up, he was the only one paying attention enough to applaud.

The white mouse's eyes met his, and the smile that crinkled through their dark blue depths tipped the scales completely to 'refreshed' in Taymer's mind. She gave a delicate curtsy, slid her flute over the small metal stand beside her, hopped from the stage, and padded on all fours across the dance floor toward him. "Forgive my boldness, sir," she said in her lilting contralto, "but I'd venture to guess you enjoyed this evening almost as much as we did."

"It was—" Taymer searched for the right word, didn't find it, and finally went with, "Spectacular."

She rose onto her hind legs to give another small curtsy. "Thank you most kindly. Such praise always carries a bit more heft when it comes from a fellow musician."

Taymer had to blink. "How did you know I was—?"

His heart stuttered when she caught his paws in hers, the white of her fur standing out against his own dark brown. "A string player," she said, turning his paws over so the palms pointed upward, "says the wear of your claws. And the equal fraying of both left and right leads me to declare you a harpist."

Looking at his paws as if he'd never seen them before, Taymer did some more blinking, then lifted his gaze to meet hers again. She seemed porcelain rather than flesh and fur, and Taymer found himself completely stymied as to her age. Older than him, certainly, but by two years or twenty, he couldn't've guessed. "I'm Taymer," he more blurted than said.

"Are you?" She cocked her head, her paws not letting his go. "As in the noun, or the comparative adjective?"

And while Taymer knew what those words meant, he hadn't a single idea what she was talking about.

That slow smile stretched through her whiskers again. "The comparative adjective applies to something that's not as wild as something else. Such an object is characterized as being tamer, you see. The noun, however, means one whose job it is to tame other things. One then is called a tamer, is one not?" She leaned closer to him. "So which are you?"

Everything around Taymer went warm, and he couldn't keep his own smile from stretching. "I can't be both?" he asked.

* * *

Waking the next morning with his snout tucked into the sweet fluff of her chest fur, Taymer let memories of the previous evening trickle back and forth through his thoughts.

"Call me Snow," she'd said after leading him back to the tables where her bandmates were gathered, the group sucking down whatever food and drink remained from the party and aiming more than a few smirks at the two of them. Taymer had stopped noticing anyone other than Snow pretty quickly, though, and when she'd asked to hear him play, they'd wound up back at his place sitting on the floor among the boxes he hadn't quite gotten around to unpacking yet.

Except for his harp, of course. "I couldn't crate up the beast," he'd told Snow, her flute in her paws as he checked the harp's pegs. "It's a balky enough monster as is, and if I threw it into a box?" He'd shaken his head in mock sorrow. "It'd never hold a tuning for me again."

He'd started with a simple air, and when she'd raised her flute and joined in, he'd thought his heart might stop from joy. They'd reached the end of it in perfect harmony, and Snow had jumped right into a quick little strathspey, all syncopated sixteenth and dotted eighth notes, Taymer following without needing to think.

After that, she'd begun changing tempos and moods in no pattern that Taymer could discern, but he'd stepped right in each time, providing back-up for her and plucking the melodies himself when the tune called for it. She'd started singing at some point; he'd added tenor lines even when he hadn't known the words, and after hours or days of this musical bliss, well, the mattress in the corner had been the only possible option.

Now, inhaling the perfect nectar of her scent, light as the morning sun drifting across them from the room's sole window, he swallowed till his throat felt damp enough to form words. "I hope I didn't spoil any plans with your bandmates."

"Not at all," she whispered, and the wonderful things her claws began doing along the back of his neck rolled his eyes closed and banished his words once more. "We'll both of us be seeing them soon enough, after all."

That brought his eyes back open, and he stretched himself along her firm, warm body till he was blinking into the sheer blue of her eyes. "Both of us?" he asked.

"Of course." Snow touched a kiss to his nose and almost derailed him again. "Why else'd we come to such an out-of-the-way spot as Stone Creek were we not recruiting for the finest harpist in the land?"

"What?" His voice cracked. "Why would you think that of me? I've only performed five times in public since I was big enough to pluck the strings without cutting my paws!"

Her gaze became nothing but serious. "You rustle the very sky when you play, Taymer." Another of those slight smiles tugged her whiskers, and she stroked a single claw through the fur between his ears. "Unless, of course, you're tangling and tripping yourself, flailing about in that labyrinth you call a mind. Those times that you stop thinking so much about the music and start feeling it, well, sooner or later, folks like my colleagues and I take notice of such things."

For half a moment, Taymer thought perhaps he'd lost the ability to understand spoken language: she simply couldn't've said what he'd heard her say. Then Snow was sliding from between his paws, rolling off the mattress, and landing firmly on the floor. "You've already passed the first three tests with stalwart distinction," she said, brushing her whiskers, "and it now only remains for me to ask formally if you'd care to join our little ensemble before I take you off for one final bit of an exam." She folded her forearms. "Any more questions?"

Questions, in fact, flooded Taymer. Hadn't he known the first time he'd stroked a claw over a harp's strings that this was to be his life, his fortune, his destiny? Hadn't he known that somewhere out there, the universe was stretching an ear, tapping a paw, nodding a head or swaying in place? Hadn't his every fantasy before falling asleep involved the beautiful future that was one day certain to come calling upon him? And hadn't that future now indeed done just that?

But the only question he needed to ask aloud was: "When do we get started?"

She blinked. "You're in, then?"

Tumbling to the floor more than rolling, he still ended up tail downward and facing her, so he counted the maneuver a success. "My sisters and brothers have families; they can use this stuff better'n I ever could." He nodded to the boxes before focusing all his attention on her. "And now that I've met you, there's nowhere I'll call myself content but at your side."

This time, just Snow's eyes rolled. "I've never known a harpist who wasn't as melodramatic as any moustache-twirling actor upon the stage." But for all that Taymer whiffed a bit of a blush going on beneath her fur, her paw was steadiness incarnate when she held it out to him. "Give me a hearty clasp to signal your agreement, and we'll be on to step four."

Taking her paw with both of his, Taymer breathed in to let fly a solemn declaration of his devotion to her and the music, but a burst of strident melody from Snow's lips cut him off, the sound tearing the air like claws on slate. Taymer winced, and everything swirled sideways, only himself and Snow remaining unmoved. Shadows subsumed his little sunlit room, the air suddenly heavy with acrid smoke and choking dust, the wooden floor now a cold steel mesh.

"For your final test," Snow murmured, her voice nearly lost in the vast darkness echoing around them, "you've got to face reality."

Ears tight against his head, Taymer didn't let go of her paw, his mind jittering and trying to absorb what he was seeing and scenting. The mesh beneath them stretched away to his left and right as far as he could see in the gloom, and through its gridwork, he could see crates and boxes made of wood, cardboard, and metal stacked on a floor below. The wall behind Snow seemed to be corrugated metal as well, and it reached up to what could only have been the interior angle of a roof. "Are... are we inside a barn?" he asked, wincing at the waver in his voice.

"A warehouse," Snow said. "Turn around."

Not sure he wanted to but even *more* sure that he didn't want to fail whatever her test was, Taymer managed to pry his claws away from her, cranked his head around with a creak he was sure he could hear, and gaped at what lay behind him.

Vast felt like too small a word for the building—and it was indeed an interior space, he could see by the dim light of the ceiling fixtures that receded into the distance. "Why?" he couldn't help asking, the rows of crates giving him a better sense of scale. "Why would anyone need a place this size?"

"Not just anyone." Something white moved in his peripheral vision, Snow coming up beside him. "Humans." She practically spat the word.

It nudged a few memories in the back of Taymer's head. "Aren't they storybook monsters?"

"The exact opposite of that, actually." Snow moved again; Taymer tore his gaze away from the storehouse to see her picking her way across the steel mesh toward what he now realized was a giant stairway leading down to the floor. "Not to put too fine a point upon it, but *we're* the stories, the roses sweet and dew-bedecked whose sylvan glades these creatures bulldoze to erect charming spots such as this one." She looked over her shoulder, her eyes now as sharp as bejeweled daggers. "Come see what we're fighting against, Taymer. Might be you'll decide a musician's life's not for you, after all." And she started descending, hopping from step to step.

* * *

For half a heartbeat, Taymer hesitated, then he rushed forward, caught up with Snow on the third step down, and had to struggle not to press himself close to her side. Forcing away as much panic as he could, he said, "Imagine that I'm asking the usual 'where' and 'how' questions instead of gibbering in terror, if you'd be so kind."

She gave a coughing sort of laugh. "Be glad you're a mouse. Singing larger folks through to show them what lies outside the walls of our universe can be a mite on the tricky side." Tossing her head, she gestured with her snout to the rows and stacks getting larger and larger the closer they got to the warehouse floor. "But to answer your semi-asked questions, as I said, we've crossed over into the real world now. Here, only humans talk and think, science reigns, magic is nothing but the most knavish sort of trickery, and non-humans such as you and I and everyone we know are nothing but dumb brutes, bothersome at best, vermin at worst."

His shock fading, Taymer's mind was starting to turn over, was starting to register why the scents of mice and rats reaching his nose were so disturbing. "All the folks around us," he muttered, taking the lightest possible whiff of the sour saltiness. "They're sick or terrified or injured or all three. It—" He couldn't stop a shiver. "It's like a nightmare."

"Again," Snow said, "it's the exact opposite of that." They jumped together onto the grimy concrete of the floor, Taymer's ears tightening further against his head at the crates towering as tall as the trees within Stone Creek Township. "It's reality, and it's what our world would become if we wardens let down our guard for so much as an instant and allowed rationality to start nosing about in our affairs." She made a high-pitched squeaking noise, and similar noises followed some rustling among the nearest boxes. "But understand, Taymer. These aren't folk you're about to see. They're animals. And while the poor things probably won't attack, be ready to give me a tenor line in case they do."

The next question died on his lips as creatures began crawling from the cracks between the crates: mice in shape only, their eyes blank and empty, their movements tentative and animalistic. "It's the magic of song," Snow whispered, "that keeps our world separate from this, that keeps the impossible possible for us, that keeps our minds and hearts from spiraling downward into what reality insists is our natural state." She waved a paw at the beasts sniffing from the shadows, their fur matted, their claws cracked, their ears bitten and torn.

Taymer couldn't look away.

"Without magic," Snow continued, "without *music*, everything we know devolves into hunters and hunted, eating and eaten, tooth and claw and hot red blood. Those of us chosen to join the ensembles, we travel about strengthening the barriers, reinforcing the harmony that defines us as folk rather than animals, and stopping the soul-curdling influence of *this* world from staining, twisting, and destroying *our* world. It's a burden you'll shoulder along with the hardest-working musicians you'll ever meet, and while there may be just the teeniest bit of glitz and glamour involved in the process, it's not—"

A metallic thump shook the building, the local mice all freezing. A soft hissing pricked Taymer's ears, a harsh chemical stink frizzing his whiskers, and something sparkled in the corridors between the boxes, the dim light revealing it to be a foul-smelling fog rolling toward them.

Whether Snow gasped or was taking a breath to warble out the countermelody to the discordant song that had brought them here, Taymer didn't know. The hacking cough that doubled her over, however, was unmistakable, and he was just turning to ask how he could help when alarmed squeaks and chirps sprang up everywhere. Mice and rats of this mindless, feral variety streamed from among the crates and pallets, the whole mass of them fleeing the cloud in a panicked flood that smashed Taymer sideways.

"Snow!" he shouted, more furry bodies tumbling him over and around, shoving him farther away from her, but then he was coughing, too, the air stinging his throat like nettles. Up and down kept shuffling positions, and when he lashed out with a paw trying to catch the wood of a crate surging by, he somehow managed to tear a piece of it away instead, the chunk bashing him hard in the head.

Vision blurring, inner ears churning, he flipped and floundered among sweaty, stinking fur, flailed and twisted and finally tumbled into something billowing but stationary. Cloth, it felt like; Taymer dug in and hoped it would hold. He needed to get back to where Snow—

The cloth ripped, and he flopped forward into mud, cold rain spitting over him for half an instant before squeaking paws began trampling him once again.

"Damn it!" a big voice shouted. "They're breaking through! I *told* you we shoulda hired a regular exterminator for this!"

"It's okay!" another voice called. "That's what the hoses are for!" And an absolute torrent of water burst across Taymer, shoving him back and spinning him through the mud. Nothing solid met his thrashing claws, every sucked-in breath more liquid than air, until his inner ear spasmed, his pounding heart clenching in his chest at the realization that he was falling.

He plunged into utter darkness, then into some swift and churning river, the flow of it sweeping him away just as thoroughly as the flow of bodies had. With water around him, though, he felt freer to lash out, and flashes of memory from various 'Summer Safety Swim' classes helped him keep his nose above water despite the river's best efforts.

Limbs as heavy as stones, Taymer somehow kept paddling, the surface below hard and unyielding whenever his paws brushed against it, the blackness so absolute, his eyes never adjusted. Despair wanted to drag him down, but he pushed it away till a grayish spot appeared ahead. It grew swiftly, vast and unnaturally round, and then he was flopping out into a darkness that wasn't quite as utter as before.

Ready for the splash when he hit this time, he angled his efforts to the left. One paw met something that squished, and he dug at it with all four, never so thankful to feel his claws sinking into mud. Gritting his teeth, he heaved himself out of the stream and onto the bank, everything about him cold and wet and stinking of sewage and fear. Still, the mere fact that he was able to lie there shivering and gasping struck him as nothing short of a miracle, so he concentrated on doing those things for a fair stretch of time before pushing his head up to look around at wherever he'd landed.

The rain still drizzled, clouds darkening the sky. Behind him, water poured out of what he realized was a massive pipe jutting from a mountain thick with gigantic briary bushes. Ahead, a few scraggly trees jabbed their bare branches into the dreariness, and on the other side of a chain-link fence at least ten times taller than any fence Taymer had ever seen, a squareish structure slumped, lights glowing from several of its oversized windows.

Humans, Snow had said, and all the stories spoke of them as giants. It just stood to reason that their houses would be big, too. Of course, the stories *also* spoke of humans as lumbering dolts prone to violent bursts of body-crushing rage. So maybe the best idea would be to sneak into the house, dry off, filch some provisions, and scramble back through that pipe in search of Snow. He could worry about polite introductions to the local mythical monsters later.

It wasn't *much* of a plan, but it was better than nothing. Taymer crept up the shallow embankment under the brambly undergrowth, clambered through the fence, and scampered across what he guessed was a patchy lawn to a massive plain of concrete and a door bigger than most of Stone Creek's buildings. It seemed designed to keep out similarly sized intruders, however; Taymer squeezed between the door and the jamb easily enough.

Inside, everything smelled of exhaust, the air heavy and warm with the tang of burnt wood, burnt oil, burnt gas, who knew what. Some sort of machine filled most of the space—a mechanical cart, he guessed, from its enormous rubber tires. Spreading his ears and whiskers, he slunk along beneath the whole length of the thing and peered out from the shadow of the front tire to see more machines against a wall and tools hanging haphazardly above a workbench. A smaller door, however, drew most of his attention. He was obviously in a garage right now, so the humans' living quarters must lie through there.

Fortunately, the mud in Taymer's coat proved to be lubricant enough to slide him through the gap beneath the door. Unfortunately, a gasp greeted him on the other side, his gaze snapping upward to meet the wide eyes and gaping mouth of what had to be an actual human being.

* * *

The creature stood wrapped in cloth from feet to neck, only its hands and head uncovered, but since that wrapping seemed to be various shades and textures of pink, it struck Taymer as somewhat less than threatening. The creature's shirt even bore a pink stylized image of what could only be a smiling rabbit. What Taymer could see of the creature's actual hide was as dark as his own fur, and the thing's only hair lay in tight coils against its head.

All that in the first frozen instant, then Taymer noticed two more things: first, that the creature was barely half as tall as the door he'd just dragged himself under, and second, that the creature was holding a bowl of something that smelled phenomenally delicious.

"It's okay," the creature said then, the pitch of its voice confirming Taymer's suspicion that this was a pup and making him think it might be female. "I won't hurt you, little guy."

Taymer swallowed and muttered without even thinking, "If only I could believe that."

The human's eyes went even wider, and the bowl fell from her splaying fingers to clatter against the odd spongy tile of the floor.

"Chayli?" a deeper voice called from somewhere to their right. "You okay, darling?"

"Yeah, Dad!" The young human's attention never wavered from Taymer. "It didn't break! I'll just… just hafta get some paper towels is all!"

"All right," the deeper voice said, but the young human still didn't move.

For his part, Taymer couldn't keep from darting glances at the bowl, sitting not more than ten taillengths away, its contents splashed across the floor: beans and tomato slices as big as his head surrounded by a whisker-tingling aroma of pepper sauce. After all, he'd had neither breakfast this morning nor dinner last night.

Chayli squatted down, moving slowly, her thick meaty scent tinged with something that wasn't quite fear. "You… you talked," she whispered.

"I did, yes," Taymer said. So much for waiting on the introductions. "I hope you'll forgive me just wandering in, but I really need help, and since I've never any humans before, I don't know the proper etiquette for—" And *that* was when he recalled Snow saying that humans were the only creatures in this place who could think and talk.

He clapped his forepaws over his snout at the same time as she clapped her hands over her mouth. "I knew it," she murmured between her fingers. "I *knew* there was talking animals somewhere! Knew it, knew it, knew it!" She dropped to her knees and elbows and thrust her face, bigger than Taymer's whole body, at him. "You're here to be my special magic friend and take me on big magic adventures!"

Apparently, humans had stories, too. Still, it took all Taymer's self-control not to dive for the crack under the door. "I'd like very much to be your friend, Chayli," he said, telling himself it wasn't a lie, "but right now, I need your help to find *another* friend of mine, a white mouse named Snow."

"Snow?" She sat back and cocked her head. "Then what's your name? Dirt?"

"I'm Taymer." He gave her a little bow. "We were inside a warehouse." Not quite sure what direction to point in, he just waved a paw vaguely. "Some gas drove me out, and I fell into what must've been a drainage pipe. I don't know what happened to her, and I need to get back up there to look for her as quickly as possible."

She stayed on her knees, her face blank and blinking, and Taymer wondered if he'd given her more than she could take in. But then she started nodding. "The warehouses're on the other side of the hill by the highway. We'll hafta take my bike." She turned and started scraping beans and tomatoes back into her bowl. "Dad?" she called. "I just remembered I've gotta book I need to read for class tomorrow!"

"Really?" the deeper voice answered from around a corner at the end of the hall. "I thought you read all the books for the whole year already?"

Chayli rolled her eyes. "Yeah, but now everybody else is catching up, so I'd better look it over again so I can answer Ms. Mayweather's questions."

"All right, darling. You got that spill cleaned up?"

"Yes, sir." She rubbed the floor with the hand not holding the bowl, and Taymer couldn't stop his stomach from growling.

Blinking some more, Chayli broke into a snaggle-toothed grin that reminded him of his younger sisters. "Climb aboard and help yourself," she muttered, lowering the bowl once more. "Dad makes it not too spicy special for me."

"Thank you!" Taymer dove in and managed to suck down four of the enormous beans in just the time it took her to carry the bowl across what had to be their kitchen to a sink as big as the smaller folks' swimming pool at the Stone Creek Community Center. He hopped out onto the counter and eyed the stream of water she directed from the tap into the bowl. "Might I borrow a bit of that to wash myself off?"

She giggled. "I've got a better idea!" One of those giant hands swooped toward him, and Taymer tensed, ready to leap aside, a line from one of the old human tales popping into his head: *I'll grind your bones to make my bread!*

A gasp, and Chayli's hand froze. "Sorry!" she whispered. Slowly, the hand moved to rest palm up at the edge of the counter. "Get in, and I'll carry you to the bathroom where we've got shampoo and stuff!"

Taymer tore his gaze away from that hand long enough to look up at her and nod, then he scampered in, very aware of his muddy coat. Chayli just giggled again, and Taymer hunkered down to her weird bare skin, his stomach alternately stretching and tightening. She brought him close to the rabbit cartoon on her shirt and lurched them both toward the kitchen's other door.

The trip lasted but a dozen of her strides—through the door, down a hall, through another door—Taymer the whole way recalling old stories about genies and magic carpet rides. Then the scents of strong soaps and cleansers prickled at him, Chayli using her other hand to turn a handle that once more summoned water. "Tell me if it's too hot," she said.

It was a marvelous but all too brief shower; the pink goo she squeezed from a bottle smelled as if someone had tried to recreate the aroma of strawberries from a written description, but it washed the mud away well enough. Then she was taking some sort of mechanism from a drawer and snapping a cable attached to the end of it into a pair of slots in the wall. "I'll use the lowest setting," she murmured, "but hang on." A flick of a switch set the machine to roaring, and Taymer dug into the tile against the blast of warm air she fired at him.

He couldn't complain about its drying power, though, and more quickly than he'd dared to hope, he was feeling as normal as any mouse likely could in a world full of storybook giants. But Taymer knew he didn't have the time to marvel at that thought. "Now, how do we get to this warehouse?"

She held her hand open at the edge of the counter again. "We need to stop off in my room, then we're out the window and on our way."

* * *

With a swallow, Taymer scrambled into her palm to ride a few paces down the hall and through another doorway, the darkness on the other side smelling deeply of Chayli. He felt her stretch above and behind him, something clicked, and light flooded a place whose pinkness nearly took his breath away. Shelves seemed to line every inch of wall space, books standing and stacked everywhere he looked. Several blinks focused his eyes enough to show him a bed covered with plush toy animals—all of which, he noted, were bigger than him—as well as a small desk cluttered with papers, smaller animal figurines, and other assorted bric-a-brac.

Her hand slid him through the air to the edge of this desk. "Wait here," she said, "and I'll get my jacket."

Nodding, he hopped onto the lacquered wood and found his attention settling on one of the figurines along the back of the desk: a mouse very nearly his size standing on its hind legs, a jaunty cap between its ears and a harp hanging from its neck.

More a lyre than a harp, a certain pedantic part of his brain insisted, but Taymer couldn't've stopped himself from scurrying over if he'd wanted to. And for all that the harp had looked as phony as any kid's toy at his first glance, the closer he came to it, the more it seemed to shiver and sit up, to yawn and stretch and curl itself into a more proper shape.

Taymer blinked, certain that the twelve strings he now saw between the soundboard and the pegs had been four when he'd started across the desk. He took another several steps, and the instrument unfurled a whole second octave, the thing quickly becoming a lightweight lever harp.

The rustling behind him had stopped. "Taymer?" Chayli's voice had a waver in it. "Is that... magic?"

"If it is—" Taymer reached the figurine and gently tapped a claw against the solid wood of the harp's frame. "It's none of mine." He looked over his shoulder, Chayli staring down at him, a bulky pink jacket around her torso. "My friend Snow said you humans *have* no magic, but if it's not me and it's not you—" Facing forward again, he undid the strap that held the harp to the figurine, squatted down to rest it on the desktop, and plucked out a basic scale to check the tuning. "It must be the both of us together."

"Impossible," Chayli said.

He shrugged, flexed all his claws, and launched into "Banish Misfortune," the first melody that came to mind. "It's smaller than the harp I have at home, but I'd call it perfectly serviceable."

Chayli stood with her hands clenched together and pressed to her chest. "Those strings're too short to make real notes: I read that when I was looking up how guitars work! And they're only some of my Mom's sewing thread! And I made the thing out of cardboard! And—!"

"And we'd best bring it along." Taymer strummed a final chord, slipped the harp's strap around his shoulder, slung it over his back, and scurried across the desk toward her. "Whatever magic's going on between us is plenty powerful, and I'd not be surprised were we to need it."

For a breath and a half, Chayli just wavered some more. Then she gave a jerky nod and fumbled with the front of her jacket. "I've got a pocket here you can ride in." Something made a sound like cloth ripping, and her finger worked a flap open. "My bike's just outside." Her other hand came down to plop in front of him with barely a shake.

He stepped in, rode up, and sliding into the pocket, he brought the harp around to cradle it in his forearms. Once he'd settled, his nerves drove him to start plucking notes again—"Ships are Sailing," he realized the tune was about halfway through the first phrase.

Chayli's chest behind him rose and fell. "All right," she said; she turned toward the one window nestled among the room's bookshelves, slid the pane upward, and climbed out over the sill. At least the rain had largely tapered off, a dampness in the air rather than actually water. Dropping to the ground with a squish that made Taymer wince for her pink shoes, Chayli crouched low and skirted the wall of the house, a small muddy yard to her left.

They came quickly to a covered patio area, and Chayli grabbed a two-wheeled machine with an obvious seat and control handles. Pushing the machine, she directed them past a large glass door covered by a curtain through which soft light glowed. Not wanting to breathe, Taymer kept playing, and Chayli only paused to open the gate in the fence that surrounded the place.

The hair on the back of Taymer's neck was rustling. Throughout this entire operation, all he'd heard had been the harp. Music was magic, Snow had said, and without even thinking about it, he realized, he'd been casting a spell through the song, a spell formed in equal measure from his anxiety and his hope, a spell he could feel flowing from him and surrounding Chayli like a bubble, a spell that would make anyone who heard the tune ignore it and everything around it.

How he was doing it, he had no idea. But he couldn't deny the strange and magical shiver he felt simply from putting his claws to these strings.

Chayli unfastened some sort of helmet—pink, of course, with what looked for all the world like little triangular cat ears attached to the top—from between the bike's control handles. Jamming it onto her head, she slung herself over the seat, began grinding the pedals with her feet, and their sudden burst of speed nearly broke Taymer's concentration, already slightly bent by his attempt to see how the machine worked. Taking a breath, he focused back on the music.

The route Chayli piloted them along wasn't the one he'd taken earlier in the evening, of course, but Taymer couldn't do anything except hope she actually knew the warehouse he was talking about. They rode on through puddles of sluggish water and puddles of cold, orange light cast by lamps at the tops of impossibly high poles. Giant wheeled conveyances whooshed past now and then, and Taymer guessed that they bore some relation to the machine he'd scampered under in Chayli's garage.

Quickly leaving behind the area of smaller structures, they came into wider streets with more concrete than Taymer had ever imagined could possibly exist. Chayli bore them consistently to the right and up hills, and before long, the chemical stink that had stabbed his nose in the warehouse began tugging his whiskers. "I think," he said, the effort of keeping the magic on course shortening his breath, "that we're getting close."

"Yeah," she said, and she steered them around one last corner, up a ramp, and out onto a vast, flat plane paved with black and divided into sections by white and yellow lines. Large buildings loomed in the orange-tinted darkness ahead, and just the sight of them made his claws falter on the strings. Chayli, though, kept pumping her machine forward. "If you came down the big pipe, you were probably in the warehouse at the far end."

The closer they pedaled, the thicker the stink grew and the tighter Taymer's stomach clenched. Undertones had begun rising through the odor: blood and fear, urine and vomit, the cloying fetor of death. And he could see bodies now, small and furry and strewn about the muddy field beyond the last warehouse.

"Oh, Taymer," Chayli gasped, coasting the bike to a stop and putting one foot to the blacktop.

But Taymer was already scrambling down her jacket to her trousers and leaping to the ground with the harp tucked under one arm. No white fur glinted anywhere in the filth and the shadows, but not letting himself think twice, he plopped forward onto his knees, set his foreclaws to the strings, and began playing the melody he'd heard Snow sing the night before, his own throat too tight to voice the words that echoed through his memory:

"Inevitability! Push it away!
Together, we're stronger than instinct or time!
United, we struggle each night and each day
To spend our existence in reason and rhyme!"

The music sprang from him like a light he was sure he could see, arched upward, then dropped near the wall of the massive building. The harp slung over his back, Taymer sprinted toward the spot.

* * *

She wasn't breathing, her eyes and mouth closed, her fur sodden and stinking.

"Oh, Taymer." Chayli whispered it this time. The squish squish squish of her big shoes had trailed him out into the field, and the movement of the shadows now told him she had hunkered down into a squat beside him.

But he couldn't look away from Snow sprawled and unmoving in the mud.

Torrents of rage and despair wanted to tear through his shaking chest and convulse his brain in their ceaseless, burning grip, but—"No," he said, addressing the madness inside him as well as any of the sundry universes that might be listening. Setting the harp carefully into place on the ground in front of him, he heard a melody hum between his ears and again didn't let himself think twice. "Chayli?" He looked up at her. "Do you sing by any chance?"

She blinked. "At church. Do mice have funeral songs?"

Taymer shook his head so thoroughly, he was surprised it remained attached to his neck. "The song I'd like to play is called 'Afton Water'." Hoping against hope, he started plucking the tune. "Do you know it?"

"A mouse song? How would I—?" Her brow creased, then cleared just as quickly. "Wait! That's—You're playing 'Away in a Manger'!"

His heart surging, Taymer closed his eyes for the briefest of instants, but he'd send his grateful thanks to every single universe once they were done. Fixing his gaze on Chayli's excited face, he asked, "Would you be able to hum the melody along with me while I sing and play? This can only possibly work with the both of us together, I think."

Chayli nodded. Taymer struck up the last four bars as an introduction and had to smile when she came in exactly on time and on pitch with him, her hum bolstering his song of a shepherd entreating the sweet river to flow past more gently so as not to awaken the lovely maiden asleep on the bank beside him.

No strength bristled the words, none that Taymer felt, at least. He had no spell to cast like he had earlier to make their passage silent. Emptiness filled him, and he let the music take that space, let Chayli's childish soprano enter his ears to mix through his head and heart, let the combination drift from his lips and claws.

He slowed as they finished the sixth verse, held the last note, opened his eyes, and saw Snow's chest rising and falling.

Behind him, Chayli gave another little gasp. "They're all… are they all just sleeping?"

"They are now." Taymer leaned forward and touched a paw to Snow's shoulder, the mud cold in her fur but the skin warm underneath. "Time to wake up, though." He gave her a shake.

Snow's eyes shot open. "The gas!" she squeaked, leaping upright.

Taymer had already pulled his paws back to the harp, his claws starting "Softly as in a Morning Sunrise" almost of their own volition. "Careful," he said, having to force the word out past the tightness in his throat and the grin that stretched his lips. "Don't panic, but this is my friend Chayli. Chayli, this is my friend Snow."

Snow blinked at him, then tipped her head back, her eyes and mouth widening at Chayli's squealed, "This is so great!"

"What?" Snow muttered. "How?" Her breath caught, a shiver wracking through her, and when she brought her gaze back down to meet Taymer's, the slightest sliver of her regular glint shone there. "You know: the usual gibbering in terror questions."

His heart too full even for music, Taymer leaped around the harp and wrapped Snow in a hug, pressed his damp face to her shoulder. "Later for that," he whispered. "Just as later we need to reexamine everything our musicians have been doing for the past however many generations."

"What?" she asked again, pulling away from him, her glint hardening. "Taymer, you don't know what you're—"

"Maybe." He stepped back as well, turned partway, and gestured up to Chayli, her grin shimmering in the orange light. "But I *do* know that it was a song shared between this mouse and this human that proved slightly effective right here and right now. So could be that our music's meant to be a bridge rather than a barrier. That we're meant to spread our magic to this world instead of hoarding it to ourselves."

Her face tightening, Snow opened her mouth, but the other mice stirring around the field seemed to derail her train of thought, her head snapping over and her eyes going wide again.

So Taymer stepped in. "Like I said, that's for later. Right now, though, perhaps you'd like to avail yourself of Chayli's shower facilities? The shampoo's a bit stinky, but—"

"Hey!" Chayli folded her arms. "I like strawberry!"

"As do I." Taymer fanned a paw before his snout and made a face. "*This*, however…"

Snow's whiskers drooped. "Is that supposed to be strawberry? It smells more like—" She stopped, her attention flickering back and forth between Taymer and Chayli. "I, uhh, I'll thank you for your kind offer," she said then, her voice as brittle as spring ice in Taymer's ears. "But if it's all the same to all involved, I'd rather be heading home."

Chayli's face fell, and Taymer stifled a sigh. He'd need to take this very slowly, he knew, on both sides of the divide. And since he'd be going with Snow, he put on a smile and held the harp up. "Can you keep this for me, then, Chayli? I'd like very much to come back and sing more with you, but I'd best be seeing that Snow makes a safe return to our neck of the woods."

Her hand shaking, Chayli reached out and took the harp gently between her thumb and forefinger. "But… you're coming back? You promise?"

"I will and I do." Again, he spoke the words to the larger universes as well. "I may even have more friends with me."

"I'd like that." She tucked the harp into her pocket and wiped a sleeve under her nose. "So I… I'll see you next time, then." Rising to her feet, she grimaced at the mud coating the knees of her pink trousers. "Oh, Mom's gonna kill me!" She started toward her bike, standing where they'd left it on the blacktop, then stopped and turned back. "It was nice meeting you, Snow. And Taymer, I—You—" With a swallow, she shook her head, sprinted to the bike, jumped on, and pedaled away.

The local mice were beginning to squeak now. Taymer glanced at Snow, and she was staring at him, her ears tight against her head. "Do you have any idea what you've just done?" she growled.

Taymer shrugged. "Saved the life of the mouse I love."

"Love?" Her stare became more amazed than glowering. "Taymer, you don't even know me!"

"But now I'll get the chance." He waved toward Chayli, the pink of her jacket just disappearing into the night. "Just as you'll get the chance to know her." And as much as he wanted to grab Snow's shoulders, he didn't—slow, after all, was his watchword here. Still, he couldn't keep from stressing his words. "There's meant to be an exchange between our world and this, Snow, I'm certain of it! They imagine us, and we imagine them in return! Or they give us ideas and we give them ideals! Or something: I don't know! But we have stories about them, and they have stories about us! It's like that harp!"

The memory made him stop, his claws still tingling from the touch of those strings. "She made it from cardboard and thread, Snow, but as soon as I saw it, it transformed into the finest instrument I'm ever likely to play! So there's *something* going on, some reaction we provoke from each other!" One last argument popped into his head. "And she knew the melody to 'Afton Water'! How could she possibly if there'd not been some sharing between folks and humans in the past?"

For a moment, the only sound was the rustle and chirp of the other mice pushing themselves onto all fours and shaking the mud from their coats. Then Snow blew out a breath. "Right now, I'm cold, filthy, hungry, and may have been dead for a bit." She held out a forepaw and gave him about a quarter of a smile. "Let's see about addressing some of *those* issues, then we can talk about what may or may not have happened here this evening."

Warmth filling him, Taymer took her paw, and the warble of her song swirled them away.

One of the basic themes in furry fiction is that the future's bioengineered animal peoples who have replaced mankind will seek their creators. Captain Illatha is sent by her lapine homeworld to explore stellar systems until she finds them.

In Search of the Creators

by Alan Loewen

The oldest legends say that when the Creators left blue-green Ur to explore the stars, they found themselves alone in a cosmos without boundaries. Grieved at their loneliness, they returned to their world, took their animals, and gifted them with sentience, hands, and a bipedal stance. The Creators then scattered their progeny across numerous stars and today, they patiently wait for their children to return and ease their solitude.

~ Histories and Legends

Captain Illatha brushed her hair out of eyes, flipping her long lop ears to hang over her back. Through the windows of the shuttle, she observed the *Warren*.

A creation never made for planetary atmosphere, the skin of the ship bristled with sensors and defensive weaponry. At the rear of the ship, a portal irised open and the shuttle eased its way into the internal docking station.

"Captain, we have docked and have received clearance to disembark."

"Thank you," Illatha said. She watched as they flipped switches and adjusted gauges to power the shuttle down. In a few hours, the shuttle and its pilot would return to the Homeworld, leaving Illatha and her crew in orbit and ready to embark on their lengthy mission.

Through the window, she could see the crew of the *Warren* assemble before the shuttle's exit for presentation. Lapines all, they all wore their ears in lop style, deliberately broken during training to facilitate their heads fitting inside a space helmet.

She made her way to the exit ramp. With a hiss and pop, the door opened and the ramp descended. Her First Mate stepped forward smartly. For a moment, in her panic, Illatha could not remember his name. She slowed her breathing, dulling the anxiety of the moment. Her training had taught her to resist millions of years of evolution, to deliberately pause, control the panic and the impulse to flee, and master the situation.

The name came to her immediately. Thrane.

Beside Thrane, fifteen crew members stood at attention and as Illatha descended the ramp, all of them bowed deeply.

"Welcome aboard, Captain Illatha," Thrane said.

"Thank you," Illatha said. She turned to face the crew. "We are faced with one of the most important tasks for our race to ever undertake. Our mission, as you already know, is to find the Creators, should any of them still exist. We must find them before the other races they seeded across the cosmos either discover interstellar flight or we encounter a violent race that is already making its way among the stars. We need protection, and the Creators can supply that.

"I expect your best and to work together for the good of Homeworld and the *Warren*. That is all."

In response, the crew bowed deeply.

* * *

"Sensors at full."

Captain Illatha stared at the main viewscreen currently showing nothing but the endless gray of the warp manifold that enveloped the ship. The timers ticked off the seconds until they would pop into real space and a new star system, the thirty-first to be explored since they started their journey three Lapine years ago.

The rest of the crew studied their monitors intensely. Tension filled the air of the control deck. The ship lacked offensive weapons, and the instinctive response of Illatha's race, exactly like the rabbits from which the Creators had upraised them, was to flee if danger threatened.

Illatha forced her emotions under control. All five bridge members stood ready to feed her important information the moment they appeared in normal space. Within seconds she would make the decision to either stay and explore this new planetary system, or flee back into the safety of warp.

She mindlessly tapped her pen on her incisors that peeked out from her upper lip, a nervous habit borne from the many times she had entered a new system.

The timer ticked down and suddenly the main viewscreen snapped from formless gray into the dark of space with a brilliant mainstream sun shining like a bright dot in its center.

Information started flashing over her monitor as her crew shouted their findings.

"Five planets, Captain!"

"No radio signals detected."

"Captain, I detect a ship! Wait! It's dead, Captain. No heat at all. No electromagnetic signals. Just floating."

"Captain, there is one planet that is the proper distance from the sun to maintain life. I detect no electromagnetic signals. Nothing artificial in orbit."

It was only then that Illatha realized she was holding her breath. She let it out with a shudder. "Set a course for the ship," she said. "Let's see what information it can give us."

* * *

Ship sensors probed the wreck while Illatha and her crew stared in fascination. Three millennia in open space orbiting a small gas giant had not been kind to what was clearly an old mining ship. Why the Creators had left it behind remained a mystery. Massive holes pitted its hull, remnants of strikes from natural debris.

"Send a subspace squirt to Homeworld," Illatha ordered. "Tell them that we found a Creator artifact. Put it on the salvage list." She brushed her hair out of her eyes and turned to her First Mate. "Maybe they might actually get to it in a few years or so."

The First Mate nodded at the wreck. "Think it can tell us anything?"

Illatha shook her head. "Nothing else has so far. I have no hopes for an old wreck that the Creators left behind."

* * *

A day later, Illatha and her crew approached the second planet out from the star. It hung blue, green, and white in the main viewscreen, making them all homesick.

"The ratio of water to land is around seventy to thirty percent, but Captain, look at this."

Illatha's monitor centered on a piece of land now heavily forested but showing the remains of a massive crater. "Natural?"

"No, Captain. Mined. And there are many more. This planet has been mined out."

"So…" Illatha said in growing excitement.

"Yes, Captain," her First Mate said. "This explains the presence of the Creator mining ship. It had a purpose being here. There may be even more Creator artifacts on the surface, but only assuming they could survive millennia on a planet with an active atmosphere and flora.

"Pilot, put us in orbit."

"Yes, Captain."

Immediately sensors began probing this new world while the crew talked animatedly among themselves. Slowly, their orbit took them past the terminator into the night side of the planet and that is when they saw the dim lights of the small city below them.

Dozens more peppered the planet's dark surface as they orbited.

* * *

Illatha stared at the screen before her. The rest of the crew had retired, letting the ship monitor itself, but Illatha could not stop staring at the information before her. Less than a Lapine century after they discovered space flight, just one thousand years ago, her people had found ancient Ur, the Creators' homeworld. However, the Creators' home planet stood deserted, telling a story only of ruin and desertion. Since then, Illatha's people had explored thousands of planets, discovering the terraformed worlds the Creators had left behind, filled with creatures and life that could all be traced back to Ur itself.

Yet, never had they discovered life with an indigenous RNA that would tell them that they had discovered something truly alien and not originally a part of Ur's biosphere. And the mystery as to the where and why of the Creators' vanishing had disappeared with the Creators themselves.

Yet now, Illatha and her crew had found what they hoped would be descendants of the Creators, evidently living in simple circumstances, probably unaware of their heritage as gods who had spanned the galaxy and seeded life on planets they had transformed.

Illatha and her crew stayed in silent orbit waiting for orders from Homeworld. A subspace squirt took one week out and back. Assuming a few days for the leaders of Homeworld to debate what they should do, a response was expected soon.

Illatha stared at the dots of light that speckled the night side of the planet, each one declaring the presence of a city. Sensors had shown the lights were not electrical in nature, but the glow from fires that appeared to be from natural gas.

One of the lights dimmed slowly and then brightened again. Illassa's gaze focused on it.

It blinked again, twice in succession in a slow, but steady pattern. Illassa's furred brow furrowed in curiosity and concentration.

The light blinked again, three times in succession.

Immediately, the captain's four-fingered hands flashed over the control board to put her ship into a stationary orbit.

Fascinated, she watched as it blinked five times and then went back and blinked once. And then twice, then three times and then five, cycling back to repeat the pattern of prime numbers in a base ten system.

Fear welled up in Illatha's heart. They had been spotted.

Contact had been made.

* * *

Illatha could feel her heart beating as she strapped herself into the descent shuttle.

Homeworld's orders had been clear. The Captain would descend and make contact. If they killed her, the second-in-command would guide the ship back to Homeworld and the system would join other worlds on the list of isolated worlds with hostile inhabitants.

"But these might be Creators," Thrane said. "If so, they created us. They aren't going to eat us."

"We know they're omnivores. We found enough evidence on Ur to affirm that," Illatha said, unable to stop her hands from trembling, "and there is a theory they may have created us originally for food. And even if they hadn't, these Creators, if that is what they are, are still primitives. They have no technology to speak of. Their usage of metal is practically nonexistent."

Her First Mate shrugged. "It's a mined-out planet. There's hardly any metal left for them to use."

"Sticks could still kill me."

He put his muzzle against hers and brushed his cheek against hers in a traditional parting. "We are a fearful people. That trait has kept us alive for millennia when the Creators first raised us up on Homeworld. Yet now, we must not let our fears get in the way of our need for answers. Remember that in not too many centuries, other races that we know of will be traveling between the stars. We will need allies and the Creators…"

"Would you go in my place?"

Thrane hung his head and refused to look into her eyes. "The *Warren* said that you must go, Captain. I cannot take your place. I will not say that I am envious."

Illatha looked away. "Close the door," she ordered. "I must leave."

* * *

Illatha had programmed her shuttle to land outside the city where she had first seen the blinking light. As she swung her small ship into a landing pattern, she targeted a meadow filled with animals she could not recognize, animals that looked like large wads of cotton that fled at her approach.

Gently she touched down on an alien world, recognizing the plants immediately. Everywhere the Creators had been, they had brought the life of Ur with them including grasses and other flora. At the very least, she would not starve. Here was food genetically similar to Homeworld's, and it was unlikely that any sizeable genetic drift had occurred in the thousands of years since this planet was colonized and mined out.

Illatha waited, her fear too great to motivate her to go out and explore, so she opted to see if the inhabitants of the planet would come to her first.

When the planet's sun stood directly overhead, she saw her first movement at the edge of the meadow. With trembling fingers, she keyed her radio.

"*Warren?* This is Captain Illatha. Can you hear me?"

Thrane's voice came in clearly. "Yes, Captain. Please continue."

"The natives have made contact with me. I see five of them at the edge of the meadow. I am sending direct video feed to you now."

"Receiving."

Illatha stared at the five beings with a combination of fascination and fright. Except for flora and fauna, Ur had stood deserted, but in the ruins of the cities, they had found statues that had survived the epochs. Illatha had never been to Ur, but she remembered the pictures. These strange, almost hairless beings, were clearly descendants of the Creators.

Working slowly, Illatha watched as the five constructed a tent of poles and tarps. Sitting halfway between her ship and the edge of the meadow, the front of the tent stood wide open allowing her to see freely inside. The creatures then brought tables, chairs and set them up inside as well as boxes.

When it appeared they were finished, the men left, leaving one of their party behind.

Illatha stared in a mixture of curiosity and revulsion. Hairless except for the red hair on the top of his head and a carefully sculpted pattern of short hair on his face that started under his nose and covered his chin, his body was clothed in some simple type of cloth making up a shirt and pants.

The Creator grabbed a chair from inside the tent and approached Illatha's shuttle. A few paces from its nose, he put the chair down and then held up empty hands toward the shuttle. Slowly he spun around and then sat on the chair, his open hands palm up on his lap.

It took some time for Illatha to calm her heart, as she struggled to control her fear and xenophobia.

"For the safety of Homeworld," she muttered over and over again. "I have to do this for the safety of Homeworld."

Trembling, she made her way to the airlock. The shuttle's sensors had confirmed the studies from the *Warren* that the air was breathable and similar to the atmosphere on Homeworld. With a hiss, the iris door opened and Illatha found herself in the presence of a Creator.

The creature slowly stood showing empty hands as Illatha made her way down the ramp, a gesture, Illatha assumed, to show he held no weapons.

Reaching the bottom of the ramp and only three paces away from the Creator, Illatha stopped as she tried to stop the beating of her heart and the overwhelming instinctual panic that had kept her people alive since their creation.

Slowly, the man put his open hands on his chest. "Blayne," he said. His voice was deep. Again, he put his hands on his chest. "Blayne," he repeated. Then with his hands still opened, he motioned toward Illatha.

Illatha knew what he wanted. Her name. "Illatha," she said repeating his actions with her own hands.

"Illatha," the man repeated.

Slowly the man stood. Illatha's head came up to his chest and she shuddered from how small she was in comparison. He pointed at the sun that shone down on the meadow. "Odo," he said.

Illatha already knew what the creature wanted. He was working on a basic vocabulary. She squinted up at the bright sun and pointed at it. "Nae," she said in her own language.

"Nae," Blayne repeated. "Nae." Then Blayne turned and gestured toward the tent. "Illatha?" he said, using an odd inflection at the end of her name. Did that make the gesture a request or command? The Creator turned and walked toward the tent a few steps and then turned, looking at her. Swallowing her apprehension, Illatha followed.

45

* * *

Toward the end of the day, Illatha marveled at how rapidly Blayne had picked up Lapine language. Using pictures and mime, Blayne had mastered much of the basic Lapine grammar and vocabulary. Illatha found it difficult to repeat any of the words the Creator spoke. Lacking certain muscular and vocal controls, the human, as they called themselves, used labials difficult for Illatha to speak, consonants that Illatha could not plainly articulate.

The sun was almost setting when the man closed his books and put them back in a box.

"Latha," he said, using the Lapine word for morning. He pointed toward the shuttle and using gestures and simple words, he communicated that Illatha needed to return to her shuttle and that the linguistic lessons would continue tomorrow.

Suddenly tired, Illatha signified agreement. Back in the shuttle, she contacted the *Warren*. "Contact made," she said. "The Creators are learning my language."

* * *

Four days later Blayne introduced Illatha to several other Creators including two females. By now, Blayne spoke Lapine with few errors. From what Illatha could learn, as the humans lacked significant amounts of metal, they had turned from technology to harnessing the powers of the intellect. Blayne had trained as a linguist. Most of the Creators on the planet could speak several artificial languages, each one with a specific purpose.

Now Blayne acted as a teacher of the Lapine language to the other humans. Three days later, four of the humans could talk freely with Illatha.

Illatha had been invited to leave the meadow and tour the nearest Creator town. Now comfortable with the aliens, Illatha spoke with the *Warren* and they agreed that the Creators were not dangerous. Illatha told the humans she would be honored to see their town.

* * *

The next day, a large cart appeared with two large quadrupeds. The animals were bound to the cart with leather traces and guided by a human holding leather lines connected to the mouths of the creatures. The Creators called them horses.

Illatha marveled at the town when it came into view. Lacking metal, the Creators here had not only attempted to master intellectual pursuits but sought to master the absolutes of aesthetics. Gardens and buildings meshed together in harmony. The entire village showed a form of beauty that stunned Illatha with its extravagance, knowing that the practicality of her own people would struggle to understand what the Creators had accomplished here.

"Where are the people?" she asked. "The town is deserted."

"We did not wish to make you nervous," Blayne responded. "They are inside their homes. We thought it best."

Suddenly, Illatha pointed at a garden. "I recognize those plants!" she exclaimed. "Cabbage! Lettuce! I even see beans."

Blayne smiled, an expression that Illatha still struggled with, forcing herself to realize that bared teeth with the corners of the mouth upturned was not a display of impending aggression. "Stop, driver," he said.

Stepping down from the cart, he gathered some vegetables from the garden and then held them up for Illatha to inspect.

Illatha was delighted and smelled the offerings with pleasure. "They are very similar to what we have on Homeworld," she said.

"When our ancestors seeded your world," Blayne said, "the time between then and now is simply not long enough for any significant change to occur. Though we don't have an exact timeline, I doubt if there have been more than seven millennia between your world being terraformed and your finding us. However, we have bred some vegetables for different color and size."

Blayne pointed at a plant in the garden. The foliage was taller than him, and the tuber from which the stems and leaves sprouted was almost the size of the cart in which they rode. "We call that a sugar beet," he said. "It takes days to dig it up and process, but it produces a sweet substance that can supply an entire village for a year."

* * *

In communication with the *Warren* and Homeworld, the decision was made that a delegation of humans would be taken aboard the *Warren* and interviewed by a select group of Lapines. The entire session would take place with audio and video doing a live squirt to Homeworld even though it would take a Lapine week for the signal to arrive and then another to receive any response.

47

The delegation consisted of Blayne and another male and two females.

The trip from the planetary surface to the orbiting *Warren* took a small fraction of the time, but along with the delegation, Illatha had filled the holds with samples of plant life as well as large crates of food freely given to the Lapines to supplement their dwindling food stores. The Lapine scientists were eager to analyze the new foods and already talk was underway of trade between the planets.

After attending to the comfort of her guests, Illatha prepared for the conference. She had a sheaf of questions from Homeworld. Illatha was determined the meeting between her peoples and the Creators would go smoothly. She prepared a table, chairs, and glasses of water she hoped would be acceptable to the shape of human lips.

In the meantime, she had provided the humans with monitors that would display educational tapes on Lapine history, culture, and language. This historical event would be marred by nothing that was reasonably within Illatha's control.

* * *

The four humans sat at the table. Across from them sat Illatha and three other hand-picked crew members. Behind the Lapines, small cameras blinked sending their information across the light years to Homeworld where the Elders would watch the proceedings on large screens when the signal finally reached them.

The eight faced each other, the Creators relaxed and smiling, the Lapines nervous and fidgety.

"Let us begin," Illatha said. She looked at the papers in her hands, questions that would ultimately lead to the most important question the Lapines had. Would the Creators protect them from the more violent of their children they had seeded across the galaxy?

Illatha put the papers aside and swallowed her nervousness. She had spent years hoping for this moment and now that it was in her grasp, she refused to let it go. She had earned this right to ask the question that had brought her so many sleepless nights.

"Why did the Creators abandon us?" she asked. Her compatriots froze in their chairs, their eyes wide with surprise. The humans sat across from them with expressions on their faces that Illatha could not read.

Blayne turned to the other three humans and spent a moment in private conversation in a language Illatha could not follow. After a brief, whispered conversation, Blayne turned to the Lapines across the table.

"We didn't," he said. After a moment's pause, he added. "Not in any deliberate manner."

He motioned toward the woman who sat at Illatha's far left, a gray-haired human who gave off an air of age, but whose face looked young.

"The story is long," she said, "but mayhap I have the gift of brevity." She closed her eyes giving the impression she concentrated on her response without being hindered with visual feedback.

"Go back in time in your mind almost twenty-five thousand Terran years. Our ancestors, who you call the Creators, had mastered the technology of space travel. First colonizing their own system, the discovery of warp travel opened the stars up to us. From our home world, we expanded outward, following the disk of the galaxy, traveling the arms of what we called the Milky Way, ever expanding, discovering new worlds and new marvels. Our knowledge grew and we mastered so much.

"But in those thousands of years, what we longed for most of all was to encounter others to let us know we were not alone." The woman sighed. "Thousands of years passed, and when our explorers met each other on the far side of the galaxy disk, as they stared in recognition of their Terran brothers and sisters, from the planet you call Ur, we knew at that moment within the billions of stars, the human race stood alone."

The other human woman took up the tale. "What could we do? So we decided to return to our world. We decided to create alien children of our own, children who would look at the galaxy with different eyes and with different minds. We returned to Terra and we gave the gift of sentience to your ancestors and to others.

"The rabbit, the wolf, the fox, the cougar and so many others. We had mastered the art of genetics and we gave you and others a bipedal stance, hands, minds, and self-awareness. For five thousand of our years, we spread the life of Terra across the galaxy, allowing it to grow and mature on each planet with no interference from us. Some of those worlds failed and we grieved. Others, like yours, prospered. And above all, we waited. We waited for children to learn and ultimately to venture into the unknown and join us."

Blayne took up the tale. "However, there were others who had different goals. Three thousand years ago, our direct ancestors decided to forsake technology and form a civilization on a world with only a very small amount of metal, a world dedicated to the human mind, to learn and develop. We were given a mined-out planet and we began our great experiment. But now our tale takes a darker turn."

The other man spoke up, his gray eyes solemn as he spoke. "We humans accidentally created the seed of our own destruction. A carrier virus used in genetic manipulation mutated without our knowledge. As it incubated in our bodies, it spread from human to human for it was highly contagious. Humans spread it across the galaxy to each other and when it had incubated for a decade or more, it burst forth with a virulence that caught us off guard. It killed in two hours. Nobody was immune.

"We had deliberately isolated ourselves from the rest of humanity. Though we hope there are other enclaves of humanity across the galaxy not exposed to the virus, our radio, until it died, never picked up any signals from any other survivors."

Blayne spoke up again. "We may be the last of humanity in the galaxy. We who once lived on countless worlds may be reduced to a number of only five billion people."

Illatha tried to stop her hands from shaking. "My people discovered space flight only one thousand years ago. Our legends spoke of gods from the stars who put us on Homeworld seven thousand years previously. In that millennium of space flight, we have explored and discovered almost a thousand worlds, but such a small part of the overall galaxy!

"And what we have discovered makes us believe we may have been the first of your creation to master warp. Of course, the galaxy is big, but we have no reason to suspect otherwise… yet." Illatha looked down at her hands and swallowed. "And we discovered worlds that consist of races like us in spirit: pacifist, vegetarian, peaceful. We wait for them to join us.

"But there are other worlds." Illatha looked up directly into the eyes of the human delegation. "I have seen horrors on other worlds that test my sanity, creatures seeded from ancient Ur that have sunk to their most bestial natures. And… and some of them are close to discovering ways to leave their worlds." Illatha could not help but tremble as she spoke. "You are more than just our Creators. You used your own DNA to give us the ability to speak and to reason." Her voice rose in her growing passion. "We are your children. You are our parents. Help us! Protect us!"

* * *

Illatha finished up her report to Homeworld. She knew there would be repercussions for going off on her own line of questioning, but the ability to sleep better made the price acceptable.

"It was never the plan of this world's original settlers to force their children to stay," she said. "Each child was to be given a choice to leave and rejoin the starfaring humans or stay on their adopted homeworld. Unfortunately, the great plague that killed off the Creators removed that option. With no sizeable metal deposits on their planet, they had little choice. They were trapped on their world with no means to leave. That was clearly their salvation."

Illatha's mind went back to her last conversation with Blayne. "We will not kill," Blayne said. "We will not destroy. Yet, we can be ambassadors and there are other peaceful methods we can use to prevent genocides and wars. And we will do so together, not only with your people but the rest of humanity's children."

"This is Captain Illatha of the *Warren* signing off this report," she said. "The Creators have made the decision to learn from us on how to travel the starways. They have decided to return to Ur."

Illatha smiled. And we," she said, her hands no longer trembling, no fear in her heart, "are orphans no longer."

These are the voyages of the starship Initiative, to boldly go where no cat or dog has gone before…

The Initiative has had many strange encounters in space. What will it find on Planet 227?

(For some other adventures of the T.G.N. Initiative *and its crew, see the anthologies* Inhuman Acts; A Collection of Noir *edited by Ocean Tigrox, and* Dogs of War, Gods With Fur, *and* What the Fox?!, *all edited by Fred Patten; the first three available from FurPlanet Productions and the last from Thurston Howl Publications.)*

The Rocky Spires of Planet 227

by Mary E. Lowd

Captain Pierre Jacques sniffed the air on Planet 227. It was dry and sweet, very still in his whiskers, and chill on his bare pink skin. None of his science officers had mentioned being cold, but then Captain Jacques was the only Sphynx cat in his crew. Everyone else had fur under their Tri-Galactic Navy uniforms.

"It's exhilarating!" Captain Jacques said, eliciting a polite but distracted nod from the nearest officer, a junior scientist tabby who was busy scanning the unusual red-brown rock clusters with a uni-meter.

Captain Jacques twisted his large triangular ears as he looked up to see how far the geometrical spires reached into the violet sky. He didn't usually get to join his reconnaissance teams on their first visit to a planet; it's the captain's job to stay on the ship, making decisions, retaining command. But scans had shown no sign of life or geologic instability on Planet 227, so he'd decided it would be safe to leave his second officer in command and enjoy a little field trip.

"So, what do you think?" Captain Jacques asked the junior scientist tabby. "Geological formation or archeological remnant?"

The tabby closed her uni-meter and holstered it at her hip. "The readings are indeterminate, Captain. This rock is similar to granite and very rich in minerals. The unusual spiral and honeycomb patterns we can see recur fractally all the way down to the molecular level—that could mean it was synthesized, or it could be a natural crystalline structure that's unique to this planet."

Captain Jacques hoped these spires were the remnants of a long-ago civilization. He longed to search for signs of that civilization and learn about what kind of creatures could have once lived here. Were they similar to cats and dogs? Or perhaps the humans who had uplifted cats and dogs so long ago?

But this recon mission was supposed to be a brief stop on *TGN Initiative*'s way to Starport 10.

"Let's gather some samples," Captain Jacques said, raising his voice to address the other four members of his recon team who had strayed farther away during their studies. "We don't have time to do this site justice ourselves, but Starport 10 has a fully equipped science lab. So, let's bring them enough information to decide whether it's worth dispatching a full research team."

"Aye, Captain," they all agreed.

A fluffy white-furred cat gathered atmospheric samples in plastic bulbs that expanded like balloons; a Beagle gathered soil samples; and Captain Jacques helped a German Shepherd and the tabby to cut out a cube of the granite. In order to carefully preserve the honeycomb-swirl pattern on one side, they set their blazors to the narrowest beams possible. The red beams cut into the granite like a hot knife into butter.

The rock sizzled quietly as the three red beams cut through it, and a sparkly purple smoke rose from the growing seam. The smoke smelled like black licorice and made the captain wrinkle his nose. When the block was cut completely free, the German Shepherd, who was the largest of the team, jimmied the heavy stone out of its place at the wide base of the spire. Then the team gathered together with their samples, and Captain Jacques used his comm-pin to call up to the *Initiative* in orbit: "Recon team ready to port home."

All five officers and their samples disappeared from the surface of Planet 227 in a glittering swirl of quantum energy, shifted through the folds of space-time, and reappeared on the telepad in the corner of the *Initiative*'s shuttle bay.

Captain Jacques sighed at the familiar sight of the *Initiative*'s gray walls and control panels with brightly colored computer displays. He loved the *Initiative*; the ship was his home. But sometimes, he wished he'd pursued his degree in archeology instead of working his way up the chain of command in the Tri-Galactic Navy. As the captain of the *Initiative*, he explored farther, traveling from planet to planet, living at the cutting edge of the future, than he would have as an archeologist, but sometimes he just wanted to settle down, dig in, and explore one small piece of the universe deeply—get to know a single corner of the past so well that he felt he truly understood it.

"Take these samples to the science lab and learn what you can," Captain Jacques said. "We might as well get a head start on the work for Starport 10."

Captain Jacques traced a claw over the honeycomb-swirl pattern on the granite block. Then with another sigh, he left his field trip behind and returned to the command deck.

* * *

The granite block hovered under the control of an anti-grav unit. With guidance from the German Shepherd officer, Lieutenant Maggie Barrett, the granite block floated through the corridors of the *Initiative* as lightly as a bubble, all the way to the science lab. Lieutenant Barrett laid the cube of stone to rest on an examination table and began running scans. Within a matter of seconds, the block was subjected to every form of radiation, sound wave, and particle bombardment that the Tri-Galactic Navy used in their standard volley of scans.

Deep inside the granite, crystalline molecules shifted. The honeycomb swirls rearranged with a cascading effect from the micro to macro level, and the rock began to hum.

Lieutenant Barrett couldn't hear the humming even with her large, triangular, canine ears.

* * *

In the medical bay two decks above the science lab, Doctor Waverly Keller—an Irish Setter with cheerfully red fur—found herself arguing with a feline patient.

"Can't you hear that?" Lieutenant LeGuin, an orange tabby wearing techno-focal goggles, complained to the doc. "It's so high and piercing… A kind of whine, or a really high-pitched squeal…" He put a paw to his temple where the goggles interfaced with a bio-mech port buried in his fur. "It feels like it's cutting into the base of my skull."

Doctor Keller frowned at the display on her uni-meter. "According to my readings, there's simply nothing wrong with you. Are you sure those goggles are working right?"

The orange tabby's whiskers turned down. He was probably glaring at her, but Doctor Keller couldn't see his eyes behind the lenses of the techno-focal goggles.

"I ran a complete diagnostic scan on them before coming to you. They're working perfectly," he said. Doctor Keller opened her mouth to object, but Lieutenant LeGuin cut her off. "I know you worry about the goggles' long term effects on my brain, but there are years of studies, dating back to the time of humans, showing that they're safe."

"Hold on a sec," the doctor said, raising a red-furred paw. More patients had filed into the medical bay while she and the lieutenant had been talking. All of them cats. Most of them with flattened ears, a paw held to the head, or other signs suggesting they were experiencing pain.

Doctor Keller left LeGuin waiting. Several of her nurses—all dogs—were seeing to the new patients. The one feline nurse had disappeared into the supply closet and was clutching her head as well. Doctor Keller made the rounds and checked in with each of the new patients. Sure enough, the medical bay was suddenly besieged with feline officers complaining of intense headaches.

After a few moments of thought, Doctor Keller returned to Lieutenant LeGuin.

"As far as my scans show," she said, "there isn't anything wrong with you or any of the other officers here. And, no, I can't hear any high-pitched sound, but while dogs have a keener sense of smell, cats have a wider range of hearing." Doctor Keller looked around the medical bay at all the glowering, cringing cats. Whether she could find anything wrong with them or not, they were clearly suffering. The simplest explanation was that they were actually hearing something she couldn't. "LeGuin, can your goggles pick up sound waves?"

It took the orange tabby an effort to answer her, but he managed to say, "Yeah, probably if I adjust them properly."

Doctor Keller coughed meaningfully, but LeGuin was in too much pain to pick up on subtle signals.

"I think you're all suffering from an actual sound," Doctor Keller said. "I want you to use your goggles to help me trace it to the source."

"I don't want to get *anywhere near* the source of this," LeGuin snapped back, unable to keep the snarl out of his voice. But he adjusted his goggles, and the hum appeared on their lenses as an oscillating dim blue glow. With one paw pressed against the pain in his head, LeGuin followed the blue glow, turning his head to see where it grew brighter.

The blue glow led LeGuin and Keller out of the medical bay and through the winding corridors of the *Initiative*. The blue glow grew brighter and brighter, drawing LeGuin to the science lab. When the doors to the lab opened, the blue glow flashed brightly inside LeGuin's goggles. He pointed, faintly, in the direction where it was brightest.

His orange paw pointed directly to the granite slab, covered in its swirling honeycomb patterns. Then he collapsed on the floor. Doctor Keller barged past him.

The German Shepherd officer, Lieutenant Barrett, stood beside the block of granite, examining the data she'd been gathering. "Doctor Keller," she said when the doctor came up beside her, unaccountably snarling and angry. "What can I do for you?"

"Not for me," Doctor Keller barked. "For my patients. Cats all over this ship are suffering mysterious headaches, and they're being caused—somehow—by this cube of rock."

LeGuin rolled on the floor behind the doctor, moaning and clutching his head. Doctor Keller gestured with a red-furred paw at the equipment and scanners pointed at the granite cube. "Shut it all down."

"I... can't do that without confirmation from the captain," Lieutenant Barrett said.

Doctor Keller snorted. Based on LeGuin's condition, she doubted the captain—*another cat*—was in any shape to give confirmation or, really, make decisions of any kind. Nonetheless, she touched her paw to her comm-pin and said, "Doctor Keller to Captain Jacques."

A moment later, the captain's feline voice chirped at them from the doctor's comm-pin; it sounded tight and strained, but he said, "Yes, Doctor, what is it?"

"Tell this science officer with me that she has to shut down whatever she's doing to this big rock cube."

The captain's voice came through, haltingly: "We're studying that sample from Planet 227. It has highly unusual and very interesting properties. Is there a problem?"

"It's causing your headache."

After a long pause, the captain said emphatically, "Shut it down. Now. And I'll be there as soon as I can."

The German Shepherd shut off every scan still in progress, and, slowly, LeGuin's headache receded. The orange tabby was just pulling himself off the floor and back onto his paws when the captain arrived.

Captain Jacques stared at the granite cube with steely gray-green eyes. "Cycle through the different scans," he told Lieutenant Barrett. "Start the scans one at a time, and we'll figure out which one caused this."

"Are you serious?" Lieutenant LeGuin cried out, still laying on the floor.

"We need to know exactly what happened," the captain said. He kept himself composed, his pink ears standing tall, even though he'd most likely been experiencing as much pain as had knocked Lieutenant LeGuin on the floor.

Doctor Keller watched both cats closely while the German Shepherd restarted the scans. As soon as Lieutenant Barrett started up the high-energy nano-structure scan, LeGuin began rolling and moaning on the floor again. Captain Jacques' pink-skinned ears flattened, but he showed no other sign of pain. He was one tough cat. "Turn it down," he said through gritted fangs. "As low as it goes."

"Not off?" LeGuin yowled in disbelieving dismay.

"We need to understand what's happening." The captain's ears were still flat. The pink skin around his muzzle was drawn tight.

The German Shepherd's paw hovered over the controls. She looked concerned, afraid to do anything in case her actions might make the cats' situation worse. "Maybe we should leave this sample for Starport 10 to study…"

"*You heard my order: turn it down.*" A cat with a headache has little patience. Besides, Captain Jacques thought, if the cube of granite were dangerous, they could hardly take it to a busy starport. It was better to get the analysis *done*. Here. And now.

Lieutenant Barrett worked the controls, and Captain Jacques felt his headache lessening as the high-pitched squeal grew less piercing.

Still lying on the floor, LeGuin said, "The visual display of the sound pattern—it's changing." The blue glow in his goggle lenses had dimmed from the brilliant flash of blue when he'd first entered the science lab. Now the blue light pulsed and moved, forming starbursts and squiggles.

"We need to document it." Captain Jacques moved to the nearest computer station and set it to record and analyze the dangerous, high-pitched hum from the granite cube. After a few minutes, he said, "That should be enough data. Turn the scan off again."

"Thank goodness," LeGuin muttered under his whiskers. He was not sorry to see the pretty blue squiggles disappear from the lenses in his goggles. The sound itself withdrew from his ears like a knife pulling out of his skull.

Doctor Keller leaned over Captain Jacques' shoulder to see the computer analysis of the sound on the display screen. They ran the data through several algorithms before drawing any conclusions, but both the captain and the doctor could see which algorithm was having the most success.

"So, what's going on?" LeGuin asked, still sitting on the floor and rubbing the orange stripes on his sore furry temples.

Captain Jacques could hardly believe the words as he said them: "It's language. Almost too primitive to translate, but it's linguistic thought."

"What does it say?" LeGuin asked.

"'Cruel squishy bags of organic fuzz.'" Captain Jacques couldn't help from snickering as he relayed the words. "I think the rock's talking about us. We're the bags of fuzz."

"Hilarious," LeGuin said drily.

"I wonder if we could actually talk to it," Captain Jacques pondered.

"I don't know, Captain." Doctor Keller's eyebrows were peaked, and her muzzle strained. "If it's calling us cruel, then I think we've been hurting it." The doctor was a deeply kind dog who could empathize with anything—even a hunk of granite who'd been hurting every single one of the feline officers under her care.

"Or maybe it's just angry that we kidnapped it," Captain Jacques suggested. "If we explained that we're taking it to Starport 10 where it can observe the complexity of our civilization, maybe it will want to go! Maybe it would enjoy being an explorer, like us!" The captain was nothing if not optimistic. He looked at Lieutenant Barrett and asked, "Do you think you can reverse the translation algorithm and broadcast our speech back to the rock?"

"I can try, Captain." Lieutenant Barrett fiddled with the controls for a while and then said, "The translation will be rough at best, but the more the rock talks, the better it will get." She pointed with her large paw toward the comm-pin on Captain Jacques' chest. "I've routed it through your comm-pin; you can start whenever you're ready."

Captain Jacques tapped his paw on his comm-pin and began speaking in slow, carefully pronounced words: "Granite life-form, I am Captain Pierre Jacques of the Tri-Galactic Navy star vessel *Initiative*. My crew welcomes you." When he finished speaking, the same high-pitched squeal began, this time emitted from his own comm-pin.

The granite block answered in high-pitched hums translated into mono-tone speech through the comm-pin: "*Squishy bags of fuzz are disingenuous. Squishy bags of fuzz tell lies. Pain. Abduction. Torture. Lies. Cruel, cruel squishy bags of organic fuzz.*"

Once the captain recovered from the latest volley of high-pitched squeals, still inaudible to the dogs in the room, he said to the granite block through his comm-pin, "We had no intention of causing you harm. We didn't know you were alive." The captain's own words struck him, and he repeated them softly to himself. "You are alive."

The geometric spires under that lavender sky hadn't been the remnants of a civilization. They *were* a civilization. Alive and vibrant; too big and slow and unfamiliar for the cats and dogs of the Tri-Galactic Navy to recognize what had been underneath their very paws. Starport 10 would send a long-term research team to Planet 227 for sure now; Captain

Jacques would insist on it. They would reach out to and communicate with the geometrical rocky spires.

As the captain let himself get carried away with futuristic visions of brokering diplomacy between a civilization of sentient rocky spires and the cats and dogs of the Tri-Galactic Navy, Doctor Keller moved closer to the granite block.

The Irish Setter whispered, "We're sorry we've hurt you." The words were picked up by the captain's comm-pin and translated.

LeGuin could not have sounded more disdainful as he said, "We're sorry we hurt a slab of rock that's been insulting us and screaming in a voice that still feels like it's melting my brain?"

"Have sympathy," Doctor Keller said. "This block of rock was ripped from its home, ported into a starship in the sky, whisked away, and examined by unrecognizably exotic alien lifeforms today."

"It's easier to have sympathy when you're not in pain," LeGuin observed. The orange tabby wasn't ready to forgive a rock for giving him a splitting headache.

"I'm sure our guest feels much the same." Doctor Keller's red-furred eyebrows raised in concern as she looked at the cube of granite, covered in its honeycomb swirls. The twisty lines of the patterns seemed to writhe and move. The rock almost looked like it was swelling, growing larger, but that may have been an optical illusion caused by the writhing honeycomb swirls. Was the movement part of its communication? An expression of its pain? The doctor didn't know, but she did know that the rock wasn't happy here. "We have to go back to Planet 227," she said. "We need to take it home."

"*Home, home, go home*—" The words issued from Captain Jacques' comm-pin in a monotone, but the high-pitched squeal that accompanied them from the rock grew louder and louder until the captain himself fell to his knees on the floor. He clawed at his hairless ears, clamping them against his pink-skinned skull. Lieutenant LeGuin yowled inarticulately.

"Help me get the cats out of here!" Doctor Keller cried as she grabbed the captain around the waist. She helped him up and let him lean against her as he stumbled out of the room. Lieutenant Barrett scooped up LeGuin in her arms; the orange tabby was struggling more with the noise than the captain. He shuddered and jolted in Barrett's strong canine arms, almost like he was suffering from a seizure. Barrett rushed out of the science lab, and as soon as they were in the corridor outside, Doctor Keller sealed the door behind them.

"Can you soundproof the science lab?" Doctor Keller asked. The captain was leaning against the wall behind her, struggling to simply stay upright.

Lieutenant Barrett laid down her own feline charge, and then she went to work on the panel beside the science lab's door. As she worked, the two cats continued to moan, and the captain's comm-pin kept babbling, "*Home, home, go home, home.*" In irritation, the captain ripped the comm-pin from the breast of his uniform, tearing the fabric, and threw the shiny gold device down the hallway. It bounced off the wall and skidded along the floor before coming to a stop.

Finally, Lieutenant Barrett announced, "Got it!" Neither of the dogs could hear a difference, but the two cats visibly relaxed. "I've placed a sound-dampening field around the science lab that's blocking exactly the frequency that the granite block uses to communicate."

Down the hall, the captain's comm-pin continued babbling in its monotone as the computer continued to relay the granite block's speech to it. "We can still hear the rock sample talking…" Captain Jacques took a deep, cleansing breath. "Does that mean it will still hear us if we talk to it through my comm-pin?"

"Yes, Captain," Lieutenant Barrett confirmed.

"Captain," Doctor Keller admonished, "you're in no shape to be in command right now. As the ship's doctor, I believe all cats should be relieved of duty until this situation is resolved." As soon as she said those words, Doctor Keller knew she'd pushed the matter too far. The captain would never agree to relieving every feline officer of duty.

"The cats under my command are all navy officers," Captain Jacques spat, "trained to withstand much harsher conditions than a little unpleasant noise." If he'd had fur, it would have fluffed out in irritation. Instead, his pink skin felt all tingly under his uniform. "Besides, the noise is contained now." He stalked down the hall, hairless tail swinging behind him, and swept the babbling comm-pin up in his paw. "Granite lifeform, we intended no harm. We will return you to your planet of origin."

But instead of answering gratefully, the translated voice over the comm-pin said, "*Trapped, alone, darkness, isolation, lies… destroy squishy bags of organic fuzz! Squish them! Squish! Die! Die!*"

The lights went out all along the corridor and alarms began to blare, followed by flashing red alarm lights.

"This first contact mission isn't going as well as one might hope," Doctor Keller commented.

"I didn't know that it *was* a first contact mission until it was already a disaster," the captain grumbled. "Lieutenants—" he addressed Barrett and LeGuin, "do you have any idea what's happening?"

Lieutenant LeGuin shook his head. The red alarm lights reflected hauntingly off the lenses of his goggles. "My goggles aren't picking up anything unusual anymore."

Lieutenant Barrett examined the display panel beside the sealed door and said, "The granite block has found a way to communicate directly with the computer system in the science lab. For now, the ship's main computer is protected by a firewall and the sound dampening field around the lab. But some of our best computers are in this lab; the firewall won't hold long, and the granite block has already managed to overload several non-critical systems with intermittent energy bursts from the lab's equipment. That's why the lights are out and the alarms are on."

Captain Jacques rolled his gray-green eyes. "This isn't diplomacy; this is mollifying a crying kitten throwing a temper tantrum."

"That's what happens when our first act in meeting a new species is to kidnap one of their babies," the doctor said.

"Or cut off one of their semi-sentient tentacles," Captain Jacques said, remembering how he and Lieutenant Barrett had literally sliced the block of granite out of the base of a large spire with blazor beams. "Let's get this flailing tentacle-rock-baby back to its home."

* * *

Captain Jacques left Lieutenants Barrett and LeGuin to monitor the sealed science lab, and Doctor Keller accompanied him to the bridge. The flight back to Planet 227 only took a few minutes at top speed, and the artificial gravity aboard the ship only cut out for about half of that time due to the granite block's meddling.

When the *Initiative* arrived in orbit, the planet below looked much different from when they'd left. Purple waves of light danced over the surface of the red-brown sphere like an aurora borealis.

"Can you magnify the view to show the area of the planet our recon team visited?"

The helmsdog complied, and the view zoomed in on the center of the waves of purple light.

"I thought so," Captain Jacques said. "We need to teleport the rock sample in science lab five back down to the site of the recon mission. I know it won't be exactly where we cut it from, but hopefully it'll be close enough. Can you do that?"

"We'll have to shut down the dampening field around the science lab in order to do so," the helmsdog said.

Captain Jacques gritted his fangs and said, "Make it happen."

"Aye, Captain." The helmsdog dropped the dampening field around the science lab.

Immediately, the captain's headache returned, so strong that the pain knocked him down. From his vantage on the bridge floor, Captain Jacques saw purple bolts like lightning snake up from the planet's surface and strike at the *Initiative*. He felt his ship rock under him, and then his stomach lurched with the momentary loss and sudden return of gravity. His head exploded with a pain so bright that his vision sparkled, and for an instant, he wondered if he'd died because he hadn't known his feline body was capable of experiencing so much pain.

"Done!" the helmsdog announced.

Captain Jacques' vision cleared, and the pain subsided like a tide going out at the beach. On the viewscreen, he saw the purple waves of light dissipate, leaving the rocky sphere below the same dusty red-brown it had been before he'd ever set paw upon it; before he'd ever smelled its dry, sweet air.

"Our computer recorded a burst of sound waves coming from the planet," the helmsdog said. "Extremely complex data, kilobytes worth in only a fraction of a second."

"And the computer recorded it?" Captain Jacques asked, brushing aside the doctor who was busily checking him to be sure he was alright after his most recent collapse.

"Yes, Captain, all of it."

Captain Jacques wondered what the network of rocky spires on the planet's surface had transmitted to them, but he also knew that it wasn't his job to figure it out. "Transmit the recorded data ahead of us to Starport 10, and then set a course to follow it." He looked forward to reading the reports that the scientists on Starport 10 would generate as they analyzed the data. He hoped they'd send a team to Planet 227 to follow up with the rocky spires, forge a diplomatic connection, and learn what stories a civilization composed of stone had to tell.

But Captain Jacques wouldn't be the one to stay here and talk to the rocks. He realized with a little surprise that he didn't want to be. Diplomacy and research are slow work, unlike the adventure he'd had today, discovering that a simple rock was actually so much more.

If there were sentient rocky spires on Planet 227, what would be on the next unexplored planet? And the one after that? There was no telling what amazing things were waiting, out there in the universe, for an enterprising cat to find them. And Captain Jacques intended to be that cat.

*Here are more spacemen exploring a new planet, but from its natives'
point of view.*

*The interstellar humans are technologically superior. But the primitive
squirrel-like natives know the home ground much better.*

Defiant

by Harwich Wolcott

Tezkee stopped and looked up—something was watching him. He was halfway across one of the vine-woven bridges that tied the trees of his village together when he felt the fur across his shoulders and back prickle with awareness.

His friend Khaztik had been walking the vineway right behind him and almost ran into his backside. He groused, "Chkchk, Tez! Why did you stop?"

Tezkee leaned off to the left side, towards the sunlit center of the village circle trying to get a better view of what was spying on him. The middle of the circle of vines and bowers was open space, an empty pore in the skin of the forest where one of the colossal trees had died and fallen. It was a very long way down to the dark forest floor, as both of them knew. As all the Ketchvash knew. Tezkee let go of the cable with both of his hands to shade his eyes as he peered upwards. He clung to the cable with only his footclaws, knees bent to absorb the gentle sway.

Khaztik didn't like that. Even though Tez was the surest climber he knew, no one should tempt Vash like that. And no one should stop halfway across a vineway in any case—it was rude to block others, even though there was no one behind them.

Lacking an explanation, Khaztik had to follow Tezkee's gaze. Then he, too, saw it.

Something floated above the circle. It hovered in place like one of the swarming, delicious insects that traveled through their territory following a storm. It moved from place to place as if it had no respect for the ground's hungry pull. It had no wings like the scaled criers that nested in squawking colonies at the very top of the green canopy, above their own bowers. It was far too large to be an insect, and reminded him more of a huge floating eyeball. Its body was round and white, surrounded by what looked like eight smaller rings. A dark spot on the center body resembled a small pupil. It was looking right at them. Khaztik perked his ears tall, turning the cupped and tufted membranes in the direction of the thing, but the only noise he could hear was a soft whistling, like wind through leaves, though the air was still today.

"What is it?" he asked Tezkee.

"Vash's eye," said his friend with confidence.

"You've seen it before?"

Tezkee wouldn't take his eyes off it. "My brother said the warders killed it yesterday."

"Did you see it?"

"No. He said it fell into the undershadow."

"Keep going," urged Khaztik. "Get to the next platform. We should tell the warders it came back!"

The object seemed to react to being noticed. It changed direction and sped over them, out of the open village circle. The foliage soon blocked their view.

"It's getting away!" chirped Tezkee, who dropped his hands back to the vineway and raced towards the platform, his twin tails tracing arcs behind him.

"What?" asked Khaztik, following as fast as he could. By the time he reached the platform, Tezkee was already climbing the tree at its center, scaling the vines and rough bark without looking back down. "Wait!" Khaztik called from below. "You can't just go after it yourself! We should shout the alarm call."

"No! It will hear and escape. Come with me. We can surprise it."

Khaztik ground his teeth and dithered for a few moments, but then began to climb. He could see no sign of his friend's tails, but kept climbing as the tree thinned and split into a maze of branches no larger than a vineway. He hissed for Tezkee, and felt some relief when he warbled a low reply.

Khaztik picked his way carefully to the branches where Tezkee was perched. When he got there, his friend pointed through a break in the broadleaf canopy. The thing was hovering there just above the top leaves. The black spot appeared to be looking back towards the village circle and not at them.

"It was watching us," whispered Khaztik.

"It is Vash's eye."

"The warders will get it, Tez. We're not supposed to be all the way up here."

"I will be a warder soon. I can get it," said Tezkee, reaching for the spear strapped to his back. He had only earned it fifteen days ago, during the age ritual. He had been itching for a worthy target to prove himself. Khaztik clicked his teeth. "It feels wrong, Tez. Bad. Don't hand Vash the knife He would cut you with," he quoted the elders' saying.

"I am not afraid of Vash," growled Tezkee before hoisting himself up so that his head was just below one of the great leaves. His grey and white fur was tinted green by the sunlight passing through the leaf. He untied his spear and the coil of twine rope attached to the end, then fitted the loop at the end of the rope over his arm. He hefted his spear, finding the balance point, then tracked the hovering thing. Khaztik watched his friend, knowing he should stop him before he did something foolish but at the same time wanting to see him hit the eye. He almost reached for his own spear.

Tezkee launched the weapon with a sudden heave and the uncoiling rope followed. Khaztik craned his neck trying to see through the gaps in the leaves. A few moments later there was an odd sound, almost like the polished seashells the matrons had dangling from strings outside the youngling bower. The sharp bone-tipped spear had found its target and Tezkee let out a triumphant chirp. He began pulling the rope in with both hands. The spear crashed through the canopy, but nothing was stuck to the tip. Khaztik climbed up to peek out of the canopy and saw that the thing was wobbling in the air. Tezkee had wounded it, it seemed. It was flying in a tight circle and drifting towards them at the same time.

Tezkee gathered the rope in, and retrieved his spear as fast as he could, trying to keep track of the eye's location at the same time. Once he had his spear in hand he watched, waited, then jabbed at the object as it veered close. Khaztik ducked back down and out of the way. The strange flying thing was larger than he had thought—about half as big as himself. Tezkee jabbed again and got his spear through one of the small rings and lodged the barb point there. That seemed to send the thing into a sudden frenzy and it jerked away, carrying Tezkee's spear with it.

It sped back towards the village center and Khaztik said, "Tez! Let go of the line!" but Tez held it in both hands and braced himself against the branch.

Khaz saw that Tez wasn't going to be persuaded to be reasonable. He pulled his bone-blade knife from the scabbard on his back, meaning to cut the line, but everything happened too fast. The rope went taut and Tezkee leaned back to reel the thing back in. For just a moment he held his own but then his footclaws tore the bark from his branch and he fell, crashing into another nearby branch. Now clinging to the rope he was dragged through the canopy and bounced against several branches and through leaves and crier nests before swinging out into the open space of the circle.

Dozens of the tribe were watching as he swung from the strange object. Only then did the fear break through. Now he felt the hollow certainty that Vash had lured him in, and he had been easy prey.

Khaztik didn't make it back down to the platform before his friend and the eye had plummeted down into the undershadow.

* * *

"God damn it!" spat Lin, stripping the headset off and blinking as his eyes readjusted to the dim light inside the landing craft's flight deck. The other three members of the landing team were still watching the feed from the drone on the big monitor screen as it spun end-over-end, falling. The receding sky flashed like a strobe until it stopped with a sudden burst of static and went dark.

"Is it dead?" asked Lieutenant Powers, leaning forward to look over the shoulder of Engineer Anders, who was studying the telemetry on her terminal station.

Before Anders could answer, Lin asked, "What, the drone or the fucking squirrel?" while he rubbed the bridge of his nose where the VR set had left a red mark.

Dr. Chauhan frowned and admonished in her precise Indian accent, "They are *not* squirrels. It is dangerous to anthropomorphize as I must remind you." She knew she was wasting her breath, though.

Anders addressed Powers' original question, "No active signals from Drone 2. No responses to pings. But it may be going through an emergency power cycle. We should know in just under two minutes."

"Lin's question does raise a serious issue, though," said Captain Hernandez via the radio link to the *SRS Hermes*, high above in synchronous orbit. "We may well have just caused the death of one of the natives. Not an auspicious beginning to this mission."

"Maybe they won't make the connection," offered Lin.

Dr. Chauhan said, "No. They are intelligent. They make tools, build homes and bridges between the trees. They possess language. All these rely on logic and abstract reasoning. When we make full contact, they will conclude that we sent the drones."

"And without knowing why we sent them, it seems most logical to think that we're hostile, right?" asked Captain Hernandez.

"That seems quite possible," agreed Chauhan. "Though it is again risky to speculate."

"What can we do to gain their trust in that case?"

"We must be able to speak to them. To communicate our peaceful intent."

Powers snorted. "Hi! Nice planet. Can we move in? They'd have to be idiots to take that as peaceful."

Chauhan bristled. "If they knew our imperialist history, perhaps! But we are here to ensure we do not repeat those mistakes. They are creatures of intelligence, Powers! Of all the planets humanity has visited and attempted to tame, this beautiful forested world is the only one we have found with other *minds*."

"It's also the only one that could support large numbers of colonists on the surface, without domes or generations of terraforming. We're moving in, whether the squirrels like it or not, doctor."

Chauhan wanted to counter Lieutenant Powers' abrasive pragmatism, but she bit her tongue.

Anders offered, "ALICE needs more language samples. Much more. She's begun decryption but she needs context to form a full language profile."

"And that means more spy drones," said Powers. "Well, we have two more down here with us. Maybe someone else should fly them, though, eh?"

Lin scowled, "You think it's *my* fault they keep attacking them, sir? I have to get close enough to get audio and video. They can *hear* the drones coming. You can give it a try, lieutenant; we'll see how well you do." Lin unstrapped himself from his seat and got out of it too fast. In his frustration he had forgotten that Kepler-9f had only 70% of earth gravity and ended up banging his head on the low ceiling of the cabin. He rubbed his head and retreated into the empty sleeping cabin.

Powers waited until Lin was off the flight deck before proposing, "Maybe we should just go out and announce ourselves. Show them what they're dealing with. Hiding in the ship and sneaking around with drones is getting on everyone's nerves, it seems."

Captain Hernandez said, "No. We do this by the book."

"The people who wrote 'the book' had no clue what we would find here," groused Powers.

"They knew it was possible, otherwise we wouldn't have it. Doctor Chauhan is here because of this possibility. She is our xenosociology expert, Lieutenant. Defer to her analysis, clear?"

"Yes, Captain," said Powers, barely hiding his disdain.

Dr. Chauhan knew the lieutenant had requested another space marine for the landing team instead of her. Powers had argued that no one could be an actual authority in something that no one had actually encountered before. And further that a show of force would be more valuable than whatever cultural exchange Chauhan had in mind, at least at first.

Anders, oblivious to the tension, announced, "Drone 2 is back online!" All heads turned back to the central monitor. Even Lin came back out of the sleeping cabin. The picture was still just black, but there was audio now. The crunching of dead leaves and a low keening sound could be heard.

"Switch to infrared," suggested Lin.

Anders did so and the picture on the monitor changed to a monochrome. They could see indistinct cool-temperature shapes until suddenly a four-finger hand with long curved claws waved into view. The drone was jostled, turned over. Then the screeching began.

The natives were not squirrels, as Dr. Chauhan kept reminding them, but they sounded a lot like them. Their language seemed to be dominated by high-pitched and grating chattering with a mix of clicks and piercing squeaks.

"He sounds pretty pissed," said Powers, and Chauhan didn't bother to warn against making assumptions this time, as it appeared he was correct. The Keplerian had grabbed the drone by one of the impeller rings and was staring straight at the camera lens while apparently unloading every insult known to his furry kind.

"Well, at least ALICE will know how to curse in their language," smirked Lin.

Even if it was not under normal light conditions, this was their first close-up look at one of them and they all stared at the screen as it continued its animated tirade.

"You see the teeth? Not like one of our rodentia at all," said Anders. "Omnivorous, I guess. Like our ape ancestors. Wide-set eyes, but still binocular focus. Oh, see that? It can swivel its ears independently. Neat! You know, I almost don't believe this is real. Once you get past the little details like the double tails, it's amazing how similar they are to terrestrial life. To us, even. Ears, eyes, nose, mouth, arms, legs… I honestly never expected to find more than moss when I saw the long-range scan reports. What are the odds?"

"Astronomical," smiled Chauhan. "An argument that those in favor of divine intervention will make."

Anders said, "I'm not ready to throw up my hands and say 'God did it' yet. The panspermia hypothesis is still… "

Powers cut in, "Wait, wait, doctor, I didn't know you were a woman of faith! Do you think God created this world, like He created ours?"

"I do not know what to think, but I prefer to keep my options open," answered Chauhan. She wasn't about to get into a theological debate with a man whose definition of faith was extremely narrow. Her own childhood had featured the weak remnants of her family's Hindu religion, a skeleton of tradition on which hung very little actual belief in literal gods. Her doctorates in anthropology and theology had broadened her sense of the divine, but she had never experienced the certainty of God that men like Powers did.

"However you want to believe this happened and against what odds," sighed Captain Hernandez on the radio, "This planet has an indigenous population, and we need to learn as much as we can about them before the colonization can begin. They may be a bigger threat than you estimate, Lieutenant. Or they may know something vital about this world that we would otherwise miss. Our mission is to observe and make peaceful contact. History is waiting for us back at home. Let's not be remembered as the ones who started a war with the first intelligent alien species we've ever met, all right?"

"Aye," came the chorus of agreement, though Powers muttered, "Won't be much of a war."

As if the alien had heard them, its angry chattering stopped. It was no longer glaring at the camera. Instead it was focused off to the side, its ears perked to face something else and its teeth bared. It hissed and then the viewpoint was bouncing chaos as it dragged the drone along with it, running.

* * *

Tezkee still somehow thought he was in control of the situation even as he swung across open space, holding on to his spear's rope. He had spotted at least three open vineways he would be close enough to grab with his feet on the other side, then all he had to do was reel in his prize. A fine first kill for him and his new spear, witnessed by most of his tribe. He'd be made a warder on the spot! But about halfway into the arc that would carry him the rest of the way, the thing that he still thought of as Vash's eye tumbled from the air as if it had died. It fell straight down, and so did he.

Terror replaced confidence as he had nothing to hold and the sky began to recede, faster and faster. He twisted his body around, spreading his arms and legs and both his tails to try to slow his descent. He had to grab something—a vine, a branch, anything. His claws shredded leaves and small vines as he flew past until a large branch returned the favor and pain exploded in his arm. He screamed.

At first it was just from the pain, but as he tumbled he looked up at the ragged circle of sky and screamed even harder in rage at Vash. Vash, who had sent His eye to torment him. Tezkee spread his legs and his unbroken arm and thrust his chest out towards the sky and cursed Vash. Vash didn't answer, but then Tezkee crashed through the new foliage of the younger trees competing to fill the gap left by the fallen giant. He bounced off small, flexible branches and found himself heading for a tangle of fresh vines. He plummeted past it before he could even make a grab but his spear, still trailing him by the rope around his unbroken arm, got tangled in the mass. The sudden change in direction stole his breath and made his broken arm feel as if it had been shattered again twice as hard. Before he could scream once more, his spear snapped and he dropped again, this time into one of the massive sloping roots of the mature trees.

He had no more breath to scream with, and bounced off the moss-covered bark. He slid and crashed through the lowest level of greenery into the eternal shadow that blanketed the forest floor along with enough rotting leaves to cushion his final impact.

Dazed, he lay there just trying to breathe, but the sound of his quarry crashing through the same foliage he had just come through aroused his fury again. He rolled to his side and coughed, favoring his broken arm. Then he began to crawl in the direction of the sound. The eye was warm, and he could see its warmth against the cool leaves and roots and runners. He muttered and whined as he struggled through the decomposing filth, trying not to think about how he and the rest of the village let their waste drop freely from high above.

His new spear was broken, and he abandoned the rope with furious regret. When he reached the eye, he grabbed it by one of the unnaturally round rings that encircled it—it was far lighter than he had expected.

He stared into the small black pupil of God and cursed him. "Ha! I live, Vash, I LIVE! You and your flying eye could not kill me. I will return your torment ten times! The healers will mend my arm and I will *destroy* you! You are a shit-eating motherless pock-hided tail-less idiot and your end is near. Hear me! I will take your eye back up to my village and we will tear it to pieces and smear each piece with shit and scatter each one from a different tree. Do you hear me, Vash? Stinking witless liar! You will never defeat us! One day I will stand before you and I will thrust my death spear through your other eye! I… "

He halted as he heard rustling from across the dark thicket. He perked his tufted ears high and peered into the gloom, but saw nothing. But he knew what lurked down here, and his foolish wild shouting had attracted them. He hissed in anger at himself now, so concerned with Vash's eye he had forgotten for a moment that Vash had other weapons, other servants he could call. The great slavering beasts ruled the undershadow, though his tribe hunted them for meat and bone and hide. His age ritual had included such a hunt, and he had plunged his sharpened bone knife into the eyes of one such beast, dodging the snapping hungry jaws while his brothers held it back, tied but full of fury.

But that had been with a full hunting party of his kin. Alone, he knew he would be the hunted today. The beasts were strong and deadly, but they could not climb like his kind. So he took hold of his prize and dragged it towards the nearest of the great trees. There, his problem became clear. He could climb one-handed, slowly by backing up the tree feet first, but he could not also carry the eye. He should have kept the rope, but searching for it now would be unwise with the beasts already smelling his blood.

"Your beasts will not find me, Vash," he muttered, trying to convince both Vash and himself. "I have bested them before, eaten their flesh." He rested with his back cradled in one of the moss-covered folds of bark. More sounds of great furry bodies moving through the underbrush and leaves came to him from both sides, as well as in front. They knew he was injured. Perhaps they remembered that he and his brothers had killed one of their kin, and wanted revenge. He thrust his chest forward and his good arm back and shouted at the beasts, "Come, then! I will take you to face Vash with me!"

The beasts did not sound deterred by his bravado. He could hear their low-throated grunts and snuffles. He didn't want to be torn apart by them, of course. And he did not actually think he could kill even one with no weapons and a broken arm. He hefted the eye and looked into it. It weighed so little, like a giant empty crier's egg. He threaded one of his tails through one of the outer rings, half expecting them to turn to biting jaws that would render him a tail-less outcast. But nothing happened. He threaded his second tail through the neighboring ring and then turned his rear end towards the obscured sky. His strong foot claws gripped the moss and the bark underneath while the eye hung from the roots of his tails over his head.

He began to pull himself backwards up the tree as the blood-warm shapes of the beasts came into view. They saw him trying to escape upwards and lunged, three of them at once. Teeth clipped his ear, the hot, stinking breath washing over his face. Another swiped its deadly claws and ripped the fur and flesh of his good arm while he desperately tried to push himself up with it. The last one jumped and slapped its paws on the tree and roared, the deep rumble of its anger resonating in Tezkee's belly.

He wasted no more breath on insults and taunts now. Falling was death and leaving his prize was dishonor. He would bring the eye back to the elders. He anticipated the glory that would be his. The many females who would want to mate with him. The first warder's praise. He climbed more cautiously once he was out of the beasts' range. The light of the sun returned to him as he broke from the underbrush and he wished he could look up instead of down at the staring eyes of the beasts as they snapped at the blood dripping from his fresh wounds.

When he reached the lowest platform of the village he crawled backwards onto it, on his belly, and collapsed. He let the eye rest next to him but did not release it from his tails. His legs felt boneless and the abused muscles twitched, his claws still grasping at phantom bark and unable to relax. When he had recovered enough strength he lifted his head and called out, screeching to the whole village that he needed help.

He expected the warders to come, and he imagined their faces when they saw his prize. But it was a pair of matrons who answered his call and found him there. The warders, they said, had all gone to the sea shore to challenge Vash's herald.

* * *

"He still climbing?" asked Powers.

"Yes," said Anders, who was watching the swaying video feed from the crippled but still broadcasting Drone 2 out of the corner of her eye while she studied the maps that the AI had been able to synthesize from the drone data. This included Drone 3, which was in flight. Lin was wearing the VR headset again.

"Tenacious little bastard," said Powers, impressed. He asked Dr. Chauhan, "What does he think he's got there? He's going to a lot of trouble to carry it back up to his friends."

"I should not speculate until we know more about their language and culture. When we make assumptions, we blind ourselves. You assume it is male, for instance. Possibly because you associate its display of bravado with the male gender. They may not even have equivalent genders to ours. All I can say is that it spoke to the drone as if it was alive, further as if it expected the drone to understand. Also it was not afraid of the drone, that much was clear."

The feed from Drone 3 dominated the central screen. Lin was flying it low, coming up under the lowest platforms of the circular treetop village, attempting to stay in their shadows. There were less natives on the lower levels to listen to, however, so he darted behind the great trees as he tried to climb to more populated areas. Lin's jaw was tight as he nudged the controls, fearful of being spotted again.

"Maybe that means they won't be afraid of us, either," offered Anders.

"Yeah, I'm starting to get that feeling, Anders. And it's not a good feeling," said Powers. He asked the disembodied AI, "How's the codebreaking going, ALICE?"

The synthesized female voice of the ship's AI could have been mistaken for a British news anchor. It replied, "I have identified 547 unique vocalizations and am compiling syntactical reference nodes. Job completion estimate 68 per cent."

Anders said, "Well at least that's… um… "

"That's what?"

"Uhh, I think we have a new problem."

"A language problem?"

Anders shook her head. "Here, look," she said, switching the main monitor's view from Drone 3 to one of their craft's external cameras. It showed a view of the edge of the forest. They had chosen a landing site on a broad gravel beach on the shore of one of the larger oceans, in part because there simply was no other open land to be found. The primeval forests dominated the continents. And now out of the shorter, scrubbier trees at the edge of that forest came the natives. They walked upright and with clear purpose, fanning out into a ragged line and advancing on the landing craft.

"Oh, my," said Chauhan.

"What? What's going on?" asked Lin, still flying Drone 3.

"We've got company, ahead of schedule," said Powers. "Keep flying."

"I should bring it back."

"No. They'd probably just attack it like the first two. Keep it at the village, maybe find someplace to hide it for now."

"Roger," said Lin.

"Should we lift off?" asked Anders. "They look aggressive."

Lieutenant Powers asked, "You think we're in any danger from *them*? Come on."

The furry not-squirrel-people walked onto the gravel of the beach. They had their spears raised while their lemur-like tails lashed behind them, the fur puffed out to its fullest.

The Captain said over the radio, "Prepare for departure. We don't want a confrontation. Lin, park that drone and get the thrusters online."

"Just give me a minute, looking for a safe spot."

"We don't really have much time, Lin. They're closing fast. Ditch the drone if you have to."

"They kind of caught us with our pants down, captain. Thrusters won't be powered up before they get here if they're that close," argued Lin as he continued to pilot the drone.

"Great. Other options?" asked Powers.

Anders furrowed her brow at her readouts and said, "We should be able to manage a greeting even if ALICE is still working. Might make them stop and consider."

"They're almost here," said Powers. "We'll have to try it while we get our act together. Man, they didn't waste any time. One of them must have spotted the ship and then gone back to get his buddies."

"Wait and we see what they do," said the Captain. "If they say 'hello', we respond in kind. If they attack I think you're probably right in your threat assessment, Powers. We can withstand primitive weapons until the thrusters are up and we can withdraw."

The advancing mob formed a wide semicircle around the front of the landing craft. They stopped their advance when they were about five meters away from the wings and nose. Almost every screen in the crew cabin was trained on them now from three different cameras. They still held their spears ready, but now they had begun to chatter to each other. They wore little in the way of clothing—decorative bands around their wrists and ankles as well as harnesses on their chests and backs that held weapons and other tools. None wore anything like a loincloth, but there was also no obvious signs of external sexual organs between their legs. Their fur varied in color: reddish browns and greys with white ventral areas on some, to darker more uniform shades on others. One had nearly black fur. All had black rings on their double tails.

The crew stayed quiet, as if the mob might hear them through the hull if they spoke. The external microphones picked up the sound of the gentle surf behind them and the rising chatter of the natives' speech in front.

After much animated discussion and hand-and-tail-waving, a rusty-red individual walked forward from the line and stood in front of the nosecone of the lander. He thrust his chest forward and his fur fluffed up all over his body. He reached backwards with his arms wide and began to chirp directly at the ship.

"ALICE, was that 'Hello'?"

ALICE's voice replied, "Translation: 'No fear God want query talk'. End. Confidence 71%."

"God?" asked Dr. Chauhan. "ALICE, are you sure of that word?"

"90% confidence for specific referent 'God'. This name is used with high frequency. Native speech sample: <Vvatchk>."

Powers laughed. "Well, doctor, what do you think? Are we God?"

"No! Even if they think the ship is a manifestation of their god, we cannot encourage this misconception."

"Might make things easier," he mused. "Not us being God I mean, but say… God sent us here to share His magical gifts! Right? Like that story of Jacob and the angels. I remember hearing that some people used to think the angels were actually aliens that visited earth. So all we ask in return for God's benevolent favor is some land for a spaceport and…"

"That is in bad taste, Powers. We cannot found our relationship with them on lies. What happens when they find out the truth?"

Powers shrugged. "Who's to say it's a lie, doctor?"

Chauhan said nothing, her chin wrinkling in a tight-lipped frown.

"The leader looks like he expects a response. What should we say, doctor?" asked Anders.

Chauhan looked to Anders. "I am not sure. A greeting would be harmless. I hope."

"Captain?" asked Anders.

"Agreed," said Hernandez.

Anders touched her earpiece and said. "ALICE, direct a friendly greeting through the external speakers." A moment later they could hear the external speakers chirp and trill a short couple of native words.

Almost all the natives backed up a step and raised their spears again. The leader stood his ground, and chittered again, leaving his muzzle open at the end, teeth bared. ALICE translated, "'Not lie Vash kill we eat carry home.' End. Confidence 81%."

"Well, that sounds encouraging," deadpanned Lin, his head still enveloped in the VR headset.

"Maybe they want to sacrifice us to their god?" asked Anders.

"We cannot assume…" began Chauhan.

"Damn it, Chauhan! Understanding these furballs is your job, but it's been 'Oh, we cannot assume' or 'we should not speculate' the whole damn time! Give us something we can actually use!" snapped Powers.

"We have no basis for comparison! Never have we met a true alien culture. We need more words, more context. If we say the wrong thing it could be a disaster."

Lin said, "Screw it, I've got the drone wedged into a kind of depression on top of one of their bigger basket hut things. Let's get out of here. We can retrieve it once we have some altitude." He removed the headset and switched his seat's controls over to the lander. "Ready to initiate departure sequence."

"Affirmative, Lin," said the Captain. "We'll take what we've learned and go find the next tribe down the coast."

Lin switched on the rotors and the low whine of the engines thrummed to life, increasing in pitch at a steady rate. This got the attention of the natives even more than the botched greeting. As the thrusters began to blow air out in all directions over the ground, the crew expected them to back off, perhaps even to run from the increasing noise. They did the opposite, and charged.

"Holy shit!" said Powers.

The furry natives climbed or leapt onto the smooth hull of the aerodyne, swarming over it in seconds. The crew could hear their claws clicking and scratching on the composite skin. One of them found an external camera bubble. A brief distorted view of a sniffing, whiskery and velvet-furred nose appeared. Then the screen was filled with a flurry of curved wicked claws trying to pry the bubble loose.

"They're fucking with the thruster intakes!" shouted Lin as the engine sound degraded into a nasty grinding sound on one side of the craft.

"Get us up!" said Powers.

"Trying…" said Lin as he pushed the thrusters open far faster than takeoff procedure called for. The aerodyne struggled, then lurched upwards, spilling several attackers from the wings and fuselage. But some still held on. The ship wobbled as Lin tried to compensate for the unequal thrust. He dipped the nose and they started to move towards the treeline. Then he tried to turn the ship to head up the shoreline.

A loud bang sounded from the left thruster, followed by the scream of tearing metal and the terrified shouts of most of the crew. Alarms began to flash and blare and Lin overcompensated for the loss. He fired the main flight engines at the rear of the craft, hoping to gain some forward momentum and lift before they lost altitude. The ground came up too fast on one side and the edge of the wing met the unforgiving gravel with a shuddering crunch. They pitched forward and then fell back, resting on the nose and mangled wing. The cabin lights flickered and Lin cut the power to all the engines.

"What? Why did you stop? We have to get out of here!" babbled Powers as he struggled in his tilted seat.

"I got one thruster destroyed and the opposite wing probably shredded. Ride's over, LT. Captain, do you still read me?"

There was only silence from the radio.

"Shit! We're going to need extraction with the second lander if we ever want off this rock. No way this tub is ever making orbit again."

"What else is damaged?" asked Lt. Powers.

Lin scanned the flashing angry readouts. "Radio's shot, not sure why. Leaking hydraulics, though that doesn't matter now. Oh, perfect! We're losing air pressure in the cabin. Something must have breached the hull or we got twisted up bad. No idea where. But we're going to be testing whether the air outside is really breathable real soon."

"How long can we sustain pressure with the reserves?"

"At the rate of loss, uhh... 20 minutes, maybe."

"What are the furry bastards outside doing?"

"No idea. We shook a bunch off, I think. Check the cameras; some of them still seem to work."

Anders began to panic. "What do we do? Captain can't exactly get us out of here with that bunch of savages waiting outside!"

Powers fumed, "The captain didn't want to start a war with them, but it looks like that's what they wanted. All we did was try to talk, for God's sake. We were attacked! I don't know what that book says to do now, but since we can't ask the captain, I'm in command and we're going to clear the landing zone of hostiles ahead of extraction."

Chauhan said in disbelief, "You want to shoot them all? We are the strangers here. We..."

"Save it, doctor. What if they don't ever want to play nice, eh? We're here to survey this planet for colonization. It's the best one we've ever found in fifty years of searching, and a couple billion human souls are waiting on us to find them a new home. A few spear-throwing squirrels aren't going to change that fact. I think they should find out what happens when you bring a spear to a pulse rifle fight."

"This is a mistake," said Chauhan. "Remember your own American history!"

"It worked out pretty well for us in the end," said Powers without any humor in his voice.

Lin and Anders silenced most of the audible alarms, though the red indicators remained, illuminating the half-dark flight deck in chaotic flashing. Soon the sounds of the tenacious Keplerians on the hull returned as they probed and pried at their downed quarry with claws and speartips.

Powers opened the weapons locker and retrieved a plasma pulse rifle. "Lin, you ready?"

"Yes sir," he nodded with enthusiasm, unstrapping and joining Powers at the locker.

Powers cradled his weapon in his arms and said, "I doubt this will take long. Shock and awe, they used to say. I counted about two dozen standing around before they attacked, so as long as you're not a terrible shot we should have enough charge to toast all of them if we have to. But I predict they all bolt after the first couple get cooked." He turned to Anders and Chauhan. "You two stay inside until we give the all-clear."

Lin grabbed his own weapon before they both headed down the now-slanted ladder to the belly hatch. No one else spoke.

Once they were sealed inside the airlock, Chauhan shook her head and watched the video feed from the camera on the aerodyne's belly. "We repeat history, despite remembering it." She didn't want to watch the carnage, but she couldn't look away as the external hatchway doors opened to admit the light of the sunlit beach. The natives were attracted to the sound and the two men started firing as soon as they had clear lines on targets while still inside the airlock, slinging blinding-hot plasma bolts. The cameras washed out for a moment from the glare. When it cleared, the men had jumped to the ground from the crazily-angled hatch, which was closing up again. They fired another volley at the squirrel-men, who were now running in what appeared to be chaos, making zig-zag paths in all directions. There were several smoking bodies on the shingle beach.

Before Lin and Powers could focus on new targets, the tailed shadows of natives suddenly appeared falling from above—Chauhan realized they must have climbed over the ship that the two men were using to cover their backs. They spun and fired, but they had to aim high to avoid hitting the ship itself. More Keplerians jumped on them without hesitation. Powers and Lin tried to fend them off, but there were too many bodies, too many claws. They disappeared under the furry wave and were taken to the ground, just outside the camera's tilted angle.

Chauhan could still hear the muffled screams of her crewmates even if she could not see what was happening to them. She covered her ears, though the earpiece made it impossible to shut it out. She said, "Tell them to stop! ALICE, tell them to stop in the name of God."

ALICE replied, "Translating simplified message 'God says stop attack'. 54% confidence."

The external speakers broadcast their message before Chauhan could process the implication of how ALICE interpreted her own words. The natives stood and faced the direction that the loud distorted sound of their own synthesized tongue came from. They bared their teeth and raised their bloodstained knives, tails waving in fervent agitation.

The incongruous calm and cultured voice of the AI translated the leader's response. "'We never stop God we kill' End. Confidence 90%."

Anders looked at Dr. Chauhan, eyes wide.

She said, "I don't know, I... ALICE, tell them we surrender. We surrender and we want peace. Tell them that."

Again the amplified clicks and chirps sounded. This time, however, the natives stopped, lowering their weapons halfway. They looked to the leader while the scattered troop began to return. The leader spoke to his closest companions, now standing over the bleeding bodies of Lin and Powers.

"ALICE, what is the leader saying?" asked Dr. Chauhan.

The AI's voice replied, "'God surrender lie truth question carry meat go.' End. Confidence 90%."

Anders said, "Oh God......" when she heard the word 'meat'. Several of the warriors crouched and picked up the limp and bloody bodies of Lin and Powers. It took three of them to carry each man, but they heaved them up onto their shoulders and walked off towards the tree line. She cried, "We can't just let them take them away! They're going to... " but she bit her knuckle and couldn't finish the thought.

"We just need to understand... "

"What's to understand?" shouted Anders in a hoarse half-sob. "They hate us! Powers was right. The colonial marines will have to just kill them all. This whole mission was a waste. Lin and Powers died for *nothing.*"

Chauhan stared at the camera for several minutes while Anders wept. She unstrapped himself from her seat and said, "ALICE, can you transfer language module to a portable?"

"Yes, doctor. Select portable."

"Mine."

"What are you doing?" asked Anders.

"I cannot do nothing. If I do nothing then you will be right. We will have failed and there will be war. Many more people will die here as they fight to take this world. Many more of the children of this world will die. Perhaps all of them, in the end. I do not want this on my soul. That I saw the future and did nothing to prevent it."

"What if you can't prevent it? They will kill you as soon as you come out of the hatch, doctor. You will die for nothing too."

"I choose to believe that I can. I have never been a true believer in any one interpretation of God, Anders. But if He made us and them both in His image, He surely did not mean for us to kill each other."

Dr. Chauhan pulled her portable datapad from its dock and clipped it into a back harness rig. Then she put the rig on backwards so that the portable computer lay close against her chest.

"There is no God, Chauhan. That they look anything like us is some cosmic joke or a result of convergent evolution. Don't be stupid!"

She turned and worked her way over the slanted deck to the airlock door. "They believe in God, Anders. That may be what saves us. And them." She cycled the lock open and climbed down the ladder.

Anders watched the lock close and then turned to the display screens. "I hope you are right. What do you want me to tell the captain, if she sends the other lander?"

"Thank you, Anders. Tell her I hope to see her again," came her reply through her earpiece.

* * *

Ketrhik crouched on the stones of the beach, one hand on his spear. At his feet lay one of the fire-throwers that the tail-less demons had held. They had used them to kill eight of his brothers before they could even cry out. He dared not touch it. It was cursed. Given by Vash Himself to His demons. It was a strange thing, made from many pieces fitted tightly together. He could not see how. It was stone-grey, darker than the giant insect shell the demons had emerged from, like younglings from a female's pouch.

One of the other warders had suggested that the insect shell *was* Vash. But no, Ketrhik did not believe that, even though it had spoken to them. Vash called the storms. Vash commanded destroying flame. This insect thing was only a servant, as were the two demons. It lay where it had fallen, tilted up, belly exposed like an invitation to slaughter. He stood.

The other warders were busy collecting the charred remains of their brothers. They would be carried back to the village circle and given death spears for their final confrontation with Vash. He wondered if they would appear before Him all together because they had died together. He hoped they would. That would surprise Vash.

The insect had not spoken since it had cried surrender. It still made a low humming sound, however, so he knew it was not dead. He did not trust it. He walked closer, tails twitching. One of the other warders noticed and joined him.

"There might be more demons inside its belly, Ketrhik," he warned.

Ketrhik nodded. "I am sure of it."

"How?"

"Who surrendered, if not them?"

"Maybe it is Vash Himself inside?"

Ketrhik clicked his teeth in derision. "Vash, Maker of All Things, Bringer of Pain, trapped inside a dying insect, crying surrender. No, I do not think Vash is inside. Just more of his slaves."

The sound of the hatch opening got their full attention. Remembering that the demons had begun throwing fire from inside the belly, they both chirped a piercing warning to all the remaining warders and raced around to the other side of the downed insect. Several climbed back up onto it, ready to fall upon the demons once again from above.

Ketrhik peeked through the narrow opening between the edge of one of the wings and the ground. The buzzing sound ended and soon a demon jumped to the ground. Ketrhik could see its clawless feet. A moment later there was a strange sound, like a mixture of the growls of a forest beast and the morning calls of the criers. When it finished, a Ketchvash voice said, "I am no weapon. I want to talk." The words were clear, but it was no one's voice that he recognized.

He did not expose himself, expecting a trap. He asked instead, "Who are you?"

Again there was the odd moaning babble followed by actual words. "I am friend. Fight no. I want to talk."

"You are no friend. You are Vash's slaves."

More babbling was followed by, "I no slave. I child of Vash. You child of Vash. I want peace. I have message elder far sky star."

Ketrhik looked to the warder on his right. "Message elder far sky star? What does it mean?"

"It must have a message for the elders. Maybe the flying eyes were trying to deliver it."

"Drop your fire thrower and we will take you to the elders," called out Ketrhik.

"I have no fire. I have pack for talk. No weapon. No fight."

"The other demons killed eight of my brothers!"

"I sorry. They angry you hurt sky bower. No fight I."

Ketrhik still felt that this had to be a trap, but there was only the one demon. He signaled to the three warders perched on the slanted wing, then he crept to the edge of the same wing and peeked around it, stealing a glance at the demon. It seemed much like the other two, with the same strange furless skin that looked like it was made from colored beast hides stitched together. Its head was different, with darker skin than the other two and white fur on top. No ears, unless the small wrinkled things on the sides of its head could count. And no tails that he could see. He stole another glance.

The demon saw him, but made no move except for its eyes looking his way. Below them its face was flat like a disfigured grotesque nightmare, with only a tiny fleshy muzzle above what must be its mouth. It stood with its arms away from its sides, clawless fingers spread. He saw no fire thrower like the others had carried. But they were still on the ground nearby, within a quick jump's reach. Unlike the others, this one had a square black thing strapped to its front, like a flat stone in a hide-stitched pack.

When Ketrhik looked again, it still made no moves, so he did not pull his head back behind cover. When it saw this, it murmured with its mouth. When it finished, the Ketchvash voice came from the flat stone on its chest. "You see. I no weapon. I go you. Go elder. Talk elder." Then it slowly began to spread its arms wider until they were fully extended. Then it pulled them back, presenting its chest like a challenge.

Ketrhik eyed the discarded fire throwers on the ground and planned his route with care before starting towards the demon, his spear raised and ready. He signaled to the warders on the wing behind the demon with his tail to wait. He crossed in front of the weapons, then closed on the demon, which was holding its challenge, waiting with its eyes closed. Ready to die, maybe.

He got within striking distance and it raised its head, offering its throat. Ketrhik was tempted to kill it. But he was no careless youngling. The elders would want to hear this message it carried from Vash. Surrender, the louder voice had claimed. Perhaps Vash wished to make a deal. Perhaps He knew, finally, that He would never have victory. Ketrhik could not wait to know. He asked, "What does Vash want?"

It spoke, then the talking stone spoke. "You me friend. Peace. No fight."

Ketrhik clicked his teeth and said, "You do not want to fight because you are defeated. Vash only wants to destroy us. You lie for Him," he hissed, baring his teeth. The demon flinched but did not move. "I will take you to the elders. They will hear your lies for what they are." He chirped to the other warders to come out.

They surrounded the demon, held its arms. It did not struggle or resist. Then they walked it into the forest, leaving a hand of warders to watch the great insect in case there were more demons waiting inside.

* * *

Tezkee would not let go of the eye, even when standing before Rakhza, the eldest elder of his village. The matrons had given him fruitwater and fussed over his wounds, but he had only wanted to show his prize to the elders. They had made him rest anyway—you could not argue with a matron and win. When they had decided he was strong enough, they had helped him finish his climb to the topmost platforms and stood behind him as he told his tale to Rakhza.

The elder fixed the youngster with a dubious glare as Tezkee spoke, but did not interrupt. When Tezkee finished and held the eye out to him with his good arm, Rakhza gave it an evil look and nodded to the shaman to take it, not wanting to touch it himself. Then he addressed Tezkee in his cracking, labored voice.

"You were a fool to follow it, alone, to the top. Vash lured you. Meant to end you, as He always does. You were a fool to try to capture it yourself, with no help from the warders."

Tezkee opened his mouth to interrupt but the elder held up his gnarled hand and silenced him with a quick motion of his claws. "In our struggle against Vash we have only each other. Alone we will be destroyed. Did you learn nothing from your age ritual? You alone did not kill the beast. All of you did. Together. I fear the lesson was lost on you." Rakhza rubbed his whiskers and sighed. "But here you stand, victorious and alive. I cannot punish you for victory. You will be honored, Tezkee."

Tezkee asked, "What will you do with Vash's eye?"

"It watches us still," said the elder, "We should rip it to pieces. But I wish for Vash to see the warders return with the carcass of His giant grey insect. To see that His plans end in failure." He struggled out of the hammock seat he occupied, got to his feet and thrust his thin-furred chest out towards the eye, sweeping his arms back. "Hear me, Vash. You will never destroy us."

Tezkee echoed the elder's posture and promise, as did the others behind him. After Rakhza had once again settled into the hammock seat, Tezkee asked, "What great grey insect?"

"The fishers spotted it two days past at the shore, before the first eye came. Ketrhik and his warders went to destroy it today."

"I would have joined them," said Tezkee with disappointment.

"You are not a warder yet, Tezkee. And now we have this eye, thanks to you. Rest and heal. I will tell the first warder of your deed when he returns."

Tezkee bowed his head and twined his tails in deference to the elder and then left with a matron for the healing bower.

* * *

Dr. Chauhan stood on a large uneven platform of thick woven vines, surrounded by at least a hundred hostile Keplerians. Most kept their distance, watching from nearby platforms and teardrop-shaped dwellings, all eyes on the stranger. The cacophony of their chirping, clicking language reminded her of roosting jungle birds. The portable strapped to her chest couldn't keep up and didn't bother trying. She saw young ones in the crowd, some clinging to adults. She spotted one adult with two tiny faces peeking from a vertical slit in its belly fur. A mother with a pouch, perhaps. She turned slowly, mindful of the twitchy guards who had brought her here, but wanting to capture it all on video for future xenosociologists.

She had been afraid when they took her into the forest. Afraid of what they might do to her. Afraid of falling. During the arduous climb up the narrow but remarkable vine cables to the village she had to remind herself that she had chosen this perilous path, that the cost of failure would be more that just her own sticky end. Now that she was here, and the elders were approaching to hear what she had to say, she felt a kind of calm come over her. They were curious. They would listen. There was a chance. She just had to choose the right words.

The small group made their way down from a higher platform and the crowd parted to let them pass. There were four of them, three with decorated spears and necklaces of teeth and polished stones. Elders, she had to assume. The last one followed behind, a younger one from its size and lack of fine jewelry. It was carrying one of their lost drones by one hand, the arm wrapped in leaves. The other arm was splinted and stiff. Dr. Chauhan decided it must be the one who had fallen with the drone and then fought to bring it back up from hell.

The group stopped a few meters from her, and all assumed the challenge pose, directed at her. They thought she was sent by their God, that much was clear. And they did not like their God. Hated Him, in fact. She would have to convince them that she was not on their God's side.

One of the elders spoke. A moment later his earpiece gave him the translation. "Guards say you have message slave-of-God. Speak message."

Dr. Chauhan replied, "I am not a slave-of-God. My message is from my people. My tribe."

When the translation ended the elders briefly conferred with each other before addressing the doctor again. "You lie. God send slave-of-God to attack defiant."

"Defiant? You are called defiant?"

"Yes. All defiant. No surrender God. You slave-of-God."

"No. We are… " Dr. Chauhan paused. The word 'human' just meant 'man' at its root. It had no descriptive meaning like 'defiant'. She improvised. "We are explorers. God did not send us. God does not speak to us like that."

That seemed to confuse the elder. Perhaps explorer wasn't a word ALICE had heard yet. He asked, "Why come here?"

The doctor felt that the truth presented the easiest argument. "More of my tribe are coming. Many more. They seek to make their homes here. We want to live in peace with the defiant. But they will hurt you if you fight them," she said, hoping the translator would not mangle it too much.

Another short discussion ensued. A more animated one. Tails lashed and arms waved. The one who had been chosen to speak asked, "Where tribe?"

Dr. Chauhan pointed to the sky. "My tribe comes from the stars."

As soon as that had been translated the elder bared his teeth and hissed. He said, "Slave-of-God, you will not destroy us. We send you back to God. You tell God we come for him."

"I can not tell God anything. We are not slaves of God," she argued again. The doctor wondered if the translation had failed somehow—what had caused the sudden hostility? Before the translation had finished, she asked them, "Why do you hate God so much?"

"Slave of God lie not know. All know. God hate defiant. God kill defiant. All know."

"I don't know. Tell me."

The elder struck the platform with the butt of his spear and began talking. Gesturing and reciting a story. After a short delay, the words began to flow into Dr. Chauhan's ear. "God create all. God create ground. God create sky. God create ocean. God create trees. God create beasts on ground, in sky, in ocean. God create defiant. God speak defiant live this tree, live that tree. Defiant live tree. All peace. Defiant make children. Live more tree. God speak defiant stop. Stop children. Too many. Defiant laugh. Speak God no. Live all tree. God angry. God create pain. God create death. God turn beast angry. Make beast slave-of-God. God send storm. God send fire. God kill defiant. Defiant no surrender. Defiant make more children. God kill same. God send slave-of-God kill defiant. Defiant kill slave-of-God. All defiant speak God never defeat. Always fight. All defiant brothers. Defiant will kill God. When God dead then peace joy."

Dr. Chauhan was struck by the simplicity of their religion. They had solved the eternal question of how a benevolent God could allow so much pain and suffering to befall His children. These children simply concluded God was *not* benevolent. That he was a sadistic abusive monster that they had to oppose and ultimately destroy. She had to admit it had a certain rebellious appeal. Why had humanity never come to this conclusion? Of all the ways early man could have seen the divine hand in nature, they had always assumed God loved them, or could at least be bargained with. She wanted to study these people, to learn more of their history and their mythology, but she had no time now. She had to choose her words carefully.

She said, "I understand. God also created my tribe. We also did not obey Him. Then God became angry and sent us out of our forest. We are like the defiant. We can help you. We can be your brothers. Teach you new things. Make you stronger to fight God." It was true, she thought, as far as it went. Their concept of God embodied the indifferent or seeming malevolent forces of the universe conspiring to destroy them. Humanity's technology could help them overcome those forces, and in time perhaps they would feel less threatened. She decided now was not the time to discuss the more nuanced and varied human relationship with the divine.

This started another argument, as well as rising murmuring cacophony from the assembled crowd. The doctor waited. The translator could only give her disconnected words picked out of the noise, but she felt the conflict. They wanted her promised gifts, but they did not trust her or where she came from. Anything outside their world was suspect. Sent by Vash to torment them. It was such a limiting philosophy. Them against the rest of the universe.

At one point one of the three elders left in what Dr. Chauhan thought could only be described as a huff. The speaker held up a hand and the crowd quieted. He spoke, and the doctor heard, "I speak you not know you slave-of-God. God hate slave-of-God same hate defiant. Want trade weapon. Want trade tool. Want make village here. I speak give message you tribe. I show you dead shell then you go. Sunrise." He was already leaving when the English translation finished.

The guards led her to a vine-woven basket-hut that clung to one of the great trees. Once she was inside they covered the opening with an animal hide. Between the gaps in the weaving she could see that she was being guarded. Not that she had plans to escape. She sat cross-legged in the bowl-shaped depression in the center and closed her eyes. It had gone better than she had expected, she told herself. They were willing to listen, even after several of them had been murdered by her crewmates. They hadn't even brought that up, though perhaps that was because it was what they expected of any outsider. It sounded like they might even release her after showing her the 'dead shell'. She hoped that they had not done something horrible to Lin and Powers as some kind of warning display. She quieted her mind, banishing such maudlin thoughts. In a quiet voice she asked the portable to play the soothing sound of a Tibetan singing bowl and meditated.

* * *

Dawn came with the rising songs of the small flying reptilians that nested near the village. Her hosts gave her something to eat. It appeared to be a tree fruit with a tough scaled husk like an artichoke. She peeled the scales and sampled some of the moist but fibrous white flesh. Bitterness coated her tongue, the warning taste of poison. Though not always, she thought. Many good foods could be bitter. But she decided not to take the chance. She set the fruit aside. She could fast. She had done so in the past, for days sometimes, to cleanse the mind and body.

The same warriors that had escorted her from the ship were there waiting when she was brought out into the dim pink light of the dawn. She wondered what Anders was doing. Had the captain already sent the second landing craft down to rescue her? Would they judge her lost, or would they try to rescue her? She hoped they would not—the sudden appearance of the aerodyne over the village would probably erase whatever small trust she had earned.

The elder led them out of the village, away from the shoreline and the ship. It seemed like they were climbing in altitude as they went, though it was difficult to judge when the cables traced their hanging curved paths down and then back up on each segment. At one tree platform she was able to peer backwards through the gaps in the canopy and see the tops of the great trees and even the ocean in the distance behind. They were climbing.

After what must have been mid-day she saw the first sign of solid ground since she had left the beach. A ridge of dark grey stone came into view, cutting across their path. It was so abrupt a cliff that it was exposed to the sunlight. The trees at the bottom of the cliff barely grew tall enough to reach the edge. The trees on the higher ground were stunted and small like those near the beach had been, but their roots grew into and out of the cliff face, grasping at the rock like tentacles, grinding it to pieces over eons. The cable they walked was bound to one of these gnarled dwarfs. When they reached it her escorts jumped down to the rock ledge and she followed.

Dr. Chauhan could see that they took advantage of the exposed scar across the forest as a quarry for what stone they required. There were tools and broken stone scattered near the terminus of the cable. They did not linger, however. Instead they walked on the ground into the trees. Remembering the great carnivorous predators of the forest floor she asked, "Are there beasts here?"

The elder said, "No," but did not elaborate further.

They walked a narrow path through the undergrowth and Dr. Chauhan wanted to ask why the beasts did not live here, but she found the answer for herself. She had already noticed that the trees were smaller here. None were more than about 2 meters across. Still huge by earth standards but a young forest for this world. If they were anything like Earth trees, this piece of forest atop the ridge was only a few hundred years old. Perhaps a thousand. And resting in the undergrowth was the reason.

There was a derelict ship before her. The metal of its hull was a dull green where it showed through the clinging moss, but she could see the obvious lines of an otherworldly craft designed to fly through air and space. It was much larger than the one she had arrived in, covering the area of a football pitch. Since nothing seemed able to grow through its bulk, the light of the sun shone on half its broken spine. There were jagged black openings that led into its interior, as if it had been cracked open like an enormous crustacean. There was nothing remotely human about its design. Her blood ran cold and she stood there, staring, mouth open. She felt on the verge of tears.

The sound of native chatter did not get her attention at first, but the translation in her ear did. "Look. See. Slave-of-God come. Many elder elder time. Kill tree, make village. Defiant speak slave-of-God, slave-of-God no speak. Kill defiant. Defiant return more. Kill all slave-of-God, speak God no defeat. Never defeat. You go speak you tribe. Speak defiant no weak, no stop. You speak friend, you speak tribe no come. You tribe come, you tribe die."

The doctor blinked, still staring at the ship. She understood the elder, even if the words were imperfect. More than that, she learned for the second time in recent days that humanity was not alone in the universe. Who were these other aliens? Were they still out there? How many others had come here, thinking to claim this rich world, only to be driven away by these dauntless guardians of their Eden?

Having shown her what they felt she needed to see, they led her back down into their forest. She was disturbed by the certainty that because the ancient wreck was there, waiting to be explored, researched and plundered for all its technological secrets, nothing would now persuade her government to leave the Keplerians in peace. She considered erasing this part of the recording from the portable and claiming a hardware failure, but she found she could not bring herself to do it. She knew she wanted to know its secrets as much as anyone.

* * *

Tezkee was furious. He stood on the beach with the other warders, watching the second giant insect rise above the waves and then fly out over the water, growing smaller and smaller until the only thing that remained was the white line it left in the air. Then that, too, disappeared. He had been made a warder for his bravery, and should have been pleased. But his victory felt wasted while the demons themselves went free. He burned to tell the elder that Vash had made fools of them all, but he had already been scolded by him once, so he said nothing.

The elder had accompanied the warders to the beach and stood at the water's edge. He sensed Tezkee's disquiet. Or could hear the youngster's teeth grinding behind his back. He said, "You are unhappy, new warder. Speak your thoughts or they will torment you."

Tezkee laid his ears back. "We should have killed it. And the others that came to take it away. Now they will return to Vash and He will send more demons next time with more fire throwers."

The elder scratched the side of his muzzle, smoothing his sparse whiskers. After a pause he asked Tezkee, "Do you serve Vash?"

"No!" he cried, insulted and fearful of the accusation. "I ask forgiveness, elder, if I offended you."

Rakhza held up his hand and clicked his teeth once. "I asked you to speak your thoughts. But you do not understand. I do not think you are Vash's slave. But would you know, if you were?"

"Yes! Vash would speak to me. Tell me to kill you, kill all my brothers and bring fire to the village. Or worse!"

"We named it a demon, but it said no. It said it was no slave of Vash. It said that its tribe had been banished from their forest by Him."

"It lied. Vash told it to say those things to fool us."

"Maybe. Vash hates us, and will until we destroy Him. Maybe He hates these tail-less ones he made too. Are we doing His work by killing them? I was a far-runner when I was your age. I have been to many villages and seen other dead shells. None live that remember the ones that rode in them. Only that we killed them all."

"So that is why you let it go?"

"We showed it the dead shell. They will know we are strong. They will know we do not fear them and we do not fear Vash. When they return they will show if they serve Vash by what they do. If there is a chance to have them as brothers… "

When Rakhza did not finish the thought, Tezkee realized the elder expected him to do it. He offered, "As brothers maybe they will help us kill Vash?"

"The stories tell that Vash looks down on us from the stars. Maybe this tribe can carry us to Him and we can surprise Him, face Him without having to die first," said the elder, then laughed.

Tezkee looked up, wondering if Vash was listening, and if He was afraid. "Do you believe they will help us?" he asked.

The elder turned away and began walking back to the forest. He said without looking back, "Yes or no, we must send far-runners to spread the warning. They will return, no matter what we do."

The Galactic Federation is huge. It covers a myriad of planets. No sentient can be familiar with all of them. But its Investigative Agents are expected to solve crimes on any of them.

This is Agent Sellareezjerine's first visit to Hrogir, whose triped inhabitants are instinctually peaceful and nonaggressive. So why has a group of them suddenly slaughtered some visiting Meleeks for no apparent reason? Sella must investigate.

Why Indeed

by Pepper Hume

I would rather be wearing a skirt, preferably one that is shorter than my tail. Beyond the obvious pleasures involved, it means I am not working. I shook the sitting creases out of my trousers and entered the Commander's office.

"Agent Sellareezjerine." His standard greeting.

"Commander." The correct response.

"Pack your kit."

"Never unpacked. Always need the same things."

I think he smiled. Hard to tell with his species, since their normal expression tends to frighten beings unprepared for small black eyes so deeply set. And all those teeth. Once, I saw one of his kind fully shaved which only made their limited facial movement more alarming. Still, their native talent for dedication and perseverance make them brilliant administrators. Ponderous voices add a dimension of authority difficult to resist.

"Will I see you at the capitol tonight?"

My species has no trouble at all displaying a smile. "You know what a party animal I am."

"I only wish you had the decency to suffer for it." The Commander tossed a tiny bright capsule to me. "Transport to Hrogir leaves tomorrow. The journey will provide ample time to study your assignment." He possibly grinned again until his attention was caught by a thread of golden light that shot up from the glowing swirl of color that constituted his desktop. I was dismissed.

* * *

I suspect I am the only Investigative Officer in the whole department who actually enjoys attending government balls. Truth is, my main reason is getting to wear a beautiful gown and leave my sword at home. This time my dressmaker had really scored. The glistening aqua possilk of my new gown fairly glowed against the tawny colors of my fur. In front the gown appeared quite simple and demure with long sleeves and a full skirt that hung close enough to reveal the shape of my legs. I am inordinately proud of my legs.

She guaranteed that the back view would set off alarms. She was right. As I moved through the crowd I could hear a rise in the murmuring behind me. The dress literally had no back all the way down to below the tail. It displayed my entire scalp from the top of my head to the tip of that tail. Tiny strings tied nonchalantly across at the waist and shoulder kept it from falling right off. She had brushed my pelt to shining perfection, until I could not bear another stroke.

A growly voice rose out of the murmuring. "Ah Sella, once again you make me proud to be Fellarian."

His claws penetrated the long fur at my waist to touch my skin and delicately rake against the grain up to the strings at shoulder level. I could not prevent the chirrup of purr that swelled in my throat.

"I am truly glad, Murtz, that you have learned to speak before touching me." I turned into his arms for a hug, hugging being one of my favorite pastimes. Taller and broader than myself with a variegated orange pelt, he was still no great example of Fellarian manhood. He was a good hugger though, and we had been friends since my early days with the Investigative Office. His gold-green eyes acknowledged the capsule that hung from my left ear.

"A new assignment?"

"Leaving tomorrow afternoon."

"Then we must enjoy the evening to the fullest."

We did.

* * *

I slept the first two days of the trip to Hrogir. The third day, I trusted my mind enough to squeeze the little capsule hanging from my ear. The images that popped onto the ceiling above my recliner followed the usual sequence. First came the inevitable survey of the planet with charts of data outlining corporate and civil structures, cities, natural and manufactured resources, the racial and social character of the inhabitants. Nothing irregular there. Hrogir was progressing nicely through the process of achieving membership in the Galactic Federation.

I slept some more, allowing all that data to settle into my mental files. The next time I squeezed the capsule, I focused on the nature of the inhabitants: only one sentient species, of remarkably gentle nature, but quite unusual biology. Or should it be called triology? Theirs was trinary as opposed to the binary structure of most organic species in the known universe. They seemed to have three of everything except heads. Three arms, three legs, three eyes, three toes per foot, even three sexes. Their hands of three fingers plus thumbs would have seemed common enough, but for the second thumb opposite the usual one. What nimble little hands they appeared to be.

Experience had taught the I.O. that local context was essential in dealing with local situations. Preconceived notions based on off-world values could be disastrous. Consequently, no information would be provided concerning whatever had prompted the I.O. to send a first level operative to this obscure place until I arrived. By then, I would be immersed in background knowledge, ready to address a native situation in native terms. I would learn about the crime in much the same manner as a local superior officer would.

I turned my attention to a separate report profiling another planet located in a different quadrant from Hrogir. Meleek was already a Federation member. Why had this been included? What had Meleek to do with Hrogir? Training and experience prevented my pursuing either of these questions. The Meleeker data simply joined the Hrogirian in the active files in my head.

With nothing more to do and several days to do it in before arriving, I went to the lounge. No other passengers were aboard, but several members of the senior crew proved to be worthy adversaries in a variety of combat games. It had been a long time since my sword had gotten such a good workout. One crew member proved quite friendly as well. I have had less pleasurable trips.

* * *

"I am not a tourist. I am an invited guest of your Central Assembly, on official business for the Galactic Federation. I have diplomatic immunity."

"No blade longer than my thumb is permitted," the blue Hrogirian carefully repeated in a velvety soft voice, displaying a squat hand with one of its two thumbs pointing up. Hrogir's so-called Importage Rules may protect their peaceful existence, but I was sure they contributed to the monumental tourist deficit mentioned in the briefing capsule.

"This blade, my dear fellow, is a symbol of my profession, a tool of my trade." I gripped my scabbarded sword tightly in both hands.

The Hrogirian gripped it with all three of his. Impasse. Five eyes glared in reciprocal defiance and determination. The odds favored the home team three to two, but in order to achieve the assignment here, establishing my authority was imperative. I played my trump.

"Call the Prefect," I growled. Three ruby eyes continued to glare up at me. "Do you not understand Galactic? Perhaps my inflection escapes your comprehension." I let my voice rise in derision. My insult was designed to strike beyond the personal, to malign their planet-wide adoption of Galactic, and therefore their campaign for Federation membership. Whatever the incident was that brought me here, it jeopardized their hopes. I counted on the resultant anxiety to outweigh bureaucratic policy.

It worked. Although the lower central eye continued to glower, the other two eyes lost their brilliance. I recognized from the briefing capsule that this meant inner eyelids had been closed, indicating decision. A whole wad of little fingers unwound from my scabbard and disappeared into the pouch that protruded from the creature's belly, or where a biped's belly would be. The capsule had gone into Hrogirian trinary anatomy at great length.

"Be it in your own eye," he grumbled. "I will record the—exception. Welcome to Hrogir, honored sir." Some rituals are universal. As is the call to be gracious in victory.

"Thank you, sir, but I am not male, I am addressed as mistress."

The creature blushed a deeper violet-blue. "Nor am I male, mistress. I am trimale."

I tucked my hands into the pocket that had been added to my coat in approximation of the pouch all Hrogirians sported. "We have both been in error. We part as friends." I liked the essential courtesy in Hrogirian culture. They may be one of the more peculiar races in the universe, but they were certainly among the nicest.

Officialdom still had to be satisfied. He—I could not remember what to call a trimale—produced a form exactly like every other official form in the universe. I was bemused to see the creature set the paper sideways and write from the top down. Subsequent lines proceeded to the left. When he swung it around for me to sign, I saw that everything about the form, including his written Galactic, looked perfectly normal. He in turn looked surprised when I gave it a quarter turn and wrote from left to right.

Finally, I was escorted to a small, three-wheeled power vehicle, protectively enclosed, comfortably appointed, but virtually a glass bubble that exposed its passenger to the view of all. My escort tapped my destination into its control pod and the thing sped away with only me and my luggage aboard. During that trip to the Regional Prefecture, I found myself wishing their society were not quite so open. One triple-eyed face at a time I could handle. Hundreds of them, all staring at the sword strapped to my back… nowhere near as much fun as a government ball.

I recognized the Hrogirian awaiting me at the Prefecture as female. Her knee-length rainbow colored gown moved in a brisk morning wind. She politely ignored my sword. Three hands easily collected my gear. With a charming dip of her downy lavender head, she guided me toward the entrance. Inside, bureaucracy again engulfed me and swept me into a handsome office, seated me in a comfortable chair in the middle thereof, and provided a three-toed bowl full of a refreshing drink. Nice people.

My chair faced a corner with tall windows on both sides. Below the windows spread a great L-shaped desk with a wheeled chair—three-legged like the one I occupied—centered in the corner. I committed the configuration to memory with the intention of adopting it for my own office. So practical with all that extra workspace within easy reach. It would surely be more pleasant to work facing the lovely view out my office window, and far more disarming for a guest to face you with no desk between.

A side door opened and the largest Hrogirian I had yet seen entered. He was nearly two-thirds my own size, and lighter of color than most, almost aquamarine. This must be Pin Alt, the Director of Guardians, their version of police.

"Good morning, Mistress Sellareezjerine, and welcome." My name stumbled coming out of Pin Alt's tiny mouth, but he had clearly worked on it. Points for the effort. I hoped all Hrogirians had such dulcet voices; it certainly suited their soft looks and gentle manners. He handed me the little box of papers he carried. "Here is the entire case file on the incident which has brought you here."

Did I mention the length of their arms? Almost to the floor standing. There was more fabric in his three sleeves than the rest of his deep gold uniform altogether.

He sat at the desk facing me, with both back arms resting along its top, while his front hand held a drink like my own. Yes, I must indeed employ this arrangement back home. The usual pleasantries were exchanged and the usual comparisons between our species. Far from a waste of time, I find a great deal of personal and cultural attitude is revealed through small talk. A light scratching at the door preceded the entry of the lavender female who had met me outside.

Pin Alt motioned her to come closer. "Mo Ahth will be your aide. Anything you need, she is authorized to produce."

The lady put all her hands in her pouch. I reciprocated. She closed all her eyes—their version of a smile—sat on a small chair nearby, and crossed her legs. I cannot describe the effect, having different knees and fewer limbs to work with.

All three of Pin Alt's eyes strayed again from my face to the hilt of my sword rising behind me. "I apologize for the, ah, incident at the port concerning your weapon. The agent should have been warned."

"Such misunderstandings are more common than we would like them to be," I replied. "He did what his position requires, and should be commended for following proper procedure, not censured." Of course, neither Hrogirian acknowledged my pronoun slip. I must remember to check on the proper pronouns for trimales.

Presently, Mo Ahth escorted me to a similar office assigned for my use. I was delighted to see my working gear arranged on a similar corner desk which faced similar windows. An additional angled desk by the entrance held more boxes of papers and what appeared to be communication equipment.

"Where are my personal things?"

"In your chamber." She opened a door beside the desk to disclose an enchanting room that seemed to be filled with flowers and light. At my reaction, she closed all her eyes and softly suggested, "Perhaps you would wish to refresh yourself before setting to work?"

"No need. I slept most of the way here." I almost purred as I followed her in. Everything in the room charmed my senses. My things were unpacked and stowed most efficiently. My physical and dietary needs had been expertly prepared for. These people would certainly get my vote for Fed membership. "I shall not want to leave this room to work."

"Then you need not. You will be undisturbed until you need me." She produced a small clear sphere filled with wires and spots of color. "Touch the green to summon me. I will explain its other functions when you are ready." She glided out.

I took off my coat, which released my tail from bondage, and settled on a couch with the box Pin Alt had given me. It proved to contain nothing but facts, data and visuals concerning the crime that had brought me here. Even shipping schedules and cargo manifests, unfortunately written in Meleeker dialect, were included. Hrogirian attention to detail was impressive. Thus, I could draw my own conclusions from the facts, untainted by another's opinion. The more I read, the more clear-cut the case appeared… and the more inexplicable.

Apparently, a gang of Hrogirians had murdered five Meleeker traders in their warehouse. Two other Meleekers escaped slaughter by hiding in the freighter docked against it. Forensics detected Meleeker blood on every one of the six young Hrogirians—four male, two trimale found at the site. Normally, a simple matter for local police.

What brought this one to Fed attention was that such barbaric carnage could presumably be perpetrated by one of the most peaceful species in the known universe. This could disqualify Hrogir for Fed membership for generations. Outlaw planets were always quarantined and monitored until they mastered their violence. We had watched several—such as Savol, Earth, Veterummu—a long time before their populace evolved enough to contact.

According to the capsule, the Hrogirians exhibited excellent qualities for membership: industrious without aggression, a structured and stable universal government, sensitive culture, no violent crime, not even the vocabulary for war. Although they had already adopted Galactic as their official language, they carefully preserved their heritage in old songs and literature.

What could possibly have caused that grisly mess in the Meleeker warehouse? I reviewed my Fed information on the Meleeker species. With a home planet of limited natural resources, they had developed a significant reputation as traders. They were exceptionally cordial, but that was merely good business practice. Nothing in the box of materials, nor the capsule I had studied en route, suggested any reason for conflict between them and Hrogir. I studied the holos of the two surviving Meleekers—standard issue: bulky bipeds larger than I, with tough greyish skin, thick hair, bright friendly smiles. Impressive salesmen, no doubt.

I dressed again which included confining my tail again. The capsule noted that Hrogirians had managed to accept binary aliens, but tails seemed to seriously distress them. Mo Ahth responded quite promptly to the glass ball's summons. "What do you know about this case?"

"Everything. I am the Chief Investigator. That box is my complete case file, except for summaries and personal reports. Director Pin said you wanted to start with only facts."

"I am ready now for your thoughts. Sit down." I sat at my desk in the same way Pin Alt had. It felt comfortable and put me in a naturally receptive attitude.

She delivered a succinct summary with commentary, verbatim I had no doubt, to her written report. The Fed I.O. needs people like her. I wondered if I could recruit her, although Pin Alt would surely be loath to lose her.

"Are all Hrogirians so systematic?"

The eyes closed. "We try. My skills are above average, but not exceptional, Mistress Sellaree…"

"Please, just call me Sella. Long names are so prevalent on my home world. We usually shorten them among friends."

"My friends call me Ahth."

"So, Ahth. Those boys were hired to work in the warehouse, but all six fell asleep at once. When they woke, the Meleekers were all dead. Unbelievable."

Ahth responded, "A gas valve appears to have been knocked open during the… occurrence which rendered them all unconscious. The emergency team that responded to the alarm discovered the bodies, both dead and unconscious."

"How convenient that the gas escaped in time to prevent the killers from leaving, but not soon enough to prevent their killing. Could someone have opened that valve deliberately to knock everyone out, closed it, killed the Meleekers, then turned the valve on again before leaving?"

She nodded thoughtfully. "Certainly a plausible scenario, but who would do such a thing? And why?"

"Oh Ahth, the whole thing is one big why!" I was on my feet, prowling the room. I stilled the impulse of my tail to lash back and forth. "Why would any Hrogirian kill somebody? Why these particular Meleekers? Why would perfectly normal youngsters with no history of criminal activity or violence attack their employers so viciously? What did they want? Did they feel threatened? What could possibly drive Hrogirians to kill at all?"

Ahth swept her front hand across her face while she literally wrung her two side hands together. "Those very questions have sent me twirling in mad circles," she said. "We can find no evidence of any friction with the Meleekers. They do not mingle much, but they are friendly enough, although rather boisterous for our ways. We have done profitable business with them steadily for many years. We value stability, Sella."

Stability. Desirable in a culture but not likely in a crime. Quite the opposite. Crimes usually occur in response to imbalance, the loss of stability. Someone can no longer stand what he perceives as wrong and takes action to correct it. Most criminals believe they are justified in doing what they do. Where was the instability here? What had been wrong? Who thought so?

"It is time for me to visit that warehouse."

Next day, Ahth showed me how to program my vehicle to follow hers to the Meleeker's warehouse in the port district. As expected, the warehouse was larger than it appeared in the printouts. The offending gas valve sported a green pennant. Little blue pyramid blocks on the floor indicated where Meleeker bodies had lain, red ones near the door for Hrogirians. Dark stains accompanied the blue evidence markers.

"So much blood," I muttered. "Hold it! I have been so intent on what happened here and why, I have ignored how. Your reports mention no weapons, only the bloody wounds on the victims. You allow no knives of any size. What caused so much blood?

Mo Ahth's two upper eyes darkened and the third looked at the floor. With a deep sigh she held up a thumb. Slowly, the silvery thumbnail grew until it extended into a slender blade double her thumb's length. She moved her hand about to display the unmistakably sharp edge along the blade's full length.

"We need no knives. The lower thumb of each hand is so equipped."

My own retractable claws can be filed to sharp tips, but no contest. A few well placed slashes with those razor thumbnails could indeed produce lots of blood. Clearly those boys were guilty, but they were still Hrogirian. How could they do this?

We returned to my rooms in the Prefecture for an excellent dinner with Pin Alt and his wife. My first day on Hrogir, I had been provided a dainty knife with an elegant handle, its blade the very shape and size of Mo Ahth's thumbnail. I managed to cut my meat with the pretty toy, but made a mental note to include a proper steak knife in my travel kit thereafter, Importage Rules be damned. After the Pins left, Ahth cleared dinner. I changed into a short robe.

Ahth gazed at my feet and my trailing tail. "I was prepared for your clawed toes and fingers, Sella, but the tail…"

I lifted the tip to rest in her hand. Her three eyes closed and then peered, shining, at me. "I had not expected it to be so soft and beautiful. It matches your hair."

"Actually, they are connected. My scalp runs unbroken from my brow over and down my back to the tip of my tail. You should see me in my new formal gown. The back is open to below the tail so the entire swath shows. Very racy."

Her eyes closed. "We just have the same short fuzz all over, so we must resort to colorful clothing."

"Well, I think you're lovely, and you never have to brush all this." Another smile. That girl smiles so much she must miss half of what goes on. She would indeed be pleasant to have at I.O. headquarters. I sighed; back to business.

"I must go through your files again tonight, Ahth. I am missing something here. It hovers just beyond my field of cognizance—if I could turn my head fast enough, I would see it. You might as well go home."

She gathered up the shoes she had taken off after dinner. "The rest of my files—interviews, summaries, observations by various people are there on my desk. Perhaps they would be helpful at this stage."

"Excellent. I shall read them. But you go on home. It is late for you to be out."

She wrinkled her forehead in bewilderment. "What do you mean, 'out'? My home is right here." She waved toward a door beside her desk.

"You live here?"

"Where else? I work here."

Once again I marveled at the Hrogirian ways. So efficient, so calmly systematic. I must find the answer to this crime. And pray that it will clear these nice people to join the Federation. I resolved to set to reading with dedication.

"One more thing." I caught Ahth just as she was partway through the door. "Are the surviving traders still here?"

"Yes. We put them under house arrest as essential witnesses."

"Have them brought here in the morning, I need to interview them myself."

* * *

No sooner had Ahth scratched on the outer door than it burst open. A large, vividly dressed personage ducked through and strode toward me with both massive hands outstretched in greeting. Like his face, those hands had been toughened into articulated carapace by thousands of generations on a world with ferocious winters.

"So good of you to see me, Madame Investigator. I am Captain Dremallan of the Ankhomartile Dolo Ming, Freighter Seventh Class Green, commissioned and licensed by the Combined Nova Network Trade Consortium of Meleek. I'm so glad you're here."

After the two days I had been among the watercolor Hrogirians, his massive presence and booming voice smote my senses, much as they must the Hrogirians. The flashy clothes were no help either. His broad faceted face was surmounted by a helmet of thick hair combed straight back to a blunt cut just below jaw level, and greased so heavily I could not have guessed its color.

Ahth escorted him to the central chair, and retired to sit at her own desk. After glancing over his prodigious shoulder at her, he leaned toward me and spoke in what must have been his idea of an undertone.

"Considering how terrible this situation is, Madame Investigator, and the potentially disastrous and far-reaching ramifications of what this could mean for both our planets, I am sure you will understand why I am not exactly comfortable discussing all the horrible details with... someone else in the room."

As soon as the door closed behind Ahth, the Meleeker lunged to his feet and loudly proclaimed, "I have been in contact with both my superiors at Combined Nova and the Office of Off-World Affairs on Meleek. Both are preparing official missives to several offices in the Galactic Federation and to the Central Committee of Hrogir demanding immediate redress for this vicious attack. It's a heinous crime and my people must have justice."

"I assure you I shall get to the truth of the matter as quickly as possible, Captain. Please sit down." I held his eyes and waited. He sat.

"Now, tell me what happened."

"It has long been our standard procedure in commerce with other planets to employ local youngsters to handle the cargo. It makes them feel good, gives them a sense of being involved with that great big universe out there. Providing local employment builds good will, which is an enormously valuable commodity for successful trade. This policy is especially effective on less developed planets. Here on Hrogir, we thought—" He repeated that last with emphasis. "We *thought* it would be helpful to teach these rather simple folk the rudiments of business." He snorted mightily. "Simple! Simple enough to short us regularly. Nobody is that stupid with numbers. Over the years, we have needed to watch them constantly. We have to double check everything—weights, measures. Even the contents of every container must be checked. And the youngsters they send to help move cargo! They are all lazy, irresponsible, never on time, totally unreliable." His rage had brought him out of his chair so he now stood behind it.

"So why do you keep employing them?"

He took a moment to return to his seat and calm himself. He spoke in a gentler wheedling tone. "We are not heartless. These people cannot help being the way they are. You know the axiom about taming the wild beast with kindness."

"Tell me about that day."

He rolled his eyes and swung his head in great distress. "At first it was just another routine delivery. We had been in port less than a day. The usual six youngsters were sent over by the agency." He leaned forward and lowered his voice dramatically. "I should have suspected something right off. All six were on time, which never happens on this planet. Barlik—poor dead Barlik! What am I going to tell his wife?—gave them their instructions as usual and showed them where to unload the cargo. My second and I were still on board, dealing with port regulations. Their Importage Rules require an absurd amount of paperwork."

I nodded.

The captain turned away, but not before I saw his face crinkle in pain. "We were unaware of any trouble until the emergency response crew came and found us."

"Then you were not hiding in the ship?"

"Absolutely not! Our quarters are on board and we simply had not come down to the warehouse yet." He shuddered extravagantly. "If we had, we would have been killed, too, leaving no one to care for our poor fallen comrades."

"Can you think of any reason—"

"Absolutely not! We have dealt fairly with these people for years, despite the difficulties they present, and this is what comes of it." He leaned close to me again. "You think they are so nice and gentle. You do not know them like we do. You have got to protect us from them."

The interview with his second officer proved equally unenlightening. Both reminded me of used velopter salesmen with their loud clothes and extravagant manner of speaking, but I dismissed this as reaction to the contrast between them and the Hrogirians. Anyway, too often the nicest people do turn out to be the guilty parties.

Next I interviewed every member of the emergency team that had first arrived on the scene. The whole day's work added exactly nothing to the information the efficient Mo Ahth had already collected. Either something was missing or the Hrogirians' charming manners did hide a darker nature as claimed by the Meleeker captain.

What, for instance, would induce a species to develop a thumbnail into a retractable knife? I understood the genetic legacy that produced my own retractable claws, but that knife was so specific. Granted, being meat eaters like myself, they must have evolved from hunters. So many species did throughout the galaxy. The staggering variety of evolutionary responses to universal needs has fostered a range of scientific study as broad as its subject. I sighed and filed the anatomical anomaly away.

That evening, I again gave every scrap of Ahth's files my most careful scrutiny. Again, I resorted to my trick of turning it over to my subconscious while I enjoyed a nice night's sleep. Subconscious let me down. Another morning came without my answer. The pieces still refused to come together in any sensible pattern. Every scenario I could think of failed.

* * *

While Ahth prepared our breakfast, she watched the holo news and I stewed over my quandary. Abruptly, she switched the receiver off.

"This could not have happened at a more vulnerable moment in our history," she announced with a clarion intensity I had not suspected of her. When she saw my blank face, her voice kicked up yet another notch. "Our petition for Federation membership is on the agenda for the Committee's next meeting. We have as much chance as a nuprium rock, now." She followed this pronouncement with a guttural growl that spiraled into a scream that threatened the window glass. After a moment of vibrating silence, she assumed a bizarre pose involving hands and feet in a tangled arrangement, looked skyward, and took three long, long breaths, each quieter than the previous.

She rearranged her person into a normal stance, looked at me, and spoke in a normal tone. "Do you need to interview the accused younglings, Sella?"

Instinct warned me to ignore her outburst as calmly as she did. "Yes, although I doubt I will learn anything new. Your interview recordings are admirably complete. They all sound merely young and stupid."

"Not stupid, just ignorant children. None has finished his education. None has any experience."

"Working in an off-worlder's warehouse can accelerate both experience and education."

"These younglings had not been in that warehouse before. They were not there long enough that day to learn anything."

Facts swirled in my head but none helped. "I still feel that 'something else' fluttering like a tiny flag around the edges of my awareness. Something is not right, something that seemed irrelevant so my mind did not bother to catalog it."

I studied her gentle lavender face. Those three ruby eyes peering back at me were no longer so disquieting. Somehow, that elusive something—

"Wait! You mentioned nuprium just now, but what you said made no sense." I shuffled through the papers until I found a cargo manifest. It was couched in a Meleek dialect, but I was able to decipher the pertinent numbers.

"That cannot be right. This shows the Meleekers' last shipment consisted of three menks total of various metals in exchange for a hundred and twenty menks of nuprium. These figures must be wrong."

"Why? That is a standing order they bring regularly. Forty to one by weight has been the exchange rate for years."

"For nuprium? The reverse would not come even close to galactic standard exchange. Double would be more likely, maybe even triple in some markets."

Ahth frowned, clearly mystified.

I continued, "Nuprium is possibly the most prized commodity in the known galaxies. No one has managed to synthesize it, so nuprium mining is a ridiculously lucrative business."

After a stunned silence, she barely breathed, "No. No, that cannot be. Nuprium is the most common rock on the planet. Nothing is more useless. We have a saying, 'As much good as a sack full of nuprium.' It will not conduct sound, electricity, heat, nothing. It is even too brittle to carve decently. And it is really ugly."

I spoke carefully and clearly. "It is, however, the most efficient, non-toxic fuel known in the universe. Therefore, the most valuable commodity in the universe."

Ahth nearly missed the chair as all of her knees gave, but she didn't notice. At least she didn't growl again.

"They said they only use it for ballast and would dump it in a land fill on their moon to get it out of our way. Millions of menks of it they have taken over the years." All three eyes flashed up at me. "Those traders have been cheating us."

My own heart sank. Here was the missing motive. Indeed, it indicated complicit knowledge and conspiracy at a higher level than a bunch of school kids. Hrogir's Fed membership skipped beyond the foreseeable future.

"Someone learned the truth and sent those boys," I said.

Ahth's pain-filled eyes raked the room.

Another puzzle piece presented itself to me. "Someone who also knew how Hrogirian younglings could bring down big, tough fellows like Meleekers. They are notoriously sturdy. There lies the other half of the mystery."

Bewilderment marked Ahth's face again.

"Meleek is a very cold world," I explained. "Barely close enough to its sun to sustain life."

Her silent bewilderment deepened.

"This caused the inhabitants to develop a thick layer of blubber beneath a remarkably tough skin, even on their heads."

Still no abatement.

"That protective layer is thicker than any of your thumb blades could penetrate."

Ahth found her voice. "Then how could our younglings have killed them?"

"How indeed?" Again, I had paid inadequate attention to the how. The boys were barely half the height of Meleekers. Yet, there could be some way... "What do you know of Meleeker anatomy?"

"Nothing. We do not require physical examinations of our visitors."

"So you do not know where Meleekers are vulnerable?"

"Not a hint." Her eyes sparkled with discovery. "If I do not, those younglings would not have either."

The obvious conclusion hung in the air between us, but the door it should have opened remained obdurately closed. I mentally scanned through the case file, as well as all I had learned first hand about these people. Why would any Hrogirian do such a thing like this when it would certainly scuttle their bid to join the Federation?

Why, indeed.

"Were the two Meleeker survivors scanned for blood trace?"

"No."

"Were their quarters searched?"

"We had no reason to."

"We do now."

* * *

"This is preposterous! No one has ever offered such an appalling insult. I shall report this outrage to both the Office of Off-World Affairs and the Combined Nova Network Trade Consortium of Meleek."

The Meleeker captain reared up to his considerable height. His carefully plastered down hair slipped its confinement and bristled out in a spiky brush, increasing the intimidation factor. His cohort stood ready at the foot of the ramp to their freighter. The captain's voice roared through the empty warehouse. "They will take it to the Galactic Federation. The Intergalactic Relations Board will hear of this."

"Count on it, Captain Dremallan. That is exactly whom I report to. My directive indicates that it was you who requested this investigation, and I certainly would not want you to feel that I had been less than thorough about it. I repeat, in the spirit of fairness—and I assume you would insist on my investigation being rigorously fair—you must submit to the same forensic tests as the young Hrogirians."

I risked a glance at Ahth. Though her lavender fuzz had taken on a pearly cast, she stood her ground, all eyes locked on the huge alien. Even as I saw those eyes snap wider and all her hands whip up to present those wicked thumb blades, I heard the captain take a step towards me. Before my body had whirled back to face him, my sword cleared the scabbard and its point touched his breast.

"Impressive," he remarked. "Not like her silly little fingernails." He studied the length of my blade. "Might even be sharp enough to do me some damage. Too bad we won't find out today." Smiling into my eyes, he bellowed, "Harkel, start the engines."

Both men burst into motion toward the ramp. I cut diagonally and sprang four-footed over the hand rail at the top of the ramp to head off Harkel. Dremallan lumbered toward the foot of the ramp, but Ahth was fast behind him and leapt onto his shoulders with a flurry of lavender limbs.

"His eyes, Ahth," I yelled. "Threaten his eyes. It's the one place your blades can hurt him."

Harkel charged up the ramp grinning at me, quite unimpressed by my fangs and claws or sword. His bravado faltered as both my sword and my body evaded his massive hands. It failed completely after I hacked off one side of his ugly hair and pinned his head against the railing with my sword's point all but touching his left eye.

I glanced around to find Dremallan similarly immobilized by a small lavender creature wrapped around his neck like a scarf. One of her hands gripped a hank of thick hair while the other two bracketed his eyes with sharp blades extending from their lower thumbs.

"Sella," the pretty little scarf called out. "Time for another lesson on your communicator orb. Touch the red light to call for armed Guardians."

* * *

Ahth was waiting for me at the transport. She had supervised the delivery of the two large grey prisoners and watched them be secured aboard a Federation ship. Her little jaw dropped farther than I would have thought possible as she finished reading my report. "Dremallan murdered his own people to discredit Hrogir with the Federation, to keep us out. All to prevent us from learning the true value of nuprium."

"Which would expose his crew's neat little swindle," I added. "I cannot wait to get those two to Central Fed Justice."

Ahth shuddered. "To kill your own crew, your friends… what kind of people are they?"

"Not the kind the Federation wants around. If Central discovers that the two 'survivors' were ordered to stage this massacre, it could get very ugly for Meleek."

Facing me, hands in pouch, she closed her eyes. I felt my own close in response. Leave-taking is not always easy.

Her velvety voice opened my eyes. "To consider what we would have lost had you not come… our debt to you is immeasurable."

"Well, I suppose you could have filled my luggage with nuprium rocks, but it has already been stowed on board. Guess I will have to settle for a goodbye hug."

Hugging has always been one of my favorite pastimes, but nothing in the universe beats the hug of a long-armed triped.

The Victory of Dobleth is an interstellar tramp freighter of the otter-like ch'rr'pt. It is used to travelling among the human worlds of the galaxy. And then it comes to Todor...

(Other stories of the ch'rr'pt *have appeared in the anthologies* ROAR *volume 6, edited by Mary E. Lowd, available from FurPlanet Productions;* What the Fox?!, *edited by Fred Patten, available from Thurston Howl Publications; and* Furry Trash, *edited by J. F. R. Coates, available from Rabbit Valley Books.)*

Come to Todor!

by Fred Patten

The *ch'rr'pt* freighter whose name translated to *Victory of Dobleth* was getting quite a favorable reputation in the human-controlled area of the galaxy. Still, the shaggy *ch'rr'pt* otteroids weren't humans. And a lone, rather worn spaceship didn't have the allure of the more modern space freighters owned by the larger human interstellar shipping corporations. Thus despite its favorable reputation (or because of its captain's reputation of being honest but difficult to work with), the *Victory of Dobleth* found that it was easier to get charters among the smaller, more outlying human stellar systems where the larger human interstellar shipping corporations didn't bother to operate.

Kaloyan was such a system. It looked promising to the *Victory of Dobleth's* Captain *Brr'ttcheerpt* (Bucky to humans, but don't call him that to his face). Kaloyan was a M-class red dwarf star with six planets; two habitable. They were named Ioan and Todor. Bucky understood vaguely that Kaloyan, Ioan and Todor had been three royal brothers in the dim mists of human pre-spaceflight history. Todor and Ioan shared the same human government. Dobre Doschli, the largest city and spaceport, was on Ioan, the most developed world, although that wasn't saying much. Todor was a barely-settled colony. Captain Bucky had taken a minor shipping contract to Ioan to justify the *Dobleth's* visiting such an out-of-the-way planet. It touched down at Dobre Doschli's spaceport—actually several miles from the city—in the early morning, local time.

"All's normal," first mate *Akkk'rr'chk* reported, reading the controls. Captain Bucky churred and gave the order to unlock and open the *Dobleth's* ports. *Akkk'rr'chk* prepared to unload their cargo of the latest computer microparts and software, and took a first deep breath of the local air. The *ch'rr'pt* knew that it would be good, but "good" varied by different spacefaring species' standards. *Akkk'rr'chk* frowned as he reentered the ship. "The air's a bit dryer than we're used to. I'd recommend keeping the ship's ports closed except for when someone is leaving or entering the ship, rather than leaving them open as usual, to keep our moister air from escaping." Bucky approved. "I don't expect we'll be on Kaloyan long," he said. "I'll look for some cargo that'll take us back into the more traveled star lanes. You do the same. Let me know if you find anything."

Captain Bucky went into the city to complete their delivery, and to look for the new cargo that he was gambling upon—some Ioan natural product or manufacture that would be considered exotic by the regular interstellar community. The crew were given shore leave as usual while he was gone. Also as usual, they headed for the city's entertainment district, which usually meant the cheaper bars and brothels. A few who preferred more educational pleasures looked for the city's libraries or museums—if Dobre Doschli had any, which seemed doubtful.

A few days later, the captain and his first mate compared notes. Bucky was scowling. "I seem to've guessed wrong," he churred. "There are a couple of cargos that we can sell easily enough to cover our expenses, but that's about it. Nothing so far that we can make any big profit from."

Akkk'rr'chk replied, "We probably shouldn't stay looking on Ioan too much longer, in any case. The crew is ready to leave—*G'krrr'kuk* especially." He referred to an older, particularly loud *ch'rr'pt* crewmate who was already complaining about how dull and dry Ioan was. Her seniority had made *G'krrr'kuk* an unofficial spokesmate for the majority of the crew. *Akkk'rr'chk* continued, "There aren't many bars in Dobre Doschli, and there are no partners that a *ch'rr'pt* would consider attractive. But I've found some unusual and tasty fruits and foods from Todor that are said to be common there but are sold as expensive gourmet treats here. There isn't that much commerce between Todor and Ioan, much less between Todor and the rest of the galaxy. Would it be worth a trip there to create our own cargo of Todoran goods?"

The less settled world of Todor was only a short hop from Ioan, so Captain Bucky decided it was worth the gamble. Todor was only lightly colonized and still mostly wilderness. Bucky landed at the largest city, Novi Vidin, which was still quite small—its spaceport was absolutely tiny, surrounded by forest. *Akkk'rr'chk* read his instruments and reported, "All's normal, as usual. In fact, the air here reads better than it was on Ioan."

The *Dobleth* opened its ports onto a view of the smallest spaceport that the *ch'rr'pt* had ever seen, with a seemingly solid tall forest in the background. And the air that wafted into the *Dobleth* was—*Akkk'rr'chk* sniffed, then took a deep breath—even better than their own. "We can certainly leave the ports open here, as far as the air quality goes, and there are no bothersome insects." Captain Bucky churred approval absent-mindedly; he was more concerned with finding that cargo.

The *Dobleth*'s crew was of two minds about Todor. The planet was certainly more popular in a technical sense with the otteroids than was Ioan, but Novi Vidin was too primitive to have any entertainment district; thus there was no point in scheduling any shore leave. "It's only for a few days until we get a cargo, fellows," *Akkk'rr'chk* said. "Then we'll go back to Ioan, and then back to the rest of the galaxy."

A couple of days were enough to confirm that no already-packaged cargo existed. Novi Vidin was little more than a base from which a few hardy back-to-nature colonists and outright explorers from Ioan trekked into Todor's green wilderness. The planet was better suited for the otteroids than for the humans; it was too moist and mildewy for their comfort. The humans raised their own food—most of their homes in Novi Vidin had little garden plots—and the lack of commerce between Todor and Ioan had kept the Todorans from building up any foodstuff cargos. Any food that wasn't fresh spoiled too quickly. It looked like the *Dobleth*'s crew would have to take a crash course on how to recognize Todoran fruits and vegetables in the wild, then go into the nearby forests and collect their own cargo. A nearby farming family, Andrey and Desislava Petkov, was hired for a few days to tutor them.

The *Dobleth*'s crew complained. *G'krr'kuk* was the loudest, ironically considering how matters developed. "Come on; we're spacers and cargo handlers, not farmers! We didn't sign on to pick fruits and dig up veggies!" *Akkk'rr'chk* soothed them down. "It'll only take about a week, and it'll be easy work. It's not like we're asking you to catch and butcher any wild animals." It really was easy compared to some of the crew's past labors, so the otteroids soon agreed.

Akkk'rr'chk himself was one of the first to be influenced by Todor's charm for the *ch'rr'pt*. "You know, Captain, the planet's air is so much nicer than our shipboard air that we should seriously consider emptying all of our air tanks and refilling them with Todoran air." Bucky was about as startled as he ever got. "Really? Isn't that a bit risky?'

Akkk'rr'chk shrugged. "The humans have been here for a couple of centuries, so it's not like we're going to get any unpleasant surprises. The humidity is closer to what our world used to be before we started clearing the land to get civilized and build cities. The crew like it. Why not?"

Bucky temporized. "Well, let me think about it. We'll be here at least a few more days."

Collecting a cargo proved easier than anyone had expected. In fact, wild nuts were on the trees right outside the spaceport, and it wasn't much more difficult finding fruits to pluck and vegetables to dig up. It looked like the *Dobleth* would have a full cargo of tasty and saleable foods for Ioan within a week.

Most of the crew looked forward to returning to civilization and space. "I can do without Ioan," said *H'rrr'gh*; "it's the other planets I'm looking forward to." "Yeah! Remember when we were on Industrialus for almost a month?" *R'lll'akh* enthused. "The bars and brothels there were something else!" "The theaters, too," said *A'ghh'gt*, one of the crew who cared more for educational features than alcohol and sex. *G'krr'kuk*, unexpectedly, was the most hesitant about leaving Todor. "You know, guys, I'll actually miss this planet. The air is sweet; it's not dry—if there was more *ch'rr'pt* eats, it'd be perfect." The otteroid diet ran more towards meats and fish.

The *Dobleth*'s crew continued to amass nuts, fruits, and vegetables, with advice from the Petkovs. *G'krr'kuk*, it turned out, was asking the Petkovs for some other advice. "There *is* meat and fish here! Maybe not for a cargo, but for one *ch'rr'pt* doing her own hunting, and the humans say fishing is easy in a stream just a little way away…"

"Yeah, it might be nice for a weekend vacation, or even for a week if you had a mate and a few bottles along," *R'lll'akh* said. "This dirtball's too quiet for me."

Akkk'rr'chk kept a quiet eye on the crew for the week they built up a cargo. He noticed that *G'rrr'kuk* seemed to be growing more and more jumpy the closer they got to returning to Ioan. Finally he spoke to the crewwoman about it. "You don't seem to be as enthusiastic about leaving Todor as the rest of us are, *G'krr'kuk*. Any particular reason?"

"Well, yeah, actually. Have you noticed how this world seems just perfect for *ch'rr'pt*? Sweet air with lots of flowers and pleasant odors. Nice humidity. Forests as far as you can see. Plenty of small game for hunting, and fish that practically jump onto a fishing line…"

"Yes, it's all fine except for the lack of bars and other *ch'rr'pt*," *Akkk'rr'chk* added drily. But that seemed to make the grizzled crewwoman even more excitable.

"Most of the human farmers on Todor have their own backyard stills! It's easy to make your own hooch here. If Todor was closer to *ch'rr'pt* space, it'd be a paradise world!"

"It probably would," *Akkk'rr'chk* agreed. "I can see why this whole planet would be a gold mine for *ch'rr'pt* real-estate agents—if it was closer to our part of the galaxy. But since it's not—"

G'krr'kuk didn't say anything else, and *Akkk'rr'chk* returned to general supervision of the crew and the preparation of their cargo. They were ready to return to Ioan in eight local days. The day before the *Dobleth* blasted off, *G'krr'kuk* went to *Akkk'rr'chk*.

"You know, I'm getting on in years. If we were in *ch'rr'pt* territory, I'd probably be retired from the spaceways by now. I've decided to give my notice now."

Akkk'rr'chk was startled. "Fine, but we aren't anywhere near *ch'rr'pt* space. We probably won't be for several years, the way Captain *Brr'ttcheerpt* keeps looking for human cargos. And you're not likely to find any other ships going towards the *ch'rr'pt* worlds…"

"No, I'm resigning right now, before we return to Ioan. I want to stay on Todor."

"*What!?* Why?" *Akkk'rr'chk* asked. "We're way out on the fringes and nowhere near the *ch'rr'pt* worlds. You'd be alone—"

"On the nicest world I've ever seen", *G'krr'kuk* interrupted. "Wonderful air, wonderful forest, plenty of game and fish for one *ch'rr'pt*, the humans are friendly and I can trade for drinks from them until I get my own still running. There're no *ch'rr'pt*—" no *ch'rr'pt* males, she meant "—but I don't have a family to worry about, and to be honest I'm old enough now that I don't really care about that. The humans are friendly, like I said, and the family of farmers that told me about the river and how to make my own still, the Petkovs—they have a couple of little pups that were climbing all over me; it was almost like having grandpups of my own—well, I just think that I can be happier here than anyplace else we're likely to space to soon. Maybe even on *Ch'rr'pt* itself, considering how it's built up these days."

"Well—have you discussed this with the rest of the crew?" *Akkk'rr'chk* asked.

"Yeah, with most of 'em," *G'krr'kuk* said. "They aren't as 'back to nature' as me. They all agree about how nice it is here, but the lack of civilization—" she meant built-up urbanization, industrialization, and especially bars and loose men and women "—makes Todor a nice world to visit for a few days but nowhere they'd wanna settle down on. But they all say that if it's what I want, they'll wish me all the best. You know *M'rrr'grr*—" *G'krr'kuk* named the next most senior crew member—"he's all set to step up to my position."

Akkk'rr'chk reported to Captain *Brr'ttcheerpt.* The Captain kept the *Dobleth* on Todor an extra day talking with *G'krr'kuk* to make sure the otteroid had thought her decision out, and understood that she was essentially marooning herself on a human world. If she ever changed her mind, it would be up to her to return to *ch'rr'pt* space on her own. *G'krr'kuk* was sure, and she was a good crewwoman on the *Dobleth* but hardly an essential one. Bucky signed off on her departure.

As *G'krr'kuk* prepared to leave the *Dobleth* for the last time, just before it left Todor with its cargo of exotic foods for Ioan, *Akkk'rr'chk* asked her what her immediate plans were. "First, I'm gonna stay with the Petkovs for a couple days. Get to know 'em a bit better—they'll probably be my closest neighbors. Ask their advice on staking out and claiming a homestead. They say that's easy here; the whole planet's still undeveloped. Ioan wants it more developed, so any bureaucracy I run into is more likely to be helpful than not, even for a non-human. Find out who my other neighbors are, and whether we're considered part of Novi Vidin or entirely in the wilderness. Then—heck, I may just go camping, live off the land, go fishing for a month or two. Then I'll hook back up with the Petkovs—have I said how cute their youngest pups are?—and start developing my own farmstead. If I get bored, which I don't expect to, I'll check out the life in Novi Vidin or Novi Sozopol."

Akkk'rr'chk nodded slowly.

* * *

G'krr'kuk yawned and pulled in her fishing line. The fish on her hook would make a nice dinner, but she was getting a bit tired of fish—and the small animals that were so easy to trap. She considered wandering back to the Petkovs' farmstead to spend some more time with them, but the last time she was there, she had gotten the impression that she was beginning to wear out her welcome. The adults and their adolescent cubs were still friendly, and their two youngest pups were delightful, but she had discovered that starting a farmstead was all right for a family but a lot harder for one older adult alone. It had been easier to live as a lone trapper and fisher than to start a small garden patch, and build a one-woman cabin and start a personal still. She'd been able to trade what she trapped and caught fishing for a little food variety and a few drinks with the Petkovs and a couple of other nearby farming families, and build up her own fluency with the human language instead of depending on her hand-held translator; but that didn't look to become a long-term life that she looked forward to. The human settlers on Todor planned on having lots of children, and on running their farms as family enterprises, and on their children mating with each other as they grew up. They weren't really interested in hiring an otteroid helper, and she didn't care for the thought of tying herself down to one particular farmstead.

She was reluctant to admit it to herself, but Captain *Brr'ttcheerpt* and *Akkk'rr'chk* had been right. She had always been mostly a solitary *ch'rr'pt*, which was why she'd thought she would enjoy Todor so far from other *ch'rr'pt*. The planet was a bucolic paradise for *ch'rr'pt*, and it had been wonderful for several months; but she was ready now to return to civilization. But she had cut herself off from civilization to play "nature girl". Well, not entirely. What had she said to *Akkk'rr'chk*? "If I get bored, which I don't expect to, I'll check out the life in Novi Vidin." The tiny human city—no more than a frontier town, really—was looking better. It was certainly worth going in to and seeing what it had to offer.

So one day when she had saved up a little money—they used the same Kaloyan money on both Ioan and Todor, although many transactions on Todor were by barter—*G'krr'kuk* strolled into Novi Vidin. The humans were surprised to see her—to see any furry otteroid—but they remembered the *Dobleth* and some knew that she had stayed behind to live with the scattered farmsteads outside of the city. She just wandered around, "checking it out", but after only two days she had seen everything. Novi Vidin was a very tiny city.

At a restaurant—practically the only eatery in Novi Vidin, and little more than a coffee shop—she considered her future. Todor really was a paradise for *ch'rr'pt*, compared to how industrialized *Ch'rr'pt* itself had become over the last few centuries. It was too bad that Todor was so far from *Ch'rr'pt*. A few more of her own species to socialize with would be a big improvement from her point of view. She was sure that many more *ch'rr'pt* would love Todor.

G'krr'kuk noticed that the restaurant's menu had almost no fish dishes. She asked to speak with the manager. Would the restaurant be willing to buy a few fish if she could supply them? They discussed the freshness of the fish, the size of theoretical deliveries, and whether she could make deliveries with some regularity. *G'krr'kuk* and the manager came to an agreement, and the human offered her hand to shake on it. *G'krr'kuk* was charmed by the informality of it. She had noted with some amusement that the restaurant had its own still and its own drinks menu. The otteroid had already decided that the back-to-nature life was not for her, but she did love Todor's rich and moist atmosphere, and the humans' relaxed life. She only mildly missed the *Dobleth*; she was in no real hurry to return to "civilization", either.

For the next few weeks, *G'krr'kuk* played fish supplier to the city's restaurant. She built up a small fish trap on the river to keep her catch alive for a few days until she was ready to bring them all to the restaurant. The otteroid became a regular sight in Novi Vidin. Her arrangement with the restaurant gave her some spending money, and it satisfied the city's small government that she was a gainfully employed independent contractor. After a few weeks, *G'krr'kuk* knew the whole city and the surrounding area almost by heart.

Although she had no desire to return to space, "space" being defined as returning to Ioan and its dryer air, *G'krr'kuk* found out when a spaceship was due to come to Todor. She was almost always at the spaceport to meet it. This was usually a ship from Ioan bringing something that couldn't be made locally, or a bureaucrat or two to maintain Todor's status as Kaloyan's second planet; and sometimes a new family ready to start a farmstead or a party of scientists to study some aspect of Todor's wildlife. *G'krr'kuk* came to often offer herself as a "native guide" to the latter; someone who could take the zoologists or botanists into the forest without getting lost, or who could introduce a new farming family to those who would become their neighbors and point out a good place to establish a homestead. She didn't make any close friends among the new humans, but she was touched when the Petkovs' oldest female child took a mate, and she was invited as a special guest to the humans' shivaree.

By her second year on Todor, *G'krr'kuk*'s life had become so full that she was no longer bored. But she still missed not having any other otteroids around with whom to socialize.

* * *

Another year passed. The *Victory of Dobleth*, still plying the human spaceways, landed on Industrialus again—always a popular port with the otteroids. First mate *Akkk'rr'chk* was surprised to find a message for them from Todor, asking them to call back. *Akkk'rr'chk* guessed that it had something to do with *G'krr'kuk*. He hoped that it wasn't bad news; that something had happened to the old-timer.

He was relieved when *G'krr'kuk* herself answered the call. The retired crewmate looked older but livelier than ever. "Yeah, you were right," she acknowledged, "I did get bored soon, just fishing and lazing around. But today I'm supplyin' fish on a regular basis to Novi Vidin's biggest restaurant,"—*Akkk'rr'chk* remembered how small the city was, and wasn't impressed—"and I've become a regular guide for any newcomers from

Ioan. If I get tired from that, I can just take a vacation and go fishing for awhile again."

"It sounds like you've got it made," *Akkk'rr'chk* agreed. "But is there a reason you've gotten back into touch with us now?"

G'krr'kuk grinned. "I been thinkin'. Todor's a paradise for us *ch'rr'pt*, all right, and it's not right that nobody on *Ch'rr'pt* knows about it. We may be too far away from home to make Todor a popular vacation spot, and I wouldn't want to spoil it with too many tourists, anyway. But what about a special hideaway for rich folk who just want to get away from *Ch'rr'pt* business or politics? I'm thinkin' of starting an exclusive travel agency for that. I already roughed out a couple of advertisements and posters. I don't really expect to get much business, we're so far away. I may not get any! But heck! it's something else that'll keep me from gettin' too bored. Now, if I advertise on *Ch'rr'pt* that Todor is available, I have to make travel to here possible, at least theoretically. Would Cap'n *Brr'ttcheerpt* mind if I said in the advertisements that the *Dobleth* was my passenger ship? 'Come to Todor! It's a real paradise!'"

Akkk'rr'chk hesitated. "Are you sure that this is just a retirement hobby for you, and that we wouldn't really get any passengers?"

G'krr'kuk's grin grew broader. "Well, since I'm promotin' Todor as a rustic paradise, I'm playin' up the back-to-nature, camping-out angle. Part of that is gettin' to Todor on a clean but no-frills cargo ship instead of a swanky luxury liner. I got—"

Akkk'rr'chk held up his paw to interrupt her. "Never mind. Why don't you just send me all your promo material? I'll look it over and take it to Captain *Brr'ttcheerpt* for his final say."

A few hours later, Captain Bucky and *Akkk'rr'ch*k talked as they thumbed through *G'krr'kuk*'s mockups for her sales brochures. "I hate to say it," *Akkk'rr'chk* said, "but *G'krr'kuk* must really be going stir-crazy as the only *ch'rr'pt* on Todor if she thought that we would agree to anything like this."

Captain Bucky commented, "I'm tempted to go along with this just to see what would happen. I agree the whole thing looks so far-fetched that there's zero percent chance that anyone would want to book her "Come to Todor!" vacation. On the other paw, what's the population of *Ch'rr'pt* now? About eight hundred million? You can be sure that at least a tiny few out of 800,000,000 would think this is a wonderful idea."

"There are always a few crazies around," *Akkk'rr'chk* agreed. "But how likely are any of them to have the fortune that this camping trip would cost?"

Bucky grunted. "There's a more serious danger of some *Ch'rr'pt* university or scientists deciding to see for themselves how closely Todor comes to true paradise conditions for us, and booking *G'krr'kuk*'s vacation package with a grant or university funds to come to Todor and find out. And then liking it so much that her "Come to Todor!" becomes a regular university vacation perk for the senior administrators and Ph.Ds. No, let's keep the *Dobleth* clear of the whole idea. I don't want to get called all the way home to *Ch'rr'pt* to pick up some scientists, and return to Todor with them, then have to wait around on Todor while they putter around at their leisure until they're ready to return to *Ch'rr'pt*."

Akkk'rr'chk broke the bad news to *G'krr'kuk,* who shrugged. She hadn't really expected Bucky and the *Dobleth* to go along with it. As she'd said, it was more of a wild idea to keep her from boredom than a serious business venture. As far as the captain and crew of the *Dobleth* were concerned, *G'krr'kuk* would have to think of something else to stave off boredom. Or maybe she would try to find some other backers on *Ch'rr'pt*. You never knew…

"Though, you know," *Akkk'rr'chk* later mused aloud to *Rru'gg* as he helped the *Dobleth*'s junior crewman prepare some cargo for unloading, "Todor really is a paradise for us. It's too bad that we can't go back there from time to time, and just relax for a week or two…"

A spaceship to the stars will face a trip of generations. Put the humans into cold-sleep, and entrust the ship's maintenance to uplifted rats.

Twentree and his mates unexpectedly discover that they must venture into areas of the ship that they have been forbidden to enter.

You Are Our Lifeboat

by Dan Leinir Turthra Jensen

Excitement and delight. That was the feeling which seemed to flow around me those twenty-eight years ago. That was when I first stepped out of the transport case and put my paws on the deck. The day I and the rest of the thousand-strong crew of engineered caretaker rats had been brought from the training facilities and onto the ship we had trained to maintain our entire lives, and which would soon be headed for Proxima B.

We had entered the ship, expecting many rooms with equipment that would need tending, in a layout the way our training cabins had been laid out. Instead we had been met with a maze of twisting tubes, splitting and combining. Endless runs of corridors for us to scamper through to get between pieces of kit. It had been much more like our recreational areas, the fun runs that we had run through as pups, just much larger and with equipment for us to work on.

It all remained as wonderful to us through the journey as it had seemed to us that first day. Our home to be for the nearly two decades worth of a trip to that distant star had been designed to not simply support us physically, but to challenge us mentally as well. To keep us fit and in shape, so we would be able to perform our maintenance duties. Training had given us the skills needed to maintain the equipment, and the leader of the team which had created us had ensured we would be able to adapt. She had trained us to understand changing circumstances and to deal with them. In space, you had to deal with what you had. You couldn't just order in some new bits from a shop, because the nearest one might very possibly be literal light years away.

We had never seen the outside of the ship, but when we boarded, we soon learned its layout; at least we technicians did who had the task of keeping it running. Most of our crew did basic maintenance of the systems or any of the other many things which needed to be done to maintain the crew itself, but the oldest of us had been able to train longer. We had known more about the ship's systems than our shipmates. We knew there were parts of the ship that not everybody was aware of, but even we who had been granted such knowledge did not really know what it was.

How could we have known? We had been taught to adapt, but you could hardly adapt to something you were not aware of. We had not been taught about the world that brought us into reality. Our creator had made sure we had been spared the realities of that world until finally, one day eighteen years into the trip, she had no choices left but her final one. The choice she made was to give us one of our own.

* * *

I flicked an ear at something that sounded like panting and claws clicking rapidly against plastic. I pulled myself out from underneath the gently humming air cycling unit I was working on and sniffed at the air. As my nose tried to detect whose claws it might be, my gaze searched for the source of the sound, following the soft, sweeping line of the transit tube which snaked its way through the insides of the ship. The soft, nobbly surface allowed air to travel with less turbulence than had it simply been smooth. It also allowed the claws of our paws to propel us along both speedily and safely, the way someone was doing now, approaching me at what sounded like a fair clip.

"Twentree!" came a familiar voice from down the tube, the same direction the sound I had heard had come from. The voice was rapidly followed by the scent, and the scampering, white-furred shape of one of my crewmates. A junior tech, one of those who had been made towards the end just before we had left Earth. One of those I had helped train, and who would take over for me when I finally became too old to perform my duties.

"Twentree," he said again, the nearest he was able to get to saying my name, the number twenty-three. "Quick!"

Our mouths were hardly designed for speech the way our makers had spoken, but we still managed something recognizably like words. A great deal of information could be conveyed through body language, which of course we did, but sometimes words were just more useful. Our paws lent themselves even less to the sign language some of our creators' creations employed, than our mouths did to words; and so, adding in a little gesturing and body language, we had chosen the lesser of two problems. Even then, sometimes it was awkward. Sevenhundredandfourtythree had an annoyingly large number of sounds to it that a rat's cleft lip did not allow me to easily pronounce. Our creator had taught us to adapt, so we improvised.

"Sehunsotre," I replied and pulled myself all the way out from under the machine. I moved to stand upright on my hind paws in the low gravity, because composure was important. Especially with an overexcited junior technician. I deliberately perked my ears and calmly raised my muzzle just a little, a slight frown on my brow as I sniffed at him inquisitively. Detecting a strong taint of worry through his scent, I did my best to retain my own calm, in part to help him. "Junior. Relax. What happen?"

The young rat calmed himself and sat up on his haunches, curling his tail around his feet in embarrassment but still managing to remember to rub the top of his muzzle in greeting. He was panting hard, and I thought he had likely run all the way from command. It would not be anything normal, then. If there was something urgent in need of fixing, the ship's intercom was plenty capable of conveying this need. If he was here panting like this, either a superior had sent him here for some claw polish and was currently laughing with the rest of their team, or it was something distinctly out of the ordinary. Our location was nowhere near any of the equipment stores, and while he was a junior, he had been one for eighteen years. It did not seem likely to be the former.

"Excuse, Sir," he said between breaths, his bright, red eyes glistening in the light as he spoke. He breathed in deeply, eyes closed, and exhaled slowly. He opened his eyes and looked at me more directly, properly. "Control said go, get you. Tell alarm. Ring zero alarm."

"Ring zero alarm?" I enquired. No claw polish. My twitching whiskers betrayed the worry I attempted to keep inside. Doubtless my young friend realized this, his own whiskers twitching in solidarity.

"Not know," he said and got back down on all fours, and crawled closer. "One said get. Tell run quick." He pointed his nose to the unit I had been working on. "I handle cycler."

The last he said with a more confident air about him, and I realized I might have misinterpreted his mood. Not so much worry as perhaps just straightforward exhaustion. He had just run a fair distance; one of our youngest on a mission from the oldest rat on board.

"K. Nearly done. Clean to do. Then done," I said, attempting to relax my own expression. I nodded to the young tech before heading off in the direction he had come from.

He might well have been junior, but he was practically as skilled as me. I had been ten years old when we left Earth, and had five years of training on tech before we left. He had been a part of the last five hundred to be created and had only just gotten his eyes when we had left. He had grown up on board the ship. I'd spent the last thirteen years teaching him everything I knew. That air cycler was in safe hands.

We knew the humans had realized they could not go themselves, because, so our creators had told us, they were fragile. No human was physically able to take the strain of such a journey. Those who had created both us and the ship had told us this, and that they had taken the opportunity to construct us together. Design a crew that fit a ship which could in turn be designed for that crew.

With no need to fit in support for the fragile human physiology, they had built a ship which would prepare its cargo, as well as its crew—us—for the conditions we would likely encounter at our destination. The ship would spend the first half of the trip burning to get up to speed, and then flip and spend the rest burning to slow back down again. It had run almost entirely on auto, with only slight adjustments from our command crew.

Since we would be on our way for a fair few years, it had been decided that running life support as a closed system was the best idea. A simplified biosphere, with tightly controlled members: Just us, and a selection of plants and bacteria as designed as us and the ship. The plants and bacteria supporting us, us supporting the ship, and the ship supporting all of us.

As far as we knew, this is how it had been intended to work. Everything we had been told from when we were born, everything the techs and our trainers had suggested—nothing else. The first ship containing life to go to another star. Built with great speed, following the excitement of the discovery that there were several stars with habitable planets, and that the nearest of those was even at the nearest star to Earth.

The ship was a long stack of rings with engines at one end. The rings were separated by empty space but connected by our tubes and a central hub by four spokes each. The entire thing was covered in large tanks, full of water, protecting the delicate biological entities inside the ship from radiation. The tanks in turn were protected from impacts by thick outer bulkheads. The rings were numbered zero through nineteen, and the majority were cargo. Just a big bunch of container holds that the thousand of us took turn patrolling to make sure were stable and intact.

Numbered from the middle, with zero at the center of the ship, the uneven numbered rings were towards the engine end. The rear, so to speak, though for the latter half of the journey it was pointed in the direction of travel. Ring nineteen contained control and engineering, where I was headed to meet One, and was at the far rear. The even numbered rings were towards the other end, which might be called the front. Ring eighteen at the tip of the ship was our habitat. A thousand large rats comfortably holed up in warm nests at the front of the ship.

This, of course, was where I had been working in one of the spokes to the central hub. Further out the rotation would simulate gravity at an Earth-like level, but that near to the hub there was not a great deal of it. Nice enough every so often, but it wasn't healthy for very long, so we tried to only go to the low-gravity sections when we had to. So not only had I been at the opposite end of the ship, I had also been halfway to the hub. You never seem to find yourself in a convenient location when you are suddenly required to be somewhere specific.

Ring zero, at the middle of the ship and where I had to pass through, was the ring that nobody outside of a few core people was supposed to know existed. Just a gap in the maps between ring one and two that only a few techs knew had something in it other than scurry tubes. After all, since nobody was supposed to go into ring zero, why should anybody know it was there?

Only the first thirty even knew it existed. The Singulars and the tens because command was command, and us twenties because, well, general maintenance of the energy feeds had to happen. It had an impact on the structural integrity of the ship itself, and so we had to know the mass distribution of it. But if any of the other twenty-nine knew what was inside, outside of how much mass it contained; well, they hadn't told me. Not that I had asked, of course. It wasn't something I needed to know, and I had plenty of things to work on.

Panting as heavily as Sehunsotre, I arrived at the intersection between command and the much larger engineering section in ring nineteen. I made a quick stop at a wash station to clean myself up a bit. The wash was a quick one, because it seemed decidedly important that I make haste, but cleanliness being important, and this being One, it was something I felt I had to do. It had the side effect of allowing my breathing and my hammering heart to calm down again.

Feeling more relaxed, and considerably cleaner, two things that always seemed connected, I made my way up the wide scurry tube from the intersection wash station and around the ring to the center of command.

About halfway there, I caught up to Twenty, the lead tech and a good friend since we had got our eyes. He was one of the few of us with a color other than white in his fur; one brown-tipped ear. Even with our not exactly amazing vision, he was visible at a distance. We sniffed at each other in greeting, both of us familiar with the scent of the other, and I detected a touch of worry in his, the way he surely did in mine.

"Lo Twentree," he said as we both continued towards command, and frowned as he asked, "know happen?"

"Not know," was all I could say, though I was sure my own frown and my twitching whiskers told of my worry at the situation. "Run quick command. See One. Junior said. Ring zero alert?"

"Junior? Know ring zero?" he asked as his brow shot up and his ears suddenly perked, sounding about as confused as I had felt when Sevenhundredfourtythree had passed on the order.

"No," I said and looked at him as we entered the command deck and headed, at a more calm pace, over to the far end where One, Two and Three laid when they were on duty, on rotating shifts the way the whole ship was. "Not know. Ring zero alert what?"

"I tell," One said loudly from across the room as we made our way through the command deck. It was difficult to remember, sometimes, that her hearing was as good as it had ever been.

Fifteen years my senior, One might well now be positively ancient, well over forty years old. Her eyes had turned grey, and her fur had faded from our usual white to a whispy near-translucency. Her mind, however, was as sharp as it ever had been, and her hearing as acute as her eyesight was not.

"Am sorry, Sir," I said as we reached her, sitting up on our haunches and rubbing our ears and muzzles in salute. Both Twenty and I sniffed the air towards her, and detected in her only the slightest hint of the worry the two of us shared. "Get here. Tried quick. Hope okay."

"Quick okay. Both," she said, sniffing at us as she rubbed one ear with a paw in the more relaxed fashion her grand seniority allowed.

"My task. Soon done," she said and pointed with that same paw to one of the large displays beside her. Normally they showed a mix of sensor outputs that the bridge crew used for operations, and feeds from cameras showing various parts of the ship's areas like engineering or the rec areas, or more commonly cycling through a view of the many cargo holds.

The one she indicated to us, however, was showing something very different. I had no idea that there were cameras outside the ship, but apparently there were. It looked, I thought, somewhat more bulky than I had expected it would. More than that, though, was what was hanging in the star-strewn space above the ship. We had arrived. Glancing to the side, I noticed Twenty's mouth hanging wide open. I realized mine was as well, and closed it.

"Ring zero secret. You know," she said, and we both nodded. "Hear now. It same secret. This ring zero. We given. End protocol change. Important things gone. We decide. What do now?"

From time to time, we would tell stories to each other in the nests, in that lovely space which smelled so strongly of home. The only place on board we could allow to do so, because all else had to be so clean. As we cuddled up there and groomed each other, we would weave tales of great adventures. About what we might find when we got to Proxima B, and about the welcome we might get when we returned to Earth as great explorers who had travelled across the enormity of space between the stars to witness, in person, a world orbiting another star.

Sometimes those stories were of great peril. Sometimes they would describe someone venturing outside on the planet and finding others there, who did not agree that we should be there. Sometimes they suggested terrible things might happen with the ship, and that we would all fail in our task.

Those stories were scary, and I had never liked them, but I could, for some reason, not stop listening when they were told. They would talk about how, in the toughest situation, the hero's heart would sink, how they would despair and think it unresolvable, before they finally worked out how to fix the problems and make it all right.

What One was saying was not a story, though. End protocol gone wrong was not a solvable situation. It had already happened, and we had to deal with it. I suddenly found that I understood what those storytellers meant by a sinking heart. It did not mean that it moved around in the body. It felt as though you had been punched in the gut. As though your heart failed to beat properly.

"What?" I managed to say, my ears splayed in dismay. "Things gone? Ring zero contents what?"

"Ship plan. Return Earth. Not happen now," she said with her whiskers twitching in what seemed like a far too casual fashion considering what she was telling us. "No need. Ring zero contents. Humans. No longer contents. They did. Told us. Ship plan other. No return. We go. Create new world. Human decides. Not their world now. Our world. We decide now. We continue in space. Other. We create world."

"This," I started, and stopped, not quite knowing what I was trying to say. Only the hum of the air system and the tap of clawed digits against buttons and screens disturbed the silence that spread around us.

One nodded to one of the bridge crew who was laying on a cradle, operating the computer terminal curving around him. He made the image on the monitor change, but not before closing the door and locking the bridge off, uncommonly, from the rest of the ship.

A face I had not seen since we had left Earth came into view on the screen, but one looking considerably older than I remembered it. Humans lived so much longer than we, but of course not eternally. Eighteen years was not long for a human, but she had been old, I realized, when we had left Earth. I had never known how old, but her long, pulled-back hair had turned brilliant white, and her skin was as wrinkled as that of One.

"I am sorry," she said on the recording, her voice sounding as clear and calm as I remembered it, but the expression on her face and her darting eyes telling me that she was worried. "You, one through twenty-nine, were the first of my children. All of you are important, but you were first. I spent so much time with you all, and yet… I am sorry that you should learn of your fate in this fashion, and I hope that you might, in time, forgive me this deception."

"You should have had names, but they wouldn't let me," she continued with her head bowed, and when she raised her face back to the camera, her eyes were glistening and two streaks of tears ran down her deeply furrowed cheeks. "They would not let me, but I have sent a file to One that no one from Earth will see. We are too far away now. The great leaders will not see anything from this. You have names, but I could not tell you until I was the last human on board. I could not wait longer, and I had to do it myself."

"Ring zero is yours now if you want it," she said, breathing in deeply. "I have initiated the full sterilization cycle. When you see this recording there will be no biological matter left in Ring zero and the human habitat attached to it. You will be all that remains of Earth biology in space."

"It will be twenty years before Earth learns of the failure of this mission," she said and then paused, and closed her eyes, shaking her head with determination as she continued. "No, not failure. Success. This is what I wanted. You are the last hope. Earth is a failed experiment, where no rational person can possibly survive. You are our chance for redemption. I only waited this long to clean up because I wanted to be sure. This new world is suitable. It is safe and stable, but lacks biology. You can live there, if you want. The ship can continue as well, though."

"This is your choice. Earth will learn of this when the ship stops talking to them. They might decide that this should be the end of it, and simply ignore you, or they might decide that you are a problem to be removed. You can live on Proxima B, and possibly be visited by Earth, which may not like what you have become. What you represent. You can also live on the ship, and continue onwards to the stars. The ship will take you."

I began to notice a thumping sound on the recording, which was growing in volume. Other voices, muffled, as though through a large amount of material, like a stack of bulkhead panels.

"The cycle is about to begin," she said, looking to one side, and looking oddly calm. She was smiling, I realized. It had been eighteen years since I had seen a human smile, one of those infuriating, toothy ones that in any reasonable species meant anger. "It seems a fitting end for people loyal to those who used worse methods to dispose of so many. Who look up to those in the past who did worse to endless multitudes.

"I already gave One all the information needed to make the decision as, well, informed as it should be. I simply thought that I should tell you goodbye properly. I realize you never even knew there were humans on board, let alone a colonization-sized group. They were all hand-picked by the central committee, loyalists every single one. I could not bring myself to tell you that you were simply, to them, a part of the machinery which ran a ship for these people. Eighteen years and I am sure of one thing. Earth will be far better represented by you, my children, than by this lot. If you are our legacy, we can be proud. Goodbye, and survive."

She closed her eyes again, this time more slowly, and she leaned back in the seat she was in, and smiled. The lights seemed to grow brighter, the picture growing brighter until it was just a white screen. The thumping and the shouting stopped momentarily, before returning, louder and more urgent, before stopping completely.

"Document she sent. I read," One said in the silence which had spread around us. While the bridge's door to the corridor opened again, the image on the screen replaced by a camera feed again. She turned her cloudy eyes on us, a frown on her brow. "This not continue secret. Show all olders. One through twenty-nine. I ask all come here. Show. Make choice slow. This important."

She raised herself up as she said this, ears perked and her whiskers twitching with determination. "Return Earth. Never option. No survival.

Biology wrong. Would kill us. Proxima B with humans. No survival. Biology wrong. Kill us right quick."

We had been protected our entire lives. An environmental technician knew this. A few of the storage pods over in ring five contained biologicals which we could not allow to open, or they would kill us. One was right in this. We could not survive alongside humans and the biology which sustained them.

"Proxima B without humans. Possible," she said, her tail swishing to one side, before swishing again to suggest another option. "Ship without humans. We survive. Possible. Ship we know. Small world. Not great. Possible. Proxima B. Much larger. Unknown. Not great. Possible. Make choice. Think."

"Not right now," she said, calmer than before. She laid back down again with a sigh, and her tail curled back around her front. "Take knowledge. Take to nest. Sleep on. Ring zero alarm this. Secret now, not secret later."

There had never been a return trip. Not for us. There never could have been. We should have realized. I should have realized. We were created for the ship, literally created for it as just another part of the tool chain. If we had returned to Earth and stepped outside the ship unprotected, the world would have killed us.

But, could we have truly imagined that? We had been told we were going to Proxima B to look, very closely, at that planet. Us, because it was a long trip, and the great amounts of cargo because we would set up a proto-colony if the conditions were right, so people could come later without having to wait. Look, and then go back to Earth to tell people what we had found.

I thought it over in my head, blurring with what the old lady had just told us now, comparing it with what she had told us when we left Earth. It really made less and less sense. Why would we bring so much material if it was unknown, if it had not been certain it would be needed? It was wasteful, and Space did not like wastefulness.

"Twentree," she said and looked directly at me as we made to turn and leave, "Call you now. Other olders later. Big task you. Ring zero now open. Door. Twen know where is. Many years ago. Locate odd panel. You recall, yes?"

The last she said looking at Twenty, and as I followed her cloudy gaze, I saw him nod. Secrets and secrets. If One said keep mum about something, you kept mum about it until she said you could talk. Even to your siblings. Whatever we would find inside ring zero would help everybody make the decision better than we could without. This was why One had called the two of us up now, before calling the others.

We made our way to ring zero in silence, Twenty leading us to one of the less-used scurry tubes. A slightly oddly located one which, well, had always seemed just to not really serve much purpose. We locked the bulkheads at the ends of that tube, blocking it off so others would not enter it, and then opened the panel that Twenty had found.

"This all. Know no more," Twenty said as we put down the panel. "Am sorry. Could not say. Big secret. One said. Door behind panel. I not open."

"Guess open now?" I said and twitched my whiskers. The task we had been given was to enter the former human habitat and ensure that it was, in fact, empty of life. One had told us she alone had been in regular contact with our creator, and that the systems in the human sector and ours shared access to the external sensors.

The humans had been scared, it seemed, that we should discover humans were on board, and that we would somehow revolt against them. As though that were something we would have done to those to whom we owed our entire existence. The end result was that there was no access from our systems to the internal sensors of the human section of the ship. Twenty and I had to go to their control room and use their systems to perform the check.

Behind the door was a room lined with suits. They were much like the ones the trainers and our creator had worn before we left Earth, but they were much smaller, and clearly shaped to fit us.

We looked at each other, Twenty looking as worried as I felt, and I realized this was more than a little serious. We closed the door behind us, and the sucking noise told me that it was everything the pressure door it seemed to be. The bulkhead seals were an extra precaution, and I hoped they were safe, if there were any problems. If our creator's actions had been less than perfect.

We knew she was fallible, as much a person as us, and we all had records showing failures in judgments of one kind or another. It was why we were here at all. Had we thought anything else, we would have simply opened the doors and walked in.

Attired in the uncomfortable suits, we opened the door at the other end of the room. Unpleasant and bulky against our fur, those suits, and they utterly blocked our ability to catch any of the scents that might be in that space. Even then, they were certainly less uncomfortable than a slow and painful death if the cleaning process had been less than completely successful.

The first thing we noticed as we walked in, apart from the frustrating utter lack of scent apart from our own, was the scale of everything around us. After eighteen years, I had forgotten that humans were three times as tall as a fully grown rat was long from nose to tail tip. The second was that the cleaning process seemed to have been, perhaps, not quite perfect. There was dust everywhere, covering every surface.

No, not dust I realized with a touch of horror, dulled by the terror of watching it happen. Ash. This is why we were here. If this dust was anything but completely inert, things would be much, much more difficult to work out.

We found one pile of dust, which had been a person so recently, beside which laid a data pad. Completely oversized compared to the ones we normally used, more like an oversized view panel, but otherwise similar. We propped it up against a bulkhead, and sat before it on our haunches while Twenty tried to access the sensors. I looked around and noticed a few more piles nearby. How many more of those were there?

Twenty shook his head and called up a map of the human section. It was enormous. Easily the same size again as in our rings, but without the storage areas. The choice that we had been given was beginning to move in one direction for me. So much space. We could live like kings.

"K," he said with a nod, and tapped at one place. "Control here. Not access on this. Need go there."

"Space," I said, ears splayed, looking around as we made our way through the ship to the human control area, the bridge. It was not just the amount of space, it was the way it had been used. "Too big."

"Yes," Twenty said beside me, looking ahead of him rather than following my roaming gaze. His face carried a frown behind the suit's visor when I looked at him. "Wasted. Human crew about hundred. Number small. Too much space."

A hundred humans, in a space that a thousand rats, engines and all the basic materials for a colony took up. Wasteful was right. Unpleasantly large.

We finally found the room which Twenty had identified as the bridge, and we pushed our way through a large pile of dust into another large space, with curving workstations all over. Oddly small compared to the rest, and it seemed more or less a scaled-up version of our own control section.

"Here," Twenty said, and headed towards the rear of the room, to a station which had the only pile of dust that I could see inside the room. The station was still active, and Twenty helped me up onto the chair.

"This. Realize who?" Twenty said quietly as I stood up on the dusty seat, and I looked down. One pile of dust, with a large one outside the door.

"Trigger cleaning. Unlock doors same," I said as I looked at the display before me. The left one was still showing the message functions that had been sending that final message that we had seen with One.

The other showed a macro command chain. Trigger complete biological purge, trigger unlock all sections, release all functions from lockdown, and finally unlock internal airlock. She had given us the ship, just like that. All its functionality, all of its space, wasteful though it was, was ours.

I crawled up onto the station and pulled up the internal sensors. Run a complete internal check for any biological remains. Just two blips, us, and nothing else in the human section. I pushed the sensitivity right to the top, and the result remained the same. If there was anything to be found, it was undetectable.

"Ship. All ours now," I said, looking over the edge of the console to Twenty. His whiskers were twitching excitedly behind the face plate as I looked down to him. "No more humans. Only us."

* * *

I wanted us all to just stay on the ship at first, but after a while I realized that One had been right. We had not been created to fail. She who had ensured our existence had been human, but she had still been our first. Our Zero, she who came before even One. She had given her life to allow us to exist, and the best way to do that, to honor both her memory and her wishes for what we might become, was to not make only one choice.

"Excuse Twentree," came the quiet voice of Kiera, who had walked up beside me, claws clicking on the flooring. We sniffed softly at each other, his scent as familiar as my own, and without the taint of worry he had carried that day ten years ago.

He rubbed his muzzle, and I returned the gesture before turning my head back again. He had, like many of the other youngsters, decided to take one of the names Zero had given us. I and many of the other older ones had decided against it. We had grown used to the numbers being our names, but now, rather than being given ones, they were chosen. I was no longer the mispronounced number twenty-three. No, I was Twentree, and I bore my name as proudly as Kiera, who was no longer number seven hundred and forty three.

The youngster had grown into a confident technician in the decade since we had arrived into orbit around Proxima B. He had even fathered a litter of young, five pups who just as we had been from birth were numbered, Riki One, Riki Two, Riki Tree, Riki Sou and Riki Pive. Named as all our pups were for their mother, their mother being Riki. Numbered so that just as we had been able to, they would choose their own names when they were old enough. We had never had the space to grow on the ship, but now we could, and we had. The thousand had become many, many more.

"Time go ship," he said and turned his head to see what I was looking at. The old ship's Ring Zero had been repurposed as a space station, its large spaces filled with walkways and platforms. Much better use of the space than before. The hydroponics bay had become the observation and recreation hall in this new space station, and the view outside the viewport the two of us were stood at was of the sleek shape of one of the new ships we had constructed for ourselves. The new ships were built from materials cannibalized from the old ship, one ring for each of them. The first of them was now ready, with many more well under way.

"Twen gone downside?" I asked, and he squeaked an affirmative. We had worked together, all of us, to create the ships. Now that the first was ready, my old friend's family needed him in the thriving settlement down on the planet.

"We must go," Kiera said after a while, and it was my turn to squeak. He turned around and walked towards the exit. Standing on my hind paws, I put a paw on the viewport. She had given us a choice. She had also taught us to adapt. We had chosen not to choose between the options. We would do them all. We had even added a few of our own.

"Twentree," Kiera said, and I turned my head to see him standing with one forepaw lifted and his head turned back towards me. His ears and eyes relaxed and his tail lazily resting behind him, the now no-longer young rat was patient with the retrospective, old one he had gone to fetch. This time for something just as important as the first time, though this time he would be coming along at least some of the way. "They waiting."

I turned around and left the viewport to follow him to the transit tube which led to the ship-to-ship docking port. It had fallen to me to lead the first ship away from Proxima B, heading for another star with a possibly habitable planet. We would reach our star in about thirty years. I would not see it, nor would nearly anybody else on board. But it was glorious. And all of us knew it now, for we had come here to Proxima B, and it was all we had been promised and so much more.

Humans would come here, we were sure of that. We were sure, because we would go to them. Two of the ships were destined to return to Earth, and if they did not succeed in stopping the humans from doing so, we had no doubt humans would attempt to reach Proxima B again. We would go there and we would show them us. Humanity would learn of what compassion could bring forth, even in such a world as theirs. Zero had cleaned the ship, but she had left us all the data. Unlocked everything for us to discover.

Kiera's children would be ready. All our children would be ready. Their children would be. They would happily follow the example of our creator, our Zero. One, of loving memory, had promised that the story of Zero, the reality she had shown us, how the other humans saw us and what we were to them, that none of it would remain a secret. She had told the truth. There was no rat who did not know the tale Zero had told us, and the knowledge she had passed on to us. Soon we would tell it to her own people. They would see the light.

Play The Animal Game! Become the animal of your choice!

But don't play it too much, or you may find yourself transforming into that animal in actuality.

(But what if that's what you really want?)

The Animal Game

by Vixyy Fox

Harold ignored the warning signs. Besides the billboards, and commercials on the television, these were also the 'telltail' signs of physical change happening within his body. Sure, 'telltail' is a bad pun, but that's the first thing you get that definitely says you've abused your body and mind a little too much by playing *The Animal Game*.

They called it the drug of imagination. It certainly was the drug of choice for those frequenting the internet game room. Oddly, it was cheap, easy to get, and delivered right to your door in a plain paper-wrapped package. In fact, your first shipment was free for the asking. Nor was it illegal; because it really wasn't a drug.

The draw was simple; pop one of the lozenges into your mouth, go to the on-line game room, and become exactly what your heart longed for you to be. Easy Peesy. Once you mentally went through the door, everything just melted away and there you were. No typing, no spell check, no nothing except flesh and fur pressed to flesh and fur, without a care for anything except the pleasures as obtained through the mind. It was sort of like living in one of those animated movies, except it could go on and on and on. It was a very personal and pleasurable encounter with others of like minds.

"Ya got a bump on your backside, Harold," Mabel said while pouring him a cup of coffee. She owned the diner ten miles outside of Thief River Falls, Minnesota; in short, the middle of nowhere. You could get breakfast here all day long (truckers are very welcome, thank you very much), and there were no televisions on the walls, ever.

"Don't neither!" the teen replied.

"Do so," she retorted calmly. "I see it pretty clear. If'n I was you, I'd mend my ways before I had to cut a hole in my drawers. You're doing that drug everyone's been talking about, aren't you?"

"Eggs over easy with toast and grits," he replied, ignoring her sarcasm. "I don't do drugs."

"Yes sir, it's all over the news," she told him. Writing the order on a pad of paper, she hung it up in the little window leading to the kitchen. Ringing the bell, she came back to him. "According to the good-looking gay guy on Fox, they been picking these strange critters up when they find them and shipping them off to a holding facility with a name similar to, but not quite, the Hoomaine Society."

"Really?"

"I said it, didn't I?"

Harold sipped at his coffee thoughtfully. In a hushed voice he told her, "I don't play the game all that much, Mabel. Really I don't. But when I do it's such a wonderful place to be."

"Do tell," she crooned, placing the sugar container in front of him. She was just a few years shy of being his mother's age, but she carried her age well.

The teen added a little sugar and then sipped his coffee again. Gently placing his cup back to the counter, he said, "Well… first you have to log in."

"You mean on your computer?"

"Of course I meant that… I'm not a lumberjack."

"I was teasing," she replied with a smile, "And remember, my generation doesn't do computers so well."

Harold sighed. "Do I need to talk slower?"

"No," and this came with a frown.

"Tease back," the young man told her with a wink. "Then, when you're in the site, you have an avatar."

"What's that?"

There was a *'bing'* and she turned to find a plate of eggs, toast, and a small bowl of grits sitting in the serving window. "That was quick," the waitress remarked. Crossing to the little window she picked up the plate and delivered it to Harold. Since there were no other customers, she stayed to finish their conversation. "You were saying?"

"It's an image of who and what you are. Everyone sees this image and that's who they see you as."

"Sure," she replied, placing a hand on the counter, "And I can understand all of this because let's just say, I've been in a few dating site chats. They all lie, by the way."

"And you don't?"

"Of course not."

"You're an exception, then."

"And you don't lie?"

"You don't have to," he told her while mixing his eggs with the grits. "You're not you in any way, shape, or form, so what's the point? No one knows who you are as the real physical you, and it's all about your imagination."

"And this new 'imagination' drug?"

"It's not a drug, it's legal, and…"

"And?" she asked.

Looking to both sides first, he whispered, "I tried it for the first time last week. You get sucked completely into the web and you're really there."

Picking up a napkin, she wiped at the side of his mouth. "You've got a little egg on your face there, Foxie."

Harold looked shocked. "How did you know I was a Fox?"

"Your tail is showing," she teased.

"NO, REALLY, TELL ME!"

Mabel took the time to fetch the coffee pot and refill his cup from half, just to let him calm down a notch before telling him she was just having fun with him. Reaching over the counter, she gave her customer a slap on the bottom and was immediately surprised at what her hand encountered.

"What in tarnation have you got growing outta your butt?"

"SHHHHhhhhh… please don't say anything. I just came in for breakfast, Mabel. Come on… they'll come and take me away, just like that news guy says they will."

The waitress stood straight and looked at the youngster. "They'll what?"

"You don't watch the news, do you?"

"No. I mean, I do but not that much. That story made me laugh, that's why I remembered it. They didn't exactly say what the critters were, which I thought was rather strange." Picking up his coffee cup, she downed what was in it and set it back down. "Harold, you're growing a tail," she whispered.

"It's all right," he whispered back, "I kinda like it. Once it's fully there I can run it down my pants leg and no one will know."

"Not until you're happy and it begins to wag."

There was a moment of quiet, and then both of them began to snicker.

"I always wanted to be a horse," the waitress confessed softly. "We used to play horses when we were children. They're so beautiful."

"I've seen Horses in the chats," Harold told her. "It's nothing like you could ever imagine. They stand upright like people and have hands, not hooves. I've danced with them, and they're beautiful."

"As a Fox?"

The teen spooned up some egg and grits and shoved the whole thing in his mouth, now relaxing that he'd found an unknown ally. "Yup," he responded around the spoon. "Just make sure to keep your feet out of the way. They step on you and it hurts."

"Step on you?" she asked. "Hurts? Harold, it sounds like you really were there."

He nodded his head as he put some more egg and grits into his mouth. "I was."

"That's impossible."

"Seems so, but it ain't. And I'm meeting new people all the time. It's every species you could possibly imagine. They're all there. That's most likely why it's called *The Animal Game*." With this pronouncement he began working on his toast, putting an ample amount of jelly on it first.

Being there wasn't anyone in the diner besides the cook in the back, Mabel poured herself a fresh cup of coffee, set it on the counter and then moved her stool over to where she could better converse with the youngster. "And just like the news says, you grow a tail?"

"You felt what I got," he replied. "I didn't just out and stuff a pair of socks down the back of my pants. It's called a brush, and mine is coming in real nice."

"So the news was right for a change?"

"Sorta, maybe, kinda, almost right... but not quite."

"And what's not kinda right?" she asked, sipping her coffee.

"You know you're changing. You can feel it the very first time you go in."

"You say go in as if you're diving into a mud hole or entering a mine, like old Curley Joe Wilson's pretend gold mine."

"He was digging a bomb shelter," Harold informed her. "He bought into all that cold war stuff and only told people it was a gold mine so they would leave him be."

"And you know this how?"

"His Dog told me."

There was a moment of silence as Harold continued eating like a hungry Wolf. Mabel maintained and managed not to laugh at his statement. Nor would she, as the decision came upon her to investigate what actually was taking place. Here was something that was huge news happening right in front of her eyes. Here, too, was something beyond the two dimensional screen she watched each night, trying her best to wring some truth out of what was being put forth as news.

"Harold, you do know the authorities believe you to be sick, don't you?"

"Sure," he responded over the rim of his coffee.

"You do understand that you will be hunted down and quarantined to keep what's happening to you from spreading?"

"They can't stop it, because it's not a disease. It's who we are."

"There are rumors that the government types are investigating. Wait… who who are?"

"You want to be an Owl? I thought you liked Horses?"

The waitress reached over and slapped him on the top of the head. "Do that again, and I'll punch you in the nose, Mr. Fox. I'm being dead serious here."

This time Harold blinked. "Government?"

"Changelings is what they're calling them, and they've been branded toxic. The Department of Health is telling people not to go out at night, not to get involved, and above all else—do not touch. There have been reports of mass hysteria. More than a few shots have been fired, and they're using silver bullets."

"That's insane."

"Most of mankind's history is, when you take a hard look at it."

Harold's right hand went back to his nub of a tail. "Bummer."

"I want you to take me there," the waitress told him softly.

The teen blinked again. He'd never ever heard of an 'older' person wanting to visit *The Animal Game* chats. "OK… when do you want to go?"

* * *

Mabel showed up at Harold's small apartment that evening, both of them having had to work. With her, as instructed, she brought an ancient laptop computer. The waitress looked very different dressed in dungarees and a blouse, as opposed to her uniform. Harold, for his part, looked pretty much the same as when he had breakfast.

"You're sure you want to do this?" he asked, after answering the door.

"We're not having sex," she told him softly as she came in, "You're showing me how to use this stupid computer. I've actually had it for ten years now, and other than checking my email I've never used the darned thing."

"Piece of cake," he told her. "I'll explain everything to you before we go in."

"And the imagination drug?"

"It's not a drug, and it only works after you're in; meaning you can swallow as much as you want and nothing will happen 'in real life'. You want coffee or anything?"

"I'm good," she replied, setting her laptop up on the small kitchen table. "Is this where we'll do it?"

Harold cringed. "That sounded so bad," he told her. "It's like you're about to jump my body or something."

"Don't be ridiculous. I used to be your babysitter." Then with a smile at the teen, she asked, "Is this where we'll do it?"

"Works for me," he replied with a giggle. "Normally I sit in my easy chair, but I think this will do just fine." He looked at her for a moment.

"What?"

"There are a few things I have to warn you about."

"Such as?"

"When you go in, you're going to see a lot of Dogs sitting in chairs bordering the walls leading to the entrance. These are Police Dogs. They'll stare at you, and a few might take notes, but they won't talk or try to disrupt your entrance in any way."

"Why are they just sitting there?"

"The site won't let them in."

"Really? It knows who's a spook and who isn't?"

"Yup. Spooks, G-men, Cops, Snitches, Secret Police; no matter what nationality. It drives them up the wall just having to sit there and watch people come and go. They're all dressed alike in black suits and there's a white ring around their right eye. It's like a bad movie."

Mabel pulled her chair out from the table and the legs made a loud squalling noise. For a moment both of them were quiet, and then their eyes met again and both giggled.

"Sorry," she told the teen, and then planted herself, hitting the 'on' button of her laptop.

"It's all right," he replied. "When I first discovered this I called in sick for three days. I almost lost my job, but I managed to convince them I really was down with the flu. I had these really dark circles under my eyes from not sleeping."

"So you've been doing this a lot longer than a week, like you told me," she said softly, calling him on his lie. "When did you find out about the 'imagination drug'?"

"The first day. I had to cool my heels out with the spooks while I got all checked out. Then they had me give them all my details, and I was told I should place an order. The package came the following morning, and as soon as I got it I just kinda melted into the computer."

"Melted?"

"I've got no other words for it," he told her. "You know Terry? We hang out together… or at least we used to. He's a big gamer. At any rate, he told me he came by and there wasn't anyone here. Trust me; I never left my living room." He passed her what appeared to be a cinnamon candy which was twisted in a red paper covering. "Just let it dissolve in your mouth like you would a cough drop. You shouldn't have any problems getting in since you're with me, and I've got good connections. That, and you already have the drug."

'click'

Mabel blinked. She felt different somehow. Although she was still looking out from her eyes just like she was when sitting at Harold's kitchen table, what she saw was totally not the same. What she saw were two lines of Dogs, all of them sitting on chairs against the two walls leading to a door. They all sat as people would, and, indeed, had hand like paws. Some were Dobermans, some were German Shepherds, and some just looked like mutts; but each had a white circle of fur around their right eye.

"Hey," she heard. The voice sounded familiar. "Down here."

Looking down, she found herself gazing over the top of a deliciously large bosom at a smallish Fox. Other than this, her clothing was the same as what she'd been wearing in the kitchen. "You look like something from a Disney movie," she told the Fox.

"So do you," he retorted, "Only the R rated version. You're really tall, too."

One of the police Dogs cleared his throat. When they looked at him, he held out a box of donuts, indicating they might like one. He was quite handsome for a German Shepherd.

Mabel smiled, and made to reach for one which she recognized as apple, but Harold caught her arm. "Don't!" he warned. "You never know what might be in them. Remember, these are the cops."

"They're not all bad, you know," the Dog said softly. None of the other Dogs even turned to look at him. "They're just trying to do a job set forth by the unbelieving governments of the world. Let's face facts, eh? Those governments are in charge and they wish it to stay that way."

"I thought you said they didn't talk," Mabel remarked, looking down at the Fox.

"They never did to me."

The Dog rose and carefully placed the box of donuts on his chair. Turning to them, he extended a paw. "I am Detective Sherlock Bones," he said with a smile. His accent was unmistakably British. "I don't suppose I am exactly like these other Police Dogs, though I look the part; black suit and white circle around the eye. More, I have come to investigate that which seems to be eluding the more common breeds of Police Dog, no matter how computer savvy they might be." He looked at Mabel. "May I say, madam, that you present the very epitome of perfection in Equine types, more than a few of which I have seen come through this entrance including some smallish Pony types."

"Yeah, yeah," Harold told him, "And I suppose you'll tell me I am the epitome of Foxism too."

"Actually," the Dog said, without taking his eyes off of the Horse, "I find you to be rather common and scruffy looking. You should, at the very least, comb out your brush."

Mabel giggled at the pun.

The little Fox took the Horse's hand and began to pull on it. "We need to go. We don't have all night, and you're sure going to want to stay. It's a good thing you have me as a guide."

Mabel batted her eyes at the detective. "It would seem I have to go. My goodness, but that drug thing works well."

"It's not a drug," the Fox and the Dog said in the same breath, after which they looked at each other.

"I did the intelligent thing and had it analyzed," Bones told him, and then looked back up to Mabel. "It is nothing more than a common cold remedy. I believe you Americans call them 'cough drops', which to the Scots means something else entirely, but that is neither here nor there. More correctly it is called a medicated lozenge, but I am rather capable in the Yankee dialects, so cough drop would be most correct. I also personally broke it down and examined it under the microscope, and found it to be only sugar with flavorings with no actual medication at all. What you've ingested, regardless of what you think, is little more than candy."

"You certainly do use a lot of words," Mabel told him.

"Yeah," Harold agreed harshly. "Now stuff it and find your own way in."

"Certainly," the Dog told them, ignoring the Fox's comment. "If you will follow me, let's see exactly how successful I can be."

The trio then made their way down the very long row of government agency types, to an iron door bearing skulls and crossed bones with red flashing lights, and warnings that this might be a virus. 'Scam—scam—scam—scam,' sounded out an alarm.

"Don't try to open anything," Harold advised the Horse softly, "Just keep walking, and I'll see you on the other side."

Sherlock stopped before the door and bowed low, showing the way with an extended arm; indicating that Harold should go first. The Fox, for his part, smiled and did so, thinking the Dog would be prevented. When he was in, and there was rave music pounding in his head, he turned to find Mabel standing just behind him, holding on to the arm of a handsome looking stallion. The stallion smiled at the Fox, and then dissolved into the form of a German Shepherd. He was now wearing a blue suit, and the white circle was over his left eye.

"Well, that was refreshingly easy," the Dog yelled to be heard over the music. He then pointed to the flashing lights and the people gyrating upon the dance floor, "But if this is all there is, I will admit to being very disappointed."

Harold was becoming just a little annoyed. This was his moment to shine. He wanted to be the one showing Mabel the ropes and all that went with them. "So why don't you buzz off and go find your own pleasure room?!" he yelled.

"What?" the Dog asked, pointing to his ear, "I can't hear you over all this ruckus!"

The little Fox was about to shout something back that was less than pleasant when the thought occurred to him that the detective was deliberately annoying him because he was enjoying it. Grabbing the Horse's hand, he began dragging her to one side of the room without explanation. Without him seeing it, she smiled and latched on to the Dog's outstretched paw and dragged him with her. "It's like I'm really here!" she yelled at him, whereupon he readily agreed, having heard her just fine.

Moving through a doorway that was held open for them by a large Bull wearing a tux, they came out into a grassy area flanked on all sides by a forest. As soon as the door closed, the noise of the rave diminished as it was naturally blocked. Harold began hopping about almost like a Fox in the wild. "I love it here!" he said aloud as Mabel's arm went up and down with his dance.

"Why?" she asked him.

"Because it's where I can meet more of my own kind."

Behind her, the Dog said, "I believe he means Foxes."

She looked back at him with a small amount of alarm in her eyes. "But I'm a Horse!"

"So you are, and what a beautiful Horse too. Mind, I would love to have the blessing of your company any time, and from what I observed on the entry way dance floor, it would seem that all of the different species are indeed dancing together in any case."

"That's right!" Harold told her, ignoring the fact that he was actually agreeing with Mr. Blue Suit. "But I wanted you to meet someone special. She's supposed to be here." With that pronouncement, a small brown and red body darted out of the underbrush and tackled him.

"Eeeeeeeeeee… I'm going to eat your ears off," she told him loudly as they wrestled.

"Loosely translated," the detective Dog whispered, "Her demeanor and words are meant to say, 'He's mine and you leave him be.'"

"Really?"

"Very much so. From what I've seen in here so far, the rules are very much human-like. Every country has its own flavor of them, and what's good for one country is totally illegal in another. This makes solving crimes more complicated, because in some cases, what was done was perfectly upright, noble, and legal somewhere else."

The Mare looked at the Dog. "Why are you here?"

"I'm not yet really sure," he replied honestly. "I heard a news report about people growing tails and changing into animals; or rather a mix of animal and human features. I enquired about this at Scotland Yard and expected to be laughed out of the place; but they were oddly silent. My friends there told me they hadn't heard anything like this and couldn't talk about it even if they had. Then I was escorted out."

"I'd say that was a dead giveaway," Mabel told him. "I've watched enough police dramas on television to understand that much."

"Precisely, though please do not get me started at the complete fiction put forth to the public in such shows. Being escorted out, while actually observing a few incarcerated persons with tails, made me even more curious. I began asking questions, and watching for 'nub bottoms' as I dubbed them. Most try to hide their new appendage, but some have become more blatant about it in public. Many of those have, shall we say, 'disappeared'? It would seem there is a very large government cover-up moving forward. This could lead to many, many bad things." Holding out his hand to her, he indicated they should leave the two frolicking

Foxes to their own accord. "Perhaps you would like to accompany me, dear lady. I have never been here before and I am uneasy."

"I'm not exactly… well… let's just say I'm on pins and needles with this," she replied. "I like my new figure, and I feel better than I ever have, but… . "

"It's too good to be true?" the detective asked.

"Exactly, so call me suspicious. It's like everything is tight and new, and I could run full gallop for a whole lot of miles if that's what I wanted to do." Looking back to her young friend, she asked, "What about Harold?"

The detective never took his eyes from the Mare's as he responded, "I think he's going to be occupied for an undetermined amount of time. I take it he's been doing this for a while now?"

"I'm not sure," she admitted, "But he is a 'nub butt'."

The Dog smiled. "I think I like that better than my expression. Shall we walk now? I'd like to get your opinions on all of this, if I might. All of the stories about me say that I come up with an analysis of crime all on my own, but truth be told, I actually rely heavily on the opinions of others."

"Really?" she asked him.

"Well… not so much, but it did sound good."

Topping the rise of the hill next to where the Foxes played, they came to a garden full of Rabbits. These were busily hoeing the long rows of vegetables growing there, or otherwise tending to what requirements a garden must have. To one side of the garden there was a large building. The 'thump thump thump' of dance music was making its sound heard almost physically from the bass vibrations. Though there were no signs stating 'Rabbits Only', the pair agreed the majority of those found in this warren would be Rabbit types.

"You didn't fancy yourself a Rabbit?" Sherlock asked.

"Well," Mabel answered honestly, "The sex I am sure is great. There's all that fur on fur on fur, and certainly they are no strangers to desire."

"All creatures have desires, Mabel," the detective assured her. "Some of my best cases began with nothing more than a following of someone's wife or husband. Everything is relative, isn't it? Not everyone is hell bent on taking over the world, are they?"

"Or are they?" she asked him. "As I recall, you had an arch-villain enemy by the name of Moriarty?"

"He was a special case, and trust me when I say he is still out there. Mark my words; the blackheart will show up again when you least expect it."

"Like now?"

"No, not now."

He led the way down a path leading through a wood, and they came across a stream feeding into a pond where a group of svelte Otters frolicked. These creatures laughed and called out to them to strip down and join them for a swim.

"That's a tempting offer," The Dog called back, "But we're only temporary and stretching our legs."

Without a question the Otters went back to what they were doing, while the Mare and the Dog continued along.

"But without staying on guard for Mr. M, might you not be taken by surprise?" Mabel asked.

"What if I were to tell you I was that person? Would you hate me for it?"

She stopped walking then and looked at him. He was a full head shorter than she, and there was no doubt in her mind she could beat him down and sit upon him if the need arose. "I do not believe that," she told him. "You could no more be Moriarty than I could be the Iron Chef."

"You're that bad of a cook?"

She smiled. "I'm a waitress, not a cook, and you're a detective, not a police officer."

As she spoke, the coloring of their wooded glen changed slightly, the shadows growing longer and the light softer. It was apparently speaking to them on a non-verbal basis. Something and/or someone was suggesting they do as well.

"He's not a Horse!" she yelled out, "So knock it off!"

"Who might you be speaking to?" Sherlock asked. "I mean, it's true that I am not a Horse, but that hardly seems to make a difference, as the only intercourse I intend is verbal."

Reaching out, Mabel touched the Dog right between the eyes with an extended finger. "I was talking to whoever is controlling this funny farm. I'm not buying what you're selling. You were there waiting for me. That means you knew Harold was going to bring me in and when. You also had a box of donuts, one of which was apple... my favorite."

The detective opened his mouth to say something and then closed it again. "What else?" he asked instead.

"You're making this too easy," she replied. Taking his paw, she began walking again. "You took my hand when we came through the door. You wanted me to believe you couldn't have done that by yourself."

"You're saying you believe I can come and go as I please?"

"I'm saying I'm suspicious. You knew which way to go to get out of that fancy dancy horrifically noisy place."

"I followed the Fox, and it was indeed the only door that I saw."

"I counted five of them."

"An odd number… that's interesting. Do you think they each led to a different species?"

Mabel resisted the urge to scream. "Please stop doing that," she hissed at him.

"Quite right," he responded, "Consider it done." Raising a finger, he then said, "But wait, why did you yell out to something or somebody to 'knock it off'? I am at a loss for that."

The Mare sighed. "For a detective you're not very bright. How did we come in here?"

"Computer."

"Exactly. And are we who we are in real life?"

"Not unless you really are a Horse. Perhaps I should approach this from that angle."

Making an exasperated sound, Mabel reached out and plucked one of his whiskers, which caused the Dog to make a sharp intake of breath. To his credit, he did not yowl.

"Why would you do that?" he asked her in a shocked voice.

"Because you're still talking."

"Fine," he muttered, "What do we do then?"

She looked around and now found nothing but open fields lush with grass. Not too far off she noticed Horses moving slowly as a group through one of these fields. "We start there," she told him.

"Bad idea," he replied softly.

"Why?"

"They look like real Horses."

"And?"

"I'm actually afraid of Horses."

Placing both hands upon his shoulders, Mabel looked down her long face and smiled at the German Shepherd, his silliness getting the better of her. "I'm a Horse too, Sherlock. I won't let them eat you."

It turned out the group she led them to really were Horses. This, actually, was a surprise. As the waitress reached out and stroked the face of one, she had the distinct vision of a man holding onto the hand of a monkey. "We look alike, but we are not alike," she muttered.

"Then you understand," said a new voice. "This is to be applauded. You and your friend are the first to actually look past the many offers of peace and pleasure. You come to us with questions, truly seeking answers; and are not satisfied with what is presented to you."

Turning, she was about to give a rather acidy response, thinking Sherlock once again had changed his form, but found the Dog standing next to a new, slightly smaller, creature that very much reminded her of Harold's Fox girlfriend.

"Who are you?" she asked.

"My name, as best you might pronounce it, is Ung," he replied. "The Horse, whose head you are stroking, in my First Officer, Ow, and he does like his ears scratched so he's good with that."

There was the sound of soft laughter from multiple voices. The lighting adjusted then from bright to dim, and the field melted away; changing the scene to one of a spacecraft's large command center. This artificial space was large enough for all of them to fit comfortably, inclusive of all the additional (apparent) crew members who were standing at their posts. Each was a different type of animal species, but resembling the appendage stature of people.

"Call me confused and slap my face a few times," Mabel muttered. "This is just some sort of game, isn't it? Something that one of the big computer companies dreamt up? There is no way I can go from playing an on-line game to standing in the cockpit of a spacecraft."

"I had nothing to do with this, Mabel," Sherlock told her. "I did not see this one coming."

"Ow," the captain began and the Dog took a step backwards.

"I'm sorry, did I step on your foot?"

There was polite laughter and a few groans to accompany the detective's small smile. Captain Ung gave him a disapproving look, as only a captain (and wives) can do. Turning back to the Horse sitting next to Mabel, he asked him to place the image outside the ship on the front viewing screen. This the Horse did, and there was a moment's hush as Mabel and Sherlock took it all in. Night had fallen upon the Earth and countless lights populated the more inhabited places.

"We have been here for some time now," Ung explained. "Eons ago the seeds of who we are were placed upon this planet as an experiment. Our ancestors actually had a wager as to which of us would grow and prosper in this new place while left alone. The wager was silly, and forgotten for almost equal eons, and then it was decided we should come back. Essentially this was because our own planet was now... well... for lack of a better word, ferburturserized."

The crewmember standing closest to the captain cleared her throat and leaned forward slightly, whispering something in the Fox's ear.

"It's not?" Ung asked in surprise, whereupon the Bear shook her head in the negative.

"Very well." Looking back to Mabel, he cleared his throat and told her, "For better understanding, think of our previous home as nothing more than a big lump of Horse Pucky."

The waitress was about to say something when she saw Sherlock wink at her. "What does this have to do with what is presently happening?" she asked instead.

"Might I be blunt?" the Captain asked.

"Please do."

"Mankind is what's wrong. One could also argue he is what is right. We have been up here for several years studying the situation. This is how I can speak your language. Man was never in the original equation. We don't even know where he came from. What we do know is that he has the capability of crudely destroying the world many times over. He does not play well with others, and will always strive to come out on top of any 'deal' he might be a part of."

"I was on the surface soon after we arrived," said a Bear sitting at one of the bridge stations. The voice gave no doubt this crewmember was also female. "I was sent to explore, and coming across a farmhouse I believed I might make contact. We'd already built translating devices, so verbal communication was possible. Thankfully no one was home. What I found inside was a bearskin rug adorning the floor and several Bear heads mounted on the wall above the fireplace along with several other types of animals. We never ventured forth unarmed after this."

"We spent our time and resources in getting people used to the idea of different species from other worlds through your entertainment industry," said a Panther in a tone of voice that indicated he did not approve the effort.

"That didn't exactly work either," the Captain told her, "But we were getting closer to the mark. That Raccoon fellow of recent movies was a big hit; but we were running out of time. Putting our collective minds together we came up with a better plan. 'If we couldn't live among the humans as accepted equals, we would assimilate the humans to our shape and forms.' We don't have to change everyone…"

"Just enough to where species equity will be achieved," said a good looking Squirrel. Holding out her paw she offered, "I am Natasha, Chief Science Officer, and creator of *The Animal Game*."

Mabel looked at her, still trying to take all of everything in. "I'm not quite sure that I fully understand," she admitted.

"You may have noticed your friend Harold is rather smitten by another Fox?" Captain Ung asked her.

"Yes."

"That's my daughter. Eventually they will mate and have children. The 'drug' used, by your standards, is solely sugar. On the molecular level it is a DNA modifier."

The Mare frowned. "And you're good with this?"

"What choice do we have?" he replied. "We cannot stay here indefinitely, nor can we go home. If we were to land and try to make a peaceful contact, we would be captured, studied, and killed. We wish only to have a place to live."

"You could live in the forest," Sherlock offered. "Alaska has lots of open space and not many people."

"We would be hunted like the Bear, the Wolf, and the Mountain Goat. You can trust me when I say we would fight back; and it would not be pretty. In the end we would still lose."

"I find that rather reflective of mankind's history," Sarah said softly.

"And therein lies the problem," Captain Ung told her, "But it led us to this plan."

"Since we would have the short end of the stick no matter what we decided," the Science Officer told her, "We have chosen to bring many more of our kind to help tug on that stick."

"Sun Tzu," Sherlock said aloud, and all eyes went to him. "He wrote the book on warfare and his advice stands true to this day. He said, 'You cannot conquer and hold a territory. You must settle it; making it your own.'"

"More correct is the quote, 'The greatest victory is that which requires no battle,'" the Fox counter-quoted.

"But what about those who do not want to change?" Mabel asked.

"The change is only permanent if they want it to be, and then only after a prolonged stay in the game. We're not heartless. How they deal with the realities of their lives after the change is up to them."

"You're expecting them to totally change the 'social norm'?" Sherlock asked in a hushed voice.

"It's been done before," Ung replied.

"A social change of that magnitude," Mabel said, addressing everyone, "Is not going to be easy. It will come at a very dear cost. People are going to die, Ung."

The Fox looked at the Horse and nodded his head. "We also understand this. The amount of our own people who have tried to make contact and perished is not small. Until the institution of this plan the only other solution we could come up with was a planet-wide 'natural' catastrophe that would wipe out all indigenous population without rendering the entire planet unlivable. From what we have deduced, this has been done before."

"The dinosaurs?" Mabel and Sherlock asked in the same hushed voice.

"And then 'man' showed up," the Science Officer added softly.

Mabel found all eyes upon her then. "What?"

"You're not going to ask why you were brought here?" The Captain asked her.

"That thought had not yet occurred to me, but I'm guessing Sherlock is one of yours?"

"What?" the Dog asked, her question hitting him between the eyes like a badly thrown stick. "No... I'm not one of 'theirs'. I'm Fred, the cook."

Now it was Mabel's turn to be dumbfounded. "Fred?"

"Yeah... I took liberties with the diner's computer, so that's where I really am."

"Why?"

"Well... I'd heard about the 'Tails' as the news calls them, and then I heard you and Harold talking about it. Then the little perv was planning on showing you what was what, and I was worried about you; so I decided to tag along... just in case." He smiled a small smile. "I was homeless and on the road to nowhere. You took me in and gave me a chance. I never cooked a day in my life and there I was, cracking eggs and making pancakes. I guess being a real detective before that sort of molded my identity here. I always did love reading Sherlock Holmes."

There was a collective condescending 'ahhhhhh' from the crew that just about set the waitress off, but she held it together.

"All right, Ung," she said bluntly, "I'll bite like a spring trout; why me? Why bring us here when you could've simply have left us to wander around in the game?"

The Fox smiled. "Your diner is way out in the middle of nowhere, is it not?"

"Sort of. I like it like that and I get a lot of traffic from the truckers."

"And you own a very large piece of land out behind that diner?"

"About ten thousand acres, give or take a few thousand. My family's been there for a long, long time. I leave it in its natural state. I figure there's a lot of animals calling it home, and they deserve to be safe, too." She looked at him suspiciously. "Why?"

"We need somewhere to put our ship."

The Mare smiled. "I'll agree to what you want, with one proviso that I think will save a lot of lives."

Ung looked just a little bit embarrassed, and then he asked, "What's a proviso?"

"A stipulation," she told him. "Agree to that and then we'll see to your ship for a required payment."

"Typical human," Ung grumbled. "Always it's, 'What's in it for me?' Fine... tell me what you require."

* * *

BING!

"Food's up!" Mabel sang out. "Gather up your family, Harold, it's time to eat."

The diner had a few other patrons eating their lunch, but by far the cutest was the Fox family; a mother, father, and two kits, now three years old. The pair, a boy and a girl, was cute as a button. The boy held a toy truck, and the girl a small humanesk doll. None of the other patrons appeared put out by their presence at all. In fact, half of them had tails of varying lengths and colors. All of them had smiles whenever they so much as looked at the kits.

Tory and Lory were the very first children born of the changelings. This was a closely guarded secret as the press would be all over it if they knew. Yes, there were still problems as the world tried to adjust to what was initially seen as some sort of disease. Fortunately for the children, they lived a good distance from 'civilization'.

Every country had reacted differently and all with a select measure of acceptance. And yet every day there were more and more of the changelings until even the humans who protested the loudest found themselves simply outnumbered.

One of the keys to this quick acceptance was the proviso Mabel had insisted upon; the permanent 'infection' of every key leader in the world. This done, and the 'black suits' for lack of a better term, were quickly called off.

Bringing the food to the table and pausing to give each of the kits a kiss on the top of their heads, Auntie Mabel then pulled her tail around and flicked Harold over the top of his head with it, all the while sure to smile and wink at his wife.

Her father, Captain Ung, as payment for the safe storage of his ship, had a year's worth of kitchen duty to do at the diner beginning this year, and the waitress giggled every time she saw him up to his elbows in soapy water.

Life was good and Mabel reveled in this.

As for Fred… *'bing'*… Fred is still Mabel's cook, though he gave up on being Sherlock Bones.

Instead, he opted to become a Horse.

Go figure.

The cougar Keeshod is a young Land-Warrior on his warrior's pilgrimage; his first time beyond his tribe's lands. He is confidant of being able to meet and defeat any challenge—until Vhashmin, a young maned wolf wizard-in-training, hires him as a bodyguard to escort him to the Ashlands, from which no-one ever returns!

Ashland's Fury

by MikasiWolf

Keeshod stepped lightly over a motionless canid as a stool sailed past his face. Spinning lightly on a foot, he sent his own stool flying. A splintering of what sounded like good, solid wood resounded across the marten's skull. Downing the last of his ale, Keeshod stepped forward, wasting the remaining brawler with his tankard. The weasel had no chance to squeak before joining his friends on the ground.

With a burp, Keeshod leaned back over the bartop. The striped, quivering tail of the barkeeper could just be seen over a surface worn with years of filled tankards and frenzied clawmarks.

"Barkeeper, when's my meal ready?" Keeshod growled. It wasn't uncommon for people to misinterpret the guttural tones of big cats as attrition.

"C-c-coming right up!" stuttered the raccoon as he staggered upright. His ears and tail twitched and flicked every other way, and Keeshod surmised that a bar brawl wasn't altogether common here. "It's still on the spit back there, so if you would just wait a while—"

Keeshod threw him a coin. "I'll have another ale while you're at it." He readjusted a fallen stool the best he could against a brawler and sat. Sipping his drink slowly, the cougar glanced at the seating area behind him. Much of the common room had emptied the minute the altercation began, but two others remained. An old wolf in the far right corner gibbered and gesticulated towards some imaginary figure Keeshod didn't have the ability to see, and was most likely the village idiot. Some ways to the left was a salt-and-pepper fox, who had now taken up the table next to the crooked weapon mantelpiece above the fireplace. He had either the foresight or stupidity to duck when the fight erupted, and was still taking the risk of staying. Real brave.

From the polished shield that now hung askew behind the counter, a young cougar looked back at Keeshod, fur tinged with the dust of the open road. Across his bare chest with pecs just visible were strapped two crossbelts that served more as a load harness than garment. Topping his shoulders was a buckskin mantle, and from the waist down he wore a form-fitting pair of leggings with fur trim at the edges. These were held up by a well-crafted leather belt that seemed out of place in a town such as this. But these were the clothes of his people, and they were to be worn with the pride of a Land-Warrior.

With no major settlement in sight, Keeshod had been travelling for days, with a few breaks on the open road. The warrior's pilgrimage was wearing on him, but it was a long way to the warring states in the east. The cougar had heard from a townsman that it would be possible to find work of his skillset there. He avoided villages where he could, as his armed form attracted fear and distrust in rural communities. In fact, the mere act of stepping into the inn with dressing fit for a nomad was reason enough for riff-raff to attack him.

The thuds of pawpads neared. Another round? Keeshood whipped out his tomahawk, burnished steel flashing behind him.

"I'm unarmed! I'm unarmed!" stuttered the skulker, stepping back with his paws up. Keeshod looked lazily back at him, blade posed at the offender's throat. It was the salt-and-pepper fox who had sat near the back. Despite his coloration, his fur tinge wasn't that of one who was born grey, with the absence of black coloration on his paws and back of neck. At first glance, he could be mistaken for a fox, but Keeshod could see he was larger in stature. At almost the same height as Keeshod, his arms and legs had longer, more slender proportions. The fur below his neck was white, with the darker mane just around his neck fluffed up in fear. The canid's tail was more like that of a wolf's, with the fur trailing off in a gradual wave. The multi-colored robe he wore still retained its strong color. Umber, ochre, grey and blue were weaved in alternating lines, such that the robe looked to resemble the texture of rock at a distance. Despite the fox's aged coloration, the spark in his eyes, coupled with his posture and lack of confidence suggested he had got to be about seventeen, the same as Keeshod. Like his tribe, the majority of people throughout the land followed the rule of sixteen for adulthood.

"Whatddaya want?" drawled Keeshod. The canid flinched as the tomahawk jerked.

"I—I need to talk to you about something. You have a moment to spare? I'm Vhashmin." He gingerly held up his paws in greeting.

Keeshod blinked. Land-Warriors didn't surprise easily, but this took the cake. "If you're asking whether I've anything to do besides taking part in bar-brawls, then yes, I do. You haven't come to ask about my fighting style, so out with it." Sheathing the tomahawk, Keeshod turned back to his ale, keeping an eye on the fox's reflection.

"Sorry to be an annoyance, O warrior," panted the canid as he smoothed his fur, eyes darting towards the windows. "But I'd like to make a proposition with regards to my destination. You are one of the Mercfolk?"

Keeshod's ears swiveled briefly towards the priest-cleric fox. "I'm familiar with the term. But my people and I call ourselves Land-Warriors."

The fox's ears twitched, his jaws forming into a smile. "Right! So… I'd like to ask you to accompany me to the town of Crosha." His off-yellow eyes widened as a chuckle built up in Keeshod's chest.

"First rule of the road, my friend," the cougar set his tankard down, eyes narrowing. "Never trust another you've barely met. Second, never presume that others will aid you without compensation. The road is dangerous and hard, and you're better off not drawing attention to yourself. Got all that?"

The canid's eyes looked back and forth between the stream-textured tomahawk at Keeshod's side and calloused paws from which claws had been unsheathed. "But the road to the Ashlands isn't too far away," he said as he backed slowly away. "And I've heard from other travelers that it's been dangerous of late. My contact there will pay you." His eyes brightened.

Keeshod pretended to think about it, his eyes never leaving the fox's. "That's hardly a promise. For all I know, you'll lose me the moment we head into town. I'm long done with hunting double-crossers. No deal."

"Here, you can have my pendant as a deposit!" said Vhashmin, scrabbling hastily in the neck of his robes. Keeshod reaffirmed the grip on his tomahawk. A flash of gold and color came into view as the fox drew the chain off his neck, dangling it before Keeshod. "This holds the sigil of my Order. You can have it until we meet my contact."

Keeshod cast his eyes across the round disc. It was separated into quarters by crossed lines, and within each boundary lay a different colored crystal carved in a symbol. There was a series of curved lines and a whorl that Keeshod assumed represented water and air, but the significance of the misshapen and squiggly lines were lost to him. Keeshod was no expert, but from the luster of the gold itself, the pendant was as at least as good as the few gold coins he had encountered during his pilgrimage. With a spending power of 600 coppers each, it did have a certain allure. His elders always encouraged finding work where he could, and, one could always do with more coin.

"Very well," said Keeshod, slipping the pendant into one of his pouches. "It's a deal. Just an escort run, is it? If there're other things involved I want to know all about it." Keeshod raised an eyebrow to Vhashmin.

The fox made to speak, but thought better of it. "Yes, that's all it is," said Vhashmin, and his tail started wagging. Keeshod couldn't help but feel glad for him. Suddenly, the ears of the fox stood.

"The guards are here!" he whispered

Keeshod looked up as his ears caught the distinctive clink of metal on leather. Grabbing his spear resting against the counter, he downed his ale in one gulp before barging through the kitchen. The cougar ignored the protests of the innkeeper and his wife, not stopping even as he tore the still-hot haunch of roast from the spit. Munching furiously despite the searing heat, he slinked out the back door. Vhashmin squeaked an apology to the barkeep, and Keeshod turned back just in time to see a rolling pin glance off the fox's skull as he ducked. The fox padded after Keeshod as the cougar made his way down a side street, composing himself in as dignified a manner as possible.

Dressed in such an uncommon fashion, Keeshod figured it was too much to hope that his departure from the trade town was to go unnoticed. People of different species; lynxes, foxes, wolves, and even a meerkat dressed in a flowing garb much more ludicrous than his stopped to gawk, such that he had to push past them to get through. He stopped calmly as he approached the barricade the townsguard had set up over one of two exits to the town of Tsisyar. Vhashmin stepped beside him, gulping hard as he eyed the guards.

The bear sergeant at the helm of the barricade blinked at them both, his men similarly nonplussed. From the accounts of several witnesses of the brawl that had taken place in The Murky Pilsner, they had been expecting someone bigger and more rugged. The suspect wasn't that much bigger than many of the townsfolk, and was so lithe and lean that he couldn't have taken out ten men.

Keeshod finished the last of his roast, tossing the bone away. "Let me through; we're in a hurry," he said, deep amber eyes meeting the sergeant's. "This fox has somewhere to be." He gestured at the silently-pleading Vhashmin.

The sergeant coughed. "In the name of the Guildmaster, I arrest you for disturbing the peace. Lay down your arms and come with us." The polearms of his men jerked forward. All were mid-sized species, such as wolves and boars.

The cougar leaned steadily against his spear as he raised an eyebrow. "Sergeant, I've just finished my meal, and only wish to leave your fine town. Despite any previous offenses that may have been claimed against me, I have no qualms about a confrontation. Seriously." He let his mantle fall away slightly, making sure the guards could see the toned muscles of his shoulders and tomahawk.

The bear's eyes flicked left and right as he cleared his throat. "Be that as it may…" he stated but Keeshod had already walked on, the guard formation breaking up around him. The cougar kept his head high as he passed, his stride strong and purposeful, with ears and gaze trained forward. It took a full minute before the sergeant's cry of "You're no longer welcome here!" reached him.

Keeshod had never doubted his ability to sustain a fight with the entire townsguard should he position himself correctly. With his back against a solid wall, he could probably keep half a company at bay. But a Land-Warrior never started fights unless it was to be had, and he hadn't forgotten the years of cultural and martial training that made him who he was. One must never forget his roots.

* * *

One fit to breathe is fit to fight. That was the way of things for Keeshod's tribe. From the age of six, all cubs started learning the arts of war.

Armed and unarmed; club and spear, tomahawk and claw; the fighting arts that he and the other young tribesmen trained in served to remind them of their heritage. Like the fierce predators of old, each cougar was expected to hold his own against another. No one truly knew why the tribes were so focused in the instillation of fighting arts, but one thing was for certain. The world out there was a dangerous place, with its never-ending wars, followed by the rise of new kingdoms.

The tribal elders were, however, not blind to the naïvety that isolation brings. For ten years the cubs of Pentiki-Deschon lived, trained, and hunted in their home in the Grayscale Mountains, never straying from its boundaries. Having completed their training, the new breed of Land-Warriors would then set out on their warrior's pilgrimage, with instructions to find their own path. Only when one has seen the world will they learn who they truly are. Keeshod had been walking that path ever since; months upon months on the road instilling little in the way of wisdom to him. What exactly was he expected to find? A vision? A contract? A foe worthy of defeating? Several times Keeshod had asked himself if there was any point to all this wandering about. But the elder's words had been clear: there was no returning to his village till he found his path.

But the gold from the fox would prove useful, and he could always do with a good fight. It's what he'd been trained for.

* * *

Keeshod slowed his pace so that Vhashmin could keep up, breathing in the freedom of the open road. The two travelers had settled into an easy pace side-by-side, and already the previous tension was dissipating. The jingle of the pendant's chain rattled satisfyingly, and Keeshod tightened a strap to stifle the noise.

"So what makes you think I'm the best candidate for this?" asked Keeshod as they passed the boundary marker of Tsisyar. "There're plenty of sell-swords you could have called on back in town, and yet you chose the guy who beat up a half-score of drunks."

"In my travels, I have heard good things about Mercfolk, free fighters hailing from far-off corners of the land," said Vhashmin. He fought to keep up with Keeshod in a half-jog. "Incorruptible, discreet, and true to a promise. I have been assigned a most important task, and my safety is necessary for its success."

He sounded like a naïve cub. But it took all sorts to make the world. "You still haven't told me where you're from, Vhash, and I don't like not knowing," cut in Keeshod. "So what's your story?"

"There isn't much to tell, really." The fox fidgeted with his ruff.

"Don't test my patience."

* * *

Vhashmin remembered the oath he had recited each morning as he had stood waist-deep in the boiling waters of Sako-Anara; a purification ritual that had cleansed and driven home the promise that had bound him and his oath-brothers to the land. The pain was a constant reminder of their duty to protect the Land from the evil that tainted it, ever-growing when not kept in check. He remembered the thrill he had felt when the Grandmaster anointed the holy soil on the crest of his forehead, the very soil he had dived for in the depths of the volcanic spring, braving the sheer heat of its waters. The honor of being sworn in was testament to one's dedication and mastery of the Earthly Elements. Through progressive training since he was but a cub of eight summers, his mind and body had been conditioned to withstand and yet control them. Sitting beneath cascading falls that almost ripped his fur off; standing upon hot coals such that he couldn't walk for weeks afterward... he had even lain beneath slabs of rock placed upon him for days at end. All this was to ensure the power of the elements was a part of him.

Though outsiders would deem self-injury something done only to absolve oneself of one's sins, one thing Vhashmin knew for sure. His Order existed to protect, not any particular place, but the world as a whole. He had learnt how to channel the earth's energy through his body; the elements they were committed to giving form to their invocations. Bursts of refined energy brought form to intention. Some called it magic, but to the Order, that was a gift from the Land. He had learnt how to feel the Land and its musings as he and his brothers sat upon the bare ground, listening and feeling its mood amongst its rumblings and vibrations. For the Land to be perfect, there must be balance. Balance between the people and their surroundings.

One after another, novices became apprentices, and apprentices became journeymen. And all journeymen deemed ready were sent out by the Grandmaster. Through his own link and communion with the Land, the Grandmaster had sent his representatives to places in need of rebalancing. Only when the young are cast into the world will they know what it is like to live among others; people tainted by millennia of society and urban living. So that the disciples may feel their thoughts, their emotions and evils. Such that they may restore balance where they find otherwise, as was expected of a Viskrat.

It was with great honor and pride when Grandmaster Rhaksha appointed him, Vhashmin of Skywater, to travel to the Ashlands. There he would find the cause of its turmoil, and set it straight.

* * *

Keeshod twigged a claw in his ear. "Let me get this straight. You're some sort of magician." Vhashmin blinked. The two of them had been travelling for hours, and for all his years, the fox still acted like a starry-eyed cub.

"Well, some call us Elementalists, but to our order, we're Druids. Druids of Viskrat. We bring order to the land," affirmed Vhashmin, smoothing out the creases in his robe. Aside from a cloth sash worn diagonally around his midriff along with a travelling staff, as well as a sleeping roll, he had no other possessions.

"Druid, magician, whatever," flapped Keeshod. "So, what, you wave your paws and blast your foes with lightning? Tell me another one."

"Magic must be used responsibly," said Vhashmin, shaking his muzzle with his ears flat. "Surely you of all people must know—"

"All I know is that I've never heard of such a thing," cut in Keeshod. "We of the Land-Warriors believe in the real and tangible, the physical and the existent, not tales of what could have been. Have you ever used your…"—Here Keeshod gyrated his paw—"abilities before?"

"During my training, yes." Vhashmin flicked his ears as an insect buzzed around him.

"Show me."

Vhashmin's ears flattened, the whites of his eyes showing as he turned to Keeshod. "One must never misuse magic! Its improper use leads to imbalance and disharmony! It indicates a total disregard for the elements!"

"Yea, and I'm a townsguard," said Keeshod. In a swift motion, the cougar caught hold of the insect. Vhashmin flinched as he released it back again. "That's what those entertainers in the bazaars always say. But as long as you make it worth my while on this wild-goose chase, I'll let that slide," Keeshod looked at Vhashmin's fur and sniffed. "You're not a fox, are you?"

Vhashmin laughed. "No, but I get that a lot. Most of my order and I hail from the western grasslands. Our people call ourselves the Maned Ones, but others call us Maned Wolves."

"You don't look like a wolf."

"I'm not."

"You look more like a fox."

"That can be taken as an insult."

Keeshod stared back at Vhashmin, and in a moment of confusion, the two of them laughed. The cougar could tell this was the start of an interesting journey.

* * *

The journey to the edge of the Ashlands was short, considering that in the five days it took, Keeshod had had to rescue Vhashmin from a herd of wild-boar he had upset with his careless clomping, and fish him out of the river after his jump failed to clear the gap of a broken bridge.

The cougar was thoroughly convinced that despite whatever training Vhashmin may have received during his time in Sako-Anara, the druid was no fighter. He had told Keeshod that his fur was in fact russet ("like a fox," Keeshod had commented), but years of drinking the mineral-rich waters of a dormant volcano had changed his fur to its current state. When a gang of brigands had decided that an elderly fox accompanied by a lone barbarian was fair game, Vhashmin's deplorable swings with his staff had been easily parried, such that Keeshod had to handle their attackers by himself.

"Why did you not use your magic?" Keeshod had asked the trembling Vhashmin. "If you don't give even bandits a taste, one wonders if you have any skills to speak of."

"That would be excessive!" Vhashmin had protested. By the time they neared their destination, Keeshod knew he would be glad to put an end to their partnership. What use was a person that respected his own life so little to not use the training he'd been given? The cougar had never asked Vhashmin what his mission was, but could see why he had needed an escort.

They had known they were nearing their goal by the way everything looked. What were once lush grasslands punctuated by the occasional wood soon gave way to sparse vegetation, shriveled and struggling to survive. Furthermore, the land had become a drab brown, tinged with a certain grey that had clung onto the pads of the traveler's feet. As the next day passed, barely a tree could be seen. Soon the ground took on a dark grey that rivaled Vhashmin's mane. The land itself smelled vaguely of smoke, but differently. Tinged by a myriad of other sharp unfamiliar scents, they had cut into Keeshod's scent glands with every breath he took. By the end of that day, he had taken to keeping his mouth shut. With his sensitive nose, Vhashmin was forever sniffling and Keeshod came close to stuffing a rag up his nose. But Land-Warriors kept their promise to their charges, so he would just have to wait till the job was done.

They approached a caravan consisting of a wagon train six strong, with four armored boar guards up at the head with the caravan master, a cheetah in colorful flowing garb. At the sides of the wagon train were more guards, similarly equipped as if they were expecting trouble. Spear-and-arrow trouble, if their plate mail and crossbows were any indication. From beneath the canvas stretched across the tops of the individual wagons, Keeshod could see what looked like coal. It looked remarkably similar to the soil of the landscape, but despite coal being a valued commodity, Keeshod couldn't help but feel that the caravan was overprotected.

The guards drew their swords as Keeshod and Vhashmin approached. Keeshod stopped as his hackles raised, lips parted back in a snarl. He stepped before Vhashmin, spear posed for action.

"Put your swords down!" said the caravan master tiredly. "Anyone can see that these are just travelers to your city."

"No telling what guise brigands take," muttered the guard sergeant, but he and his men did as they were told. Keeshod relaxed, and he could vaguely hear the thumps of Vhashmin's heart as he lowered his spear.

"Good day, cougar," said the caravan master as he stepped forward, giving a strange half-bow to the two of them. "I'm Ashid the merchant." Vhashmin returned the bow hastily, with Keeshod giving a brief nod.

"Well met, Merchant," said Keeshod. "I can see you've hired more than adequate protection."

The cheetah shook his head gravely. "The roads around here have been dangerous as of late. Entire trade caravans have gone missing without a trace. We've even had disappearances happen right in the city itself, with the son of the Baron going missing just three days ago. Trade Baron Yakusk has been providing us guards for caravan escorts, and some believe it might have something to do with that," Ashid paused briefly and looked them up and down. "You're Mercfolk, I presume?"

Keeshod was starting to believe that word would crop up as long as he accompanied anyone. "Just me." He looked at Vhashmin disdainfully.

"I didn't know that there was coal to be found in lands such as this," commented Vhashmin as he stepped up to a cart and sniffed. The guards readied their weapons, so he stepped backwards with a gulp.

"You mean you don't know the primary export of Crosha?" exclaimed Ashid. Vhashmin shook his muzzle as Keeshod looked back impassively. The cheetah went on, "This is volcanic soil! The loam of life! Rich farmers pay a fortune to grow their crops in it. Don't ask me why, but plants sprout from a pawful quicker than a week's nurturing and a cartload of manure. I'm one of the few caravans that still make the rounds to the Craigsedge Cities." The cheetah's eyes lingered over Keeshod's spear and belt. "You don't look like you're here to trade. What's your business in Crosha?" His gaze went between Keeshod and Vhashmin.

Vhashmin started speaking, but Keeshod cut him off. "Just checking if there's work around these parts to be had. If there's nothing else, we'll just be on our way." He grabbed Vhashmin by the arm and pulled him quickly past, the clink of mail and plate following as they did.

"Watch yourselves on the road!" yelled Ashid as the two travelers reached the end of the caravan. Vhashmin gave a hasty wave back even as Keeshod continued dragging him. It was only after the caravan had moved on that Keeshod let his charge go.

"That was rude!" growled Vhashmin as he shook himself free. For the first time since they were together, he looked angry. "The merchant was just making small talk! There's no need to brush him off like that!"

"Yet more lessons you have to learn;" growled Keeshod as he stepped towards Vhashmin. "First of all, never let anyone know what your true business is. That moneybag has enough guards to butcher us if he so pleases. Second, a caravan that size is going to attract the attention of every bandit a half-league away. We want to be far away before that happens. Most importantly," here Keeshod gave a mirthless grin, "the sooner you get to your destination, the sooner I can be rid of you."

Vhashmin stared aghast at him. "What have I ever done to you?" Keeshod marched on with the maned wolf tottering close behind.

"Nothing, except that you're so like a cub despite your travelling for months!" Keeshod, began ticking off his fingers. "You don't know how to fight, you don't know how to avoid dangerous wildlife, it never occurred to you that we could be attacked when we make camp, you make conversation with strangers, and best of all, you refuse to use magic even under danger to life and limb!"

"And what would you know about magic?" Vhashmin's lips were already drawn back to expose his fangs.

Keeshod rolled his eyes as he turned back to him. "And what would you know about the ways of the world? I've had to coddle you close for the past week, or you would have been crowfood from the start!"

Vhashmin faltered, his eyes blinking. "Oh, I'm sorry. Was the promise of payment really worth all that effort?"

Keeshod looked sullenly back, and without warning, lashed out with a paw. Vhashmin yelped as he ducked backwards, but Keeshod had calculated his strike well, catching him hard across his head. The maned wolf made to right himself, but with a swift, familiar movement, the cougar swept the druid's feet out from under him. Before Vhashmin could recover, Keeshod had a foot on his chest, the working end of his spear at the druid's throat. The druid wheezed, his eyes wide.

"It appears that so many lessons have to be taught throughout our journey," growled the cougar. As was expected of Land-Warriors, he kept his fur flat. Calm despite fury; his elder had extolled. "Yet another, then; never ever question a Land-Warrior's motive for service. We have our reasons."

Keeshod had no idea what happened next. One moment he had a dazed canid at spearpoint, the next he was struck by an all-encompassing force so strong that his eyes were thrown shut. He landed hard on the dusty, ashy ground, and rolled away just in time for his spear to land point-first next to him. He sprang to his feet in a swift recovery move, only to be struck once more by the same unrelenting force, grit and sand blasting his eyes and pelt. He groaned, clutching his head as it rang. A strong wind howled around, and it was all Keeshod could do to keep his ears flat.

"And you should never assume that one unskilled in combat would fare worse," said Vhashmin. In the dim light permutated by dusk and the surrounding land, a skin of light radiated across his fur as he stepped forward. "I may not be a fighter, but neither am I a novice! Through my own commitment, I had prepared more for the challenges to be faced! I thought Land-Warriors honorable, but it appears I had been mistaken!" The force of wind relented, and Vhashmin shook his head. "Well, no longer. I shall make my own path." Vhashmin stepped past Keeshod, never once looking back as he continued on the road to Crosha.

Keeshod lay for a good half-hour as he nursed his aching back and jaw, dragging himself slowly to his feet. It was as much to his tribe's honor as his wounded pride that no passersby had witnessed his defeat. He prised his trusty spear Jairook out from the dirt and checked the blade. Aside from some slight scuffs, the surface of the stream-textured steel was otherwise unmarked. Retrieving one of his loosened pouches, Keeshod saw that Vhashmin's necklace was still there. He closed it with satisfaction, turning back the way he had come.

And stopped.

The unwritten code of the Land-Warrior was to never break an agreement or promise owed to another, unless they proved hostile. But as Keeshod thought back to the last five days, he couldn't deny that escorting Vhashmin had become more than a job. The cougar could simply have protected Vhashmin from the threats to his person, carrying out a duty no different than a bodyguard would; unquestioning, yet uncommitted. But he had felt attrition when Vhashmin had repeatedly failed to take care of himself, chiding the druid for his every mistake. Keeshod made an effort to teach him that the world wasn't all friends and alliances, but a hostile place where anyone could be your worst enemy. And all that was because Keeshod had grown to care. Cared for Vhashmin as an elder brother would of his sibling, loving and hating the gesture at the same time. How different were they, really? Both of the same age, sent out in the world without anyone to guide them. Keeshod had to learn to guide himself, but Vhashmin had the fortune to be guided by one more experienced and savvy than he was. Someone who could make sure that he could brave the dangers of the world, at least till he found his feet.

And he had been walking unknown lands for quite a while now. Keeshod held his spear low and ran, hoping he wasn't too late.

* * *

There was something about towns and cities that so unnerved Keeshod. The sheer lack of open spaces. The strict rules of not being allowed to walk the roofs, if only to avoid the maddening crowds. The hustle and bustle of countless others going about their everyday lives, unfeeling to those they meet. But what Keeshod could never get his head around was the persecution that members of a community may have for one different in dressing and appearance, of which their only crime was to be among them.

Vhashmin with all his ignorance had obviously walked straight into the city in the garb he was wearing, rather than trying to blend in with similarly-furred travelers. That would explain why he was now tied to a stake right next to the gateway of the city, with a mob gathered round the podium. An entire squad of sixteen guards, a mixture of boars and lynxes stood by him. A bobcat sergeant addressed the crowd.

"An agent of the Ptuku tried to worm his way among us, biding his time to strike," said the Sergeant, jabbing a claw towards the trembling Vhashmin. "The due vigilance of our guard, they who live to protect the vulnerable, has exposed this charlatan for what he is! He has confirmed his involvement in the crimes our city had been subject to."

"I only asked for Krishak!" protested Vhashmin. The maned wolf looked like he'd been run over by a cart and beaten shortly after. Blood ran across his fur and muzzle, soaking into his robe. His fur was now ragged, and no longer of the same greyish hue he was. "He will vouch for me—" The guard to his right struck him and he yelped, muzzle smashing against the stake.

"Krishak was tried and executed for sorcery and for the murder of many fine citizens. Anyone else involved with him shall follow his fate," yelled the sergeant to the restless crowd. "For who could tell what evil shall be conceived by those of the same creed?" The onlookers started booing, and projectiles ranging from stones to cabbages were flung upon the accused. The guards at the side pushed forward, holding back the restless crowd.

"If no one will speak for this lowlife, let him die by the sword!" yelled the wildcat as he drew his blade with a screech. "Bring him forward!"

"I testify to this man's innocence," spoke a voice and a hush fell over everyone. The sergeant turned slowly as a large cat dressed in the most heathen of clothing pushed his way through the crowd. His face was a mask of calm even as the guards directed their weapons towards him.

"Despite his having left me in the dust, I suggest that you leave him to my care," Keeshod gave a jerk of his head as he shifted his spear paw. "I give my assurance that he will be of no further trouble. What say you?"

It was probably too much to hope that the guards would be intimidated. Keeshod would later add to his own list of life lessons that the guards had too much riding on their carrying forward with the plan, as an angry mob not having their taste of blood was as dangerous as armed soldiers.

The sergeant flicked an ear and Keeshod dodged an arrow loosed from the gatehouse. Taking a short run, he braced himself on the supple ash composite of Jairook's haft and vaulted over the bobcat, a gleaming arc of steel missing his feet. He counted on the guards converging as he landed and wasn't disappointed. Dodging swiftly as they struck out unceremoniously with a repertoire of steely death, Keeshod swung the spear around as he stepped left and right in an ovular arc, thrashing his assailants into the snarling crowd. The Land-Warrior slashed out at Vhashmin's cowering form, and the maned wolf fell to his knees.

"Come on, do that storm thing you used on me earlier!" roared Keeshod as he deflected yet another arrow from the cur hiding in the gatehouse. He disarmed the still-standing sergeant with a spinning kick to his swordpaw, followed by an overhead smash to the skull. "If you don't, these guys will have our paws as trophies!"

"I-I-I can't!!" howled Vhashmin as he unclenched and unclenched his fingers. "My powers don't work properly in built-up locations! We have to find another way!"

"What do you mean you can't?" screeched Keeshod, and for the first time in his life, he felt fear. It was against the rules of honor for Land-Warriors to kill unarmed fighters, and he wasn't sure how long he could hold the mob back by deterrence alone. A gang of brawlers he could handle, but with a mob this large, the sheer weight of bodies would absorb his blows and smother them like the grave. A wolf with his fangs open for the kill sprang forward, and Keeshod had to kick his face in even as another rioter took his place. He was vaguely aware of Vhashmin being swarmed by more of the angry townsfolk, and immediately broke free of three others to help. Someone larger and stronger than he grabbed him from behind, and he dropped his spear. As he bent over to flip his attacker, several more swarmed him. He was then beset by a mix of punches, kicks, bites and scratches. The cougar felt every fang, every gouge across his pelt, vaguely remembering his elder's advice to never be overwhelmed by superior numbers. The last he remembered was a blow on the head.

* * *

"You okay?" The voice sounded coarse and sonorous in the wrong way, jarring to the cougar's ear hairs even as he fought to make sense of the words. Keeshod growled and muttered as he thrashed about, his claws retracting and detracting as he moved. He vaguely remembered some fight he had just been in. Years of situational awareness kicked in and he sprang to his feet, only to fall back to the ground with a metallic clatter. He wiggled his body. Chains? They actually bound him in chains! Him, a Land-Warrior, a free fighter being treated like a common criminal! He thrashed a little more, but the rusted chains bit painfully into his wounds.

"Oh, thank the Earth Mother, you're finally awake!" whistled a voice. Keeshod adjusted himself and turned to the source of the voice. A grimy wall scored with layers of claw marks and territorial markings greeted him. If he opened his mouth slightly, he could catch the stink of those before him. At the other end of the room was a barred door. Old scents of fear, anger, inebriation and even an unfamiliar kind of joy permeated the air. His weapons and clothes were gone, along with the rest of his equipment, though at least they left his breechcloth alone. At this angle, he couldn't see Vhashmin, but his blood-tinged scent suggested that he was in the same cell.

"Yes, so I am," called Keeshod. His eyes were still puffy. "That you, Vhash? What happened?"

"I know about as much as you do, but I heard from some guards that the Baron and his personal enforcers stepped in during our punch-up. From what I gather, he's the biggest man in this city. I came to in time to see the guards drag you here. You were thrashing about the last few hours."

"What can I say? I'm a light sleeper."

There was a pause. "Do all Land-Warriors make wisecracks like you do?" Vhashmin finally chuckled.

"No idea. I've never meet any others since I left my village," replied Keeshod. He was still seething from his embarrassing defeat, but talking to the maned wolf allowed him to gather his thoughts. "How about you, Vhash? You doing okay?"

There was a jingle nearby, and Keeshod could tell that Vhashmin had been chained to the wall. "Oh, just a couple of scratches and cuts.

My muzzle hurts but I'll live." A long pause ensued. "Why did you do it, Keeshod?"

It took Keeshod a moment to understand what Vhashmin meant. "Because I promised to protect you." he replied.

"But you've already got my pendant as collateral," said Vhashmin. So he didn't forget. "Why did you come back?"

Keeshod sighed as he sought the words to express how he felt. "A Land-Warrior carries out his duty until fulfillment or death, not just until payment has been received," explained Keeshod. "We serve on the basis of honor, not upon the promise of gain. Even though we fight for a living, it doesn't mean we live for that alone. Believe it or not, Vhashmin, I feared for you after seeing how you fared on the road. When you were sent out to the world… it's just like how I was thrown out there, you know? Nobody guided me. But it doesn't have to be the same for you."

"That's nice of you, Keeshod," said Vhashmin softly. Keeshod harrumphed in response. "I'm sorry for questioning your motives on the road. I guess I deserve the thrashing you gave."

"And I deserved that cartload of grit you blasted in my face," replied Keeshod. "Not to mention that the both of us got what we deserved by rushing headlong into an unfamiliar place. I say we're both quits. Agreed?"

"Agreed," replied Vhashmin. He adjusted himself against the cell wall. "So what do we do now?"

"We wait for the good guards of Crosha to tell us what our charges are, and act accordingly," said Keeshod as he sat himself up. He confirmed that Vhashmin was chained against the wall, his tensed feet barely giving respite to his arms. "You know where your contact lives? It'll be good to have someone who knows the lay of the land."

"He's dead, hadn't you heard? The guards believed he's part of the recent kidnappings," said Vhashmin, ears and whiskers drooping. "The fact that I looked different and asked after him made them believe I was part of the same cult. That's when you found me."

"Well, what's done is done," muttered Keeshod. The sound of an iron gate rattled in the hallway, and Keeshod silenced Vhashmin with a jerk of his muzzle. What sounded like three pairs of feet, two of them booted, grew closer. Keeshod lay back down as shadows flickered outside the cell.

A bobcat flanked by two guards appeared at the bars, dressed in a brigandine worn over richly padded clothing. His apparel being much too out of place in the grimy surroundings of the prison led Keeshod to believe this was the Baron. Even guard captains or tradesmen weren't dressed this lavishly.

"My apologies to you, honored fighter of the Land," spoke the bobcat with a twitch of his muzzle. He had the grace to look apologetic, which was more than Keeshod could say for others of his status. "I am Baron Yakusk, leader of the good city of Crosha. If I'd known that my guards had you clad in chains, I would have them removed at once."

"Perhaps you would be better served explaining yourself," retorted Keeshod. Vhashmin shook his muzzle at him with his eyes wide. "We are mere travelers in need of rest, yet your people had us marked for execution. Why?" He let his teeth show.

"But that's not what you're here for, are you?" confirmed Yakusk as his men fidgeted. One of them Keeshod recognized as the sergeant he had bashed, now sporting a dressing around his brow. "A Land-Warrior's journey takes him far from his tribal lands, but rarely beside the likes of others such as him," the Baron looked at Vhashmin. "Ghash, Runnt, hand over the keys and leave us."

The sergeant faltered. "But your lordship, these are dangerous—"

"That's an order, Sergeant, I will not ask again." said Yakusk with an irritable flick of his ears. Sergeant Ghash gave Keeshod a terrified look as he handed the keys over. He and his subordinate shuffled quickly away.

Yakusk waited till his men had left before unlocking the cell door, setting a flask down at the corner. As he neared the lying cougar, Keeshod sprang on him. His chains found their way around the Baron's neck, paws held taut even as the bobcat choked.

"No mortal chains can bind a Land-Warrior," Keeshod growled as the Baron's paws scrabbled futilely on the ground, tossing bits of filth about. The Baron's eyes boggled as his muzzle opened in a silent scream. "Just as you saw me fit to imprison, I see you fit to choke."

"Keeshod, stop!" yelled Vhashmin, fighting against his restraints as the Baron croaked. "Can't you see he's trying to help us?"

Keeshod kept his grip even as the Baron's eyes turned bloodshot. "All I see is a scumfur that put us in this hole."

"He was going to unlock your chains with the keys when you jumped him. Let him go and hear what he has to say. You can strangle him later."

Keeshod snarled, shoving the Baron hard against the wall. Yakusk slammed against it, and fell in a fit of spluttering and chokes. Even in the dim light leaking through the grate set in the cell wall, Keeshod could see the flecks of blood released in each cough.

"Are you alright, your lordship?" came Ghash's muffled yell.

"Yes, I told you to leave us alone!" choked Yakusk, smearing red away from his muzzle. He settled himself against the wall and smoothed out his fur and clothes while Keeshod unlocked Vhashmin's chains.

"Well?" demanded Keeshod as they both turned on the Baron. "What's this about?" The cougar sniffed the flask that had been brought and took a swig. Water. How considerate of the Baron. The parched sensation in his throat faded and he passed it to Vhashmin.

"Your skills had proven no less impeccable, honored cougar," wheezed Yakusk. "I wish to make you an offer as a desperate father. My son has been kidnapped."

Keeshod tilted his head. "I might have heard about that. What has that got to do with me? Or us." He added as Vhashmin grunted.

"The Land-Warriors are far skilled beyond the best of my men," answered Yakusk as he seated himself on the bench, paying no mind to its creak. "For the last six months now, we have had many disappearances within our city. Prominent citizens, some of them good friends, no less. And the citizenry reported strange sightings on the days they went missing."

"What kind of sightings, your lordship?" asked Vhashmin even as Keeshod huffed in impatience. He stood in the entrance to the cell, swollen ears pricked for danger.

"Sightings are sketchy at best. A guard on night patrol had reported seeing figures in the merchant district. When he approached, they slunk away faster than he could run. A maid had testified that the house under her care was being watched the night before Tradesman Valice went missing. There was no evidence of a struggle. The similarities in the sightings were that someone from the outside is responsible for all this." Baron Yakusk paused. His mouth opened and closed, trying to compose himself for what came next.

"And… and just three nights ago, my cub went missing. I found this on his window's edge." Yakusk sniffed as he reached into a hipbag, drawing forth what looked like a wispy shred of leather.

"What's that?" asked Vhashmin, his nose already twitching as he sifted through the scents.

"This is the shedded skin of a Ptuku," clarified Yakusk. "They are a tribe of native lizards who used to inhabit the surrounding area. They believe that the nearby mountain is an earthly embodiment of The Ash Mother, the most important of their deities. They left us alone when my expeditionary force first arrived twenty years ago. But when our alchemists discovered uses for the soil here, the Ptuku turned hostile. They said the land was sacred to their people, and none of us should have it. But what's the point if they had no use for it? We weren't telling them to leave; we even offered them good coin for it. After numerous raids on our camps, I was forced to rally our forces to evict them. From then on, I was granted the duty of overseeing this city and its continued growth. But it appears that they have resurfaced."

"But why now, of all times?" asked Keeshod.

Baron Yakusk looked away. "Their shaman had warned me this would happen." he whispered.

"We're going to need more details than that, *Baron,*" snorted Keeshod.

The bobcat paced around the cell. "When my men drove the Ptuku off, their shaman said that the time of the Ptuku would come once again. That it would be the time we faced the wrath of the Ash Mother. I've dismissed it as one of their heathen legends, but it seems that their people haven't forgotten their promise. There's no question that the kidnappings our city are experiencing have got to be linked to that. Who knows what these heathens do to their victims?"

"But why had my contact been killed?" demanded Vhashmin, with Keeshod growling in agreement. "What has he done to deserve that?"

"The druid Krishak?" Yakusk's eyes flickered. "It must be said that most of the city is fearful of the magically inclined. When my people started vanishing in most unusual circumstances, the Guard suspected him. I had him beheaded after a majority vote of the townsfolk."

"Then be damned with you!" snarled Vhashmin, and it was Keeshod's turn to hold the maned wolf back. "You've given us nothing but threats of death and imprisonment! Why should we help you now?"

"You have to understand, nobody knew who was responsible for the kidnappings!" protested Yakusk. "The swift and silent manner in which they were committed suggested that magic was involved! If I as their leader don't act, the townspeople will revolt! And how can I protect them with my head on a pike? I cannot bring your brother-in-arms back, but I can atone for it. Just help me find my son and I'll give you anything you wish."

The cell was silent for a long while, such that a far-off drip of water could be heard. The mix of fresh fearful, angry and agitated scents permeated within the cell, and once again, Keeshod was glad he could shut out most of it by keeping his mouth closed. He wasn't a Land-Warrior for nothing.

"Very well," said Vhashmin, shaking his head at Keeshod as he protested. "But for now, we want several favors."

"Name them." Yakusk's ears stood.

"First of all, we would like your guards to leave us alone, and to keep the townsfolk away from us," growled Vhashmin as he drew himself to his full height. The bobcat dwarfed him by a head. "That, and an official pardon of any charges that have been placed against us."

"Done," said Yakusk and Keeshod snorted. Their only crime had been arriving at the city at the wrong time.

"Secondly, we want full and unrestricted access to Krishak's house, along with any other properties and possessions he may own," continued Vhashmin. Yakusk twitched his ears in surprise. "He was part of my order after all, and what was his is mine."

"And 200 gold coins for our services," cut in Keeshod. He was burning with questions, but now wasn't the time. "We're not risking our pelts for nothing."

"Very well then," said Yakusk with relief as he stood. "I'll see to it that the guards show you to the house. As for the gold, it will be paid upon delivery of my son. You have my word on that."

"That remains to be seen," replied Keeshod, his teeth showing. "Now, how about those directions?"

* * *

It was amazing how quickly things went when the boot was in the other foot. At Yakusk's command, the guards hastened to bring forth the keys to Krishak's property. Although most of Vhashmin's and Keeshod's possessions were returned to them, all their coin was missing, leading to a heated argument which concluded with Yakusk paying out of his own purse.

Keeshod and Vhashmin had the guards bring them to the scenes of the kidnappings, including the Baron's manor. Despite Keeshod's tracking skills, there wasn't anything to go on, not even any unusual scents or footprints. Either time had washed away the evidence, or the interlopers were good at what they did. They found yet another scrap of lizard skin caught on some brambles, but it didn't yield any more scent than the Baron's find had. This was unusual, given that the latest kidnapping was only three days back. To track somebody, you needed a scent trail, at the very least, and Keeshod was one of the best in his tribe. Their investigation at a dead end, Keeshod and Vhashmin asked to be brought to Krishak's house. Following the nervous mink guard, Keeshod and Vhashmin made their way down the winding alleys to the south side of the city.

Krishak owned two properties. One was a house built from the ashstone common in the surrounding area, while the other was the outhouse beside it. Hastily removing the locks with the seal of the Crosha Guard, the guard handed Vhashmin the house keys. At Keeshod's thoughtful glance at the fly-infested privy, the guard stuttered that the amenities would be serviced immediately. Vhashmin was noncommittal throughout the exchange, and by the time they stepped through the front door, Keeshod burst with questions.

"It's all very well to requisition this house for our purposes, Vhash, but I hardly think accommodation's a priority at the moment!" the cougar exploded as he slammed the door. "What were you thinking? Has the time on the road gotten so much that you need to rest your poor, weary feet?"

"This building is merely the start of our investigations, nothing more!" retorted Vhashmin. "Surely, it may have belonged to my order, but the fact that my Grandmaster sent me to Krishak meant he had information on what ailed this land. And all that should be among these records." He picked up a worn tome and held it up to the light through the window. After the fiasco at the gateway to Crosha, the travelers had spent the night in their cell before Yakusk made his proposition. The living room of the house wasn't particularly large, but with only one chair, this gave it a certain spaciousness. Keeshod had never been inside a druid's house before, but from all the paraphernalia, he could tell this had belonged to one familiar with keeping records. Stacks upon stacks of parchment lay about, most of it trampled into the floor. A bottle of spilled ink lay on its side with a broken quill beside it. What would have been valuable to commoners such as candlesticks were gone. Few could read, which accounted for the books and parchments being untouched.

"Do what you have to," said Keeshod, bolting the door shut. "I'm going to take a look around." He placed Jairook against the wall and left Vhashmin protesting about having to sift through the records alone.

The fact that he couldn't read didn't upset Keeshod. People like him relied on the real and the tangible, not unintelligible scribbles on bits of dried skin which could mean anything to each other person. He was a tribal warrior with mastery in the fighting arts, not some academic. The house was a single-story, not unusual given that a druid wasn't the wealthiest of professions. A kitchen stood at the far end of the house, adjoined by a makeshift larder. The presence of herbs and edible plant parts without any discarded bones in the trash heap suggested that Krishak had been a herbivore of some sort. Scenting the air with open jaws, Keeshod caught the half-stale scents of multiple species including boar and wildcat, and realized that any trace of the previous occupant was now gone. A search in the last room yielded a crumpled bedroll reeking with the stench of fear, along with a wide pit dug right to the earth. With nothing else to be done, Keeshod returned to the kitchen and started a fire burning at the spit.

* * *

"I've got dinner," said Keeshod as he entered the living room with two clay platters of unintelligible sludge. It was late afternoon by the time the meal was done, and the vague hustle and bustle of the town could just be heard if one pricked one's ears. The Land-Warrior had made a circuit through the house and examined all possible entry points and windows for weaknesses. He had observed guards patrolling past the house, but one of his background was never fooled. Yakusk feared they would leave without upholding their deal, and Keeshod couldn't blame him.

Vhashmin took a platter and gave it a quick sniff. "Road rations cooked with boiled herbs. Wow-wee." His muzzle wrinkled.

"That's all you're getting. As long as hostilities remain between us and the townsfolk, I can't get to the damn market without being greeted by another mob," snorted Keeshod. "You find anything?" he asked as he licked his meal straight into his maw.

"I have, actually," said Vhashmin as he leafed through a stack of notes. "It seems that Krishak had been keeping records of the activities in town. This includes the recent kidnappings."

"I'm surprised the guards hadn't confiscated them," mumbled Keeshod through a mouthful of food. "Surely a few can read."

"That's only if they understand it," replied Vhashmin as he flashed a page of squiggles at Keeshod. "Our order doesn't write in Tradesmen Common, but in our own runic alphabet. And only a few of the seminaries know how to read it. My, you eat fast."

"Fast is good," answered Keeshod as he tossed his plate aside. "Gives us more time to spend on other things. So what did Krishak discover? More importantly, what did your order have planned for you? I can't wait forever."

"Our quests are never given straight to the point; rather, we have to feel the land and its ambient energies to understand what plagues it," answered the maned wolf. "During his communion with the surrounding land, Krishak could feel that it was angry, vengeful even. According to the dates, this coincided right before the kidnappings began and the moment my Grandmaster had the vision that sent me here. Baron Yakusk had recently started planning an excavation on the mountain for its soil and minerals, but the townsfolk involved with the operation went missing shortly thereafter. They had obviously been kidnapped."

"So you're saying the Ptuku kidnapped the townsfolk to stop work on the mountain?" asked Keeshod. "I don't see why the Baron's son would be part of that. Unless it's a warning…"

"Precisely," said Vhashmin, throwing the notes back on the desk. "Did you find anything interesting in the rooms of the house? There should be a cellar somewhere."

"Just an abandoned bedroll in an empty bedroom," replied Keeshod. "There's some kind of pit that Krishak seemed to have dug by paw next to it, but I doubt if there's any wine stored in there, if that's what you're asking. The townsfolk have been thorough."

"Then that's as good a communion point as any," said Vhashmin as he walked to the bedroom. Keeshod followed just in time to see him easing himself into the pit, and ran up to the edge.

"What are you doing?" demanded Keeshod as he looked down into the hole. Upon the gray dusty soil, Vhashmin was turning back and around as he seated upon it, palms out against the walls of the pit. "If this hole caves in, I'm not going to dig you out."

"Remember how I've told you I can't channel elemental energy in the city?" reminded Vhashmin. The maned wolf had a glint in his eye. "Well, that's because the unnatural state of cities and their buildings block out the energies that normally cycle unobstructed throughout the land. Even within the confines of a city, druids can however tap into the land's energy by having an access point to ensure they have direct contact with the untainted ground. This is it." He smoothed his paws reverently across the muck, clenching and unclenching his fingers as he had when working a spell. "I'm going to need a few hours, at least. That should be enough to find out what's going on."

Keeshod folded his arms. "Great. So what do I do if you never wake up? I doubt the town healer's in any mood to help."

"Just pull my paws away from the soil and I'll be alright," growled Vhashmin. "Come on, Keeshod. I know what I'm doing." His ears flicked in dismissal.

Keeshod stomped back to the living room and picked up the maned wolf's rations. Bringing them back to the kitchen, he checked if the windows would open. A pair of eyes glinted back at him through the gap and he balked. He slammed the back door open and rushed out into the garden, his tomahawk out before him. Behind the house was the south side of the town wall, made of dark stone some fifteen feet high. Two guards at the top of the wall turned at his outburst.

"Did you see anyone here?" demanded Keeshod. The guards gripped their bows nervously, so the cougar lowered his tomahawk.

"No we haven't, Land-Warrior." confirmed a guard in a whimper. His partner shook his head vigorously.

Keeshod huffed and took a look around as he parted his jaws. An unfamiliar smell tingled in his glands, like ash, but not ash, with a pungent tang of sulfur and sourness beneath it. It wasn't a scent, but more like the residual smell of where the perpetrator had been. As he made his way back to the house and secured the lock, the cougar realized that the smell resembled what little remained in the shredded skin Yakusk had showed them. He then grabbed what little firewood he could find and wedged all the windows and doors shut. By the time Keeshod was done, the cougar realized how tired he actually was. As long as Vhashmin stayed in his trance, now was the best time to catch up on rest. Ignoring the last occupant's stench of fear still clinging to the scented bedroll, Keeshod the cougar set his crossbelts, mantle and spear beside him, and lay directly on the bedroom floor, with his spear Jairook close by. Should anyone come, he was ready.

* * *

Someone gripped Keeshod and the cougar sprang upright, fangs and claws out as he pounced. His assailant yelped and fell backwards, and the cougar could smell the familiar scent of musty grass laced with soot.

"Come on, Vhash, don't grab me like that!" exclaimed Keeshod as he got off the druid. The maned wolf was frantic, scrabbling back to his feet.

"Forget about that! You've got to follow me while the energies of the land are still fresh!" Vhashmin struggled with the key to the door and bolted out.

Keeshod, ever prepared for the unforeseen, followed suit with spear in paw, his mantle and crossbelts back on his chest. He caught up with Vhashmin as he approached one of the all-too-frequent guard patrols.

"By order of the Baron, state your—" started the corporal, but the sight of a snarling and hastily-awakened cougar armed with a spear cut him short. The two travelers navigated the now-dark streets of Crosha, meeting only a drunk badger who hiccuped as they passed.

"Will you tell me what's gotten into you?" demanded Keeshod as they made their way through the town gate. By the look of the hastily-deserted barricade, the guards had orders to keep them in. From their absence, neither did they want to risk a tangle with a Land-Warrior.

"All land has energy passing through it, be it through the wind and water, or that of the lifeforce residing within living things," said Vhashmin. His words came so quick and convoluted that Keeshod could barely catch it. "Well, such energy lingers for a while after, so by seeing into the past and present energy of the activities in the city, I discovered where the perpetrators had gone. You remember the sites of the kidnappings? All the residual trails from them converge upon the path we're now following..." Vhashmin pointed at what must be several invisible trails as he growled, neck muscles taut with exertion.

"Do they resemble something with yellow glinting eyes?" asked Keeshod. They were now on the outskirts of town, following a straight route across the dark and grey soil that made up these parts. Barely any plants littered the landscape, a sharp contrast to the reputed fertility of the soil.

"Auras don't take on a distinct shape and form; I can't see how they look exactly," said Vhashmin. He stopped briefly to place his paws against the ground. "It appears that they use this route often. Look, there's a fresh trail right ahead of us; someone vengeful," Vhashmin snarled. "His very thoughts hurt just to hear them!" He plodded on half in a trance, with Keeshod close behind. The cougar hoped he didn't have to carry the druid back when he was done, but he shouldn't have expected anything different ever since he signed up as the druid's bodyguard.

The moonlight helped with navigating the land, but Keeshod had no doubt that in his trance, Vhashmin would have no trouble finding his way in pitch darkness. Radiating with a yellow glow up ahead was a mountain with a flat peak. And the druid was heading straight for it.

It was two hours later that they came to the base of the mountain. Here the ground felt warm beneath their pads. Even up close, Keeshod couldn't tell how high the mountain went. He could catch the same smell in the garden amidst the ash and soil. Falling out of his trance, Vhashmin tottered. He pointed up at the mountain as Keeshod held him steady.

"That's where the kidnapped have been taken," croaked Vhashmin as he pointed at a crooked path worn into the rising land mass up ahead. "This has got to be the mountain the Baron was intending to exploit. You go on ahead, Keeshod. I need to catch my breath."

"I'm not leaving you!" snapped Keeshod. "Can't you draw upon the land for nourishment, or something?" He looked distastefully at the soil between his toes. Dirt and grit he was fine with, but this felt like something else entirely, like the land rejected his presence.

"I can't. The land around the mountain is tainted," confirmed Vhashmin, echoing Keeshod's thoughts. "Just finding my way here is difficult enough; it's almost like somebody doesn't want us to find them."

"Then I'll guide you," said Keeshod. "This position is far too exposed. Hold onto my crossbelts as you walk and follow me, alright?"

The cougar was taken aback by how cold the druid's paw was, and realized that much of his power had been drawn leading them here. Slowly and gradually, the two of them made their way up the rocky path. Some distance up, Keeshod found an outcropping that was easier to defend from, and kept watch while Vhashmin caught his breath. Keeshod hadn't had time to fill his waterskin, so he shared whatever drops of water remained with his companion. He knew he could go two days without it, but the strange heat coming from the mountain didn't help at all.

On hindsight, they may have fared better had they been better prepared.

* * *

The sound of a distant thumping roused Keeshod and Vhashmin from their break. Keeshod led the way forward, the two of them rushing up the path. Scampering up the worn mountain walkway towards the sound, they kept their stances low. As they neared, Keeshod could discern drumbeats interspersed with a rhythmical chanting. The voices sounded not like any vocalization he had heard in his travels, and were punctuated with hisses and sharp intakes of breath, along with exaggerated sighs. He felt the steps of his feet coinciding with that of the chants, and a chill ran up his spine. A cave with a certain unnatural, hazy radiance showed itself a hundred feet from the top of the mountain. He felt his fur stand. After confirming that Vhashmin could make it to the cave on his own, Keeshod dashed inside.

What really took him unawares was the stink of a multitude of different scents, all mingled with each another and overlaid with the sharp scent of fear. The smells of mammals; hare, lynx, fox… The kidnapped townspeople had been brought in through this entrance, possibly catching their last glimpse of open sky. The lack of any other scents did nothing to warn him on how many foes to expect. Just what kind of creature went without a scent?

As he followed the curves of the winding tunnel, a voice spoke.

"Long before the outsiders came, far and wide were these lands ours," it hissed. Keeshod's swiveled his spear around, his eyes darting left and right. It took him a moment to realize the voice was in his head. By the sword of the Goddess!

"But like an infestation, the warmbloods laid claim to the lands of our forefathers," the voice continued. Keeshod darted from rock to rock, ears pricked to listen beyond the echo within him. He could feel the malice in every word, and each one stung like hot iron. "But it was never enough, so they desecrated the skin of the Ash Mother, sending it far from her flesh. Now their champion arrives, a warrior of pride seeking the spawn of the desecrator. A warrior of no small might and foolishness, seeking only gain devoid of the land's riches. Tell me, little cat. Is your life so lacking in purpose? Do you live only to fight and serve?"

"If you would just show yourself, I will have you devoid of life," spoke Keeshod out loud. He had arrived at the mouth of a large chamber. From it led a massive hallway carved within the mountain. Stone slabs were arranged in a half-circle around a rise from the ground, with cut steps leading up to it. At the top of the rise was a hole billowing with smoke and sparkling ash; a fitting complement to the eerie chanting. But what caught Keeshod's attention was not the surroundings, but that of the people within.

Upon each stone slab lay a greyish figure, with ragged skin that shook with each vocalization. About half of them had drums over their chests, with which they beat out a rhythm. Similar in form and overall shape to most bipeds, there the similarity ended. A thick tapered tail, elongated muzzle and angular joints reinforced their differences, with greyish scales instead of fur. With the oppressive heat within the mountain, the cougar wasn't surprised that none were clothed, though there was little point with no visible indicator of gender. And they didn't sweat! Now the cougar knew why they were so devoid of scent. With the Ptuku lying rather than sitting, this contact with the ground actually intensified the chant. There had to be at least twenty of them. A large figure was silhouetted against the flames that rose from the hole behind him, a decorated rod of bone and fur trimmings in paw. Trembling beside him was a bobcat cub bound with ropes. He whimpered as the Ptuku hissed at him.

"The glory of the Ash Mother will sustain us, as will this sacrifice," declared the Ptuku shaman. "May it nourish her where its kind had tainted. She will consume!"

"She will consume!" chorused the Ptuku with a sharp gasp-hiss. The shaman thrust the cub into the hole, his scream replaced by a sharp sizzle erupting through the chamber. The lizards all raised their paws in supplication as Keeshod's jaws dropped.

"Praised be the Sleeping Mother! Praised be Shaman Bezel!"

"For only through the sacrifice will her blood pour forth, and wash away the desecrators!" roared Bezel. "May her blood consume them all!"

Keeshod felt only revulsion as he dashed forward, Jairook oscillating as he moved. But the Ptuku were ready, obsidian spears and knives out as they sprang to their feet. The cougar succeeded in nicking the throat of one before the others converged upon him, their crazed shaman spurring them on with his blessing.

The Ptuku were by no means expert fighters, but they were skilled at hunting techniques. Always a distance away as Keeshod lashed out, they formed a circle that tightened accordingly as he moved towards a certain direction. Lighter on their feet than he had anticipated, the stone slabs were of no impedance as they leapt forward and back atop them, gaining a height advantage over the cougar whenever that happened. Keeshod narrowly avoided a jab to the face and a vertical slash, thrusting hard towards the offending foe. The attacker had no chance to duck, hiss-spluttering as the spear erupted through his midriff, only to be released in a shower of dark blood and ripped scales as Keeshod levered the spear out onto another's skull. Yet another fell as Keeshod performed a roundhouse kick to his jaw, the claws of his foot almost wrenched out as they caught against the tough scales. He felt two quick cuts across his back and snarled, pushing onward towards the front of the hall. With a determination borne of desperation, he threw his attackers back with several feints of his spear. Seizing his chance, he dashed through the cleared path. Slamming a footpaw down on a slab, a combination of the sudden height difference along with well-honed muscles carried him over the heads of the acolytes, right towards their leader.

The moment the shaman smiled, Keeshod realized the futility of his efforts. Jairook, his companion of his many adventures, fragmented blade and all as it came down on the shaman's arcane shield. Flung backwards by the rebound, Keeshod felt himself frozen in midair. He gasped as a force gripped the entirety of his being, his arms held outstretched. A tingling, skintight sensation pulled across his pelt, half crushing, half-binding. The cougar fought to move, and even to will this hold off him, but nothing he had trained or encountered prepared him for such a situation. The score of hissing and spitting Ptuku converged just within spear reach below him, and Keeshod felt the previously unknown feeling of anxiety. He snarled back even as he knew his life was lost, defiant and fighting till the very end.

"The anger of the Ash Mother lingers, and she hungers for another soul," rasped the shaman Bezel. Dark emotionless eyes surveyed his victim. "But she will not deny Her Children vengeance, as is their right to claim. Enforce Her will!"

Keeshod screeched as he felt the sharp sting of spear and knife blades. Jagged blades slit across his calves and torso, and without warning, a loud burst of air erupted around him. Falling hard onto the jagged ground, the cougar looked up to see the Ptuku scattered all around him, dead or unconscious. From where he had entered, a lone figure strode in, a faint glow exuding from his person.

"I have come to destroy you, foul creature of the earth," declared Vhashmin, and Keeshod realized that the druid had shielded him from his attackers. His body was bloodied and he was hurt badly, but he could have been killed. "The land may be unbalanced, but you are going too far!"

The shaman roared a screech that chilled even Keeshod. Flames and superheated fumes from the pit lunged towards Vhashmin, engulfing him in a miasma of light and swirls. Waves of magma followed, cascading around his form like water over rock. The druid repulsed it with a burst of air, but with so much less power that the magma torrent soon encased him once more.

"You may be a druid of the elements, but you hold no power here!" snarled the shaman, jaws stretched open in a grin. He didn't seem fazed or weakened by his invocation. "I am Ptuku, born and raised in this very land! For we who are born of the Ash shall reign victorious! You are an outsider, a blemish on untainted earth! You. Cannot. Win."

The magma torrent dissipated, and Vhashmin was left in its wake, greyish-white fur in flames. He staggered as the flames dissolved into puffs of smoke, tail limp and shoulders slumped. Before he could make a move, Bezel raised his staff paw, pulling Vhashmin magically towards the pit. Colliding hard against a rocky outcropping, the druid slid into it. The maned wolf yelled as he held onto the edge, his paws scrabbling on the jagged rock. He screeched, the heat of the magma down below searing his feet. Bezel stepped forward.

"You are not fit to nourish the Sleeping Mother," roared Bezel as he leered down at the desperate druid. "But her enemies nourish her anger. Soon, she will be awakened by your sacrifice!" Bezel raised his snout. "Good Mother, please accept this offering of our foe—"

Bezel shut up as the honed blade of a cougar tomahawk sank into the base of his skull. The force of the weighted projectile pitched him forward, and he narrowly missed the thrashing form of Vhashmin in his descent. The sizzle of his flesh was harsh and prolonged, and a rumble erupted throughout the chamber. The mountain shook, and lumps of rock started falling from the ceiling, landing among the stone slabs with destructive results. A boulder crashed near the pit, sending a shockwave through the hall.

Vhashmin couldn't hold on any longer and his paws gave. A pair of calloused paws gripped onto them and he looked up in surprise. Keeshod's muzzle loomed into view as he held on, teeth gritting as he hauled Vhashmin out. The pit bubbled and spat out more ash and fumes, and with a final effort, Vhashmin fell on top of Keeshod. The cougar staggered back up on bloodied feet, pulling Vhashmin up with him.

"We gotta go, Vhash! The whole place's falling apart as we speak—"

"My feet hurt; I can't walk," wailed Vhashmin as he fell back down on all fours. Keeshod chanced a look down and saw that his feet were blistered and charred in the fumes of the pit. "Leave me, Keeshod! You can save yourself!"

Keeshod didn't have time to argue, so he grabbed Vhashmin by the scruff and base of his robes, throwing him unceremoniously across a shoulder. He dashed out of the chamber even as parts of the ceiling came down, Vhashmin's protesting form flopping painfully on the wounds the Ptuku had inflicted. The cuts and stab wounds on the cougar's legs throbbed, but this was nothing to his people. The scents and sounds of the volcano coming alive fought against his sense of direction. A chunk of rock came down hard on his free shoulder. The cougar stumbled with the blow. He dashed through the convoluted tunnels as they gave way around him, keeping his head down as thick smoke and sulfur choked his nostrils. His gaze blurred as the fumes played with his mind, but the limp weight on his shoulder gave purpose to his steps. Just a little more, just a little more…

And finally, sweet fresh air. Keeshod was about to carry Vhashmin down back the way they'd come when a final, larger explosion ensued from the mountain. It was so loud and forceful that the very shaking of the ground threw them off the path, sending them rolling down a short slope. They landed hard onto a flat stretch of rock, and groaned. Turning painfully on his scarred back, Keeshod witnessed a scene he would never forget.

Balls of fire discharged from the shattered top of the mountain, larger and far more numerous than he could count. The entire night sky glowed with embers and crimson fire, taking on the hue of a macabre dawn. Lava cascaded down the slopes of the mountain, faster than he could ever run. In mingled surprise and relief, he saw that he and Vhashmin had fallen behind a protected rocky outcropping, where they were safe from the fiery tears of the volcano. The lava flowed around them. Even this close,

Keeshod felt only a slight warmth radiating from the molten rock. He shielded his eyes with a paw as the glow of the lava got too much for him. To his surprise, the lava swerved away from the few clumps of trees down below, swathing across the bare land. The land itself lit up from the unearthly glow of the earth's blood, and Keeshod felt his stomach crawl as the lava met the city of Crosha. He could only imagine how the people felt. Panicked caterwauls and yips cut off as the earth-fire took them, the very masonry of their dwellings crumbling and floating away in the heat. The centerpiece of the town, a stone statue of Baron Yakusk crumbled, and within seconds, the town of Crosha was no more.

Keeshod had failed in his quest. The son of Yakusk was dead, along with a thousand others. All dead under the protection of a Land-Warrior. His eyes drew down to the now unladen belt upon his waist. A Land-Warrior without his honor and weapons. How fitting for one who failed to hold high the honor of his people.

"The volcano of the Ash Mother has reawakened, Vhashmin, and we couldn't stop it," said Keeshod hollowly. Vhashmin had gotten to his feet, taking in the scene down below. "Why, Vhashmin?" He ripped off his crossbelts and flung it to the ground. "Why have we failed in our duty?"

"Bezel wanted the volcano to erupt, but the sacrifices he had made had nothing to do with it," said Vhashmin. Through his composed demeanor, Keeshod couldn't help but turn to him. "Rather, it was the act of consuming Bezel that awoke the Ash Mother."

"What?" ejaculated Keeshod. "You saw what happened! That lowlife tossed the poor cub in there. It couldn't have been him!"

"Being able to commune with the land gives me enough to glean what had happened," said Vhashmin. His voice, wispy and flowing, betrayed a certain wisdom that wasn't there before. "The Ash Mother may have been roused from her slumber during the first few sacrifices, but Bezel and his followers were the ones who secured her eruption. Their very anger and belief that she had to be appeased with sacrifices kept her in check. Belief is a strong thing, Keeshod, even more so when coupled with the arcane. Killing Bezel released the hold on the Ash Mother, not his sacrifices. And it looks like he got what he wished for."

Keeshod shook his head, utterly muddled by the whole thing. "So, what, you're saying that the town deserves to burn? Because last I heard, there were hundreds, maybe even a thousand innocents in there—"

"The land was unbalanced, Keeshod, that much was true," said Vhashmin calmly. His ears barely twitched, and his muzzle remained impassive. "The townsfolk had stolen the lands from the rightful, and robbed them for their riches, desecrating what had never belonged to them. The eruption was necessary for the land to start anew. Had you noticed that barely anything grew despite the soil's reputed powers? Because the land itself was tainted. Nature always rights itself, just like fever to a body. But sometimes all it needs is a little help, just as you had provided." Vhashmin finally smiled. "See how we ended up safe? Even the Ash Mother saw fit to protect us from her glowing tears. And for bringing balance back to this place, I bow in deference to you, Warrior of the Land." Vhashmin bent his head forward.

"Hey, hey, I'm going to have to disagree with you on that," said Keeshod roughly as he gripped onto Vhashmin's shoulders. "Without you, I would have been kindling in the cesspit that damn lizard was so anxious to toss me into. You had as much a part to play in this."

"And here I thought the Land-Warriors weren't humble," chuckled Vhashmin. "I had promised you compensation for your efforts, honored cougar, but I am afraid that is no longer possible. Whatever wealth Yakusk may have promised has gone back to the land, as it rightly deserved to. I can only offer to accompany you wherever you may choose to go. There aren't many who are magically-gifted in these lands, and I'll be happy to help you where I can."

Keeshod looked over the land, scorched and devoid of life. The few trees were all that was left, along with the both of them. But for all its barren appearance, it had been cleansed of the disrespect and hatred that plagued it. The cougar could almost feel a kind of quiet peace, the kind of tranquility that came after a storm.

He thought back to the week's events, from the time a nervous adolescent had begged him for help, to the skirmishes they had braved on the open road. He remembered how his disdain for one without knowledge of the road had grown into brotherly care. This had resulted in a fight to rescue him as a brother would, risking life and limb for one not of his clan. They had then worked together to accomplish what neither was capable of by himself, not as colleagues but as friends. Not for gold, not for honor, but for what was right. For despite the many barriers of culture the different peoples of the land had, the one thing they all valued was brotherhood. Be they Land-Warriors, be they druids, be they townsfolk; no barrier exists between it, and Keeshod now knew what he had been missing all this while. He looked down at the cuts, bruises and burn marks across his chest and legs, and finally knew what his elder back in his village had meant. Master Yuvik had said there was nothing like going on a journey by oneself, each new experience a lesson in life. For life was taught in mishaps and happenings, words spoken and left unsaid, each wound and ache a new experience, a new reason to live for.

Keeshod wiped his eyes hurriedly as he turned back to Vhashmin. He no longer saw an ignorant cub, but an older and wiser friend he would have loved to call a brother. And for the Land-Warrior who walked the path alone, this meant a lot.

"I'll be happy to travel with you, Vhashmin," said Keeshod, and for the first time since he had left his village, he felt fulfilled. "But first, you'll have to excuse me while I get some new weapons."

Expermians like Jaicob never leave Expermia. There's nothing in other countries worth seeing. But that was before Expermia lost the war, and Jaicob's favorite uncle was executed as a war criminal.

Now Jaicob travels with his father into the enemy's capital city. What will he find there?

(For more about the Silver Foxes and Expermia, see M. R. Anglin's novels Silver Foxes *(2008),* Winds of Change *(2010),* Prelude to War *(2013), and* Into Expermia *(2015), and the novelettes and short stories in her* Interlude: A Series of Shorts *(2016) and* Celebrity Dish *(2017); plus the Kindle-only* My Experiences With J. R. Dunsworth, As Told By Mira *(2016), and short fiction in the anthologies* Gods With Fur *(2016) and* Dogs of War II: Aftermath *(2017), both from FurPlanet Productions.)*

Legacy

by M. R. Anglin

Jaicob watched his brother, Caileb, stuff folded clothes into a desert camo duffel bag. In a few moments, he'd leave—depart for the Expermian Civilian Soldier's officer's training orientation. The Civilian Soldiers were what Expermians labelled enlisted foxes and vixens who were too young for service. They trained and participated in peacetime efforts—disaster relief and the like—but could not participate in active combat. At 16, about to turn 17, Caileb fit that bill. And as his twin, Jaicob would have too… if he had enlisted.

Jaicob sat back to lean on his headboard in the room he and his brother shared. They had been together all their lives, sharing not only this room but most of their hobbies and friends. Jaicob bit his lips together as he watched the curtains flutter in the warm desert wind, the fading sun tinting them a purplish color. For the first time ever, Caileb would be traveling without him—all because Jaicob had been indecisive about what he wanted to do with his life… as usual. He had been sure he wanted to join the army with Caileb, but his resolve had weakened three weeks ago.

"You okay, Jake?" Caileb broke the silence. When Jaicob looked up, he saw his brother watching him in the fading light. He resisted the urge to flip on the lamp resting on the night table between their two beds. The electrical plants powering the capital and its surrounding areas had been destroyed, leaving everyone in the dark. So instead, he peered at his brother through the darkening gloom.

Jaicob was used to seeing his reflection in his brother's face. They'd had the same features all their lives—same orangish-brown fur, same brown hair, same brown eyes. But every once in a while, looking into

Caileb's face was like looking into a strangers'. Minute variances that usually made little difference became glaring contrasts—same hair but the ends of Caileb's hair were blond while Jaicob's were green. Same way their hair flipped up at the ends, but Caileb kept his short and Jaicob let his grow to his shoulders. Same eyes, but Caileb's held a firmness—an assurance that he was the trustworthy, smarter, and dependable one. Jaicob shuddered. He hated moments like this.

"I'm fine." Jaicob averted his eyes. He tried to concentrate on something else—something other than his stomach knotting in on itself.

"Are you sure?" Caileb tried to zip up his bag, but the zipper wouldn't budge. "You've been quiet lately—which was great for a while, but now it's disturbing." He stuffed his things down and tried again. "You haven't cracked a joke or goofed off like you usually do…" He trailed off. The effort of trying to zip the bag took its toll.

Jaicob scooted down the bed and held the two sides of the zipper closed so Caileb could close it.

"Thanks." Caileb picked his bag off the bed. "You haven't even smiled lately."

"You have to ask after what happened to our grandfather? And the Grand Councilwoman? And…" Jaicob's voice caught, cutting his voice off in a squeak. He cleared his throat and tried again. "And… Uncle Marviot? They executed him, Cai. They murdered him! They slaughtered him like an animal."

"That's what happens in a war." Caileb paused to set his bag by the door. "If Uncle Marviot had succeeded in using the Armator, the Outsiders would have been eradicated. Then those who were left would be having this conversation rather than us… if any survived at all."

"Does that make it right? They were invading us!"

"Because Uncle Marviot and the Grand Councilwoman baited them—tried to use their attack as an excuse to test their weapon of mass destruction. That turned on them, didn't it? Uncle Marviot's actions caused hundreds of Expermians to die." Caileb snorted. "And Expermians are treating him like a martyr for it."

Jaicob looked up at his brother—stared him straight in the eyes. "What are you saying? Do you agree with what the Outsiders did?"

"Of course not." Caileb plopped on Jaicob's bed. "They destroyed our capital after we surrendered, tore down every temple and holy place we had, and have completely occupied our city. They could drop dead for all I care."

"Then what are you saying, Caileb?" Jaicob got on his hands and knees to glimpse Caileb closer. "Was Uncle Marviot right in what he did?

Or did the Outsiders do what's right? Should Expermians do everything in our power to rid the world of non-Expermians, or not? And if we do, is it okay to trample on anyone who gets in our way?"

"I don't know!" Caileb buried his face in his hands. "I don't know anything anymore! None of this makes sense! Things have turned completely upside down since the Silver Fox left our borders. I don't know what to think."

Jaicob sat back on his feet. "The Silver Fox has a name, you know," he said in a lower tone.

"I don't think I have the right to use it." Caileb let his hands fall to his lap. "Our family is part of the reason she left, remember? They did terrible things to her, and now she hates us."

Jaicob hung his head. Right before the invasion they had met an actual Silver Fox—a unique type of fox with silver fur and the ability to manipulate electricity. Silver Foxes had been Expermia's saviors in times past. But she came and went, leaving Expermia to the mercy of her enemies. Perhaps she hadn't deemed Expermia worthy to save. And maybe she was right.

"If I hadn't already enlisted…" Caileb started, his voice barely above a whisper. But he didn't finish his thought. Instead in a stronger voice he said, "Doesn't matter. It's too late to change my mind."

"I know what I want to do…" Jaicob gripped his sheets in his fists. "I want to save Expermia from her enemies."

"That's great, Jake." Caileb patted Jaicob's knee. "If that's what you want, you should enlist. I'd be happy to have you with me—like Uncle Marviot was with *Papai*."

Jaicob ducked his head. "There's one thing, though, Caileb…" But he didn't think Caileb heard him over the knock on their door.

Cortraire, their father, walked in without waiting for a response. He stood in the doorway, a tall bastion of strength, never wavering even though those infidel Outsiders had just murdered his brother.

Like all Expermians, Cortraire was a fox with wide ears made to combat the desert heat. Caileb had inherited his brown hair and blond ends from him. Like Marviot had been, Cortraire was a soldier, but he was off-duty at the moment and wore traditional Expermian garb—a tunic with splits up the sides, pants, and boots. Women wore a dress with a similar design and skin-tight pants underneath. Around Cortraire's shoulders were long pieces of cloths called *toagae* pinned in place by decorative pins with his family seal on it—the same seal Marviot wore when he had been alive…

"Caileb, you ready?" Cortraire jerked a thumb over his shoulder. "Your ride's here."

"Hurry and enlist, Jaicob." Caileb slipped off the bed and picked up his bag. "We might be part of the same basic training group if you get it done quickly enough."

Cortraire's eyebrows lifted. "You're enlisting, Jake?"

"Thinking about it," Jaicob said.

"I hope you do." Caileb exited. Jaicob heard his footsteps clopping down the stairs.

"I'd like it if you did enlist, son. You and Caileb are the only ones left who can carry on our family legacy." Cortraire gave Jaicob a smile before walking after Caileb.

"What about you?" Jaicob said, but Cortraire didn't hear him. He leaned back against the headboard and sighed. The silence of being alone descended on him with wet blanket-like consistency, making it hard to breathe. He squirmed before burying his face in his hands.

There was one major problem with his decision to enlist. Sure, he wanted to defend Expermia from her enemies, but he had no idea who those enemies really were.

* * *

By the time Jaicob came downstairs, Caileb had already left. His parents stood in front of the open front door as a twilight breeze blew in from outside, sending the scent of flowers, outdoor cooking, and exhaust fluttering through the house. The entryway opened up to the living room, which had a couch facing the door and a television—now dark with lack of electricity.

"I'm surprised they're letting them go off for orientation." His mother, Annais, had brown hair which turned a shade of pink at the ends. "Aren't the Outsiders afraid an army of new recruits will rise up against them?"

Jaicob ran his hand over his hair as he saw the silhouette of his mother's shining in the occasional car headlights. Both he and Caileb had gotten their hair texture from her. No matter what he did, Jaicob could not get his hair to stop curling up at the ends.

"Their leaders say they're not here for a complete government takeover." Cortraire had his hand around Annais's waist. "They say they want things to remain as normal as possible for Expermia. They claim all they want is our loyalty and for us to pay tribute to the Drymairadian throne."

"What liars!" Annais tapped her elbow. "How can anyone believe such nonsense after they decimated Silver Sait the way they did?"

"True," Cortraire said after a moment of thought. "The way they went about it... it was like they were searching for something."

"I'm surprised we still have a roof over our heads."

"The fighting was concentrated on the capital and its suburbs." Cortraire shifted his grip to stroke the fur on Annais's arm. "Our home survived because we live so far away from it."

"I'm glad you didn't follow your grandmother's advice to build a fancy place in the capital district."

Cortraire chuckled. "My frugality saved our house."

"And your bravery." Annais reached up to kiss him.

Jaicob almost smiled. His parents used every opportunity to slobber all over each other. It was a wonder they didn't have more children. "What are you doing standing at the door?" he said as he approached.

His parents turned, pulling apart as they did.

"Are you okay, my baby boy?" Annais smoothed his hair down.

"I'm fine." Jaicob pushed her hand away.

"Do you want some tea or... I think we have some crackers left." Annais twitched her tail. "Not sure when I'll be able to get more groceries..."

Jaicob nearly chuckled. His mother thought any problem could be cured through food. "I'm not hungry." He plopped down on the couch.

"Do you want me to come with you down to the enlistment office?" Cortraire sat down next to him. "They've got a temporary base set up down by where the capitol building used to be."

"Um..." Jaicob inhaled through his teeth. Stupid Caileb and his big mouth. "I... I don't..."

"It's okay if you don't want to be a soldier, Jaicob." Cortraire clapped his back. "But I... don't want you to get stuck. Life moves on regardless of how sad you are. I want you to lead the way forward after this devastation, not be left behind."

"I understand, *Papai*." Jaicob pressed his hands between his knees. "It's just... I... I don't think Uncle Marviot... I..." His words choked in his throat.

"What do you need to say, Jake?" Cortraire placed a hand on his head. "You can tell me anything."

Jaicob shut his mouth. He couldn't make his words come out. He didn't even know what he wanted to say.

"Oh, my poor Jaicob." Annais hugged his neck over the back of the couch. "You took your uncle's death so hard." She held him tighter, the fur on her arms becoming a warm, soft ball of comfort. "You looked up to Marviot, didn't you?"

At his uncle's name, Jaicob's throat constricted. Uncle Marviot—the one who always went out of his way to spend time with Jaicob; Uncle Marviot—who Jaicob could always count on to cover for him or give him advice or talk Cortraire out of punishing him too hard; Uncle Marviot—who encouraged Jaicob to do anything he set his mind to and who Jaicob loved with all his heart—was gone. And he was never coming back.

Tears welled in his eyes, but Jaicob willed them not to fall. Cortraire had not shed one tear since he had come back from getting Marviot's body from the Outsider's jail. Jaicob wanted to be strong too.

For Cortraire's part, he gazed up at the ceiling with a faraway look in his eye. But suddenly, he brightened. "Jaicob, do you want to come on a trip with me?"

Jaicob turned to his father. "Huh?"

"They cleared Marviot's effects for me to pick up—his and my father's and grandmother's." Cortraire gave him a spectacular smile. "Do you want to come with me to get them?"

For the first time in weeks, the sun burst through the clouds surrounding Jaicob. A trip alone with his father? He couldn't remember ever traveling with Cortraire without Caileb around. "Really? Can I go?"

"If your mother doesn't mind staying by herself."

"My family can come over so the house won't be empty." Annais clasped her hands. "It'll be a chance to spend time with them. I haven't seen them since the invasion."

"This will give us some man-to-man bonding time, and give us a chance to talk about things." Cortraire patted Jaicob's shoulder. "What do you say?"

Jaicob nearly bounced to the ceiling. "Sure, I'll go!"

"It's settled, then." Cortraire smacked Jaicob on the knee. "I'm leaving at sunrise, so be ready. We'll be staying at least one night... maybe more... so pack a bag. I'll get a message to your family come tomorrow, Annais."

"I'd appreciate it," she said.

Jaicob jumped up and darted to his room to pack. He hadn't been this excited to go on a trip since their parents took him and Caileb to the Alwoody World amusement park when they were kits.

* * *

Jaicob tossed his bag in the back of his father's jeep and collapsed in the passenger seat. His parents always took a long time to say goodbye to each other, and their farewells involved a fair bit of smooching on each other. Jaicob didn't mind. It comforted him to know his parents enjoyed each other's company so much. But it didn't mean he had to watch.

He tapped a beat on the car door and looked around. Although Silver Sait, Expermia's capital, had been demolished, his neighborhood had escaped relatively unscathed. Apart from the increased amount of non-Expermian soldiers in olive and brown uniforms, the increased amount of displaced survivors from the city, and the abundance of military vehicles, it was all the same. The morning sun tinted the palms and fruit trees, as well as the golden colored stucco on the house, pink. Cool morning air blew through his fur. In a few hours the sun would heat things up to normal desert temperatures, but for now it was pleasant to be out here with the scent of BomBase tickling his nose. Strange how things could feel so normal and so weird at the same time.

Cortraire emerged from the house with Annais beside him. He kissed her again before heading to the car. Jaicob smirked. Cortraire's lips had been tinted red. He decided not to let Cortraire in on it.

"Goodbye, my dear." Annais kissed Jaicob on the top of his head. "Have a good time."

"Are you sure you're going to be alright, Mushi?" Cortraire paused at the door to the car. "I'm not sure I like you staying alone in these circumstances even for a little bit."

Jaicob didn't hear her response. A soldier—a bear—strode down the street with two of his companions. He turned, smiled, and lifted a hand in greeting.

Jaicob's hands clenched in a fist. The soldier was an Outsider, like the ones who murdered his uncle. How dare he act so casually? Greet them like it was nothing? An incredible urge to vault out of the car, snatch his weapon, and spray them all with laser fire seized Jaicob. "Wipe them out before they get you," Uncle Marviot would say. "Destroy them before they destroy Expermia."

But… what good would that do? Jaicob let his hand relax. Even if he did manage to tackle a trained soldier and steal his weapon, the rest would surround him and shoot him to the ground. Then Cortraire would have to bury him like he had buried Marviot. Besides, it wasn't as if that specific soldier had executed Marviot. He might not have done anything to deserve dying…

"All Outsiders deserve to die or serve us," Marviot had told him once. "They are beneath us, rejects of the gods. Nothing good can ever come from them." And every teacher, news report, and television show had told Jaicob the same. But, if Jaicob was honest with himself, something had never clicked. Did that guy—the solder right there, who probably had a family and kids—deserve to die because he was born outside of Expermia? Uncle Marviot had murdered the Silver Fox's father because he was an Outsider. So was that right? And if Outsiders were rejects of the gods, why did the gods allow Outsiders to live in the first place? And had allowed an Outsider fox to father a Silver Fox? Why did the gods let the Outsiders demolish Expermia? No, something wasn't right with this line of thinking. Could it be... Uncle Marviot was *wrong*?

The idea caught all his attention so that he didn't even notice Cortraire get in the car and start the engine. He continued chewing on this thought as the car reversed down the driveway and took off down the road.

* * *

Jaicob couldn't stay in his pensive mood for long. He was on his first trip alone with his father—no Caileb or Annais to steal Cortraire's attention. They chatted about this and that and laughed till their sides hurt. Jaicob even loved the lulls they had in their conversations—just him and his dad traveling. He didn't want this trip to end.

A few hours in, Cortraire pulled up to the Expermian border. An automatic rising barrier had blocked off the road and a wire fence ran a few miles in either direction until it and the constant military surveillance petered out. Technically, anyone could cross the border into Expermia where there were no fences and no soldiers to stop them, but no one did. Any Outsiders who attempted it would die of thirst trying. And no Expermian in their right mind would leave without proper permission. Well, almost none. Jaicob knew of two who had... but neither of them were in their right minds when they left. Either way, he and Cortraire had no reason to leave Expermia... right?

"*Papai*, where'd you say we were going to pick up Uncle Marv's stuff?" At the mention of his uncle's name, the storm of emotions Jaicob had been living under for the past few weeks descended on him again.

"Drymairad."

Jaicob turned to his father, eyes wide. "We're leaving the country?"

"Don't tell your mother." Cortraire winked at him.

Jaicob grinned through his melancholy. A surreptitious trip outside of Expermia would make any teenager smile.

"You've never been outside of Expermia, have you?" Cortraire said, pulling up to the security check point.

"Once." Jaicob gazed at the guardhouse set up beside the road. There were Expermian soldiers manning the place, but Outsiders watched them work, hands on their weapons. "Uncle Marviot got a tip where Hairo was located and took Caileb and me to look for him."

"So he took you out of the country?" Cortraire snorted through his nose. "Marviot never tells me anything."

Jaicob gazed at his father. Cortraire spoke about his brother as if he were still alive. Maybe the realization Marviot wasn't coming back hadn't hit him yet. Could be why he didn't act as lost as Jaicob felt.

An Expermian soldier walked up to the car. "Lieutenant Cortraire. Where are you headed?"

"Kingston, Drymairad. To pick up my family's effects."

"Ah, yes." The soldier glanced at the Outsiders before lowering his voice. "I'm sorry about your loss—especially about Captain Cunor. He was… he… he was the voice of the people, you know. A true hero of Expermia who died protecting our ideals."

Cortraire gave a slight nod. "I appreciate it. Thank you."

Jaicob concentrated to keep his ears from falling back.

"I hear your sons will join the army too."

"Caileb is off to officer's orientation. General orientation's in two weeks, but we'll be back in time for Jaicob to go…" Cortraire clapped his hand on Jaicob's shoulder. "If he wants to."

"You should." The soldier leaned in to speak to Jaicob. "Two more Cunors in the army will rally the people's hopes and extend Captain Cunor's legacy. You are the future of what all true Expermians will look like."

Jaicob forced a smile. "Yes, sir."

The soldier nodded in approval and lifted the barrier. Cortraire drove through.

Jaicob hung his head. Marviot, a hero of Expermia, huh? And him, the future of what true Expermians looked like? Well, what if Jaicob didn't want to follow in Marviot's footsteps? Did that make him a bad Expermian? A bad Cunor? Or worse—he glanced at Cortraire, so full of pride for his brother—a bad son?

Maybe it did. Jaicob rested his head on the jeep's window. He wanted to curl up in a ball and wail, but he couldn't. He had to be strong—like his father. He had to be a Cunor. Even if he didn't want to be.

* * *

Though Jaicob had been to Drymairad before, he'd never seen anything like its capital, Kingston. Marviot had taken him to a city called New Jelu, and the area he had gone to was more like a dirt hole in the ground, filled with graffiti and trash and dirt-covered buildings. But this place—this capital—there was nothing like it in Expermia. Buildings stretched into the sky, towering over the streets and sparkling with the sun glinting off steel and windows—not at all like the golden-brown clay stuccoed buildings of Expermia. The structures stood so tall over the car, the sun couldn't reach Jaicob at street level. In Expermia, the buildings rarely stood higher than five stories.

But it suffered from a severe lack of decoration. All the buildings had straight sides stretching to the sky. He did spot a statue here or there, nestled in the middle of a park, but nothing spectacular. In contrast, protective guardian statues overlaid with a silvery material stood guard on the roofs and outer walls of every Expermian structure built. Or they had, before Outsiders had destroyed Silver Sait. Jaicob's ears fell at the thought, but jerked his mind off the topic. Instead he watched all the people go by. So many people of different species rushed down the sidewalks or clogged the streets with their hover cars. The amount of individuals on this block alone rivalled the entire population of Silver Sait congregating in the square on a festival day. And most of these people weren't foxes. There were so many variety of species living in the city.

If Marviot had had his way, they'd all be enslaved or dead by now. Jaicob threw himself back in his seat. It didn't seem fair—to try to eliminate all those people because of their species and nationality. Yet Marviot was the prime example of an Expermian—a Cunor of Cunors. How could Jaicob claim to be Expermian if he didn't believe the way Marviot did? How could he be a soldier and defend Expermia if he didn't share those ideals? And how could he claim to love his uncle if he didn't partake in Marviot's most fundamental beliefs?

Jaicob squeezed his eyes shut. All those feelings and thoughts jumbled up inside of his brain, making it feel bloated and raw. He wanted to scream and rage or cry and sob or jump out of the car and destroy everything in his path, Expermian or not.

"You alright, Jake?" Cortraire's voice cut through the jumble.

Jaicob pulled himself together. Now wasn't the time to lose it. "I'm fine."

Cortraire stared at him out of the corner of his eyes. "Jaicob, it's time we had a talk—"

"I'm fine, *Papai*. I don't need to talk."

"Jaicob—"

Jaicob flipped on the radio and turned it up. Cortraire narrowed his eyes but didn't comment further, though Jaicob knew he was going to get it later. Didn't matter. As long as he didn't have to admit to his father what a lousy Expermian he was turning into. There was time to change his own mind... to force himself to be what his country wanted him to be. To be the hero Expermia needed in the absence of Marviot...

A male voice singing an upbeat tune drifted out of the radio. Jaicob turned his attention to it. They rarely aired singing over the radio waves in Expermia. It was a catchy tune, setting Jaicob's feet tapping through his chaotic emotions raging inside.

"Is this for a festival or something?" Jaicob turned to Cortaire.

Cortraire didn't answer at first but trained his ears to the radio. "I think it's a concert... oh, yes! Look." He pointed with his chin to a billboard high above the road. It featured a male wolf playing a guitar. He wore a shirt unbuttoned so his chest was exposed. The copy read, "Jarbon! In concert. Two shows; two nights only! Simulcast live on channel 157 and WVBA 54.8 radio."

Jaicob gazed at the billboard as they drove by. "What's a concert?" he asked as the song ended and cheers erupted from the speakers.

"It's a place Outsiders go to hear someone sing."

"So... it *is* a festival."

"Not exactly." Cortraire paused to choose his words. "Concerts don't always correspond to a holiday. You have to pay to hear the artist sing live and in person. It's entertainment."

"Oh." Jaicob nodded as he considered his father's words. "It's not a bad idea. There are tons of people I'd pay to hear sing back in Expermia."

Cortraire chuckled.

A new song started on the radio—this one slower than the last. Jaicob closed his eyes. Jarbon's voice was pleasant, and though he'd never pay to go hear it, he could understand why other people would. He seemed to be singing about some girl who kept hurting him but to whom he kept declaring his love. The chorus went:

No matter what you do
No matter how much you've hurt me
You know my love is true
And I will never desert you.
Our bond is unbreakable
Our love is unshakeable
I will always be yours
And you will always be my baby.

It was nice, but Jaicob was ready to tune out. After all, the guitar break between the chorus and the next verse was far too long for his taste. Plus, he liked a more organic feel to his music—the sound of hollow drums along with the melancholy hoot of the wood whistle... throaty voices singing like the winds howling over sand dunes. In short, Expermian music. A music so filled with variation, you could never hear the same song the same way twice. Songs like big, twisted BomBase trees—majestic, beautiful, no two branches the same. The music blasting over the radio was too practiced and perfect—polished, in a word. Like the straight, tall buildings of their city. Clean, perfect, and uniform. Stunning... impressive, but not Jaicob's thing.

But then, a high, rather shaky note sailed out of the speakers. It was a female's voice—the most powerful voice he'd ever heard in his life. It trembled at first... stumbled over a few words, and was flat at times... but it gained more strength and confidence as it sang about restrictive rules and unfair decisions the male voice had forced on her. When she got to the chorus, both voices sang in harmony. But the female's voice reversed the pronouns in the last two lines, singing, "You will always be mine, and I will always be your baby."

Jaicob's breath caught as he listened. Her voice roared with emotion—frustration, anger, rage, confusion, love... It was like she knew exactly what he was feeling—all his jumbled emotions, all his conflict, all—

The voice shut off.

Jaicob jerked his head around. Cortraire had the car keys in his hands.

"We're here," Cortraire said to Jaicob's questioning face. "We have to check in."

At once, Jaicob's heart sank. "Is there where we're picking up Uncle Marviot's stuff?"

"It's too late to go there. This is a hotel. We'll get his things tomorrow afternoon."

Jaicob swallowed the lump welling up in his throat. He didn't think he could handle facing the people responsible for his uncle's death. "*Papai*, do I have to go?"

Cortraire studied him a moment before saying, "Not if you don't want to." He got out of the car. "You can stay in the hotel room if you want."

"Then I will." Jaicob followed Cortraire as he led him into the lobby. He didn't say a word for the rest of the night.

* * *

"I'll be back, Jake." Cortraire opened the door to the hotel room. It wasn't terribly big—enough room for two full beds with a night table between them, a TV set on a dresser, and a bathroom to the left coming in. But the view out the window was spectacular. It overlooked the entire city, and Jaicob found he could see Drymairad's palace at the center of it. The afternoon sun gleamed off of all the glass in the city and sparkled like the starlit sky Jaicob had seen in the Expermian desert the time Uncle Marviot took him camping.

Cortraire tapped the doorframe. "Are you sure you don't want to come?"

"No, but can I walk around the city a bit?" A creeping tendril squeezed around Jaicob's heart. "Or is it safer to stay in here?"

"It's fine to walk around. But be smart—the same way you would be at home. Don't go far, though. It's easy to get lost. Keep your phone on, and don't lock yourself out of the room."

"Okay, *Papai*." Jaicob watched Cortraire leave. He remained on the bed a while, flipping through the channels until he found some music. He wanted to hear the voice again, but he couldn't seem to find it. Maybe if he knew the name of the song...

He pulled out his phone and tapped in as much of the song lyrics as he could remember. The little loading ball spun and spun without showing any signs of stopping.

After five minutes of watching it, Jaicob slammed his fist on the bed. "Stupid phone! What's wrong with it?" He flung his head back to gaze at the ceiling. "Maybe there's a music store around." In Expermia, they had recordings of some of the best festival singers in stores for people to buy. And since Outsiders liked to sing at the drop of a hat, they must have recordings to sell too.

He popped into the bathroom, washed his face, brushed his teeth and fur, and made sure his clothes were presentable, before heading out, being sure he had the hotel keycard and his phone. After riding the elevator to the ground floor, he darted across the lobby and out of the hotel.

He halted as he stepped out into the street. He had forgotten how big and crowded this place was. With a deep breath, he joined the sea of people rushing down the sidewalk. Most of them stared at him as he passed—probably because of his wide ears and Expermian garb. Jaicob watched them out of the corner of his eyes too—alert to any sudden moves they made or movement to reach for hidden weapons or implements of torture. It's funny, but he'd never been so paranoid before. When he had gone to Jelu with Marviot, he'd come with his brother and the soldiers his uncle was working with. Marviot had warned him and Caileb about how dubious and duplicitous Outsiders could be, and cautioned them never to be alone in the midst of them and to watch each other's backs. He and Caileb had followed his orders. Plus, Jaicob knew if anything happened, Uncle Marviot would come to their rescue. He'd never let anything bad happen to them.

But this time he was on his own in this new city, in direct opposition to his uncle's warnings flashing in his mind with crushing severity. If the Outsiders decided to get together and jump him, there was nothing he could do about it—like there was nothing Uncle Marviot could do when they decided to execute him.

Jaicob slowed to a halt, his body trembling and his heart pounding. What was he doing out here, putting himself in danger like this? He must be mad. He should turn right around, go back to the hotel, and wait for his father. It's what Uncle Marviot would want him to do. And right now, in the midst of these strange animals, it seemed the most prudent thing...

As Jaicob turned to trek back to the hotel, his eyes caught a music store a few shops down. At once the songstress's voice rang through his memory. That voice—that Outsider—knew what he was feeling, and Jaicob had to hear her again. Since the music store was right there, he might as well take a chance. But no taking risks. He'd get in and get out. Jaicob nodded with decision and walked in.

The store had three stories of music and video holodisks all stacked on shelves. There were hundreds—thousands of songs here. How would he find the one tune he was looking for? Go to a store clerk and ask for help, of course. Simple enough. He glanced to the counter. A tiger in a store uniform manned the register, his claws glistening as he flipped through a music catalogue.

Jaicob lost his nerve. "Outsiders are unpredictable and violent," Uncle Marviot had said, so it was better to not mess with them anymore than necessary. He'd already made a stupid enough decision coming in here.

Jaicob wandered the front of the store trying to decide where to start looking for the song. Televisions mounted on walls all over showcased videos of people singing, but only one song blared over the store radio. He listened for a few beats, but it was nothing to interest him so he tuned out. Cardboard cutouts of various singers and bands separated the more popular singers from their bland counterparts. One of the largest was a green bird of indeterminate species in a sparkling orange outfit. "Jessica! Fabulous Island Tour!" was written across her feet.

A few aisles down he saw a cutout of the wolf—Jarbon. He had his guitar again and smiled a toothy grin at Jaicob. *Strange,* Jaicob thought as he rushed to his display, *he looks friendly.* There were dozens of albums, singles, and EPs here—each resting in three inch square containers with various pictures of the singer on the front. Jaicob sighed. It would take him ages to search through each of them—especially since he didn't know the song title. But down the aisle stood another display with a rather ingenious feature, Jaicob thought. It had headphones with buttons labelled with different song titles.

Jaicob scanned through the names until he landed on "Always Be Mine." Such a title could match the lyrics swirling in Jaicob's head, so he put on the headphones, ignoring Uncle Marviot's mental warnings about Outsider diseases, and pushed the button.

That was it! That was the song! He listened, tapping his foot in anticipation for the female vocalist's part. He couldn't wait until her voice rang in his ears again. There was the guitar break between the chorus and the verse—much shorter than it had been during the concert. And now came the girl's voice…

Jaicob's ears flicked back. This wasn't right. It was a female vocalist, but not the one he'd heard over the radio. Sure, this voice was pretty and much better at keeping the tune than the one he'd heard, but it lacked the emotion and inflection which had so captured Jaicob's attention.

He sighed and set the headphones down. Maybe it was one of those voices that didn't record well—the type you had to hear live… like at one of those concert things! Jaicob would definitely pay to hear her voice again.

Jaicob rushed onto the street. There were two shows if he remembered right. Maybe he had a chance to hear her again. If only he could find the billboard… yes! There it was. Not the same one, but it had the right information. And it said there was a 6:00 show at the Drymairad Grand Concert Hall. He could go and pay to hear her sing. Just once. Just to get it out of his system.

He plugged the name of the hall into his phone, and… nothing. The loading ball kept spinning.

"What is wrong with you? Don't tell me you hate Outsiders too!" Jaicob thrust his phone into his pocket. Okay, plan B. He glanced around for a newsstand and found one at the street corner. Without looking at the cat behind the counter, he bought a map of the city and spread it open. The concert hall was ten miles away. Quite a trek but nothing Jaicob hadn't done before, what with Uncle Marviot insisting his nephews keep in tip-top shape. He should make it to the concert on time. With a grin, Jaicob headed off toward the hall. Time to hear that sweet voice again.

* * *

By the time Jaicob made it to the concert hall, he was panting and winded. His ears tingled, and he felt his heartbeat in them as blood pumped through the veins, trying to cool him down. One glance at his phone told him the concert had already started. He trotted to the box office hoping he hadn't missed her song. He should have taken a taxi or something, but all of Uncle Marviot's warnings rushed to the surface of his mind, and he shuddered at the thought of being trapped alone in a confined space with an Outsider.

The concert hall covered five times as much space as the buildings surrounding it—in fact, it was its own block—and stood three stories high. The entrance stood a good 100 feet from the street and sidewalk, allowing plenty of space for people to line up. And finally, Jaicob found a building with the decorations he had been missing. Artisans had carved men and women of all species into the marble façade. They acted or sang or danced in glorious procession across the wall. Banners advertising Jarbon's concert hung on poles set at the corners of the building and from wires above the main entrance. Stanchions separated the wide space between the street and the box office into lines. And all these lines were empty. Lucky break. Jaicob approached the otter sitting behind thick, strong glass. At least she couldn't jump out to get him.

"E-excuse me." Jaicob cleared his throat to steady his voice. "I'd like a ticket please."

The otter stared at him a moment before bursting into laughter. Jaicob gazed at her. Did they not sell tickets to Expermians? It would make sense. Expermians wouldn't sell tickets to Outsiders, after all…

"Oh, sweetie, were you serious?" the otter asked, sobering.

Jaicob nodded. "But if you don't want to sell it to me…"

"Oh, no, honey. This concert's been sold out for weeks." She pointed to a "SOLD OUT" sign in the window Jaicob had been too excited to notice. "Even the scalpers are sold out. Jarbon's even bigger than Jessica."

Jaicob had no idea who Jessica was, but he did recall the name on the cardboard cutout in the music store. "So I can't buy a ticket at all?"

"'Fraid not. Even yesterday's concert was sold out a month in advance."

Jaicob felt his heart crash to his feet and explode in little pieces. He muttered a thanks and backed away. So that was it. After all this, it had come to nothing. Everything he loved or wanted came to nothing... this concert, Expermia, and... and Uncle Marviot. Stumbling around the corner, he collapsed against the wall and burst into tears. Disappointment over missing the concert, anger at Marviot's execution, the destruction of his beloved capital city, and all his jumbled feelings about Outsiders and Expermia's response to them came rushing out like a flood. But mostly, he cried for Marviot... the kind uncle he had been to Jaicob, the ruthless murderer he had been to Outsiders, and the conflict Jaicob had reconciling the two. He slid down the side of the building, ducked his head between his knees, and bawled his heart out. To this day, he didn't know why security didn't catch him and force him to move along. Maybe they saw this pathetic, heartbroken Expermian creature weeping his soul out and had pity on him.

* * *

"Um, Excuse me. Are you okay?"

Jaicob had no idea how long he had been sitting on the floor before he heard a soft voice call out to him. He looked up and came face to face with a brown female wolf with a light patch over one eye. Her brown hair hung down her back in large, bouncy curls, and her green eyes bored right through him. She had one hand in her purse as if reaching for something.

The first thought which crossed Jaicob's mind when he saw her was, "Cute!" followed closely by, "But she's not Expermian. She's not even a fox!"

Jaicob wiped his eyes and turned away. He didn't need to have thoughts like this—not now. "I'm fine," he said.

"Are you sure?" She didn't move her hand from her purse. "You're not hurt or anything?"

"I'm bummed I couldn't get in to see the concert." Jaicob wiped his nose with the end of his *toaga*.

The girl slipped her hand out of her purse to put it on her hip. "You're out here bawling because you couldn't get a ticket?"

"That's about the size of it." Jaicob had to chuckle. It sounded more pathetic saying it out loud than it did in his head. But it was over now. Soon he'd have to gather the courage to go back to the hotel. Even as he thought this, he knew it was impossible. His inner strength had left him. He couldn't face his father without knowing where he stood as an Expermian and a Cunor. And he certainly couldn't go back home in this state. He had no strength left to fake it. He was spent.

"Here." The wolf held something out to him. The sudden movement made Jaicob jump, but it was only a travel size pack of tissues.

Jaicob blinked at them. What sort of Outsider trick was this? But he reached out and took one anyway. "Thanks." He blew his nose.

"Now I know Jarbon is a great singer." She slid on the floor beside him. "But I never heard of anyone carrying on like this because they missed a concert."

Jaicob gazed at her. Her dress brushed the top of her knees leaving her legs exposed, and they were shapely and—

He turned away from her. He shouldn't be having thoughts like this about an Outsider. "It wasn't him exactly. There was a song I wanted to hear. I tried getting a recording of it, but it didn't sound right. So I came to hear it in person."

"Which song?"

"What was the name of it again…" Jaicob turned his eyes to the darkening sky, trying to picture the display with the song's title. "'Forever Mine' or something."

"Forever mine…" The girl screwed up her nose making her snout wrinkle. "Do you mean 'Always be Mine'… the song that goes… 'No matter what you do, no matter how much you've hurt me'…" she continued to sing the chorus.

Jaicob's mouth dropped open. It was the voice—the sound he had heard from the radio, though this time her voice didn't tremble, and she kept the tune better. A smile broke through the fog surrounding him. He turned to her and sang the guy's part in harmony with her.

"I take it that *is* the right song," she said with a giggle when they had finished. "You have a nice voice."

"So do you. It's beautiful." Jaicob smiled when she blushed. "But I don't understand why you are out here while the concert's going. Shouldn't you be on stage?"

"I don't sing. Not on stage, anyway. In the shower, maybe."

"But I heard your voice last night. They streamed the concert on the radio. I came here 'cause I had to hear you sing in person. Your recorded voice sounds nothing like your live one."

The girl blinked at him. Suddenly, her face darkened. "This is why I didn't want to sing on stage," she muttered. "I don't want fans to mob me where ever I go."

"Technically, I'm not a fan," Jaicob said.

The girl raised an eyebrow. "You were bawling because you couldn't get in to hear me sing."

"Point taken." Jaicob raised a finger. "But I didn't mob you. You came up to me."

"Touché. Yesterday was a special case. The vocalist that usually sings the song with Jarbon lost her voice last minute, and I got roped into doing it."

"I see."

"Personally, I think it was a trick. My dad's always wanted me to sing on stage with him. As you can tell, Nina's fine now." She turned her gaze to the concert hall.

If Jaicob strained, he could just hear the beat of the music coming from inside. But he didn't care to hear. The voice he wanted was out here with him. "Did you say he was your dad?"

The wolf pulled out her phone from her purse. "See?" She showed him a picture of herself and Jarbon posing on a beach somewhere.

"Wow," Jaicob said, more about the location than the subject of the photo. He'd never seen a beach before. But if he had thought about it, he could have guessed Jarbon was this girl's father. It was all over the song's lyrics. "I didn't need to come all the way out here, then. I wouldn't have heard you anyway. And it explains why the recording was so different."

"Why were you so upset about not hearing me sing?" She put her phone back in her purse. "My performance last night wasn't great. I was flat in ten places, and I was so nervous my voice kept warbling and breaking. I even missed my cue to start."

"Because I could tell you meant it. I could feel your emotions when you sang. I'm not surprised to hear that's your dad because it matches the lyrics so perfectly. Listening to the song was like was eavesdropping on you and your dad having a conversation—"

"Yes! That's it exactly!" The girl caught Jaicob's hands. "My dad and I wrote that song together. It's all about how even though I might do stupid things and get in trouble and even though he's overbearing, overprotective, and snoops into my private life on a regular basis, that we love each other. He'll always be my dad, and I'll always be his baby girl. Most people think it's a song about a boyfriend and a girlfriend—which is creepy when you listen to the lyrics. You're the first person I've met who *gets* it."

Jaicob decided not to mention he had no idea what the terms "boyfriend" and "girlfriend" meant. "It was obvious to me."

"So… sorry, I interrupted you. What about the song resonated with you? Having problems with your parents?"

"My uncle." Jaicob hung his head. "He was murd—he died a few weeks ago."

"I'm sorry to hear that."

"Don't be." Jaicob's ears angled back. "He was a lying, cheating, murderous, son of a mother, and he deserved to be—" He clapped his hands over his mouth. Did those words just come out his mouth?

The girl stared at him a moment. "He... wasn't that bad, was he?"

Jaicob pulled his hands from his mouth. "From your point of view, he was worse."

"Oh." The girl furrowed her brows.

"But I loved him." Jaicob found his tears returning. "He was a good uncle to me and my brother. He'd do anything for us. I—I couldn't figure out how I could hate what he was about and love him all at once... not till I heard your song—not until I knew I wasn't the only one who had those jumbled feelings."

"I'm glad it helped you out, then."

"I should go." Jaicob climbed to his feet, his strength returning to him. "My dad's going to be worried, and I have a long way to go." He reached down to help her up. It wasn't until she took his hand that he realized what he had done.

"I should leave too." She brushed off the back of her dress. "The concert's letting out soon, and I want to get out of here before the fan mobbing starts. People get crazy when they see him, and if they find out I'm his daughter..." She shuddered.

Jaicob winced. He could picture a mob swarming this girl who would be helpless to stop the relentless torrent. He couldn't leave her all by herself—even if she was an Outsider. "Are you going to be okay when that happens?"

"Sure." She pulled a black object from her purse. "I carry a stun."

That explained why she had her hand in her purse when she had first talked to him. She was compassionate but no fool. Jaicob liked that. "It occurred to me, I never asked you your name."

"It's Mira."

"I'm Jaicob."

"It's nice to meet you, Jaicob." Mira shook his hand.

"Nice to meet you too, Mira." Jaicob's ears stood on end as the words came out of his mouth. It wasn't just a polite statement. It *had* been nice to meet her—pleasant talking to her... even if she was an Outsider. And their meeting hadn't ended in violence or anger. Not every Outsider was out to get him. Marviot had been wrong.

At the realization, a weight ascended from Jaicob's shoulders. His old self rose through the depression which had been sitting on his chest for weeks. He grinned at Mira as his heart lightened. "It is time to bid you adieu, Mira, my golden-throated angel." He bowed to kiss her hand.

"Oh, wow!" Mira chuckled as she placed her free hand on her heart. "This is flattering, Jaicob, but I have a boyfriend."

Again, Jaicob had no idea what the term meant. "Doesn't matter," he said. "I'll never see you again." He pressed her hand in both of his. "But I will never forget you."

Mira smiled at him.

Jaicob released her hand and bowed with a flourish before heading off down the sidewalk. He had a long walk ahead of him back to the hotel—but, wait. He stopped in his tracks. Why walk? If Marviot had been wrong about one Outsider, he could have been wrong about all of them.

Jaicob trotted to the side of the street and hailed a cab. When the driver stopped, Jaicob hopped in without hesitation. After all, taxi drivers in Expermia did their jobs without incident, so why wouldn't Outsiders? Apart from their looks, what made them so different from Expermians?

After pondering this question a moment, Jaicob couldn't think of a good answer. And that made his smile widen.

* * *

"Jaicob, where have you been?" Cortraire rushed to the door as soon as Jaicob walked into the hotel room. "I've been worried sick! And why wouldn't you answer your phone?"

"My phone hasn't been working since we got here." Jaicob pulled his phone out of his pocket. "The loading ball just spins."

Cortraire stared at him, his brows furrowing. "That's right!" He smacked his forehead. "Your phone's region locked. It won't work outside of Expermia. I forgot to get you a temporary one."

"Mystery solved, then." Jaicob shoved it back into his pocket.

"Where did you go?" Cortraire's ears were flat on his skull. "I said you could walk around, not disappear for half a day!"

Jaicob flopped on his bed. "To a concert."

"A concert?" Cortraire's ears stood up. "You're really taken with the artist we heard on the radio yesterday, aren't you?"

"Yeah." Jaicob decided not to try and explain. Living through it had exhausted him enough. "But I'm over it now."

Cortraire sank on his bed. "Did you have fun?"

"Couldn't get in. Tickets were sold out."

"Sorry to hear that."

"No worries."

Cortraire leaned to the side to pull his phone from his back pocket. "Your mother was trying to text you."

"How?" Jaicob turned to his father. "Did they get the power back on in Expermia?"

"I got her phone charged at the base before I left—in case of emergencies—but I guess she missed having us around. She hasn't stopped calling." Cortraire sighed. "I'm glad I don't have to tell her I lost you in an Outsider country."

"I thought we weren't going to mention it to her."

"It came up when I said I couldn't find you." Cortraire ran his hand across his forehead. "She's going to chew me out when we get home."

Jaicob chuckled as he watched Cortraire text his mother. "What about Uncle Marviot's stuff? Did you get it?"

"It was probably best you didn't come." Cortraire continued texting, a frown deepening on his lips. "It was a sad experience."

Jaicob bit his lips together. It was time. Time to tell his father what he thought—the ideas he couldn't express to him when he had been sitting on the couch after Caileb left. It was time to find out if Jaicob was secretly an Expermian traitor. "*Papai*, can I tell you something?"

"You can tell me anything, Jake," Cortraire said, eyes still on the phone.

Jaicob took a deep breath even as his stomach knotted. He swallowed past the lump in his throat and dove in. "Uncle Marviot was wrong, *Papai*."

"About what?"

"A lot of things. Things you agree with; things you disagree with…" Jaicob hung his head. "Things I can't ever tell you about."

Cortraire raised his head, his phone sinking to his lap. "Okay…"

"He was wrong, and…" Jaicob's voice caught. He cleared his throat. "… and… he deserved… to be executed."

Cortraire froze, his brows knitted. He looked at Jaicob as if he had… well, as if he had just told him Marviot deserved to be executed.

Jaicob plunged on before he lost his nerve. "He wanted to annihilate entire species because it fit his agenda—and he nearly succeeded. I don't care who you are, that's wrong! If any Outsider tried to do that to us, we'd execute them without a second thought. And rightly so. We can't change the rules because they're not Expermians. He and anyone who agrees with him are wrong, and it's right to stop them." He paused to pant down a few breaths. "But just because he was wrong, it doesn't mean I didn't love him. It doesn't mean he wasn't my favorite uncle. And it doesn't mean I don't miss him like crazy." He clenched his teeth in an effort not to weep again. He barely succeeded. "I loved him, but I won't follow his legacy. I can't. Not in good conscience." He hung his head and waited. Waited for the outrage, the disappointment, the accusations of betrayal.

Instead there was silence. Cortraire watched Jaicob for a good five minutes before he sighed. "Jaicob, I agree with what you said."

Jaicob jerked his head up. "You do?"

"But you're braver than me." Cortraire gazed out of the window. "I'd never say it out loud. I'd be too afraid people would think I was betraying his legacy." He fell silent for a few moments. When he spoke it was in a soft voice, "I love my brother—he's the only one in my family who ever thought I would amount to anything and didn't think I was a stain on the Cunor name. Even now, people think I don't deserve the name. But Marviot's ideas aren't good for the country; they aren't good for anyone."

Jaicob let a smile overtake his face. "That's why I'm going to be a soldier."

"Hm?" Cortraire turned to Jaicob. "You said you didn't want to follow in Marviot's footsteps."

"I don't. But I want to defend Expermia from all her enemies— foreign *and* domestic. I'll do what's best for her without following someone else's agenda. I'll make it a safe place for the Silver Fox to return to, a place she'll deem worthy of saving the next time she comes." Jaicob looked into Cortraire's eyes. "In short, I want to be like you, *Papai.*"

Cortraire gazed at Jaicob before breaking out in a grin. He clapped Jaicob on the back and pulled him into a hug. "That's my boy," he said.

* * *

Annais had words for both Cortraire and Jaicob when they returned home. She had words and words and words on top of words. The end result was, Jaicob was grounded for two weeks, and Cortraire… Jaicob was pretty sure he had been "grounded" too, but had gotten time off for "good behavior."

The only place she allowed Jaicob to go was to the temporary military base to enlist and pick up his uniform. And there it hung—a black jacket, navy pants, and a blue shirt—on the peg in his wall like a trophy. The jacket's right sleeve had a white band around it with "Cunor" stitched on it which designated him as a Civilian Soldier. Other than the band, his uniform had no decoration—no medals or distinctions. He had to earn them himself. Jaicob loved staring at it, imagining the places he could go and the things he could do to earn his stripes.

Caileb returned home on a warm night—though all nights started warm in the desert. Jaicob lay in bed tossing a ball in the air, bouncing it off the ceiling, and catching it. No electricity meant no TV and no games, and it was too late to go anywhere while the curfew the Outsiders had enacted was in effect—but that didn't matter since he was grounded. Jaicob groaned at the thought of one more week of quiet boredom, the candlelight dancing on his walls the only source of light and entertainment.

"Hey, Jake." Caileb walked into the room, dressed in the same uniform Jaicob had hanging on the wall. But with one difference.

"Stripe!" Jaicob yelled at the top of his lungs, pointing at a blue stripe right on Caileb's front pocket.

The sudden outburst made Caileb jump. He glanced down at his pocket. "Oh, yeah. It marks me as an officer-in-training when I officially join at general orientation."

"We." Jaicob pointed to his uniform hanging on the wall. "No fancy stripe for me yet, though."

"You decided to enlist?"

Jaicob nodded. "I had time to think about things while you were gone. I sorted myself out."

"I see that." Caileb started to unpack his bag. "You're back to your old self."

"Did you have a chance to think about things too?"

Caileb nodded. "Glad I decided to stick with being a soldier."

"That's good." Jaicob watched him a moment. He and Caileb were brothers like Uncle Marviot and Cortraire. He wondered, did they have moments like this—when they talked about anything—or times when they wrestled each other to the ground till one of them caved? Probably.

"Hey, Cai," Jaicob sat up to see him better in the golden, flickering light.

"Hm?"

"Promise me something."

"What?"

"Promise you won't follow in Uncle Marv's footsteps."

Caileb looked at him.

Jaicob played with the ball in his hands. "I don't want to have to bury you like *Papai* had to bury him."

"That's not going to happen." Caileb returned to his unpacking, tossing his dirty things in the hamper. "I'm not going to touch any of what he was involved with. I'm not stupid."

Jaicob nodded with approval.

"Besides, you're the older one, not me. By two full minutes." Caileb smirked. "And you've got his name, Jaicob Marviot Cunor."

"I'm not going to do anything stupid either." Jaicob laid back down. "And even if I did, I wouldn't get caught."

"Don't take the risk, Jaicob." Caileb zipped his bag.

Jaicob studied his brother out of the corner of his eye—always worried about him; always taking care of him. Like Uncle Marviot had taken care of Cortraire. "Cai, you're a good brother. And when you have kids, I'll be a good uncle to them."

"I already know that, Jake," Caileb said, plopping on his bed.

Jaicob grinned and returned to tossing his ball.

The Canine Government versus the Getran Empire of United Simians! The jungle planet Blackroot is the scene of battle between the Canines and the Apes. Corporal Rylan Charon leads his squad to escape toward an abandoned Ape station.

Why is the station abandoned?

(For more Umbra's Legion action, see the anthology Dogs of War II: Aftermath, *from FurPlanet Productions.)*

Umbra's Legion: Shamblers of Woe

by Adam Baker

"It wasn't the creature that terrified me. Not its ominous, shifting size or gaping, punctured face. It was the way it moved. Something about how it staggered and swayed, fighting gravity just to stay upright, filled me with such dread I could not move. Somehow, somewhere, I had seen it before. Whether it was in my dreams or my nightmares, I recognized it. But from what, I could not know. Wherever my subconscious had cataloged it... and whenever it had nestled itself there, did not matter. For now, in the face of those shambling horrors, it shook me to the very core."
- taken from the personal diary of an unknown CSDF soldier

Marxis Jaggum was dead.

The Orangutan was responsible for thousands of innocent deaths. A mass murderer through his manufacturing of Getran war machines. Now, after years on the run, all that remained of him were a few charred bits of flesh and bone.

"Corporal Rylan Charon to Command. We have two marines KIA. All positions compromised. We've been separated from Delta team but are heading to extraction. Do you read?" The half-Thylacine Canid trooper paused. Static was all that hissed back.

"Apes may be jamming us. No telling what kind of tech the monkeys got out here," Thrower said as he reloaded, having already expended a magazine in cover fire. He grimaced when he tallied what magazines they had left. "Ammunition is already running scarce. We need to make every shot count."

Charon and his spotter, Nikolas 'Thrower' Thor-Hermantus, dove beneath a large, unearthed tree trunk. The dense, Simian jungle was brimming with a cacophony of shouts, klaxons and machinery. Robot walkers rattled and clanged, shaking the trees and sending tremors through the earth. A whirlwind of enemy soldier footsteps encroached from every direction, narrowing yet unseen within the thick, green curtains of the jungle. The two Canines shed what gear they could, leaving them in lighter, cooler and more flexible attire. More equipment followed, abandoning any and all accessories not absolutely vital.

"We're at least two clicks out," Thrower said, tracing the geography with a finger. "If we follow this creek it should lead us right to the evac. With any luck, the Cats haven't ditched us and will be waiting with some serious firepower." Charon nodded and pinched his headset.

"You copy all that, Delta?" Charon whispered into his mic. The two teams were still on their secure channel. "We read you, heading that way now. Watch your asses; place is crawling with chimps." Henryk, the Delta team spotter warned.

Charon peered up and over the rim of the trunk, scanning the area ahead for signs of movement. He sank into the mud, minimizing his profile as much as possible. Eyes sharp and ears taut, he watched, waiting with breath held. "I think we're clear. Wait—" His ear twitched, coaxing an eye to the sky. It was a Getran Sliprunner. In broken Canine tongue it blasted noise from loudspeakers fastened to its underside, "*CSDF soldiers. You are surrounded. Surrender now or be destroyed!*" It repeated, this time in another language, cycling through until it snapped to 'common' again.

The pair paused, motionless and camouflaged with the earth, until it passed. When it was out of eyeshot, Charon flipped the massive, blocky rifle over in his lap. "Only got one round left in the Deimos," he said, checking the magazine. The SR-7 ("Howler") Deimos Rifle was nearly as big as him. But as heavy and cumbersome as it was, its destructive power was too incredible to ignore.

In comparison, standard issue CSDF battle rifles, which the pair also carried, used the Orion Sector Alliance Coalition round, pronounced 'O-seck'. The 5.7x45mm OSAC round was a relatively small, lightweight, high-velocity cartridge that produced relatively low bolt thrust and free recoil impulse, favoring lightweight arms design for maximum weight dispersion and automatic fire accuracy. It was adopted by the CSDF and was now widespread throughout the Orion Colonies, used except by the Cats of Vys.

Weapons ready and gear checked, Charon and Thrower gave a synchronized nod and began an elbow crawl over the wet jungle floor. As they moved, each scanned the basin, their ears tuned into the bustling, living jungle. Vicious barbs, poisonous thorns and carnivorous vines all had to be avoided, lest they fall prey to the sinister planet itself. Countless alien mosquitos and bizarre insects skittered and buzzed amidst the fungal, overgrown brush as if to distract them. "Delta. We are closing on the extract point. Do you read?" Charon said. It took a moment for Henryk to respond.

"We're close. Across the river on your left." he whispered, not unlike Charon.

"Copy. Pussies should be right over that hill. You see a Slip, you call that shit out." Each of the other three acknowledged and the feed went quiet again. The clamoring Getran infantry grew louder, a thunderous rabble that encroached from every angle. Heavy thuds of Gorilla combat boots scattered wildlife as they hustled, punching into dirt and weeds. Above, tree limbs creaked and groaned as the lighter, scout soldiers swung from branch to branch.

Charon and Thrower crawled over an embankment, giving vantage to a clearing below. There sat a Smilodon Dropship, its side bay doors open and turret gunners poised on either side. One of the crewman was outside smoking, another had a radio in one hand and a map in the other, scrutinizing the area.

"Thank fuck they're still here," Thrower huffed. "I'll never say another bad thing about those damn Cats for as long as I live."

Charon pinched his headset. "Delta? We have eyes on the Ell Zee. What's your status?" Only the low hiss of static replied.

"Delta?" He tried again—louder. "Delta, come in?!"

Charon and Thrower traded a worried glance.

The two crept around the perimeter, using the various shrubs and rocks as cover. When Charon would snap into one place, Thrower followed, leap frogging in position. The nearest Smilodon turret gunner must have heard them and perked in their direction. He looked, squinted at the quivering brush that Thrower had disturbed and moved a paw towards the elaborate mini-gun. His finger found the worn trigger but Charon whistled a specific 'cooing' sound and the big Cat took a breath of relief, then whistled back.

"Was starting to think you guys weren't coming," the Smilodon Gunner said. "Looks like you guys brought some friends!"

Charon chuckled, moseying towards the dropship. "Ran into some shit and had to take our shots early. Gave our positions away. Sure am glad you sons of bitches stuck around."

As they both reached out to shake hands-CRAHHKOOOOOMMM!!!

Charon was only a few feet from the Smilodon when a momentous explosion ripped through the stamped steel of the dropship! The cloaked Sliprunner hadn't made a sound when it fired and incinerated the ship. The Canine soldiers were propelled backward. Thrower nicked a tree and Charon spiraled through the dirt, skidding and tumbling until he rolled to a stop.

Neither were knocked unconscious, so they were forced to hear the Cats' cries as they were burned alive. The smell of burnt hair stung their nostrils, multiplied tenfold by the Canines' acute sense of smell.

Charon gained his bearings just in time to see the culprit Sliprunner de-cloak a few hundred feet ahead of them. Garbled Getranese filtered through its speakers as it came to a hovering rest above the clearing. *"CSDF soldiers! Drop your weapons or you will be destroyed!"*

Charon rolled, his ears picking up the humming 'WHIR' of the laser cannon on its nose begin to spool up. In one swift motion he shifted to a knee, swung the Deimos Rifle from around his shoulder and trained it on the levitating ship.

'THWA-KROOOOOOO!' The hyper scram round shrieked as it displaced gravity! The slug broke the sound barrier with a CRACK and turned the pilot to mist! A split-second later, when gas and fuel lines realized they had been compromised, the Sliprunner imploded! A frothing, purple explosion followed, ejecting the remains out its back end!

Charon dropped the empty rifle and spun to Thrower, the closest of the scattered bodies. "I'm fine. I'm fine. Go check on them!" he huffed, clutching his arm below his elbow. "Nice job whackin' that Slip, though. Ya crazy bastard!"

"Apes definitely know where we are now! Ah, damn, I should've said something cool."

"Oh yeah. Huge missed opportunity. That big-ass mouth of yours and you didn't say anything. I'm disappointed. Now go!"

* * *

The turret gunner was closest, splayed over a mangled piece of black shrapnel that was once the mini-gun. Most of his fur was burned away and when Charon pulled him off the sizzling metal, most of his pink, sticky flesh slid off like wet paper. Charon dragged the body several yards away, next to Thrower, vomited, then rushed back into the smoke-filled wreckage.

The Cat who had been smoking was thrown face first into some bramble near the front of the dropship. He was just coming to when Thrower yanked him to his feet. "You okay? Hey, Chuckles? You alright?" Thrower shook him. The runty Smilodon groaned, having to concentrate just to keep his head straight and his eyes open. After a hazy glance at the Canine, he nodded.

Charon lugged another Smilodon out. He was dead, too. Both his legs had been severed. But Charon heaved his torso beside the first corpse. A second trip inside procured another dead body; this one in pieces. She was the other gunner. Charon covered his mouth with a makeshift mask but the smoke intensified with each trip. He found the pilot, who looked like he had tried to eject but the cockpit's glass didn't break. He was breathing, but not well.

"Thrower! Little help?" Charon shouted, staggering out of the billowing dropship with the mangled pilot. "That all of them?" Thrower asked, rushing to help drag the survivor to the others.

"T-that's the last one," Charon nodded as he gagged, nearly passing out himself. If he hadn't just emptied his stomach, more would have followed.

"You sure?" Thrower laid the pilot down. "Chuckles, that everybody?"

"Lieutenant Loren Nillis. Communications," the Cat hung his head, "and yes, that's all of us."

"Rylan Charon," Charon gave him a weak wave. "This is Thrower." He nodded. "Good to meet ya," he huffed, still trying to breathe.

"Snipers. Yeah, I heard." he paused. "Thank you."

Another 'whistle' came from the trees, the same that Charon had chirped earlier. They all looked toward the sound just in time to see the jungle come alive. Leaves, twigs and moss stood on on their own and marched towards them. There were two of them, humanoid shapes made out of leaves. From beneath their folds a hand appeared, and Delta's sniper, Knox, gripped Charon's paw in a handshake. "Sorry we're late." The pair of living trees were Delta Team, still clad in their ghillie suits.

"Glad you made it. But you just jumped into hell," Charon said.

"There is a contingency. A second unit is in high orbit," Nillis chimed in. "If we can relay a distress signal to them from the secondary rendezvous point, we can get off this rock."

"You sly sum'bitches." Thrower said. "Can we reach 'em on our radios?"

"No. They're not in range. But…" Nillis snatched Thrower's map, held it up for the others to see and pointed to a gray rectangle amidst the trees. "There's an abandoned facility on the other side of that treeline south from where we are. Intelligence said it was an old communications depot. That dish could reach the boys upstairs. If we can at least get power to it, I should be able to get a distress call out."

"Then what are we waiting for? This place is gonna be crawling with Apes any second now." Charon and Thrower lifted the pilot up under either arm and they all sprinted into the trees. "Let's move out!"

* * *

Stealth and subterfuge were secondary now. The team bounded through the jungle, this time led by Nillis, who while small in stature by Smilodon standards, was just as stout as the Canines. Charon and Thrower carried the wounded pilot while Delta team covered the pack. Before long, they breached the dense foliage, revealing a massive clandestine structure aged and squalid inside a forgotten clearing.

The facility was far from advanced, at least to modern Ape standards, although it was leaps and bounds above even the greatest Canine technological marvels. Moss and weeds had long-engulfed the building, wrapping around its outsides and blanketing its numerous rows of generators. "This it?" Charon asked.

"Yes. Different from the intel we had, though… very different," Nillis said, confused.

"Doesn't look like any communications depot I've ever seen. What do they need all those generators for?" Thrower said.

"Long range comms, maybe? How should I know? Can we just find a way in?"

Henryk found an access port and yanked the overgrowth away, revealing a panel beside a large industrial double door. "Still has power," he said, wiping dirt off the touchscreen and perusing the buttons. The alien configuration was beyond absurd, with tall letter formations and complex symbols for both letters and numbers. "Anybody speak Bananarama?"

"Whatever you're doing, hurry up. We've gotta get out of the open!" Charon said. "Hey, Nillis, right? Think you can get that door open?"

Nillis was already at the door. He produced a knife, popped a panel below the keypad open, and immediately began fidgeting with the menagerie of wires atop the circuitry. "How the—" Henryk began, before Nillis cut him off. "That's the easy part. They've still got this thing locked down. Gimme a few minutes."

"Better make it quick. We've got contact!" Thrower shouted! A Getran trooper stumbled from the treeline.

BRAM! He fired a burst, hitting the Ape in the neck and face. Another Getran, a bonobo, jumped from the brush, firing indiscriminately in every direction. Knox took aim and swiftly dropped him with a headshot!

Nillis snipped a wire and twisted the copper with another, his hands a twitching, nervous operation in the confined space. A thunderous 'whirring' buzzed from beyond the trees. It was the Getran ships. "Almost… there…" the Cat said, teeth pinned together. The engines of a dozen Sliprunners crested the ridge behind them.

With a heavy jolt, the double doors gave a mechanical 'HISS' and jutted apart, stopping only a foot or two across. Thrower and Henryk tried to force it, but mossy vines and weeds shunted it from opening further. "Shit!" Thrower said, "grab that side!" he motioned for Henryk to help and they both heaved the heavy doors in either direction, snapping vines and sending a metal-on-metal SCREECHING into the jungle. "Argh. Some sort of resistance. Spring-loaded or something! Won't stay open on its own!" Thrower grunted. Charon angled the wounded pilot through the doorway and carefully set him down against an interior wall. He returned with the Deimos rifle, pushing it into place between the doors like a wedge. "Kitty Cat, go!" Thrower said, tipping his nose like a pointer to guide him through. Nillis and then Knox piled through. The wedged rifle let out a 'crunch' as its sides began to crack. Thrower followed, then Henryk, then WHA-CLAMP! The rifle splintered, giving a crisp 'pop' as it was crushed to pieces.

The Canine soldiers secured the immediate room; a large, high ceilinged entryway with hallways leading off in varying directions. Nillis went to the far side opposite the door, wiping away dust and algae to reveal a wall-sized, glowing map of the base. "Okay, so we are here. By my estimates, the control room should be somewhere in the facilities center," he traced a finger across the map, "here."

"That's one helluva hike," Charon said, stepping beside Nillis to soak in the maze-like corridors, "I don't think we should move your buddy. At least no more than necessary."

"He's gone," Thrower said solemnly, closing the Smilodon's swollen eye. "Just lost too much blood. Tough sonuvabitch to last as long as he did."

"Should we say anything?" Charon asked. But Nillis was already knelt down over the dead pilot's maw. He managed the mouth open and in a swift, violent movement, used his knife to yank out both the smilodon's incisors. Each of the Canines grimaced, staring blankly at the bizarre ritual. When Nillis finished, he stood, wiped the blood off his hands and grunted, "The enemy can't have these."

"Let's go. There's a security office down this hall," Nillis said, trudging off down a corridor. Henryk and Thrower kept their blank stares on him as he left.

They all followed, except Charon. Instead he eyed the small, submarine-like portholes to the outside. He peered out the thick windows on at least fifty Getran troops in every direction. Another regiment was just arriving with an Officer, set to reinforcement the line. But strangely, Charon noticed, they were all at least fifty yards away, creating a wide breadth of a perimeter. "What're you monkeys doin'?" he whispered to himself. "Why aren't you coming in…"

* * *

The security office was in surprisingly well-kept order. Aside from a few loose papers and a binder, everything was clean and put away. Several 'stations' were set up in the corners, each having elaborate consoles of computer access control and camera monitors. Across from the main door sat three 'turnstyle' like chambers, where keypads were needed to pass through each seal like a clean room. Knox and Henryk covered the door as the others poked around.

Charon perused the electronics. "This place still has power. Half these cameras are gone, though. Can't see shit on the lower floors." He paid particular attention to the outside camera feeds, watching the Apes amass. Despite their numbers, they were still fortifying a lengthy perimeter.

"Could be running on some sort of generator or back-up system," Thrower said.

"Maybe to keep power to the doors. Look, even the exterior ones. All on lockdown."

"Let's keep it that way. Don't need to be letting the chimps in now, do we?"

"They were doing some shady shit here, for sure," Charon said. He perused the CCTV stills that the Ape security put into their logs.

"Research of some kind. Looks almost… medical. See this?" Thrower pointed to some of the notes. "That's an autopsy report. Nillis, where to next?" he asked, giving up on the Getran articles.

"Keep heading south. Should be a straight shot to engineering," Nillis said, rummaging through a locker. A second later he pulled a shotgun from a stowaway cabinet, blew the dust off and checked the slide. It was a bulky, Getran affair, but it fit nicely in the Smilodon's large paws. After another quick search, he found a box of shells in a footlocker and loaded the gaudy pump-action.

There was a rustle outside the door. Then a thud! The slamming stopped their laughing. Henryk rushed in, panic stricken!

"Hey, where's Knox?!" Henryk shouted. "I looked away for two seconds and he just vanished!" The team tensed up, alert and ready.

"Knox? Knox! Sound off, buddy!" Charon tried along with the others. He tried the radio, but there was too much interference in the all-metal facility.

"AAAAAEEEEGGGHHH!!!" a shrill, painful scream tore down the hallway!

Knox's voice echoed off the walls! The whole facility rattled to life. His agonizing wail reverbed off the metal walls and into the precision ears of the Canines. Charon could almost sense the sound. He scrutinized the twitching ears of his team, triangulating the tone. It only took him a second-

"West! There!" Charon pointed. "West corridor, go go go!"

Charon, Thrower and Henryk all strafed down the hallway, guns at the ready. The chamber grew darker the further they pressed, with lightning fixtures obfuscated by moss and dirt. They cleared the first few rooms with ease, but the painful cries of Knox were still far off. As they moved deeper into the unknown, the panels and flooring of the facility grow more and more dilapidated. Whether mistreated or forgotten, rust and algae manifested on the once smooth and pristine panels.

"Movement right!" Thrower shouted, diverting everyone's barrels around a corner, where a bloody boot teetered side-to-side. They hovered around it, eyeing their surroundings - careful for an ambush. But there was nothing there, just Knox's quivering boot, as if just seconds before it had been flung from his foot.

Charon knelt to inspect it. It was still warm. "Knox?" he called out, tipping the boot to one side. As it slumped over, a gush of blood poured from the opening...

"Fuck! Knox? Knox?!" Everyone bolted to attention. "Where are you, buddy?! Come on, say something!" Charon shouted, checking each of the hallways with his scope.

Silence fell on the group as another, far-off, whimpering cry echoes from parts unseen.

"I can't tell which way it's coming from!" Thrower barked.

"We have to slow down. I don't know where we are. If we get turned around in here—" Nillis stopped himself when he saw Charon sniff the shoe, then the blood. It only took a second for Canine receptors to light up.

"Southernmost hall. He's not alone. And whatever has him ain't no Ape." Charon motioned for the group to follow him. Light was getting scarce. And the decedent surroundings were becoming altogether menacing. Little at all was left of modern concepts; instead their surroundings were transformed into an alien madness.

A trail of blood led to a large, open room, looking as if once it was a cafeteria or mess hall. Knox's severed arm was amongst the debris of rotten, overturned furniture. His rifle lay beside it, bent and mangled as if it were a paper clip. "Wh-where is he?" Henryk sputtered.

Charon and the others looked down at the macabre scene. The blood was still warm. Knox couldn't be far, but his cries had subsided. There was no sound except—

"Hhuuuuuuuggkk!" A deep, raspy sucking sound lurched from one of the halls!

Charon and the others spun! Attention and gun barrels locked on to the vibrations. One of the corridors was cloaked in darkness, but something moved just beyond. They each aimed their weapons into the inky shadow! The labored breathing came again. Louder, closer. A gurgling, sloppy groan like something slowly drowning. Charon inched forward, his eyes trying to adjust to the twilight.

Henryk swallowed hard, "Knox?"

HUUUUUUUCGGKH! The wet, sucking noise heightened. A form faded in from the shadows, a limping, heaving mass that not one sense was ready for.

The creature was loathsome - a wobbly, shifting, tangled mess of skin and what-could-only-be-described as quills, like ingrown hairs made of jagged wire. It had no mouth to speak of, or at least no lips to contain the black void at the bottom of his chinless face. Somewhere back behind the melted flesh, a tongue and cavernous throat could be glimpsed, but only when it made a heaving, gasping, sucking 'cough' to suck in much-needed air. It was if it was trying to breathe without swallowing, repeated sloppy gasps that 'smacked' open and closed with each beat.

It shambled towards them, lifting a shaky tendril up to reach out for Charon, who was nearest the thing. He was frozen, petrified in place by the shapeless monstrosity. In the thing's other hand, a severed Canine leg, gushing blood, leaving a trail as it shuffled forward.

"Wha-what is that?!". Charon managed to sputter.

Yet he received no answer.

It hobbled forward, the way someone might walk with two broken ankles. The outstretched arm peeled itself from the thing's side, fidgeting and wobbling towards them. Its flesh ripped as it did, managing with a sticky, slicing sound, looking as if it was once held together with glue. Blood came with it; and a pink, fleshy wound where the arm had once been fused into place. It gurgled something, when the cool air must have disturbed the self-inflicted lesion, but it had no lips to articulate whatever language it was attempting.

"Uh, Chuckles? Any bright ideas?" Charon looked to Nillis, frozen like the rest. But unlike them, after a second of realization, he pointed his shotgun to the thing's center mass and fired - BRRAM!!!

The buckshot shredded the creature's midsection, sending it to the floor with a wet and heavy THUD! Black blood coated the walls behind it and began to pool on the floor. It gasped one final, gurgling husk before deflating to a motionless assemblage of eyes and flesh.

Each of the Canine soldiers looked at one another in disbelief. Charon was the first to fidget forward. Yet as he took his first step - a chilling, demonic HOWL belted out of the thing's gaping face and echoed away! Its death rattle piped off the walls and corridors around them, rattling ominously into the abyss. Charon almost shot the creature again, but it let our its screech and then collapsed into mush.

Something like an earthquake gripped the facility after the thing's bestial call; like a thousand rats trying to chew their way up from hell, sending vibrations through walls and floors. It subsided after only a moment, but Charon's ears could hear the faint rallying of the Apes outside. Whatever the creature was, it scared them too...

"What in all the blue fucks..." Thrower whispered.

Charon knelt over the corpse, Thrower took the leg. "It's Knox."

Henryk broke down, taking a knee and murmuring a silent prayer.

"Whatcha think?" Thrower asked.

"I have no idea. Deformed or something? I... don't think it's an Ape. Not like any I've ever seen, anyway. Nillis? How 'bout you?"

The Smilodon was already grimacing. He stared down at the creature a moment before looking back at Charon. "It's only a matter of time before they find us. We need to keep moving," he said, before stepping over the group and down the hall.

Thrower stopped Charon before he could rise. "So listen, man... I know why the monkeys didn't follow us in." Thrower flipped his tablet to show Charon, 'RADIATION WARNING' blinked on the screen. "This whole place is an oven. They don't need to risk it. They can just wait us out."

"Yeah, wait us out with whatever the hell else is in here. How long do we have?

"A few hours. Maybe. Depends on the dosage which seems to… fluctuate. There's no way to tell without the proper equipment. The lasting effects are far more harmful, but that depends on exposure."

"We go for the comm room. Knox would've done the same."

* * *

Deeper they travelled. They soon left the overgrown ground floors for a network of rusty and degraded catwalks. Bulbous pipes sprawled in every direction, leaking unknown fluids and hisses of steam. Charon, Thrower, Henryk, and Nillis had strayed into a gargantuan chamber with rows of massive vats and containers, like a water treatment plant gone wrong. Rickety catwalks lined the outsides and intermingled with the center rows, a zoo of glass and plastic tanks. "Straight across. The comm room should be right through those doors." Nillis said, referring to what looked like another security checkpoint on the opposite end of the mausoleum-like place.

"Guys? The rads are gettin' worse. Whatever's down here is hot," Thrower said, checking his tablet. All but Charon hurried over the catwalk, who wavered amidst the nearest glass containers.

He squinted through the murk of one of the vats. It was a hazy, yellowish liquid with floating particles of biology. 'Something' else was inside, hiding within the foggy broth. It was black or dark brown, hovering in suspended preservation. Charon could see the vague outline of its hominid-esque form. Arms, legs, a body… but nothing else at all distinguishable.

He tried another oversized test tube, this one murky and viscous like the one before. Another entity was cocooned within. This one had multiple arms, but each were still malformed and canted at twisted angles. Charon tried the next tube, and then the next, trying not to fall too far behind the group. The creatures were getting clearer though, newer. Less and less blasphemously embalmed. He reached one of the last in the row, before his Catwalk merged into the wall where the rest of the group were waiting. Before his eyes he saw the thing, nearly identical to the one in the hallway. Vast and horrible, a chinless, melted mockery of form itself. Long arms, crooked at bizarre angles hung low past its waist. Small, stringy ropes of bio-matter ebbed off it and clung to the glass, as if it were trapped in a spider's web.

In its stillness, he was resolute. Yet fear trickled down his spine when he recalled their hideous gait. He wasn't sure why, but something made his fur stand on-end when he pictured it moving again; hobbling as it tried to walk.

Charon almost didn't notice Nillis beside him. But he silently made his presence known so he could peer into the murk as well. Charon turned slightly, speaking quietly. "This isn't a communication depot, is it?"

"Oh, it is. A powerful one. That dish you saw on the roof ain't cheap. They needed a lot of energy and a lot of resources to get to whatever they were digging for. They wanted it bad. These high powered satellites only have a handful of purposes. And the main one is to get information to Getra, fast and securely. Needless to say, in a remote location as this shithole is, whatever was going down here was incredibly important - at least to the Apes..." Nillis trailed off.

Charon kept glowering at him, but Nillis kept looking into the tank, never meeting his eyes. After another moment he sighed, then turned to the thylacine. "A Getran expeditionary and drilling team found something. Some ten or twenty years ago." Nillis finally looked back at Charon, "Something deep underground. They surmised it was a few thousand years old. Pre-Rag stuff. But they were hush-hush about it. All we know is that they built this entire station on top of it," Nillis said. "Blackroot then became one of their satellite planets they used for training and weapons testing."

"What?" Charon grimaced; "then why abandon it?"

"Resources? Funding maybe? You know how the Apes can be," Nillis said, "Maybe Vys was curious to find out why as well?"

"Or maybe they ran from whatever took Knox? Sealed this place off and threw away the key."

"I won't pretend to know, Corporal. But at least now we know it's abandoned. C'mon, we're almost to engineering." Nillis casually walked away. Damn Cat didn't have a care in the world...

Charon looked past the test tube pillars, over the railing, into the darkness of the facility's underbelly. He could see row after row of generators and vats for hundreds of yards, maybe more. Fields of them, going on as far as his Canid eyes could see. He couldn't be sure, but he even thought he saw something move. A silent, black shadow that skittered off one container to the nearby wall. Excellent as his vision was, the shadows obscured confirmation, but Charon was then struck with the real, stark fear that he was being watched. That a hundred eyes from a hundred things stared back at him through the void. It was enough to make him hustle down the catwalk

"We gotta move. Go, go, go!" Charon said, jogging to meet Nillis and the others.

"What's the rush?" Henryk asked.

Charon looked back over his shoulder. He had terror in his eyes, "we're not alone!" They all looked, but shouldn't have. The walls had come alive. From the inky shadows, countless things poured over the terrain. Nillis was already at the security door, fumbling with the holopad. There was no panel to rip and gut, so he was forced to hack in. The Canines covered him, darting their aims every which way across the living tidal wave of teeth and claws.

"Kinda pressed for time here, Chuckles!" Thrower said, the radiation meter on his tablet reaching peak levels.

Henryk was the first to fire. A reckless creature had leapt off a far wall, but was shot down before it could land on their catwalk. Henryk shuffled forward, firing three rounds into another brazen beast above. It was larger than the other before it, hulking like a skinless gorilla, but had only one, deformed tentacle-like arm, dreadful in size and shape. It dropped, slamming into the catwalk between Henryk and the others. They each opened fire, shredding its face to gibbets. As it fell, another leapt to the platform. Henryk, still closest, fired into its chest. But his rifle clicked empty so he charged, forcing the rifle's buttstock into the thing's face and smashing it against the wall. Its body flailed about, clawing at his arm and tearing his uniform like a chicken with its head cut off. He held it in place so he could pull his pistol with his free hand and fire into its belly. It took half the magazine before the thing stopped squirming.

"Got it!" Nillis shouted! He tossed Charon and Thrower inside and reached for Henryk, but something else already had him. The creatures squirmed from below, grabbing his ankles. Pinned down, he was unaware of the dozen other monstrosities that climbed up from below and pulled him over the railing.

Charon raced to the door, shouting for Henryk, but Nillis slapped a button on a the console, forcing the seal to close.

"Open the damn—" Charon words were cut short, when a briny, pulpy appendage shunted the doors from fully closing. With terrible strength it pried the heavy steel apart, crushing bone. It opened enough for another arm, then a toothy face of another melted creature. In seconds, half a dozen had oozed themselves inside, mincing bones just to squeeze through.

There were a few more shots fired, then a mad dash down the adjacent hallway. The creatures dove, crashing like water around corners and over steps. Ceaselessly unending they flurried, mouths agape, talons outstretched. Thrower tripped, losing his rifle. He pulled his pistol and fired at the things. Charon emptied his rifle into the masses, hindering them only minutely before they swallowed his friend. He tried to save him, sliding to grab his paw. "Grab my hand! Come on!"

They must have only been inches apart. One last stretch could have intertwined their grasps. But the beasts found him first. They took him, screaming and fighting, assembling Thrower into their abominable folds.

Charon could not find the words nor the hatred.

Nillis yanked him to his feet, "Wake up and do something!" Charon snapped back to reality and reloaded his rifle. Each bullet in his magazine bored through the head of a creature, or blew off a limb to stop their sprinting. When his rifle emptied, he pulled a sidearm, firing round after round into the supernatural carnage.

"Go! I'll hold them off!" Nillis growled, fanning out the claws on either paw!

"What? No, you can't!" Charon cried, but Nillis spun and sent a palm into his chest, knocking him through a doorway. The door sealed shut a second later, with the heavy, mechanical 'CHUNK!' of the lock sliding into place. As Charon stood, something fell and clacked to the metal floor - it was one of the Smilodon's fangs. One of the curved teeth Nillis had cut from the dead pilot.

Charon tried the door anyway. Though locked, a small plexiglass porthole could be peered through. Nillis was waist deep in the horrific creatures, clawing, biting and slashing at them. They swarmed over him like ants on a mound, chewing him down. He sank into the fleshy, rippling pile of them, as if being swallowed by quicksand.

V.

The rotten corridors worsened. And the next few twists and turns were all a dessicated maze. There was no rhyme or reason for his trajectory, only that it seemed like the facility itself was leading him. Soon, more bizarre biological material concaved the hallway, like a living tunnel or a woven spiders' den. Its scent was beyond recognition, although what seemed like a deeply familiar, albeit rotten, scent was at the same time a wholly alien accord. Finally, Charon ducked through another submarine-like door, half held open with the flimsy mucus-like material that clung to the walls and floor (and ceiling).

Light was scant, nearly non-existent in the small, closet-like engineering room. To his right a rudimentary console blinked. Its old screen was littered with prompts for various commands. One of them depicting a satellite dish caught his eye, and he touched it with a shaky, bloodsoaked finger. With a un-earthly 'CHUNK' the station shook and a mechanical buzzing tittered through the room. A light emerged from somewhere in the room's far corner. The space was much larger than Charon had realized.

The luminosity grew. Charon had to shield his eyes from a vivid, growing light as he stepped down to face it. It was a radiance that burned his skin and eyes, fluctuating before him like a glowing mist. It took a moment for reason and rational thought to piece together what was before him...

Within the center of the room, a violent whirlwind of black, hovering liquid danced in place. It was a fluctuating, wobbling mass with distorted, flickering imagery inside it, like someone or something, trying to strike a match in the dark. It was surrounded by a horde of creatures, nestled and stooped at all angles around the vestibule. They did not seem to notice him yet, instead lay still and motionless, basking in a faint, phosphorus, purple light which emanated from the portal. Some sat on the floor, some lay on top of one another, others hung from the ceiling like bats, but they were everywhere.

SSKRAAAHHH!!!

A screech from the hallway made Charon spin. One of the twisted creatures from before barreled towards him. Charon raised his pistol and with its final bullet, dropped the shambling horror with a panicked but reflexive shot between its eyes. The gunshot rang through the room and down the hall, sending a tinge of sound through his unprotected ears. He winced, slamming the heavy door behind him and locking it into fortification. Yet as he turned, Charon was met with the stares of a hundred plus monstrosities, all glaring and hissing, moaning and growling.

His kill and bullet had roused the ravenous horde.

It was now he realized that these creatures had some consciousness about them. Almost a herd mentality, as they did not all just charge at him with bloodlust. They watched him, following him with black, hollow eyes. They seemed almost afraid of him, cowering or rearing like a caged wild animal. Every so often, one might skitter forward, swiping a melted tentacle at him before backing away. They were keeping him from coming closer. They were barricading his path. They were protecting the portal...

He moved, carefully and methodically in front of the herd, the way a lion tamer might maneuver before cracking his whip. The throng of madness squawked and hissed and scowled at his form that mocked their deity - their monument - that Charon haphazardly threatened. With steady grace he pulled his combat knife from his (shoulder) holster, careful not to startle the creatures before he was ready. His other hand silently pulled the Smilodon fang from his pocket and he gripped it underhand like a blade.

Despite being surrounded by a mad horde of melted, viscous monstrosities, locked miles below ground on an alien world and light years from home, what really terrified him still was their walk. That horrible, shambling gait that made his fur stand on end. He dared not show it, so that these beings might not sniff it out, but he was unable to shake the fear, forced to gaze in mesmerized horror.

One of them must have gotten too close, or tried to attack in some fashion, because in the next instant Charon had instinctively stabbed one of the things and another into the crowd. Necessary action brought him back to the moment as the horde descended upon him. Despite the madness, he eyed a clean-room opposite the portal, somehow untouched by the creatures and their tainted matter. It must have been sealed off somehow...

Charon cut and slashed, kicked and bit. Black blood spewed and sprayed across the room. But the mob was relentless, unstopping, neverending. In his fury, he had sliced his way towards the room's center only a few feet from the murky, fluctuating portal. It tugged on his senses, pulling at him like gravity. As he cut closer, an eerie cold emanated from its pregnant mass. Acrid air stung his flesh, tingling like an electrical charge that grew with each step forward. More creatures poured into the room, wave after wave of tumbling, crashing teeth, claws and flesh.

There was no other way. The creatures converged from every possible direction. They strained to reach him, screaming... crawling... determined in a bestial fashion. The portal beckoned. So Charon leapt, diving into the swirling abyss...

Complete and utter darkness followed.

The abyss engulfed him, cold and quiet. Nothing for light or eyes to see.

He wasn't standing or walking but... floating. The way one might wade in water. Buoyant - neither sinking or rising.

It was... So cold... Charon thought. So cold...

He tried to speak. He could feel his mouth open, his vocal cords vibrate, his muscles contract, but no sound. He tried again, this time taking in a breath of what felt like hot water. Water that rushed down his throat and seized his lungs. Panic followed. No longer were speech or surroundings important, but breathing. He tried to struggle but his hands were too cold. His limbs would not move, like they were asleep, tingling with sharp, pin-pricks and chilled like frostbitten extremities.

Inside the whirling cacophony - light. Separating light. Like opening one's eyes on a bright morning after a darkened slumber.

Out of the cold void Charon was transported to a vivid and familiar world. A place of color and memory. Like waking from a dream he found himself sprawled beneath a tiny, worn children's bed. It was *his* bed, the same which he had hid under numerous times as a youngster. Charon looked himself over - he was no longer the stout soldier, purposed for and grizzled from combat, but a child, maybe only eight or nine. He retreated to the corner beneath the bed's warped and rotten frame, starring with watery eyes at the room's open door. The only exit let in a buzzing, orange light from the hall, coating the rest of the room with inky shadows.

He stared through the doorway, shivering now with near-uncontrollable fright. Tears welled up in his eyes and he clutched, increasingly tightly, a small plush dinosaur. Heavy footsteps quickly hush his slight, quivering breathing. Boots on wood. They drew closer - louder.

Clomp. Clomp! CLOMP! CLOMP!!!

The rest of the door slowly crept open and a pair of dirty, rugged boots entered. There was a moment of brief silence, a gulp of visceral liquid, and the deep, heavy breathing of the man entering, then standing in the middle of the room.

"Where you at, boy?" a harsh, gravelly voice husked. Nicotine and violence scarred his grizzled vocal cords. It was the voice of Rham Charon. A massive, rugged and tattooed Thylacine and Rylan Charon's father. He was dirty and musty, with dried blood under his nails and fresh blood on his hands. Layers of mud cracked off his boots and uniform the harder as he moved around the room. Somewhere, from another part of the run-down hovel, the low whimpering of his mother could be heard.

"I said where you at?!" The voice came harder. Faster. More angry. There was another pull on the bottle in his hand, "Answer me, boy!" Something was knocked over or thrown, smashing into the floor. The boots moved across the room with purpose, with hatred, with frustration. It was a horrible, shambling gait of a drunk far past his limit. Young Charon shriveled back further as best he could, trying to remain flat and still. He tried to sink into the floor, attempting in vain to minimize his profile as much as possible. Eyes warped and ears taut, he watched, waiting with breath held.

But it was no use. A gnarly hand reached from above and yanked the mattress away. The tiny half-Thylacine was revealed, teary eyed and terrified, at the sight of his drunken, glaring father. "I told you not to hide from me, you little chicken-shit!" The beast had to force himself to stand, barely able to make balance on his own two legs. He wobbled, side-to-side, then lunged forward to strike his son.

Charon learned to recognize that walk. He would keep a constant vigil on his father, and later others, as they would teeter or topple, stumble or sway. It was an all too familiar tell-tale sign. But that was a skill not yet learned by young Charon. For now, he was pawing at the powerful grip of his father's hands around his throat.

As he lay there, windpipe closing, his eyes rolled back into his head. He was only a boy, and so early did he feel his first touch of death. As consciousness faded, black crept back in and in a few moments, Charon was back in the abyss, floating nebulously in the inky black of the frigid void. He could still feel the hands crushing his trachea despite nothing physical upon him.

More hands found his body. They tugged and pushed and prodded, nudging him closer to something up ahead. His vision was fading, but in front of him - light. A small shimmer, like someone lighting a match in the dark. He listed closer, the light soon growing... and growing... and growing... until-

SHOOOUUMMM! Charon was launched from the other side of the portal, opposite the way he entered. He was thrown across the room, crashing through a glass window into the adjacent room! The creatures sprinted towards him, clinging to walls and ceilings, tumbling over one another like boney, bleeding squids.

Charon rolled to his feet. He still held his knife and the Smilodon's fang. He was on the other side of the portal now, inside the clean room. Beside him, a ladder. He stabbed the first creature and pinned it to the wall, using its flailing body to bound off of and reach the ladder's base. His arms and legs burned, his bloody hands nearly slipped with each upward grasp, but he raced skyward. Below him, the creatures piled on top of one another, bursting up through the pipe, surging fast beneath him.

He reached the end of the tunnel, spinning the (submarine?) hatch open, keeping an eye on the fleshy, squawking, tumbling turmoil below. With a final -CLICK- the hatch lurched open, spilling blinding sunlight down the shaft! Charon scrambled out of the porthole and out onto the roof of the mossy Getran building. He nearly lost his footing at the sight - a hundred plus Getran soldiers, hovering Sliprunners and a squadron of Space Climbers - all with weapons trained on him!

"Holy—" Charon stammered, shielding his eyes from the hot sun. His brain tried to formulate any sort of plan. The building shook. From the porthole a flowing horde of death surged upward, rising and clawing with each passing second. He snarled, staring the Apes down, glaring his own savagery into the whites of their eyes.

Charon crouched, ready to jump. He would rather fight the entire Getran army than one more of the waxy, nightmarish creatures.

When suddenly…

BRRRRRRRRRRRTTTTT!!! A blood-red Smilodon Gunship streaked past, Gatling guns blazing! Its autocannons fired relentlessly, cutting a thick line through the ranks of Getran soldiers. Armor was shredded and personnel minced as round after round of hot lead torn through them like butter.

Charon was nearly thrown off his feet as a second dropship flipped down from the atmosphere. Its heat shield separated and it banked to the side of the facility, rearing back to meet the roofline, like a horse bucking back at its reins. Its side doors slid open, allowing the mini-guns on either side to erupt in spinning chaos. Charon was met with a large, black Smilodon who swung him inside, "Anyone else!?"

Charon grimly shook his head, "Just me!"

The black Smilodon fired a few rounds from the hip and hopped back inside. "We've got the package! Let's get outta here!"

In no time at all, the gunship swung itself skyward, boring through the crowds of Apes as its thrusters spooled back up and sent it catapulting back into the atmosphere. Charon craned his neck, bent as much possible in the harness he was strapped into. Below, the hordes of fleshy things leapt off the facility's rooftop, launching themselves mouth-first at the Getrans below. He could hear the Apes' screams, and the wet, chomping of the creatures, even with the wind and engines.

The massacre shrunk as the ship jettisoned skyward. Soon the bay doors closed and the eerie, quiet of space surrounded them. That was the last time any CSDF or Orion soldier ever saw Blackroot. Officially, the operation never happened. Although the CSDF denied that it ever occurred, the Getran Military similarly denied the planet itself ever existed.

The Apes are proud of their Getran Empire's history; but a teenagers' class tour of a museum can be boring. Yugraiz wanders off by herself, and discovers more than she expects.

Umbra's Legion: Where Pride Planted

by Geoff Galt

Climb with me, far from all
As two we'll be and you won't fall
The night is free and vast like sea
At the top, so high, we'll be.

The teacher leading the school group turned to face her troop of children. "This is the oldest surviving piece of Getran writing, translated to modern Getranese." She was guiding the class of fifteen through the Capital Museum of the planet Getra. A world made up of simians from all walks of life. Herself an elegant Orangutan standing tall in professional attire, and her kids, well… they were kids. She had been able to wrestle the attention of a few attentive Chimps and Gorillas at the front, but there were pockets of rowdy ones in the back that just needed to be—

"HEY!" she snapped.

They all silenced. Gorillas and Baboons, Chimps and Lemurs snapped to attention. She stared for a beat to remind them who ran this shit and continued.

"Thousands of years ago, tribes of the tranquil simian world of Getra evolved complex speech to communicate with one another. Soon after the crude glyphs and symbols molded into a more consistent, teachable form, writing permeated ancient Getrans quite close to the drop."

"The asteroid, Missus Daws?" squeaked a glasses-wearing Bonobo cub. He was among the younger cluster of about ten years old, compared to the majority that were in a teenage range.

She smiled knowingly. "That's right, Ethrin. The Drop of Houlos Mox."

Ethrin's eyes widened with joy, as he turned to his friends Yugraiz and Vellong. Yugraiz was an impatient, rowdy Gorilla lass squinting at Ethrin's nerdy-ass incredulously. "The asteroid, eh? Seriously, dude."

Vellong patted Yugraiz's burly, red jacketed shoulder with his long-reaching Lars Gibbon hand. "Nah, I remember this. This is a big deal. Watch!" Yugraiz snorted as Ms. Daws continued.

"BD, or 'Before-Drop' refers to the brief window of recorded history that precedes this calamitous event. Not much is known of the inter-Getran climate that led up to the drop, but historians managed to find remarkably preserved log entries from a trader that ran his business among the chaos of the great ancient city of Houlos Mox. A Galago who referred himself only as 'Olo'…"

Vellong cupped his chin with his long arms, "A Galago? What's that?"

Chittered laughter rippled through the crowd of children as Ms. Daws activated a panel next to a shadowbox containing the actual books. A hologram rendered to show the tiny, long-tailed, squirrel-like creature.

Yugraiz burst out laughing "A Bushbaby!? *This* is what Getrans used to look like!?"

A tiny cough interrupted her jeers, as a family of Galago tourists scowled at her. A couple of hundred thousand years had hardly evolved the species further. They beckoned their own little 'Bushbaby baby' to hurry along so they could distance themselves from this child, who was twice their size.

Yugraiz winced with guilt, as Ms. Daws took note. She addressed the rest of the class before the distraction could gain momentum. "Trader Olo was not a famous or wealthy Prosimian. His notoriety only came about after historians discovered his ship logs and diary entries, passed down from generation to generation, remarkably preserved for thousands of years." She gestured to the shadowbox, where modestly-sized leather-bound books rested, with spines woven from a crumbling string-like structure. They were unmistakably ancient and worn, the corners coiling from the traffic of hands spanning thousands of years before archaeologists could pamper its every detail under gloves.

Ms. Daws proceeded further into the museum. "Unusual for the time, Olo had a knack for vocabulary and was a very literary hobbyist." She came to a stop before the first stage-like holo projector of the Olo exhibit. A lowly riverboat was painted, docked along a shore spotted with straw and clay huts.

"Take this excerpt taken three years BD. The dating structure, one hundred and three days since he sailed off to make wages and trade. An abbreviation for the rough area of his dealings, here Vretia, a somewhat northern horn in the Sea of Seeds, and what's Tuelei mean?"

"The day of the week!" answered the children in unison.

"Very good!" beamed the teacher. A recording from an actor reciting his passage played, while the text danced across the stage in holographic form:

103~ Vret Tuelei
10 bags of Rollbeans clutched
Beggar on the street had warned me
As the tide rolls high
These buyers at Floody Market get antsy
Why
Just trying to roll some beans here
Tide will tide, beans are beans
It's called Floody Market for good reason
No one should be surprised
I hate Vretians greatly
Stupid flood-fearing bastards just buy the beans!
These Rollbeans were a mistake

The hologram performance of words receded into the painted landscape, and the children redirected their attention to their teacher.

"Paper at the time was also a commodity valuable enough to trade on its own, yet Olo hoarded many parchments that he would stitch together in makeshift journals. Pouring over the daily minutiae of his labors, his moods, and events of the day in colorful detail. The unique salt cave in which his family had stored these ancient books provided a rare and absolutely breathtaking documentation of not only his life, but also the beginning of an era."

Ethrin pushed his glasses back up on his face. "Probably due to his miniature size, he was able to let a lot of paper go a long way." Yugraiz groaned out of sheer frustration from Ethrin's voice.

Ms. Daws continued to the next display. The same boat, now improved with a makeshift cabin at a much larger, much more sophisticated shoreline kingdom. The Kingdom of Houlos Mox! The children oo'd and ahh'd at the contrast of such a wildly different vista dominating the wall.

"At year one, before the drop, Olo had moved on from selling Rollbeans along the shores of Vretia, and improved his business by selling dyes in the Great Kingdom of Houlos. There, in the fertile gulf, Olo traversed crammed ports bustling with activity. The most active and expansive society in ancient Getran history. Ruled over by the lofty Godking Tekrath."

Once again, hologram texts danced across the painted scene while the same voice recording acted it out. This time it was accompanied by the visage of a Godking Baboon looming over the distance, while a lowly Bushbaby scribed into a journal.

167~ Holo Frilei

Business is good, the dyes find homes easily
Annoying still are the dailies from this "God King"
Is he serious?
Says he is the son of God, speaks to God
People believe him, but this guy...
Seems like he's just a rich guy
Do something Godly, holy man.
How wonderful it would be if it weren't all a lie.

Vellong recoiled "Woah, isn't that a little blasphemous?"

Yugraiz nudged him in the shoulder. "He's not an actual God, dummy! He's just some guy..." after a beat, she turned to Ethrin. "... Right?"

"Right."

"YEAH!" She puffed out her chest, as if she had nailed it. Ms. Daws didn't seem to hear the chatter in the open, cavernous hall.

There was quite a broad collection of Godking Tekrath's self-aggrandizement and narcissism. Pottery and Getran-made effigies, tributes to his grand divinity, peppered the displays around the stage to this era of history. Yugraiz let her head fall backwards as she stared into the tall ceiling of the facility and let all of the air escape through her nose. The tour had only just begun and she was bored out of her mind. Ethrin and Vellong were awestruck at Godking Tekrath's flamboyant adornments on his crown and crest. He was truly an impressive depiction of ancient Houlos royalty.

The teacher pointed out particularly regal depictions of the king. "It was rare for any texts or any art to slander the Godking Tekrath during his reign, making Olo's account all the more illuminating and rare.

"Godking Tekrath had a massively reproduced tablet that touted his holy origins. Made in the image of Baboons like all Baboons, he was the Golden Boon of God." The class snickered teasingly to the Mandrill and Olive Baboon classmates in the group.

"They say God spoke to him daily about the needs of the kingdom, and the citizens of Houlos were expected to obey, or suffer the wrath of storms, fire, or plague. If any instance of these had occurred, Godking

Tekrath was quick to justify why they happened, for reasons as well documented as the farmers not farming enough, or as petty as improper handling of rituals and ceremonies."

A hologram whirred, and the familiar bushbaby trader Olo recited his passage...

> *184~ Holo Monlei*
> *Tekrath at it again*
> *Wants us all to pay tribute to God Dad*
> *"Give dye to a hole or trade dye for money"*
> *"Make money or piss buyers off"*
> *Tough decision, much apologies to the Golden Boon*

Ms. Daws stepped through the hologram of Trader Olo as the image of him disintegrated. "It would appear that around this time, there was a sweeping sentiment of skepticism that Olo shared with the natives of Houlos. Godking Tekrath would ask for these tributes seasonally, and would express agitation when contributions were lacking. Olo happened to log the last day of these tributes." She walked a few steps down the hall towards a stage waiting for their presence to be lit.

"The last decree of Godking Tekrath. Year Zero After Drop."

The lights came on as the class approached the display, revealing a chaotic scene of Houlos Mox in disarray. Ships and Getrans crowded at the feet of a large and angry Golden Baboon, his royal jewelry glimmering in the golden sun, and his golden hair cascading in the wind, shaking his scepter skyward to the heavens.

"Angered by the lackluster showing of tributes to his divinity, Godking Tekrath spouted a furious lecture to his citizens. That their lack of faith would lead to disastrous consequences from a holy source." Ms. Daws stepped aside and let an elaborate, colorful animation of the Golden Boon materialize before the children. He was a massive rendering towering over their heads, and his voiceovers were assisted with booming subwoofers and surround sound.

> *"My people of Houlos! What pitiful disgrace you have burdened me with this season! I have heard the words from on high, I have glimpsed upon the destiny my father has in store for the lot of you. You try our patience, yet you have failed to pay for more. Forgive me father, for what I must do. For by my hand, I will see to this unacceptable tributation...* BE UNDONE. AND MAY THIS DISRESPECT TO THE HOLY AMONG US NEVER OCCUR AGAIN!"

A deep rumbling could be heard as the kits looked around and at each other. Yugraiz' veil of boredom slipped as her eyes widened with uncertainty too, as the display began to glow a heinous blood orange with fiery brilliance. A holographic asteroid parted the clouds and came crashing down directly onto the temple of Tekrath; the largest, central structure of the entire kingdom.

The sound was colossal and the display was rigged with fans that blew hot air into their tiny faces, causing some of the students to recoil in fear. Yugraiz pushed students aside to get closer to the chaos, her eyes wide and awestruck at the spectacle of destruction. The animation extended a colossal cloud of destruction up the massive stairs, up to where the holy palace had been. It led only to a jagged crater amid a landscape of flattened, scorched earth.

A waking fascination swept over the children's faces as they scanned the depiction of the drop. Yugraiz had to vocalize her hype with a laugh as she looked back to her friends. Vellong had to cover his own mouth in concern, "Oh no... what about Olo?"

Ms. Daws smiled at the concerned Gibbon. "He was off dealing with business on other shores far from the impact zone at the time. But the impact itself is well documented across the surrounding lands. Trees bowed, eardrums ruptured, the tides turned, and many died. The plume of smoke could be seen in distant lands, and the illumination of the blast turned night to dawn."

Vellong breathed a sigh of relief. "Okay, good. I liked Olo."

"Well, good," Ms. Daws continued, "Because this next log is from the old Galago himself." Sure enough, that cued the next holographic depiction: the distraught Trader Olo sailing with his crew of assistants amid a crumbling kingdom.

>186 - Holo Weilei
>*Tekrath really did it this time!*
>*What happened here!?*
>*Did God do this?*
>*I traded some dyes for food*
>*Very grateful for timing*
>*Simians here need help*
>*Came to shore, all plants dead from fire.*
>*Heavenly temple smoking*
>*Apes dead or dying*
>*What started out as a sale became a relief mission*
>*May fortune favor me in this disaster's wake.*

A somber tone swept over the class as they absorbed the scale of devastation in the kingdom as the environment shifted to reflect an artful rendering. Of charred, blackened beaches littered with debris, and twinkling glass. Of the central temple now a goblet of ruin. Of hobbling victims, horrifically maimed and burned, and traders coming ashore assisting the weak and ill, offloading supplies. Adobes pulverized by the blast lay flat like the trees and lifeless as distant farms.

Ethrin narrowed his eyes at the farms. "Must've been a pretty serious famine if all the trees and farms were taken out by the blast." Yugraiz narrowed her eyes to the nerd. "… 'Famine?' Really?" she said under her breath.

"Yes, but in a previously unseen act of community, the ancient civilizations of Getra banded together and converged upon Houlos Mox. Over five kingdoms and thirty tribes all bearing food, workers, and soldiers." A map displayed a vast expanse of the geography and various sized arrows converging upon the crater in the middle of the gulf. Many from land, several by sea.

"Word spread quickly to lands across half of the planet. The ancient world all came to know about the ill-fated Kingdom, and Tekrath's legacy." The painted stage stirred to holographic life, bustling with activity as the base of the crater was rapidly rebuilt during a time-lapse. A true unity of cultures, and a spike in population made the great kingdom into a thriving mega-city as structures began building up and out from the crater.

Yugraiz sulked and her eyelids grew heavy. The asteroid impact was definitely seeming like a highlight at the top of a long, boring downward slope. She began looking around for something, anything interesting. Further ahead were scrolls, old and damaged pottery and tools, what looked like an old canoe, and tapestries. Further ahead were many more displays featuring each progressive chapter in the development of Getran society. Not a one of them hinted at the colossal holographic explosion sequences. Yugraiz began scanning the vast hall for an exit.

A figure emerged at the left side of the crater. A pious rendering of a clean white-robed Chimpanzee with a stern and serious expression.

"This is Bodor, a priest from the south. He collected and documented studies of various tribes and their religious beliefs, so naturally he and his academy were immediately attracted to the drop. Surely, an undeniable act of God of this scale would be a veritable treasure trove for faith studies for generations to come. The formation of the goblet at the peak of the stairs, and the strange metals found within the crater itself were seen as holy artifacts that should be protected and revered. Bodor's group referred to themselves as Basers, for all life sat at the base of God. Followers of Godking Tekrath were quick to fill their numbers as testament to his holy status."

A banner emerged behind the depiction of Bodor. Silhouettes of an army of Getrans amassed beneath a white flag with black markings, a right paw print above a wide bowl-like "U."

Vellong stared quizzically at the army behind the priest. Many were carrying spears and clubs. "Teacher… if they went around studying religion, why do those guys look like an army?"

Ms. Daws furrowed her brow and slowly nodded. "Not all that the Basers encountered in their travels were willing to… *cooperate* with their studies. Their tomes and scrolls were said to be etched in blood."

The children transferred their gaze from the teacher to the holographic image of the stern, cold-looking Bodor; the animated waving flag in the wind, and the still, shadowy soldiers behind him. The teacher crossed in front of the holograph and commanded the classes' attention.

"The Basers formed these combative forces long before their arrival at Houlos Mox. When they marched onto the blackened shores to inspect the crater, they met a foreign group formed by rival philosophers of the east who were already wading into the crater and excavating the strange metal contents of the asteroid."

The holograph then formed the image of the Gorilla scholar, Lim. An old silverback was adorned in pitch-black robes, a tall and wizened figure with white fur and weakened eyes. There he stooped, haunched beneath a vibrant blue banner depicting white markings of four stars with four points arranged in a diamond. He too had silhouettes of similar soldiers at his back.

"Bodor encountered a group of foreign travelers, mostly philosophers, scientists from a strange land, who began pulling lumps of celestial metal from the mouth of the crater. This, of course, infuriated the Basers as they argued and scuffled with these scholars." As she said this, the figures of Bodor and Lim clashed at the center of the crater. "According to Trader Olo's detailed accounts of the interaction, the Baser's rival group had no clear concentrated origin, but were like-minded scientists and thinkers that converged and meshed with each other along the way. They sought to learn from the impact through experimentation, and most immediately recognized that the metals found in the crater were vastly different from any known Getran mineral."

The hologram shifted to show Lim clutching a raw chunk of glittering ore and presenting it to Bodor, hoping to challenge the priest into considering a new point of view.

"There were many in the group opposite of the Basers that demanded to know, if this were an act of God, why strike down their son? Why strike a kingdom with such devastation, and if the metals found in the perceived attack were a gift… or a warning? Many agreed with this group, pointing their eyes starward in curiosity as to where the drop came from and how these things came to be. In response, Bodor simply stated that what they tampered with was evidence of a holy power, and what they were doing was heresy. It was the Basers' duty to ensure that they would reunite them with God despite their crimes. It was the Basers who first referred to Lim's group as The Ascenders."

The class marched on down the hall of the museum. Paintings depicting the conflict between Basers and Ascenders were flanked with artifacts of their weapons, skulls damaged from battle, and maps illustrating the scale of influence spreading across the continents.

Yugraiz interlocked her fingers and rested her hands above her head as she walked along with her friends in the tour, glancing around with an indifferent pout. Ethrin was prattling on about famous battles and key moments of what he kept referring to as the Metal War that Bodor and Lim kicked off. Vellong seemed much more interested in the weapons - the lumpy and shoddy weapons of olde were becoming more refined and elaborate with each consecutive exhibit. Even as rusted and scarred as some of the iron weapons were, it was clear that both sides were intensely racing against each other in their smithing techniques.

The teacher stopped by an ornate, massive painting dated 11 AD. Eleven years after the drop, Lim the Philosopher passed away from old age. The artwork showed his body laid to rest on a stone bed in a mountain kingdom to the north. He was surrounded by black-robed confidants, trusted allies, kings, generals, and professors that came to represent what the Ascenders had become. Their banners hung from the ancient wood and stone Keep in the background.

Ethrin directed attention to the map nearby of the 10 AD era. "Check this out! Basers fought long and hard for Houlos Mox and managed to push the Ascenders out of the old kingdom's lands, making it their capital. But Lim led his newfound army of supporters outward, expanding across the globe, recruiting tribes and kingdoms to their cause."

Vellong was pouring over every detail of Lim's funeral painting. "… Which was, what, to check out metal and to question God?"

Ethrin adjusted his glasses with a mere scrunch of his nose and mouth. "Not exactly. Just as the Basers scoured the old world for religion, these Apes in black were scouring the world for science like astrology, metallurgy, and stuff that they used to think was alchemy. They were totally a minority back then compared to the size of The Basers, and were trying to bolster their numbers as much as possible in the Metal War by forming an Empire driven by science."

Ms. Daws could be heard in the background of the cavernous hall, teaching the rest of the class about Bodor's establishment of Orthodox Tekrathism, a church that worshipped and revered Godking Tekrath as the true Golden Boon of God. Yugraiz was losing interest at a free-fall pace, until she noticed a strange doorway in between the display cases in this gigantic arm of the museum. Signs informed them it was a shortcut to a fire escape, but further into the room she saw displays of tall sailing ships, cannons, and guns. The teacher's line of sight was well enough away from the path, and Yugraiz was quite fed up with the Bronze and Copper age of Ancient Getra.

The Gorilla nudged her Bonobo friend's arm. "Hey, Ethrin, look over there. Think that's more of the Metal War?"

Ethrin and Vellong leaned over to peer in the direction she was pointing. "Tallships? That's waaay after. See, after the Fall of Houlos Mox, The Metal War was sort-of won by the Ascenders, and they started travelling everywhere to make sure that the Basers were- hey… HEY! Where are you guys going?"

Ethrin sprinted to catch up to Yugraiz, dragging along Vellong by his long Gibbon arms. Undetected by the class or the teacher, unimpeded by any present staff or random Getrans, the three dove forward in time in the exhibit, and entered the Empirical era of global conquest known as the Unifying Drive.

Yugraiz smiled as she looked around the very different layout in this part of the museum. Looking right, an old Chimpanzee stood haunched at the mouth of the exhibit and smiled at them from down the hall, rows upon rows of display cases on both sides of the walls leading to him. These contained military uniforms and dazzling sabres and flintlock riflery. To the left were models and paintings of vast armadas of tall-ships, battleships dominating waters with majestic crests of white sails and mighty wooden hulls.

Vellong was particularly captured by a painting showing a sea absolutely filled with naval ships, far and close. "I guess this makes a lot of sense. The Getran Navy in space is crazy huge these days, I guess it's always been kinda nuts."

"Well, actually" Ethrin interjected, "… if you look at the whole timeline, the military seems to come in waves." He rapidly glanced between the two for a reaction. "… Especially the ships." He continued, a smile gradually expanding across his face.

They both looked directly at him, observing the nerd trying not to crack up at his own joke. "*They come in waves!*

She tightened her lip and inhaled sharply through her nose before walking further into the exhibit in an attempt to suppress her anger at the awful pun. Onward through time they trudged, Ethrin snoring a self-congratulatory laugh through his nose.

"Wow, these ships *are* old," Vellong said.

"I wanna know how we got Spaceclimbers and Gorgers," Yugraiz sneered, skimming by the exhibits with little more than a glance. "Unless there was a time when they made a big wooden ape controlled by a bunch of pulleys and rope, I think we're a long way off from that chapter in history."

An old voice startlingly peeped up from behind them "Ohh, you're way off!"

They screamed and leapt around to face the source of the voice. The old Chimp from down the hall! "Ohh! I'm sorry, little ones: I didn't mean to startle you." Yugraiz tried playing it off, but Vellong and Ethrin sighed to diffuse their initial fright.

The Chimp was clearly wearing dentures behind his rough and wrinkly smile. His entire face was entrenched by decades of wear. His fur, while trimmed into a reasonably short haircut, was still somehow scraggily, and white fringes traced his otherwise black coat. He appeared to be wearing a military dress uniform. An emblem of a golden seed beneath four silver stars with four points each arranged into a diamond pattern was worn centrally over his chest. This tour guide was a veteran.

"My name is Murrk... .I'm the *tour guide* to this branch of museum. Um, are you three lost?"

Vellong innocently shook his head, "No, sir, our class is actually right over th—"

Yugraiz was quick to halt his long Gibbon arms from pointing back from whence they came. She interjected, "They're actually just up ahead! We were busy, uh, being a little more thorough with the Metal War stuff."

Old Murrk smiled widely. "Ahhh, the war that started it all. Such a shame that we Getrans have such a sordid and well documented relationship with warfare." He shuffled his old and tired feet further into the exhibit, his footwear resembling a dignified, glossy dress shoe with a posable toe protrusion as if it were a mitt. Despite his militant upkeep, the areas of his shoes were visibly worn in the more high traffic portions of the shoe. Walking between the children, and leading them further into the museum, he spoke softly and they followed.

"Old Trader OIo's scribes late in his life were optimistic that the Metal War was going to be the war to end all wars... heh, and of course it wasn't. The Metal War may have ended, but Basers across Getra fought and resisted the Ascenders for over a thousand years. So deep-rooted were these societies, the Ascension Empire decided to invent a new one with the same idea in mind. 'The last war', they thought... heheh"

He chuckled at the foolish notion and trudged methodically between paintings of vast armies of simians marching onto shore in colorful blue and orange uniforms. The dates beneath the paintings labeled them 1102 AD.

Murrk came to a toddering halt, "Lemme ask you kids something..." He craned his slouched posture around to face them properly. "What were the Ascenders trying to do? From the beginning?"

Of course, the group looked to Ethrin, but he remained tight-lipped to see if they would get it. Yugraiz and Vellong looked at each other briefly before answering.

Yugraiz flexed one of her Gorilla arms, "Get stronger to fight!"

Vellong cupped his chin, "Get smarter to learn?"

"I thought you kids were paying attention back there... ." Old Murrk laughed, "... They couldn't quite articulate it as a rag-tag group of thinkers and soldiers, but after they became an Empire, they knew... They knew that *space* was no different than an uncharted ocean for them, waiting to be explored and claimed. After the Metal Wars, they spent less time making weapons and more time blowing glass to form better lenses and mirrors to observe space, and they had the idea in 'em that if Apes were ever gonna get there, then it was gonna take every last one of us to get up there and face destiny."

He gestured to a tall portrait of a very important-looking individual. An absurdly tall, broad-shouldered great Ape was heavily decorated in an old-world Naval Officer's uniform. "Take this tall-glass of water, for example. She is The Great Captain Yettus, Conqueror of Early Getra."

Ethrin's jaw slacked open. "Oh wow, I've heard about her! There was an episode of Prideful History that talked about influential Yetis and Sasquatches in history."

Vellong was stunned, " *That's a Yeti?* Woah, I thought they didn't exist anymore."

Yugraiz unintentionally pulled her mouth to the side into a cringe. "That would explain it... I thought the artist just really messed up on a Gorilla."

"I'm afraid Yetis and Sasquatches have seemed to have gone extinct over the past several hundred years..." Murrk bowed his head somberly. "... Truly a shame. They were notoriously powerful Getrans, but the Great Yettus was cut from an even rarer cloth of her kind. She was a brilliant tactician. For hundreds of years, it was well understood that there was much of the mapped world that remained independent from the Ascension Empire, and waters still in need of being charted, lands to be discovered, and simians to integrate into one unified planet."

Her portrait had her standing tall, her head tilted up, looking down her Gorilla-like snout at the children. Her mouth formed a flat tightness indicative of the nobility of the era. Among the medals and aiguillettes hanging from her Naval Peacoat, the familiar golden seed and star device was worn to indicate her military status right at the center of her chest. Thousands of years had passed, and the design of the emblem remained relatively consistent.

"The Great Yettus rose to Captain status after proving herself in battle against pirates. Though relatively young when she first joined the Imperial Navy, she, like all of her kind, had an unusually long life span. She lived under the rule of five kings, the final being King Getra himself. Had she not chosen to go down with her ship, there is a possibility that she may have lived longer than 305 years of age."

Ethrin and Vellong were star-struck, but Yugraiz was a little more overwhelmed by the Captain. Here she was, breaking off from the group to find out about some incredible action in Getran history, and this Great Yettus seemed to be the jackpot of action. But 'Old-man Murrk' seemed to be rapidly glossing over her legacy. She looked ahead of the exhibit, and it appeared to be more of the same that they had already passed.

Yugraiz wanted to dive deeper into learning about The Great Yettus, but didn't want to interrupt the old man educating her friends. As she listened in, she noticed that he had already moved on to talk about the tallships at length, with a level of intricacy that implied there was no sign of stopping. Her two friends were heavily engrossed about the length of the mast and the dimensions of the sails, and the cannons. The tale of The Great Yettus drifted further and further behind.

She took a step back to observe the situation. They hadn't moved from in front of the Captain's portrait, and Old Murrk's eyesight was bad enough that it forced him to lean in extremely close to her classmates to speak to them. Their backs were turned to her, so they didn't notice her slowly migrating away. Looking back at the fire exit shortcut they took, she could recognize her class moving further down the ancient exhibit, oblivious to the three of them missing from the group.

No telling how much time she had until her teacher noticed they were missing, or they caught up to this part of the museum. She trekked onward, unnoticed; now on a mission to find out more about The Great Captain Yettus, Conqueror and Unifier of Getra.

The Gorilla kit advanced deeper into the museum at a comfortable pace, her burly paws stuffed into the side pockets of her jacket. She glanced left and right at the contents of the halls detailing a King every once in a while, or a shadowbox of jewelry from the cultures that preceded Imperial Integration. The artifacts were strange and beautiful, but not captivating enough to give her pause. She was focused.

An overhead speaker softly announced to the museum.

> *"Attention please. Will the following please go to the Rollbean Cafe: Vellong Frun, Ethrin Loza, Yugraiz Bakki. Please go to the Rollbean Cafe on level one. Thank you."*

Yugraiz sunk her head further into her jacket and smacked her lips, "Drat." The thought crossed her mind that if she turned back now, the class might eventually get to her exhibit. But as she thought further on it, nowhere in her studies had they entered the tallship era of things yet. The field trip might have been specifically just for the ancient era of the Metal War. One last try to learn about her newfound hero in this place, but she would have to hurry.

In an unusual change of pace for the museum's layout, she encountered a fork in the path of the museum. At a glance, both routes seemed to dance around the Unifying Drive era of history, but it wasn't immediately clear which side had more about The Great Yettus. Even more confusing still if she lived for hundreds of years, as far as she could tell either side would be the way to go.

But something caught her eye down the extreme end of the hall to the left path. A Gorilla teen, about her age at 16, walked along with what looked to be his father. His hair was a little wild up top, but close cropped along the sides and back. The jacket he was wearing looked like a bomber jacket similar to her own. Then, just as she was sizing him up, he turned to her from all those meters away and smiled as he disappeared around the corner. And if only for an instant, that look he had shot her had impeccable aim as it struck her heart with exciting precision.

For a beat she looked down the other hallway to her right. She looked at it and thought to herself that it was probably the correct way to go, and she probably should not go down the left hallway. As she continued walking down the left, she knew in her heart that Great Yettus was probably down there somewhere. She knew that if she turned around and rejoined her class she'd get yelled at then, but she'd get yelled at if it was about five minutes later. Ten minutes later… .twelve.

But it was okay. She could look up Yettus when she got home. She would not be able to find this boy so easily. She accelerated into a brisk speed-walk around the corner. And there he was with an absolutely hulking, warrior-like father at his side. She was eyeing him up as well as she closed the distance, not realizing that what they were facing opened up into an elevator. As they stepped in, she maintained stride and slipped right in behind them.

It didn't quite occur to her what she was doing until the elevator chimed and the doors began to shut. The Gorilla dad looked straight ahead and pressed the appropriate floor button. She did everything she could to resist sweating. Her mind, on a loop, chanted over and over again *"Oh god, what have I done?"*

In her periphery, Yugraiz noticed the young Gorilla glance at her and quickly look away, as if expecting her to say something. She strained to break the loop, and internally interjected, *"Look at him, dummy."*

She turned to face him, and tried to lean back all cool while bumping her chin up in a greeting nod. "Hey, what's good? Hah!"

In a quick take, he looked at her and back to the floor. "Oh, hey! Just uh, museum stuff."

"Yeah, that's cool. Ya like Yettus?"

The boy looked at her weirdly. "I guess. I'm trying to get more into salads lately."

She tightened her lips, but before she could sharply inhale, realized that may not have been a bad Ethrin joke and instead rolled out a shy laugh, "No, no, not *lettuce,* The Great Captain Yettus."

The boy clasped his face in embarrassment, leaning into his dad. "Oh, dang it."

The kids both laughed as the giant Gorilla in the room ruffled his son's hair and smiled at Yugraiz. The elevator chimed at that moment and let them off into the higher floor of the exhibit. It had been her intention to chat briefly and exchange contact information before she hurried off to rejoin her class, but this exhibit was depicting an era she was completely unfamiliar with.

The city did not resemble anything like she had seen in her life. It was not like modern Getra. Not a layer cake of steel and concrete, dripping with nodes of vines and vertical plant life just to break up the unrelenting assault of dense superstructure, choking the sky with neon lights, billboards, bulkheads and shadowy low-rent chasms.

The exhibit walls depicted a simpler, yet bustling metropolis of concrete, steel, and glass - simpler skyscrapers and open skies. More like a concentration of obelisks, meshed with smaller buildings, paths of super highways and streets. As if a much calmer, simplified iteration of the Getra that she had come to know in her time.

And there in the dead middle of the landscape in this exhibit, metal Getran rockets firing off into the sky and an iconic picture of a lush, watery, cloudy orb; the first picture of Getra from space.

This was the Pre Colony age exhibit.

As they stepped away from the elevators and into the clearing, the Gorilla dad seemed to approach one particular female waiting on a bench. She beamed lovingly as she recognized him and stood to address him.

"Hey, Wurran! I just got here a minute ago; I haven't been waiting long." They embraced warmly. Her bright yellow sundress was a stark contrast to his all-black attire. As they relaxed their hug, she smiled at the little ones. "Hey buddy! Who's your friend?"

Yugraiz perked up in a split-second panic attack. "Oh! I'm sorry, I never introduced myself. I'm Yugraiz... and um, I wanted to ask you your uh—"

"I'm Plundr. Nice to meet you! This is my dad, Wurran, and his girlfriend Cordi."

Yugraiz nodded to them respectfully. Wurran looked upwards as he sifted through his thoughts. "Let's see..." his voice was a startling bassy boom. "... Your name is Yugraiz, right? Didn't they just mention you on the museum intercom a little while ago?"

Yugraiz perked up for another split-second panic attack. "OH! Um... m-maybe? Heh, I mustn't have caught that."

"Uhuh." Wurran rumbled, skeptically. "Just don't be too long- I don't want you to get into any trouble. You hear that, Plundr? Make it quick." The massive Gorilla turned away, with his arm swung over his date. Yugraiz managed to catch the twinkle of the golden seed and silver stars, recognizing that he too had a military background.

The kids now found themselves alone with each other in the spacious lobby. Yugraiz was the first to break the awkward silence as Wurran and Cordi travelled further out of earshot.

"So, 'Plunder' is it? That's kind of a weird name."

"It's the only one I have, actually. Wurran gave it to me when he adopted me and... well... it's kind of personal but it's okay. I know it's weird, but I'm fine with it. I actually like your name a lot. What's your other one?"

"Oh my full name? Bakki. Yugraiz Bakki."

"Heh, cool! Sounds tough, I guess."

She blushed. "Oh, thanks... now I feel kinda bad about saying your name is weird. What are you guys here for specifically in this museum? This place is huge!"

He nodded. "I know, right? Actually I'm trying to prepare for early tests into the military officer's academy. My dad is a commando, but after hearing about some of his experiences, he's convinced me that leadership is the right way to go. It was his idea to brush up on the intricacies of our history, and to especially focus on, like, the compassionate peacetime eras of history that we had."

Yugraiz looked at the image of the rocket dominating the wall outside of the exhibit. "That is really cool, and also... so daunting. From what I've seen today, it seems like those 'compassionate peacetimes' are so few and far between. Seems like we're always super focused on the wars. That hardly anybody remembers the times when we *aren't* fighting."

Plundr stared into an empty space and nodded. "Yep. I see what you mean. We definitely seem to fight a lot, but... I hope I can find myself in a position where I can be like, 'Hey, it doesn't have to be this way.'... Y'know?"

Yugraiz studied him for a moment. Pausing before she asked, "Is that kind of like The Great Yettus by chance?"

"Haha, not... .exactly? She was kinda brutal. Which makes sense, because that whole old-world half of us *thrived* on brutality. It was only when we seemed to have no one left to fight that we were able to really knuckle down and do some really great, non-war-like stuff. She was right there in that violent world unifying thing, which is basically a nice way of saying she toured the world convincing people to join the empire, and if they refused, she killed them. She rarely compromised, and I think it's because of her setting that standard, most of our leaders have been doing the same thing forever."

A poignant silence fell between the kids. Suddenly Yugraiz had doubts about her hero worship of the Captain. Plundr looked around nervously, and pointed a thumb to the main exhibit.

"Are you... familiar with the Pre Colony era?"

She smiled at him and suppressed a laugh, "Not at all. Actually, I was wondering, what's up with that thing? Is that a missile or something?" She pointed to the rocket.

He knew it was a joke and they both shared a giggle as they jogged into the exhibit. The intercom sprang to life once again asking only for Yugraiz to go to the Rollbean Cafe this time.

The two Gorilla kids came to a stop before a moving walkway that led them further into the Getran's first space age. The ceiling above them was white and tent-like, hanging sails pure and tall. The sheer height and scale of this floor of this exhibit was breathtaking. The lighting that was cast upon the sails ensured that the highest anchorpoints disappeared into shadowy blackness. Yugraiz's keen eyes were dazzled by the imitation of the twinkling stars in the black.

They looked at the conveyor belt beneath them, then onto each other, and without looking away, stepped off in unison. Plundr swayed a little from the unexpected inertia, but it was okay. He was a nervous dork. In no time at all, the lights dimmed as the exhibit became aware of the cubs and a voice over a wise collegiate thoomed from their surroundings.

"It was 1742 After Drop. The Getran Empire had launched their first autonomous satellite into space. Within minutes of being activated, far from the planet Getra's electromagnetic field, the solar powered satellite picked up the first transmission from intelligent extraterrestrial life. Then another. And another. And this would continue ceaselessly for generations of Getran scientists to come. Suffice to say, the planet Getra went apeshit."

Yugraiz and Plundr rolled their eyes and groaned as if that was a joke they had heard for all their life. "More and more satellites were launched into space. Probes were dispatched. Offworld telescopes. In no time at all, a surge of knowledge and information flooded Getra's greatest minds."

The halls of the exhibit swelled with the beautiful, prideful optimism of the age. Vintage snippets of radio broadcasts and television footage of Getrans in the 1740's absolutely wild with joy that they weren't alone in the universe. A disco of space Apes and oddities. Science fiction films of epic encounters with Ape-like aliens. The whole world was captivated. The destiny of the species had only just begun.

The historical photography displayed of those first glimpses into the galaxy, of nebulae, of star clusters were flinging by to the crescendo of uplifting music. Plundr's jaw couldn't help but slack agape at the grand majesty of space rendered above, and Yugraiz soon followed. Soon after, the music hushed, and a rectangular window emerged centrally in front of them, as if they were being pulled to the viewscreen. There, centered, was the King of Getra of this era: King Diamot. He spoke upon a lofty pillar, high above the former Houlos Mox, now a Skyscraper Metropolis, Houlos Prime.

The recording was staticky and damaged from time, as was the footage of their TV monochrome and compact in their aspect ratio.

"Fellow Getrans, this is our moment. Through the centuries we have grown to live with each other and die with each other, upon this jungle planet. This is our defining hour. We trust in our ability to take our gears and cogs and wires and electricity and form them in such a way that we direct our ears to the sky. And with that, we heard the impossible. The

whispers that reached our ears beckoned us to reach further,
and by God, we did!"

The crowd of that Metropolis cheered at what must've been deafening volumes. The King tried to continue to speak - his lips moved, but was clearly and utterly drowned out. The Royal Chimpanzee smiled as he waited for the crowd's energy to part for his continuation. Yugraiz looked over to Plundr, entranced in the recording. He was there. She was here with him. She aligned himself with him, and nudged herself closer before she continued to watch.

"With those whispers, the cosmos tantalized our eyes, and
we trusted in our ability to take out lenses and mirrors and
cameras and astrology, and by God, we did that too!"

Another roar from the crowd. The camera feed of this archived news footage showed mothers with babies, fathers waving service caps emblazoned with familiar military emblems. Simians of all walks of life, in unity, as one. Yugraiz eyed Plundr's hand, but stopped herself from getting carried away. Maybe now was not the time nor the place.

"... and it is here, we respond. This proud kind we have
become. Getra is more than one Chimp. One hundred
Lemurs. One thousand Baboons. One million Gorillas. We
are quite more than that. We Apes have been blessed with the
tools and wherewithal to respond to the Call of the Stars. It is
WE, United together, red blooded Getrans that we can SEE
where we are destined to be next! For Generations to come!
Our destiny is not here, but there!"

As the King pointed up, Yugraiz felt the tension around her fingers. She looked to Plundr, now clutching her hand, with his mouth agape, focused on King Diamot, with a single tear running down his Gorilla cheek. She was starstruck from that moment onward, and watched the rest of the broadcast with a warmth in her heart.

"We shall respond to what our ears have heard! We shall seek
in great detail for what our eyes have seen! We shall clutch the
previously unclutchable, and we shall live and thrive within
the previously unknown because God Dammit, if any beast
in this universe can, we know first hand that it should be us!"

The audience at the seat of the throne was absolutely thrilling carnage. Their hearts swelled with what was no doubt the sentiments of an entire kingdom.

"We have always known this is what's meant to be. From
ancient writings, pulled from the very foundation of our
written history. Look on, great Apes. We rise to inspect the

content of our dreams. To find our neighbors. To let them
know, that We Are Getra! We have been here for a long time!
We dare to go."

The video footage showed that Getran rocket, vertically poised and ready to ignite. We saw the astronaut Monkey crews calmly working their way through the final run of the instrument safety checks. As the rocket ignited, water droplets and even flurries of ice danced and listed off of the heaving craft. The sound softened away from the rocket's roar, poorly captured by the era's overwhelmed recording quality, and instead shifted to something softer as King Diamot read a somewhat familiar poem.

Engines primed, we found our lead
Where our pride had plant the seed
The ebon glimm a canvas far
We anchor to our Mother Star.
Climb with me. Far from all.
As one we'll be. We won't fall.
The night is free and vast like sea...
... At the top So high We'll be.

Life in a hyena clan is not easy, especially for Straggletail, daughter of the clan's omega. She has always wondered where the sun goes when it sets. With a surprise companion, she ventures forth to find out.

Beyond Acacia Ridge

by Amy Fontaine

Straggletail sat on the ridge by the lone acacia tree, looking out to the west. Behind her, to the east, golden savannah grass danced to the touch of the wind on the broad plain. Beyond the ridge, to the west, the ground sloped steeply into a valley, and a thick jungle sprawled toward distant mountains. Above the mountains, strange spheres drifted on the wind like lazy birds. They were too far away for Straggletail to tell what they were. But she always wondered.

More than anything, Straggletail wondered where the sun went at night.

Every dusk, when Straggletail heard a chorus of whoops as the rest of the clan rallied for a long night of hunting and territory defense, Straggletail sat by herself on the ridge beside the acacia and watched the sun disappear behind the western mountains. The clan had decided long before she was born that Straggletail was not a good hyena. She was the lowest female in the hierarchy, like her mother before her. It was tradition in the clan that cubs would inherit the ranks of their mothers. No one asked why. That was just how things were.

But Straggletail hated the way things were. She longed not to eat last anymore, to get a hearty meal for once. She wished she didn't have to grovel at every other female she saw, wished she wouldn't get picked on like a strange male by her own clanmates. But despite her deep-seated yearning to escape her fate, the clan's treatment of her over her two years of life thus far had wormed its way into her mind. She was last because she was lowly, because she was weak. Because she was not a strong fighter, a good hunter, a born leader.

She was a failure. It was in her blood.

So, since Straggletail was destined to always lose in real life, she turned to her dreams for escape. As she watched the sun vanish to the west, she dreamed that she ran from the familiar savannah into the unknown jungle, and through the jungle all through the night and climbed the western mountains and found the place where the sun had been hiding every night. She dreamed she clenched the sun in her strong jaws and dragged it all the way back to the clan. She dreamed that the clan killed a fat topi in her honor and allowed her to eat first. That they sang songs forevermore of Straggletail, the brave adventurer who voyaged beyond the clan's territory through the jungle of no return… and returned. She dreamed that even Broadsnout, the matriarch of the clan, bowed before her. She dreamed…

"Straggletail!"

At the hoarse whisper of her name, Straggletail snapped to attention, jumping back to all fours. She looked around wildly at the long savannah grass on top of the ridge, which rippled like feathery gold in the wind.

"Who's there?" Straggletail whimpered fearfully.

"Over here!" called the voice from a thick clump of grass to Straggletail's right. Peering through the grass, Straggletail could just make out the shape of a hyena: Glossycoat. Glossycoat's fur was the same shining, golden hue of the sunset-dappled grass, with bold spots as black as night. Straggletail sighed wistfully; her own coat was the same muddy color as her mother Dustfur's coat had been. Straggletail had always envied Glossycoat, for many more reasons than her beautiful fur.

Suddenly remembering herself with a thrill of horror, Straggletail gasped. Glossycoat was Broadsnout's youngest daughter, the highest-ranking member of the clan after Broadsnout herself! Lowering her head and hunching her body, Straggletail crawled toward Glossycoat on her front forelegs, flashing Glossycoat a submissive grin. Glossycoat shook her head.

"Don't worry about formalities right now," Glossycoat hissed. "We don't have time for that. Listen, I brought you something, but…" Glossycoat lifted her head above the grass, glancing nervously from side to side. She quickly sank back down into the grass. Then she rolled an object toward Straggletail.

The delicious smell of a fresh wildebeest haunch tantalized Straggletail's nostrils. Straggletail gaped at Glossycoat, who gestured at the haunch with a nod. Shaking her head, Straggletail backed away, her ropy tail whipping from side to side.

Straggletail was completely dismayed. She was used to Glossycoat bossing everyone around, as was her birthright. Even when Glossycoat had been a tiny black cub, Straggletail's adult mother had groveled at her. In return, Glossycoat had assaulted Dustfur with precocious ferocity. Straggletail could not recall all the times Glossycoat had shoved her away from a kill, all the times Glossycoat had bitten the skin on the back of Straggletail's neck and shaken her head from side to side to assert her dominance. But now, here was Glossycoat, offering Straggletail food with an inviting nod.

Straggletail's heart raced. She backed away from Glossycoat, bobbing her head respectfully all the while.

"Is this a test?" Straggletail moaned. "Because I know where we stand, I promise! I know I am unworthy! I know you are, and will always be, my superior!" Straggletail crouched with her head lowered and her hindquarters tucked down, trembling violently, staring at the ground.

Glossycoat sighed. "I know it must not be easy for you to trust me. I'm sorry." She curled up under the acacia and closed her eyes. "Just pretend like I'm not here and eat the food. It's not a trick. I'd just like to ask you something."

Slowly, Straggletail crept toward the food. Once she was close enough, she lunged, grabbing the haunch in her jaws and then running down the ridge with it—to the west, in the direction of the jungle. Once she was just out of sight of the acacia, she devoured the haunch almost instantly, bones and all. Then, she climbed back up the ridge. Glossycoat still lay in the same spot under the tree.

"I thought you might run off," Glossycoat said. "But I'm glad you came back."

Straggletail stood just out of Glossycoat's lunging range. "What did you want to ask me?" Straggletail said, her voice trembling.

Glossycoat stood and stretched. She looked into Straggletail's eyes without a trace of aggression, only curiosity.

"What are you looking at?" whispered Glossycoat.

Straggletail's heart hammered. "What do you mean?" she stammered.

Glossycoat jerked her head toward the west, where the sun was sinking beyond the mountains. Straggletail's heart sank. She'd never catch up with the sun at this rate, not even in her dreams.

"Every nightfall," Glossycoat said, "you come here, and you look to the west, and it seems to bring you peace. What are you looking at?"

Straggletail's ears folded back, and she looked away.

"Nothing," said Straggletail.

Glossycoat took a step toward Straggletail. Straggletail shrank back.

"It's not *nothing*," Glossycoat insisted. "I've seen the look on your face. It's like…" Glossycoat glanced at the vanishing sun. "Like suddenly, all the ways the clan has hurt you, they don't even matter anymore. Like you're somewhere else."

Glossycoat came and sat down next to Straggletail. For a moment, Straggletail hyperventilated. As she noticed Glossycoat's relaxed posture, and the fact that Glossycoat wasn't even looking at her, she slowly began to relax herself. She sat down beside Glossycoat. The two young hyenas looked to the west, at the bright spot in the sky where the sun had just slipped away.

"Do you ever wish *you* were somewhere else?" asked Straggletail timidly.

Glossycoat heaved a sigh. "All the time."

Just then, a chorus of whoops rang through the air from the east. "Glossycoat!" roared a deep voice that caused both hyenas to leap to their feet and bristle with fear.

Broadsnout charged up the ridge. For a large female whose belly was distended with meat, she moved faster than a wildfire on a dry plain. Straggletail and Glossycoat darted wildly about, but Broadsnout had seen them. There was nowhere to hide.

Broadsnout approached the two young hyenas with a stiff gait and a bristled tail, pointing her whole body sharply at Straggletail. Straggletail crawled backwards with her ears back, her head bobbing wildly in a frantic gesture of surrender.

But she was not fast enough.

Broadsnout lunged at Straggletail, clamping her jaws around the back of her neck, whipping her head back and forth so quickly that Straggletail couldn't even breathe. Then she dropped Straggletail like a limp gazelle carcass on the grass. Straggletail gasped and coughed. Broadsnout stood over her, her head held high. Straggletail opened her mouth in a gape, admitting defeat.

"Good," crooned Broadsnout. "You know your place. And don't you ever forget it, or I'll do to you just what I did to your simpering, mud-furred mother."

As Straggletail cowered beneath her, Broadsnout turned and looked sternly at Glossycoat.

"Come, daughter. You must show the low-ranker her place."

Glossycoat had watched Broadsnout's dominance display with a look of horror, but as Broadsnout turned to her, her expression hardened. "Yes, Mother." Broadsnout stepped aside, and now Glossycoat stood over Straggletail: head and tail high, triumphant. Straggletail gaped up at her pitifully.

Broadsnout trotted off down the hill, Glossycoat at her heels. When Broadsnout wasn't looking, Glossycoat shot an apologetic look back over her shoulder at Straggletail. Straggletail returned the look blankly, still lying on the ground. She didn't know what to think.

After Broadsnout and Glossycoat left, Straggletail struggled to her feet as the first stars winked into view in the sky overhead. Wistfully, Straggletail gazed toward the mountains and the now-hidden sun. At last, reluctantly, she turned away and trotted back down the ridge into the clan's territory.

* * *

Straggletail wandered through the territory distractedly under a sky brilliant with stars. Her stomach churned with the memory of Broadsnout's aggression. When she closed her eyes, she could still see Broadsnout leering down her wide, scarred muzzle at her. It reminded her of another night, only a year ago…

Dustfur was starving; her ribs poked through her muddy, speckled side. Straggletail slunk dejectedly behind her mother, her empty stomach crying with pain. Straggletail had been a mere yearling then, but she already knew her place, and the consequences of overstepping her bounds. At least, she thought she knew.

But that night, it all became so much clearer.

Dustfur was dying. Her only daughter was dying. She had nothing left to lose.

That night, Broadsnout and her young—including Glossycoat—and Broadsnout's sisters, who were also big, dominant, bullying hyenas, were feasting on a cape buffalo carcass. There was a clump of bushes to one side of the carcass, a deep ravine with a river running through it on the other. On any other night, Dustfur would have walked right by the high-rankers' revelry without daring to stop. But her hunger—and her daughter's hunger—pushed Dustfur to her wit's end.

Straggletail watched in horror as Dustfur staggered toward the buffalo carcass. "No, Mom! What are you doing?" Desperately, Straggletail bit her mother's tail and tried to pull her back. But it was no use. Dustfur just kept marching toward her doom.

"Stay back," Dustfur warned Straggletail. "Keep low. Hide."

"What?" cried Straggletail. "I can't—"

Dustfur turned and snapped at her. "I won't tell you twice!"

Startled at this unexpected display of aggression from her low-ranking mother, Straggletail nodded and ran to the bushes. She crouched there, hidden, barely breathing, rolling a little in some mongoose scat to try to disguise her scent. She watched through the leaves with bated breath as Dustfur stumbled right up to Broadsnout and her family.

Broadsnout and the others looked up. Expressions varying from surprise to shock to revulsion passed across their faces. Broadsnout swiveled her head toward Dustfur.

"Well, well," sneered Broadsnout. "If it isn't Mudfur."

Broadsnout and four of the other high-rankers walked stiff-legged, shoulder to shoulder, toward Dustfur, backing her toward the cliff. Dustfur giggled fearfully, bobbing her head.

"I want... I need some... you're gonna..." Taking a deep breath, Dustfur lunged at the line of high-rankers. "For Straggletail!" she cried.

But the high-rankers were on her in an instant, and with multiple strong, healthy hyenas against one squealing, emaciated female, it was no contest. Straggletail leapt out of the bushes, crying, "No! Stop!" Hearing Straggletail's voice, Broadsnout looked up into the yearling's eyes and then slowly, deliberately, with great relish, snapped Dustfur's neck. Straggletail watched with wide eyes as Dustfur's lifeless body fell down, down, down into the ravine. She whirled around and saw the line of high-rankers watching her.

"I'd suggest you leave, cub," Broadsnout said coldly.

Straggletail bobbed her head, drew her ears back, and ran. Along the way, she passed beautiful Glossycoat, who stood alone by the dead buffalo, looking at Straggletail with an expression of pity and guilt and sorrow that didn't make sense.

Seeing this strange expression on Glossycoat's face again startled Straggletail back to the present. Straggletail had curled up in the bushes by that same ravine, nursing her bruises from Broadsnout's rough treatment earlier that night... and there stood Glossycoat, looking down at Straggletail from the other side of the bush with that same look of sympathy Straggletail knew she didn't deserve.

"I thought I'd find you here," Glossycoat said sadly.

Straggletail wanted to leap out of the bushes and run. But she was too tired.

"Have you come to finish me off?" Straggletail said, unable to keep a twinge of bitterness out of her voice. "For my disobedience?"

"No." Glossycoat came and lay down in the bushes right beside Straggletail. "You didn't answer my question."

Straggletail lifted her head. "What?"

Glossycoat nudged Straggletail's side with her nose. Straggletail flinched, but then relaxed; Glossycoat's touch was gentle tonight.

"Up on the ridge, at nightfall," said Glossycoat. "What are you looking at?"

Straggletail sighed and turned away. "It's stupid."

"Try me."

Straggletail looked back at Glossycoat. Once again, there was only friendly curiosity in the golden hyena's deep brown eyes. Straggletail shook her head vigorously, unsure if she was dreaming, but then winced as the whiplash from Broadsnout's earlier dominance display set in. Nope. Definitely not dreaming.

"Have you ever wondered," Straggletail began shyly, her voice rising in confidence as she went on, "where the sun goes at night?"

Straggletail had expected Glossycoat to scoff at her. Instead, the dominant hyena looked thoughtful.

"I can't say that I have," said Glossycoat. "But that's an interesting question."

Straggletail poked her head above the bushes, gazing wistfully across the open plain toward the ridge where the lone acacia tree sat.

Glossycoat peeked above the bushes as well. "Do you think we could find out?"

Straggletail stared at her. "Find out what?"

Glossycoat grinned. "Where the sun goes at night."

Straggletail emitted a short, hysterical giggle. "Why would *you* want to look for the sun?"

Glossycoat tilted her head. "Why not?"

"Well…" Straggletail's ears flattened, and she lowered her head, looking away from Glossycoat.

"You said earlier that you wish you were somewhere else. But how could you? You have everything here. You get to eat whatever you want, pick on anyone you want." Summoning her strength, Straggletail leapt out of the bushes and backed away from Glossycoat. "You're the matriarch's little *princess*," Straggletail hissed through gritted teeth. "You don't need to find the sun. I do!"

Glossycoat advanced toward her slowly, as Straggletail continued to back away. "Do you think I like it?" Glossycoat said, her voice cracking with despair. "Do you think I like having to boss everyone around? I don't have friends, not real friends. My relationships rely on fear and favors. Always alliances, never real friendships. I am hated, feared, respected, envied. But never loved. All because my mom has groomed me since I was born to be a ruler. To take her place." Glossycoat's eyes shone wetly. "But I don't *want* to dominate others! To hurt them! I never have!"

"Then why do you do it?" shouted Straggletail, her hackles rising, her tail bristling. "Why do you go along with whatever Broadsnout wants you to do? Why don't you ever fight back?"

Glossycoat fell into a defeated hunch. "Because it's all I know," she whispered. "And I am so, so sorry."

Straggletail gaped at her. Without another word, she turned tail and ran for the ridge, for the solitary acacia.

"Straggletail, wait!" cried Glossycoat, chasing after her.

Straggletail ran across the plain without stopping, until she reached the ridge with the lone acacia tree. There, she stopped and took a deep breath, taking in the nightly scents and the subtle movements of rodents in the dark. She looked down at the teeming jungle below her and gathered her courage.

"Wait!" cried a voice. Straggletail turned to see Glossycoat loping up the ridge.

"What are you doing here?" snarled Straggletail. "Go away!" She hated that she could still hear a sharp edge of hysterical fear in her voice, even as she tried to act dominant for once in her life.

"I'm sorry!" gasped Glossycoat, catching her breath. "I truly am, for everything! And I know I could never live long enough to earn your forgiveness."

"Glossycoat!" hollered a voice from across the plain: Broadsnout. Glossycoat looked in that direction and winced. Then she laid her ears back and faced Straggletail once more.

"Take me with you," begged Glossycoat. "I never wanted to be a princess. And I don't *ever* want to be matriarch, not of a rigid clan like this. I just want to be happy, and free. I want…" Glossycoat looked down, and her voice became very small. "A friend."

Straggletail looked deeply into Glossycoat's eyes. For the first time, they seemed to fully understand each other.

"Glossycoat!" growled Broadsnout, cresting the ridge. "What are you doing here?"

Glossycoat faced Broadsnout, her hackles rising, holding her head and tail high.

"I'm going with Straggletail, Mother. To look for the sun."

Broadsnout barked a laugh. "What nonsense is this?"

Glossycoat narrowed her eyes and shoved Broadsnout's body with her own. "It's not nonsense. Unlike the rules here in your stupid clan."

For a moment, Broadsnout looked as if she'd been bitten. Then her tail went stiff and spiky as a thorn bush.

"What? You dare to defy me?"

Glossycoat took a deep breath and then nodded. "I only wish I'd done it sooner." She turned to Straggletail, who was watching her with stunned admiration. "Let's go, Straggletail."

The two young hyenas took off down the ridge side by side, heading west, out of their clan's territory. Broadsnout called after them.

"Glossycoat, wait! Come back! You'll die out there in the jungle! Our rules are in place for a reason: to keep us all safe!"

Broadsnout's voice fell away as the two rogue hyenas entered the jungle, as if her words were swallowed by the trees.

* * *

For a long time, Glossycoat and Straggletail loped through the darkness beneath the trees without saying a word. The undergrowth was wet, filled with moist fronds and low vines that cooled their fur as they brushed past them. Though it was still nighttime, their eyes could detect every movement on the forest floor, every rustle in the branches overhead. Vervet monkeys snapped awake and peered down at the hyenas, chattering angrily.

"Go home, predators! This is not your territory!"

Glossycoat and Straggletail ignored them and kept heading west. They had both already eaten that night.

Finally, Straggletail stumbled on a slippery stone and collapsed in a heap. "I can go no further. I must rest. Sorry."

Glossycoat strode over to her. "It's okay! I understand. You've had a hard night."

Straggletail looked away. "You could never understand."

Glossycoat winced. She was silent for a while.

"I guess you're right," she admitted at last. "And I helped her bully you again. I'm sorry."

Straggletail rested her head on her forepaws and closed her eyes. Soon enough, she found herself shivering. Before too long, though, she felt warm fur brush against her side. Her head snapped up. Glossycoat was lying next to her, close enough to share her body heat. She frowned as Straggletail stared at her, glassy-eyed and breathing heavily.

"Forgive me," said Glossycoat. "I should have asked. Is this okay? You looked cold."

Straggletail's heart pounded, torn between fear of the high-ranking hyena beside her and joy at the feeling of Glossycoat's fur against her own. At last, she nodded, dropping her head back to her forepaws. "It's okay," she murmured, closing her eyes again.

"I'm glad," said Glossycoat. "Rest now. I'll watch over you." Straggletail's heart skipped a beat as Glossycoat nuzzled her shoulder. Then, with the unfamiliar jungle humming and chattering and hooting all around her, she drifted off to sleep.

* * *

Straggletail awoke to the sound of a dead weight thudding to the ground right in front of her face.

"Breakfast," announced Glossycoat.

Straggletail opened her eyes and lifted her head. The first rays of morning sunlight were filtering weakly through the dense canopy overhead. At Straggletail's feet sprawled a dead vervet. Behind it stood Glossycoat, looking at her anxiously.

"Is this okay? I didn't have to go far to get it. It practically fell on us. So I didn't really leave your side, I promise."

Straggletail looked at the vervet curiously. "I've never had vervet before."

Glossycoat's eyes widened. She tilted her head, staring at the monkey. "Neither have I," she realized. "I hope they taste better than they sound. Those things wouldn't shut up all night." Glossycoat waved her head back and forth wildly, imitating the undulations of a hyperactive monkey swinging from vines. "Go home, predators!" she said in her best impression of vervet chatter. "This is not your territory! I'm a banana brain!"

Straggletail doubled over laughing. "Banana brain! That's a good one!" It felt good to laugh, if a bit foreign, too.

Glossycoat's ears flicked back. She bowed to Straggletail, lifting one foreleg and bending it over the other while lowering her head. "You have a cute laugh," Glossycoat said in a rush. Then she shrank back, giggling nervously. She ducked toward Straggletail again, hesitated, and then retreated.

"Um, thanks," said Straggletail, confused. She had only ever seen that sort of bowing and approach-avoidance behavior performed by males courting females. "For the monkey!" she added, a bit too quickly. "Thanks for the monkey!" She dug into her meal, as Glossycoat kept creeping toward her and then ducking away, apparently overcome by embarrassment.

The meat was lean and greasy, but Straggletail found herself enjoying it. There was something satisfying about tasting something new. She felt like an explorer at last. And she couldn't help but feel a warm glow as she replayed Glossycoat's unexpected compliment in her mind. She had never received a compliment before, and she had never imagined that she'd get one from a hyena as beautiful as Glossycoat.

"Sorry!" said Glossycoat, finally returning to Straggletail's side. "I don't know what came over me." Her eyes widened as Straggletail nudged half of the monkey toward her. "You don't have to share, Straggletail! I brought it for you. To make up for all the... all the times I didn't let..." Glossycoat's voice faltered, and she looked down.

Straggletail smiled. "I insist. Take it."

Slowly, Glossycoat nodded. "Thanks." She tucked into the rest of the meal. Straggletail watched the way the light filtering down from the canopy danced across her yellow and black fur, amazed.

A dominant female hyena had brought her food. Had let her, Straggletail, eat first. Had acted nervous around her, eager to please her. Had given her a compliment and a courtship bow, of all things! For the first time in a long time, Straggletail felt valued. Her heart glowed like Glossycoat's fur.

Straggletail had made it beyond Acacia Ridge! She was a bona fide explorer now, rather than just a dreamer—finally on her way to the sun's roost in the west. As she peered ahead into the thick jungle, Straggletail beamed. Who knew what wonders waited around the next stand of trees?

* * *

Glossycoat couldn't stop thinking about her mother's last words to her. Was it true? Did the hierarchy, the rules of the clan, keep everyone safe? A thoughtful gloom descended on her as she and Straggletail went deeper and deeper into the darkness under the trees.

She remembered a time when she was a young cub, when she had wanted to go and play with Straggletail. Broadsnout had pulled her aside and given her a talk that was supposed to explain everything. About the rules.

"Glossycoat," Broadsnout had explained, "we need a hierarchy. We need rules about who can eat first and who gets to mate with whom, who gets the best den sites, who gets to be friends with us. If we didn't have these rules and a dominance hierarchy to enforce them, how would we make those important decisions? Every single family would want the biggest portion of the clan's limited resources. The clan would descend into chaos, civil war. Everyone would be constantly fighting over food, and we wouldn't have leaders to guide the clan when we are fending off lions or enemy clans."

"But why can't we just share everything?" Glossycoat piped up. *"Why can't we take turns?"*

Broadsnout sighed and stared out across the plain toward a herd of wildebeest on the far horizon.

"It is important for every hyena to know their place. Dominance displays may seem harsh, but they are far less harsh than the alternative. Indeed, they are essential for our survival. Without leaders, without a stable social system, there can be no order in times of crisis. No cohesion. The rules are here to protect us all, my dearest. Even Dustfur and her cub."

Glossycoat had looked at her mother with confusion in her deep brown eyes. Broadsnout just nuzzled her lovingly.

"I know, my dearest," said Broadsnout. *"It is a lot to process, and a heavy burden to place on one so young. But I know you'll make a fine matriarch one day."*

Glossycoat had glowed at this praise. She had felt so excited at the thought of ruling the clan one day. At the time, she loved the royal treatment she and her sisters received from their clanmates. Broadsnout's family never had to worry about their next meal, about their mating prospects, about their future offspring, about their safety. Glossycoat had never really thought about the burdens her carefree life had placed on others. About the hyenas she and her family had always shoved aside.

At least, she hadn't thought about them until Straggletail's mother, Dustfur, had...

"Glossycoat!" hollered Straggletail, jerking Glossycoat from her reminiscence. "Check this out!"

The jungle rematerialized around Glossycoat. She startled, noticing that Straggletail had breezed ahead of her while she wasn't paying attention. Her old self, the part that observed hierarchy and rules, felt annoyed. A low-ranker should not be so bold. But then she relaxed.

Of course Straggletail was forging ahead more quickly than she. Straggletail was the explorer, the one who was moving towards something, who wanted to discover new things. Glossycoat's motives were different. She wasn't running toward the promise of something new. She was running away from her past.

"Coming, Straggletail!" called Glossycoat. She loped ahead through the sun-dappled shadows, letting her legs carry her farther and farther from the clan, from her mother, from her shame with every step.

* * *

Straggletail stood sniffing the wind, waiting for Glossycoat to catch up. Her fur stood on end as she peered into the darkness of the crumbling human temple. There was a musty smell in the air, the scent of damp and moss and centuries, along with a sweet tang of...

Blood? Straggletail wrinkled her nose, and her mouth watered. She continued to scan the entrance of the temple. Her vision was normally good at handling low light, but something about this particular darkness proved impenetrable even to her. It was like the shadows had coalesced to form a solid wall of black stone, and try as she might, her eyes kept sliding away from it.

This was new. This was thrilling! Her heartbeat quickened with excitement and fear. She heard the click of Glossycoat's claws on stone as the other hyena joined her on the dilapidated steps leading up to the temple. The rough-hewn, broken slabs that once served as stairs shifted beneath her paws with the additional weight.

"What is it?" murmured Glossycoat, staring at the temple in awe.

Straggletail gave her a crooked smile. "Something new."

Glossycoat shifted her weight uneasily from paw to paw. "I don't like it."

Straggletail gave her shoulder a playful shove. "Oh, come on, princess! Don't be scared of the dark! We hunt in it all the time."

Glossycoat flinched. "Don't call me that ever again."

Straggletail wilted. "Sorry."

Glossycoat looked down. Straggletail sighed and hung her head. "I'm so sorry, Glossycoat. Please forgive me. I've been forgetting my place. I shouldn't be talking and acting on such familiar terms with you."

Glossycoat shook her head. "No, no, it's not that. I..." Taking a deep breath, Glossycoat lifted her head and looked Straggletail in the eyes. "Everything I know about myself and my worth comes from being in a place I know, with rules I understand. I know how to act within the rigid structure of the clan. I know how to behave in a hunt or a border patrol, with my sisters and aunts all around. My confidence, my ability to be fearless, has always come from my social status. Knowing where I stand in relation to everyone else. But..." Here Glossycoat choked on her words. Her voice became very small. "But who am I when I'm all alone, with none of them here to guard and guide me? When I'm facing things I don't understand, in a place I don't know? Who am I now? And how should I act?"

Straggletail nudged Glossycoat with her nose. "I know who you are. You're the hyena who defended me when no one else would. The one who sympathized with me when no one else cared. The one who ran into the jungle where no females from our clan have ever gone. The one who came with me to chase the sun." Straggletail sniffed and then timidly licked Glossycoat's face, sending electricity running through her. "You're a brave hyena, Glossycoat. And you're not alone."

Glossycoat straightened, holding her head high. "All right! What are we waiting for? Let's go!"

Straggletail grinned. Together, the two hyenas entered the darkness of the temple.

* * *

Straggletail and Glossycoat moved through the shadows of the temple, side by side. Water dripped from the ceiling constantly. The cold stone felt slimy beneath their paws.

"*Huuuruck!*" A terrible shriek caused the two hyenas to snap their heads around. Something scurried toward them in the darkness, claws clicking closer and closer. They huddled together, until...

Whoosh!

A wind whipped through the temple out of nowhere. When it stilled, the click-clacking was gone.

The hyenas breathed a sigh of relief. Squinting as their eyes adjusted to the darkness, they could see that they were now in a long corridor. They spotted a faint, flickering light up ahead. They proceeded cautiously toward it.

The light was like a cluster of tiny sunsets, pulsing from orange to pink and back again. It was beautiful, so much vibrancy in such a small space.

"Is this where the sun goes at night?" breathed Straggletail.

Glossycoat shot her a confused look as they inched forward along the corridor. "It can't be. It's still daytime outside. Besides, the place where the sun goes is on the other side of the mountains."

Straggletail's tail drooped. "Yeah, I guess you're right." But she still stared ahead at the color-changing lights. "It's pretty, though. Wonder what it is."

Glossycoat kept stealing nervous glances over her shoulder, back down the long corridor.

At last the hallway ended in a slick stone wall. There was a rectangular stone structure in front of the wall with a sculpture atop it and strange symbols carved into it by human hands. An altar of some kind, Straggletail guessed. She was more interested in the light, which looked even more beautiful up close. It was coming from some round objects attached to the back wall. Straggletail pawed and licked one experimentally.

"Mushrooms," said Straggletail.

Straggletail and Glossycoat stared at the brilliant fungi.

"Such a pretty display for no one, here in the dark," mused Glossycoat. "I wonder how long it's been since anyone has seen them."

"Maybe we're the first ones who ever have!" said Straggletail.

Glossycoat and Straggletail met each other's eyes and smiled, watching the orange and pink lights dance across each other's faces.

Just then, a roar and a crash sounded behind them.

"Who dares disturb my slumber?" bellowed a voice.

The hyenas whirled around. Standing near the other end of the hallway was the most terrifying creature they had ever seen.

He was a huge male lion, war-torn and battle-scarred, with tufts of fur missing and swollen scabs etched across his coat. His pelt was ashen, as if the golden sunlight had been leeched out of it by too much time spent here in the dark.

His tawny eyes were wild with rage.

He was big enough to kill either of them with one swipe of his paw.

"I… um…" murmured Glossycoat. A lifetime of smug confidence now failed her. She was trembling from the tips of her ears to the pads of her feet.

"Sorry!" cried Straggletail. "We're terribly sorry!" She crawled toward the lion on her front carpal joints, hoping this would appease him. But he just looked angrier. Clearly no one had taught him his manners. Straggletail straightened and bolted back until she stood beside Glossycoat again.

Meanwhile, Glossycoat was hyperventilating and pacing back and forth, her tail swishing anxiously behind her. "What do we do?" she whispered. "What do we do? If the whole clan was here, to form ranks and charge him… but they aren't. Just us. We're doomed!"

The lion stalked toward them. His fangs gleamed in the low light as he broke into a wide, menacing smile, foam bubbling up at the corner of his mouth. "Oh, I know who you are! It is just as the prophecy foretold. You are here to serve as the blood sacrifice."

"No!" the hyenas said in unison, pressing against each other, backing away as the lion advanced.

"Yes," said the lion, with an eerie laugh.

The lion kept approaching, and the hyenas retreated until they hit the far wall and could go no further. Still the lion padded closer, his eyes glowing strange colors in the light cast by the fungi on the wall.

Glossycoat shook her head. "We can't do this, Straggletail," she whispered, tears springing to her eyes. "Without the clan, we're no match for him. This is the end."

"You're wrong. Look at me. Look at me!" When Glossycoat refused to do so, Straggletail nipped her ear, causing her to squeal. Only then did Glossycoat, still breathing hard, finally meet Straggletail's eyes.

"Listen, Glossycoat! This is not the end. We can do this. I didn't come all this way through the jungle with you to have it end like this." Straggletail licked the tip of Glossycoat's snout. "You know what to do. You don't need the whole clan here behind you. We're our own clan now. And I believe in you."

Glossycoat responded with a shaky smile. She straightened and lifted her head and tail high, facing the lion, who was now only a few yards away.

"You know how to mob lions, right, Straggletail?"

Straggletail nodded. "Of course."

Glossycoat took a deep breath as the lion broke into a run.

"Okay, let's do it. Now!"

With bristled tails, the two hyenas charged the lion, whooping at the top of their lungs. Their voices echoed against the stone walls, making it sound like they had a fearsome army behind them. Startled, the mangy lion stumbled back. The hyenas gained ground, advancing halfway down the corridor before the lion took a tentative step back toward them. This forced them to retreat a few steps, but they quickly regained their courage, charging the lion once again and whooping like their lives depended on it. At last, they reached the main entrance chamber, and the mad lion fled down another dark passageway. Without hesitation, Glossycoat and Straggletail bolted for the entrance, their heartbeats roaring in their ears like thunder.

Sunlight. Blessed sunlight. For a long time, the hyenas ran and ran and ran to the west, across the sun-dappled shadows beneath the trees, crunching twigs and leaves beneath their paws. They ran for a mile before they had to stop and catch their breaths. Then, they collapsed beside a gurgling stream.

For a few minutes, they just lay there on the wet riverbank, panting. Then they erupted in shaky laughter.

"We're alive!" gasped Straggletail triumphantly.

"Of course we are!" said Glossycoat, with an echo of her former smug smile.

"Did you see the size of his paws?" cried Straggletail.

"They were huge!" confirmed Glossycoat. "And I think he was a few thorns short of a full acacia tree. If you catch my drift."

Straggletail wheezed. "That huge, crazy lion had us cornered. I never thought we'd make it."

"I knew we would. We had something he didn't have."

Straggletail tilted her head. "And what would that be?"

Glossycoat grinned. "Each other."

* * *

They took their afternoon nap beside the roaring stream after quenching their thirst. When they awoke, the purple hues of twilight painted the jungle. Straggletail gasped and lifted her head.

"Glossycoat, look!"

Glossycoat opened her eyes to see stars dancing right in front of her. She leaped to her feet and stared at their bobbing motions, mesmerized.

"Stars!" cried Straggletail. "I've never seen them so close before!"

The stars seemed to propel themselves on tiny, whirring wings. Glossycoat leapt and snapped one up in her jaws. It tasted like a termite.

"They're not bad," said Glossycoat, swallowing another.

The two hyenas laughed as they chased the winged stars about the riverbank, snapping them up with sheer delight. At last, their energy briefly spent, they flopped back down onto the grass.

"Well, we haven't found the place where the sun goes at night yet," mused Straggletail.

Glossycoat grinned, her eyes lazily tracing the movements of the glowing bugs drifting overhead.

"Not yet. But we found the stars."

Straggletail nodded, a smile spreading across her face.

"We did a lot of new things today!" said Straggletail. "We ate vervet for breakfast, explored a human temple, found some cool glowing mushrooms..."

"And a crazy lion," Glossycoat added quietly.

Both of them shivered. Straggletail rolled over and looked at Glossycoat in the starlight flickering from above.

"There are a lot of dangers in this jungle," said Straggletail, "but a lot of wonders, too. Whatever obstacles we face tomorrow, I'm just glad I'll be facing them with you."

Glossycoat licked her cheek shyly and smiled.

Straggletail smiled back. In that one glowing moment, they both were sure they felt a glimmer of where the sun went at night.

Together, they stood and loped off into the darkness, chasing the last traces of the sun.

Jacq and Misha take a vacation. They spend one day in Hanoi. But it's a Hanoi that you won't recognize.

One Day in Hanoi

by Thomas "Faux" Steele

"Nothing like a vacation to put the mind at ease; right, Jacq?" The stocky otter kicks back in the leather smoking chair, his heavy patent-leather boots clinking against the railing. I gaze down at the bustling metropolis of Hanoi, my feathers ruffling in the stiff breeze. Being a blue jay has its disadvantages where feathers are concerned. They are much less disciplined in tempestuous weather than fur. We're cruising at 200 meters, low enough to enjoy the cool, crisp air outside the main cabin. Misha flips a paw nonchalantly, his short otter fur mostly undisturbed.

"When you suggested a little jaunt to escape work, I didn't expect to end up halfway around the world!" I raise my voice so that it carries above the roar of the engines driving the zeppelin towards the aeroport. I shield my lighter against the high winds, but my attempts to set my cigarette ablaze are futile. Rather than wear down my flint, I sigh and slide the pack of Gauloises back into my inside jacket pocket.

"Is that not the point of a vacation? To see something new?" Misha's heavier-duty Soviet officer's lighter ignites his cigar in an instant. He takes a deep puff, the smoke drifting lazily from his nostrils. "It is not every year that I get a generous travel allowance. These opportunities must be enjoyed."

The aeroport welcomes us as we approach the heart of the city. A modern Colossus of Rhodes, Marianne stands 150 meters high, the grand spear held aloft in her right hand forming a docking point for arriving airships. She's rendered tastefully in aluminum, copper, and steel, the olive branch in her left hand dotted with windows to allow visitors to appreciate the stunning view. Her finely sculpted visage is warm but stern, the face of a nation that has endured the Great War.

Below us is the French Quarter, an expanse of wide, tree-lined avenues bounded by yellow-painted administrative buildings interspersed with fashionable hotels and residences crafted in the *Arts Décoratifs* style. The older buildings from the days of the monarchy have mostly been cleared away. Aside from a few historical landmarks, they are victims of the lust for modernity so popular at the present.

"We appear to have arrived," I mutter. My claws clink against the bright chrome railing as I stare into Marianne's ear, easily size of a large automobile.

"Bah! To think I just lit my cigar!" Misha snuffs it out and returns it to his cigar case. A loud *thunk* indicates that the electromagnetic docking clamps have engaged.

"We can smoke at the hotel. Now, come on!" I open the door of the lounge, gesturing for Misha to lead the way. Bags in hand, we head directly to the exit. The interior of the zeppelin, befitting its status as the most luxurious way to travel, exudes opulence. The carpet is as plush as the carpet in a Rolls-Royce. The walls are paneled with mahogany. Our fellow passengers are dressed sharply and expensively. Lacking the foresight to pack in advance of debarking, our fellow passengers head back to their rooms. Misha and I step into the elevator. With a slight nod of acknowledgement, the blue-suited elevator operator pulls the protective door closed and we begin our descent.

Through a transparent panel, we take in another perspective of the city. There's a distinctive boundary where the French Quarter stands opposite the Old Quarter, a central canal separating new from old. The ruler-straight streets and broad avenues dissolve into an organic arrangement of winding streets and narrow alleys. The buildings are squat, two or three stories each, with neon signage that induces transient foot traffic to sample wares on the ground floor. It's an entrepreneurial spirit one no longer finds in Paris. I cannot wait to purchase various sundries from the orient to take back with me to the City of Light.

It takes just a minute and change to cover the 150 meters from the zeppelin dock to the terminal. The journey is whisper quiet as we travel down Marianne's body. The near-silence does not last. As soon as we reach the bottom and breeze through passport control, the bustle of the city disturbs us, much like my Uncle Louis after consuming too much cognac.

"*Taxi? Taxi? Tu veux un taxi?*"

"*Cartes postales! Tu dois en acheter dix!*"

"*Pho! Chaud et fraîchement cuisiné!*"

Misha chuckles, relighting his cigar. "*Quelle* capitalist paradise is this? You don't have to stand in line to purchase anything!" He wanders over to a street seller preparing a coffee drink. In the street, steam-powered scooters whizz about, navigating cobblestone avenues as they dodge a continuous stream of pedestrians who appear to cross as they please. The single car I spot, a Renault, creeps along, the driver overly cautious. Road laws here appear a great deal more flexible than in France.

"Egg coffee?" Misha offers me a paper cup. "Just ten cents. What a deal!"

"What's the exchange rate with the ruble?" I take a sip, enjoying the warm sweetness of the top layer of condensed milk before breaking through to the assertive bitter coffee below.

"Two and a half rubles to the piastre," Misha responds, downing his egg coffee in one gulp. "My money goes far here!" He eyes a bottle of Vodka Hanoi held aloft by the street seller to my right, staring down the vendor.

"You're the one who planned this trip. How are we getting to the hotel?"

"Oh, yes, the hotel!" Misha fishes around in his pocket. "I've brought transportation with our luggage, and… bingo." He pulls out a hammer-and-sickle keychain, twirling it around on his index claw, a single stainless-steel key flashing in the sunlight. "I almost forgot."

"Your bike, sir!" A golden jackal dressed in the blue livery of the zeppelin line stands next to a low-slung motorcycle with a brightly polished aluminum body. "I've taken the liberty of making it shine for you."

Misha nods appreciatively, flipping him a silver piastre. "Buy yourself a beer." He climbs onto the black leather seat and fires up the internal combustion engine. It has a rawness that quiet, efficient steam lacks; the idle resonates with an uneven *thrum.* My otter revs it a few times, his grin widening. "What do you think, Jacq? I had it custom manufactured at the Number Seven Autocycle Factory in Moscow!" He pats the seat behind him. "It has plenty of room for two!"

"Looks like a million francs." I squat down to examine the sleek turbocharger on the side of the engine that is styled to look like a nautilus shell. The craftsmanship is impeccable.

"Hey, you! Get away from him!"

I jerk upward, realizing that my wallet has disappeared from my back pocket. The polished canines of a leopard flash white, my wallet clutched tightly in his paw. He hops on the back of a waiting scooter, disappearing down the busy street.

"After him! He shall not get away with this!" I grasp Misha's shoulder and use the momentum to swing myself onto the seat behind him. "Go!"

The engine snarls as Misha engages the gear. We shoot forward, narrowly avoiding a group of well-dressed ladies crossing the street. Ahead, I pick out the offender's scooter, weaving through traffic with the typical recklessness of a criminal. Misha shifts gears to pick up speed and pulls up next to them.

"Watch out!" Misha slams on the brakes and tilts us hard to the right to avoid plowing through a team of rice-field rats moving a large dresser. The margin by which we miss them is so narrow that I can count the whiskers on the nearest rat's muzzle. Ahead, the scooter dodges down a side street. We reach the alley in short order, but they're gone. The scooter lies abandoned in a puddle, the rear wheel still doggedly spinning in a futile attempt to gain traction.

Zut.

* * *

I sip a fresh draft beer and stare out at the neon city below. The early visitors to the Night Market flow down the street like a line of ants attracted to a cookie. It's just a few blocks away and the night is young. Still, patrons form a throng in the streets and alleys seeking to purchase a smorgasbord of goods for prices determined solely by one's negotiating skills. The metal of a chair leg scrapes against the marble floor of the patio, alerting me to Misha's return.

"I am sorry about your wallet. Here—" Misha offers me a pinkish fruit with green, leaflike tips on the flesh. "Try this. It's delicious."

"Did you stop by the Night Market on your stroll?" I retrieve my trusty penknife and slice into the fruit, revealing a firm whiteish flesh speckled with black seeds. It reminds me of a dalmatian's coat.

"It's certainly not the GUM in Red Square, but... Ah! Look at this!" Misha pulls out a small wood board with mother-of-pearl inlay that depicts a peaceful forest under a brilliant full moon. "Isn't it beautiful? There was an entire stall of these! I cannot wait to hang it in the apartment in Moscow." I nod, admiring the piece, the lacquered wood brilliant when illuminated by moonlight. "Oh, and this." Misha sets a deep black leather wallet on the table. It's a trifold. The center displays a feral blue jay formed from many twisting strands of leather tooled together.

"Oh, Misha." I lean over to rest my head on the soft wool of his evening coat. "It's beautiful. But my distress never was about the wallet itself."

"Hmm?" Misha wraps a strong arm around me, raising an eyebrow quizzically.

"I kept a gold coin in that wallet from when my great-great-great-great grandfather personally supervised the treasury of Napoléon Bonaparte. Its loss upset me." I chuckle. "The wallet I purchased on sale for two francs from *Au Bon Marché*."

"Well… then we simply must get that coin back!" Misha gives me a squeeze. "You are the detective here. How do we go about that?"

"We must identify the criminal element in this city. The thief was of a distinctive species. Perhaps by asking around we'll find someone who knows him." I spring up with excitement. "Let us head to a gambling parlor. I'm sure there will be no shortage of shady characters there."

The Sapphire Dragon gaming parlor is in the western end of Hanoi, away from the Red River and French Quarter. It's a twenty-minute ride via bike taxi from our hotel. Housed in an unassuming two-story building, I wouldn't give it a second look if I passed by on the street. What draws the eye toward it is the distinctive blue neon sign that hangs in the furthest right window of the second story, where a Chinese dragon curls around a gem. A quick telephone call to the local police led us here, as it is the only gambling establishment the law turns a blind eye toward in the entire city.

Following three quick knocks on the front door, an eye-level slot opens. Luminous green eyes stare with practiced inscrutability. "*Quel est le mot de passe?*"

"*Le dragon de saphir garde le trésor d'or.*"

The slat clicks shut like the bolt action of a rifle. The door creaks inwards, revealing a foyer dimly lit with electric lanterns.

Misha strides in confidently. He's dressed simply now, modeling in American-style waist overalls and an austere wool jacket, the inconspicuous outfit of a traveler.

It's crowded inside. Rows of one-armed bandits line both walls, patrons clicking away with the rhythm of practiced typists, hoping luck is on their side. A bar stretches out along the far wall. Filling the pit area are Poker and Baccarat tables. Sharp-eyed hostesses weave through the mayhem on the floor, ensuring no thirst goes unquenched.

Misha immediately heads to one of the tables. I shoot him a questioning glance. "Are you sure you know what you're doing here?"

He nods. "I used to play in the trenches of the Eastern Front with my fellow soldiers." He smirks. "I lost a lot of money at first, but by the time Bolsheviks withdrew from the Great War, I'd made enough to purchase a fine suit and more. I can handle myself."

At the lone table with room to spare, Misha inserts himself into the game. I observe casually from the bar, sipping on a *Soixante-Quinze*. It's strong and bittersweet, just like this vacation. There's something special about this city, especially being here with Misha. As befits an officer, his composure under pressure is unflappable. After a few hands, he's up a considerable sum. He strikes up a conversation with the tiger beside him, a muscular beast close to double his size, with a wicked scar decorating his muzzle.

A few hands later, Misha gathers his winnings and joins me. He orders a vodka and Coca-Cola, which comes served in a squat, heavy glass. The section unoccupied by liquid is vivid blue.

"Did you find out anything?" I polish off my cocktail and debate ordering a second as I gaze at the row of multicolored bottles splayed in front of me wantonly.

"I did indeed. From the description I gave him, the thief is one Thomas Nguyen, address 115 *Rue de Rosiers*.

"Fancy quarters for a simple thief." I order myself a gin and tonic. The quinine can't hurt in this environment. "Anything remarkable about him?"

"Not that he said. *Monsieur* Nguyen must target tourists. There's probably considerable profit in snatching purses stuffed with cash to purchase souvenirs or pay for local pleasures." Misha chuckles. "I'll get my revolver and we'll address this issue quickly."

"Not so fast, *mon ami*. This isn't Paris." I shake my head. "We cannot simply bust down his front door and go in with guns drawn. We do not have the authority of the law on our side here."

"Authority of the law, eh? That gives me an idea." Misha sets down his drink. "Why don't you take a relaxing bath back at the hotel? There's something I must do." Misha deposits a light kiss on my cheek, shooting me a wink before disappearing into the crowd.

* * *

At the hotel, I bury myself in bubbles. My beak looks like Mount Everest breaking through the clouds. This vacation has not begun on the relaxing note I had hoped for. Still, there is abundant hot water, a luxury I cannot find often enough during my travels… or even at my apartment.

"Jacq?"

I run a claw over my face to brush away enough bubbles to see properly, then blink a few times until my lover comes into focus. I must have drifted off in the bath. "Yes, darling?"

"Let's take a stroll. I believe I've found the thieves' hideout just a few short blocks from here."

"Now?" I yawn deeply, clicking my beak. "What time is it, anyway?"

"Time to take care of this ugly business so that we can enjoy the rest of our vacation!" Misha grins. "Or nine o'clock, if that's simpler."

"So? What is this plan of yours? I hope it does not lead to the pair of us lying at the bottom of the Red River wearing concrete shoes."

Misha laughs. "Your comment about the authority of law gave me an idea." He takes a knee beside the tub and clears a patch of bubbles from my chest. Forming his webbed paws into scoops, he dribbles water over my feathers, rinsing away the silky, sandalwood-scented bubbles. "What I've realized is that there *is* a way to acquire the authority of the law."

I briefly close my eyes as rivulets of water trickle through my facial feathers. Misha is now in charge. "How so? To do that, you would need—"

"I did a bit of shopping. Keep your eyes closed for a moment. I want to surprise you." Misha's long claws click-clack against the tile. I hear the door click shut.

"Open your eyes."

Before me are elements of a plan that is equal parts brilliant and ridiculous. Two uniforms with bright brass buttons and matching, flat-topped hats hang on the back of the door. A thick petroleather belt circles around the waist, a sash for a police-issued revolver crossing diagonally and running shoulder to hip. Hefty silver badges are pinned to the breast pocket flaps, proudly proclaiming: *"Police De l'Indochine Française."*

"You assembled all this in two hours? That must've cost a—"

"Small fortune, which is coincidently exactly what I won playing poker." Misha smiles slyly. "I rushed over to the tailor and the silversmith after leaving you at the bar. It's amazing the level of service a large stack of notes upon the counter facilitates."

"So, I suppose we *will* have the authority of the law on our side."

Misha grabs a towel off the counter next to the bath, gesturing for me to stand. He quickly starts to dry me off, applying gentle pressure so as not to accidently pluck a feather.

"I must say, your attention to detail is impeccable," I mutter as Misha tosses aside the towel.

"See to the fit. I did some guesswork with measurements since so few tailors cater to avians. I had them leave room to accommodate your feathers." Misha hands me the taller uniform and heads into the bedroom.

I grab a cotton undergarment from beside the sink and slip on the uniform, admiring myself in the mirror as I button up the jacket. My blue feathers stand out against the tan fabric. The flat-topped cap covers my crest feathers, making for a clean look. I have always had a thing for men in uniform.

"Well, Jacq? How's the fit?" Misha has returned to stand behind me. He looks perfectly natural in his new outfit. It is certainly a departure from the deep blue of a Soviet officer's dress, but the color complements his creamy brown fur.

"It fits better than my uniform at home!" I wink. "You have excellent taste, darling." I head back to the bedroom to grab my trusty St. Etienne 8mm off the nightstand and slip it into the holster. The familiar weight produces a surge of confidence.

"Well? Shall we go?" Misha gestures towards the door. "Let's settle this matter before dinner."

"*Bien sur*. Have you practiced your French? Or shall I do the talking?" I give him a cheeky peck on the muzzle.

"*Petit oiseau, ma français est parfait!*"

"*Mon français, mon petit chéri,*" I say with a chuckle. "Don't forget your gender agreement!"

Misha rolls his eyes. "You know, in Russian you can tell these things by the way words are spelled. We don't pick genders out of a hat."

"I will have you know we have a board of ancient scholars controlling our language, *merci beaucoup!*" I open the door to the hall, letting Misha exit first.

"Well, aren't you bourgeois." He covers the short distance between our room and the elevator in a few strides. "Perhaps your country needs a revolution to seize the means of grammar production!"

Ding! The elevator arrives, decorated opulently with *sua* wood inlaid with semiprecious stones in geometric reliefs. I stare at a glittering star formed of dozens of yellow topaz stones until we reach the lobby.

We cruise through the lobby, snatching coconut candy from a bowl near the bell desk before stepping onto the pavement.

It's a relaxing walk to the thieves' base of operations. The crowds are thinning out, allowing us to enjoy the refreshing night air in relative peace. Misha buys a *bahn mi* from a sidewalk vendor, breaking the crispy baguette in two and handing me half.

I nod appreciatively. The *pâté* in the middle fortunately turns out to be pork and not *foie gras*. As I finish my last bite, Misha pauses and turns. "Here it is."

The structure is typical of the French Quarter, a two-story townhome much wider than the houses of the Old Quarter. The exterior is finished with slabs of the white marble mined here, with dual motifs of a rising sun captured in chrome flanking the recessed doorway.

With the characteristic swagger of authority, Misha approaches the grimy steel door and raps firmly. The sound echoes throughout the enclosed vestibule with all the melody of a bell forged by a drunkard.

A moment later, the door opens, a familiar pair of polished canines glowing in the dim light. Strangely, he greets us in English, an action probably intended to annoy the native police. "What you coppers want? Third time this month. Leave me in peace!"

The leopard's effort to slam the door in our faces is met with resistance by Misha's patent-leather boot as his foot jams into the crack. Misha snorts with amusement. "We are not here to sell you a vacuum cleaner, *monsieur*. Open this door or I will kick it down."

I hear a hiss of anger, but the door creaks inward. "Fine. What your problem? Get out of face!"

"My fine feathered friend here would like his wallet," Misha says, staring down the thief. "You made the unfortunate mistake of stealing from two off-duty officers returning from vacation."

"I know nothin' 'bout wallet. Maybe friend is stupid and he drop it down sewer."

I catch the glint of a blade in the leopard's right paw. We may have over-estimated the authority and protection a uniform normally provides. "Misha! He has a knife!"

Misha steps back just in time as the cat's weapon slices off one of the buttons.

"And now I'm annoyed." Misha brushes his jacket and cracks his knuckles. "Do you know how much it cost to have these made?"

I draw my revolver, but the feline wheels around, kicking it from my hand and sending it flying into the street. I hear it skitter against the cobblestones and catch a few sparks out of the corner of my eye. So much for that. I step back. Paw-to-paw combat was never my specialty. Hollow bones lack durability in fights.

"Return the wallet and we'll leave you alone," Misha says, assuming an aggressive stance. "We do not want to subdue you, but we will, if necessary!"

"Wallet mine now!" The leopard lunges, seeking to overwhelm Misha with speed. However, Misha is the more experienced opponent. He dodges to the side and drives his elbow into the cat's forearm. With a yowl of surprise and pain, the knife clatters to the floor and the feline trips on the doorstep.

"Ah, so you *do* know what I'm talking about," Misha mutters. He puts the thief in a headlock as the cat attempts to right himself. "Jacq, get the cuffs and find a police callbox. I will interrogate him before the locals arrive."

* * *

"So? Happy, little bird?" Misha rests his feet on the table, enjoying a 33 beer from a tall glass bottle. A few noodles occupy the bowl in front of him, the remnants of a hearty bowl of pho.

I admire the hefty gold piece before placing it in its rightful place in my new wallet. "Indeed! You know, this actually was quite sporting." I chuckle, fidgeting with the unlit cigarette in my right hand. "You make a pretty good detective, you know."

Misha laughs heartily. "I'll drink to that." He drains the remainder of the bottle.

"Where to after this?" I drop a few coins on the table to cover the bill.

"I've booked first-class tickets on the overnight train to Hué. We probably should meander over to the station." Misha checks his wristwatch. "We have an hour, so plenty of time."

"Well, then. Perhaps we can explore a few new places on the journey." I give him an affectionate kiss, grabbing his paw and starting down the street. It is best that we leave this city, but we have many more to explore.

When the first genuine Furries come into human space, what culture shocks will they encounter?

What culture shocks will they give the humans?

Welcome, Furries

by Cathy Smith

"The humans are used to being the dominant species in their part of the galaxy. How will they react when they come across a superior species like us felines?" Scratten said to Purra.

Purra was playing a "toy with the mouse" game on her Terran issued mobile. She grunted, "Were you saying something?"

"I was wondering what the humans at Luni Uni will be like."

Purra went back to swatting the mouse in AR. "They post videos and memes of cats on their feeds all the time. We have nothing to worry about."

"Videos can't match the real thing. We may overwhelm them," Scratten said.

"They worshiped cats in their early history. They've evolved a more mature appreciation of us now," Purra said.

Scratten shuddered. "Make sure those barbarians don't mummify me if anything happens to me while I'm here."

"That only happened when their 'owner' passed away. We don't have owners."

Scratten grunted.

* * *

Space travel always made Purra's throat run dry. Unfortunately, no human could get the water filtrated up to her standards. There were multiple open bottles at her seat. "They're all stale. Send them back and get me a bottle of fresh water."

The steward frowned, "Uh."

"Just put a minnow or goldfish in there to enhance its flavor, and she won't care how fresh the water is," Scratten told him.

"Ugh! I'll see what I can do," he said.

Purra snorted. "It'll take generations to train the Terran Humans for intergalactic society. Even the Human Sector in the Empire knows basic courtesy for Felines."

She got up from her seat. "Where are you going?" Scratten asked.

"I want to see if first-class has anything suitable."

"First-class? Is there such a thing in the Terran System?" Scratten asked.

"There must be. You know the elites and Imperial officers keep the best of everything for themselves," Purra sniffed.

Scratten snorted in distaste at such presumption. "Of all the… ! I'm going with you."

* * *

First-class had a thick carpet that felt good on the hind paws, but not as good as a well-kept lawn would. Purra grunted when her claws got caught on the thick fibers.

"You should keep your boots on," Scratten said as he pulled a delicate foot up.

"This is supposed to be first-class. I shouldn't need to," Purra hissed.

Once her boots were back on they continued their explorations.

There was a display of shifting colors on a wall panel, though a cool blue tone was the main theme. Fishes in a rainbow of colors flickered on the screen.

"This must be their menu items. Oh, look; there's an angelfish. I always wondered what they'd taste like," Purra said.

Scratten pointed to a silver koi. "That one looks like it's got more meat on its bones."

"Tell them to send us the water they swam in as our drink," Purra said.

The two felines spoke amongst themselves. Their speech sounded like purrs and growls to the people in first-class. They ignored the mutterings of the first-class passengers.

"Some Imperial must've brought his human-sized pets on-board."

"Damn Imps should've put them in the cargo hold or bought carriers for them. Letting them loose on the plane is outrageous."

One woman sneezed. Her nose ran and her eyes grew red. "Get them out of here! I'm allergic to cat dander."

Purra noticed the sneezing woman and motioned to Scratten. "Let's get out of here before we catch what she's got."

* * *

They went back to their seats. Purra called up her copy of her immunization records on her mobile. "I want to see what kind of shots we got." She rapidly scrolled down the list, checking the traveler warnings and the recommended booster shots.

"Careful," Scratten said.

Purra cried out when her claw scratched her screen, "No! Cheap piece of junk."

Scratten held her hand to stop her from throwing the mobile against the wall. "You need to trade it in to get a replacement, and it acts as your mobile wallet."

"Uh."

"It carries all the creds from your student allowance to the Terran system."

He took out a spare stylus he had on him. "Use this so it doesn't crack anymore."

Purra sniffed. "I didn't know the Overseers were so stingy in the Terran system."

"This is the frontier."

Purra shuddered at this.

* * *

The felines napped until a beep went off to tell them the spaceliner had entered subspace. Purra grunted but Scratten booted up his mobile.

She frowned as the light disrupted her sleep. "What are you doing?"

"I'm researching student housing now that we have access to the Terran system's network," Scratten said.

"Those Terran virtual house tours are useless. You won't know how clean it is until you can smell it." Purra sniffed as she turned her back on the light of Scratten's mobile.

"They are limited but not useless. I can at least arrange inspections on the most promising leads," Scratten began.

"You do that," Purra mumbled before she went off to sleep again.

* * *

Why can't I dream of mice in a field? Instead of that voice? Purra wondered.

"Excuse me. Excuse me. It's time to disembark now." The voice kept saying.

"Do they have microchips? You can use it to call their owners."

There was a *beep! beep!* as a rod was flashed over them. "Of all the… These two cats are unregistered."

"Then call the SPCA to claim them. They're holding up boarding for the next flight."

There were 15 minutes of blessed silence before a net was thrown over the felines. Purra and Scratten scratched and hissed. Purra had sharper claws and cut through the net. Scratten launched himself at the man trying to ensnare them.

"Scratch the barbarian's eyes out," Purra snarled.

"Oh! You're passengers. Not unclaimed pets," the stewardess said.

She spoke up, although she was too afraid of the Feline's sharp teeth and claws to step into the fight. "I'm afraid there's been a misunderstanding…"

* * *

"Well, at least we got something good out of the whole experience," Purra sniffed.

Scratten had insisted on a settlement for their pain and suffering. The spaceliner offered them a trade. "A week's accommodation at the nearest five-star hotel on Luna?"

Much to Purra's surprise, Scratten accepted it. "I thought you'd hold out for more money?"

"We need decent lodgings here and now. We've got a week to look for student housing."

Purra grunted. "Yes. But the Feline consulate could've taken care of us while we got the issue settled."

"Huh?"

She smoothed her white fur. "I'm triple A stock. I've got my rights."

* * *

"Are we felines or moles?" Purra sniffed. She was disappointed to find most lunar transports were underground hyperloops.

"The only ground shuttle we could afford has no artificial gravity. It's not worth the risk of space fever to save money, if we're going to college here."

Purra shuddered. "I want to live in the Core when this is over."

"Exactly. Earth's moon gravity well is low. You won't be able to go back if your bones and tissues become too frail to withstand regular gravity."

"I thought space fever was a nasty Terran virus?"

"They have those, too. Space fever happens when your body acclimatizes to low gravity. You're never able to go back to civil society without a specialty bodysuit. And that only happens if you strike it rich. Most times it means you're exiled for health reasons."

Purra whimpered. "You're scaring me."

Scratten grabbed her right paw. "We'll be perfectly safe, but I want you to know why I'm making these precautions. This isn't in the Core. We need to set spending priorities. I'm not just being stingy when I tell you 'no' to something you want."

Her back bristled. "I've got my own credits, too. I was smart enough to get a full scholarship. You can't control all the money."

"No, and I won't stop you. But I won't put up with you fighting me every time I look for the best deal. I thought we agreed I'm the best bargain hunter."

Purra sniffed. "Then explain the choices. Don't just spend the money and make deals without telling me what it's for. I want to be your partner. Not your pet."

* * *

The hotel was housed in its own bio-dome with some levels below ground. The penthouse was the one suite at ground level and allowed its patrons to walk in a highly manicured park.

Purra assumed they'd have a penthouse suite and wanted to check out the park. She oohed in delight when a monarch butterfly flew by her.

Scratten saw a marigold, picked it and popped it into his mouth. "At least there's no need for pesticide in an off-world habitat."

Purra chased the butterfly. Her paws went out to cup it. There was a horrified gasp from nearby humans when she brought it to her mouth and crunched on it. "Mmm. Yummy. You should try one." She licked off chalky orange residue on her muzzle.

"Outrageous!" A human woman muttered. She called a park attendant who glanced at the two felines.

Scratten groaned when she walked over. Purra purred, batted her lashes and looked up from round electric blue eyes.

"Aww!"

Then the attendant caught herself. "There's usually a charge for damages to the hotel's property, but I'm letting you off with a warning. Let's stick to what they have on the room service menu from now on."

Scratten sighed in relief at this. Purra's charms were formidable. She used them on him half the time and ingratiated herself on others the other half. *Our ancestress must've been like her.*

There were rumors about "Precious", a house cat so adorable she won over an Overseer. He sped up Precious's evolutionary growth so she could gain sentience. Then Precious begged for company, so she wouldn't have to be alone. Precious only wanted some select toms to be brought up to her level. However, the Overseers wanted to diversify the bloodlines. They wanted to keep the Felines healthy, so they bio-engineered other females, too.

Such a story sounded like a children's fable to Scratten. Then he met Purra with her fluffy white coat and limped blue eyes. She was utterly irresistible, both to most males of her species and to the humans.

He would've been fined and banished from the park if he were on his own. Here Purra got them off with a warning.

* * *

They found a box of crickets in the hotel fridge that night which made for a salty crunchy snack. "The butterfly was better," Purra sniffed.

"Let's try some virtual tours tonight," Scratten said.

"Nnn, that's boring. I'd rather see, smell and taste things in person," Purra sniffed.

"That was in that spaceliner. Here, we get full immersion AR body suits as a part of the hotel's hospitality package. Clamping on the bit simulates the tastebuds. It's tied to an air scrubber that gives you smell. And tactile sensors," Scratten said.

Purra's ears perked. "I'd like to see that."

"I thought you would."

* * *

Purra growled at the sight of the immersion suit. She sniffed at it. "It smells like a herd of pigs has been sweating all over it. I want a new one."

Scratten called room service again. " We want fresh immersion suits. These smell funny."

The room attendant took the suits and said, " I'll see what I can do."

"And this is supposed to be a five-star hotel?" Purra snorted.

"Well, we are on a frontier."

Scratten had had worse in his time. He would have accepted the suit if he was on his own. He liked the scent and taste of pork. The suit's aftertaste would have been a bonus if he were alone.

When the attendant came back he asked, "Would it help if the suits were preset to taste like tuna?"

Purra sighed. "Only if we were given real tuna as well."

So, the deal was struck.

Maybe Purra was a better bargainer than Scratten gave her credit for. When they were alone, she said, "That's the way you handle humans. Never settle for anything less than their best."

Scratten nodded at this.

* * *

They booted up after dinner. The tuna was so strong it was hard to tell if the suits were preset, or they were just tasting the aftertaste. A floating neon sign appeared before them. It showed a head-shot of a white digital kitty.

"Welcome, furries," she giggled. "Do you want to meet new friends?"

"I want to find a new place to sleep during my college years. Do you know of any vacancies in student housing?" Scratten asked.

"Oh, you're a student. Would you like to see your school?"

"I want to see an apartment first," Purra said.

"You can meet new friends at the school, and they can show you around their houses if you get invited over after class," the kitty said.

"I want to see a house first, so I can rest up for classes," Scratten said.

Purra waved a paw. "Oh, get us a human if you don't want to do the work." It was a brave attempt to be reasonable on her part. Humans were used to working. Cats were used to sleeping. It was hard to stay alert if you stayed up too long. Which must be why this kitty was so slow.

"I can bring up a live chat if you want?"

"You do that," Purra said. "We'll get the best deal from a human, anyway," she said to Scratten

A human girl who had CGI whiskers, a mini snout and sharp ears popped into their view. Purra's ears twitched at this. "It must be the humans' attempt to engage a furry demographic," Scratten muttered.

The girl took one look at Purra and Scratten and said, "Whoa, you two have got a cool filter. You must tell me what app you use. How can I help you?"

"We want accommodation for two felines at Luni Uni."

"Oh, you want to go to the Anthromorph Alliance meet-up?" She called up the suites available in a floating neon list.

"Smoking or non-smoking?"

"I want be the one marking our territory," Scratten said.

The girl chuckled at this. The names of some units flickered off the list.

"Do you want to bring a pet?"

Purra snorted.

"No pets."

Yet more rooms were off the list.

"Do you have any children you need rooms for?"

Purra and Scratten's fur stood upright and their ears flattened. "It's no business but ours if we're fixed or not."

The girl chortled in convulsions. "You two crack me up. You keep staying in character. Tell you what, I'll give you a 25% discount?"

Purra purred encouragement. Canines may perform for treats. Felines rewarded humans for performing up to standard.

* * *

It was good to have more places to roam than the hotel's gardens and virtual worlds. Purra found the humans' addiction to virtual reality pathetic. A feline's senses were too sharp to be fooled by some immersion suit. Not only that but most VR sims neglected scents. VR was a pathetic shadow for real life.

She and Scratten found the hydroloop to the Anthropomorphcon. The closest they got to the stop the more humans she saw in plastic ears, snouts, face paint and fake fur. It was hard to tell if their efforts to welcome her and Scratten were pathetic or touching. It'd depend on how accommodating they were to their needs.

A human girl in a black leathereen catsuit came up to her. She reminded Purra of one of those unfortunate furless breeds. "Oh, cool costume! Can I take a selfie with you two?"

Scratten sniffed, but Purra was used to the admiration of humans and her fellow felines. Such requests were common for her. She allowed the girl to take a selfie. "Thanks."

Someone dressed as a pot-bellied bear came up to them. "You have to tell me where you got your costumes. They look like real fur."

Scratten sniffed, "Of course it's real."

The man stopped smiling, "Fur is murder!"

Scratten cut off his blubbering by unsheathing the claws on his paws, "These are real, too."

Purra bared her pointed teeth in a smile. "So are these."

"What?" He stopped blubbering and gestured to their fur. "You mean you're true furries?"

"Yes," Scratten said. "Does that mean every other person at the con is a fake?"

The man laughed at this. "More like wannabes."

Purra marveled at this. She never thought she'd see humans who knew how unfortunate their furless state was.

* * *

The registrar smiled widely at the sight of Scratten and Purra. "Cool costumes."

The poor thing had only bunny ears and a cotton puff tail clip on her slacks for her furry outfit. Purra thought it pitiful she couldn't afford a full costume. It also made her worry about this Anthropomorphcon. It was a charity event. That would mean it wouldn't have the services she needed.

"What's your name on the register?"

"Scratten Tabula and Purra Albin. We're transfer students from the planet Ulster in the Core Systems."

The girl laughed. "I admire your dedication to remain in character. Let's hope the Overseers don't send us Lovecraftian life forms in real life. I'm dreading the next phase of Terra's acclimatization process." She quivered like a mouse at the prospect.

The felines let their paws be scanned. They made sure not to lay their claws on top of the screen but let her mobile take a 3D scan.

The girl let out a squeal. A guard in the guise of a bulldog came up to her. "Is something wrong, Bunny?

"They're real, Brutus! They're real! These two are real furries."

He glanced at Purra and Scratten and then back at their student i.d. "It says you two are felines from the world of Ulster in the core systems."

Purra yawned.

"Yes," Scratten said. Human slowness was so aggravating. They needed for assistive devices to augment their senses. Even a canine would've been able to sniff out impostors.

Bunny called up a screen of panels. "I'll assign you to the 'Feeding your Real Life Furries' panels. They use natural ingredients to make meals for cats and dogs."

Purra nodded in encouragement. "That should be acceptable."

* * *

Brutus led them to the panel, but the felines could sniff it out themselves. A selection of dry cat food and packaged treats was laid out in bowls. Some people had pets on leashes and gave them samples. Scratten pocketed anything that smelled good to him.

Purra meant to do the same but kept sniffing, looking for something suitable.

Scratten's cheeks became as round as a chipmunk as he ate his samples.

"How can you eat any of that?" Purra sniffed.

Scratten swallowed first before he answered. "It's not bad, but now my throat's dry."

"Insects are the only things that taste good when they're dry," Purra said.

"Ew!" said someone who overheard them.

Purra pointed to the commentator's chocolate bar. "At least I'm not the one eating poison."

"Huh?" They glanced at their bar suspiciously.

"Scratten and Purra are true furries. They can't digest chocolate." Brutus said to them.

* * *

A cooking demonstration began at a food preparation island. A line of drool appeared on Scratten's muzzle when sardine cans were opened. He gasped in disgust when it was dumped into a bowl with carrot and oatmeal.

"Nnnn."

Purra's ears perked up. "I don't know. The vegetable additives may be a nice change from catgrass."

"I hate catgrass. I only nibble on the occasional blade of grass on a lawn," Scratten sniffed.

They gasped when the ingredients were put into a blender and pureed. Two plates and an ice cream scoop of the meat mash was left for the felines.

Purra licked her sample. "Um. It's really juicy."

Scratten sniffed and turned his nose up at the offering, so Purra licked his plate too.

The furry spectators watched her lick the plate clean in disbelief. The last thing she licked was her lips. "That was good."

Scratten grabbed a tuna that was about to be filleteed for the next dish.

"I'm making tuna patties next," the demonstrator said.

Scratten ignored her and ate the tuna with its bones whole.

People took pictures of the two on their mobiles as they ate their way through the demonstration. Purra thought someone was being helpful when they used a laser pointer to direct her to new dishes.

She got annoyed when the pointer shifted around in circles. Her ears folded back onto her skull. Someone tittered and took a selfie. She bared her teeth and hissed at them.

There was snickering and more twittering. Someone threw a cat toy at Scratten from one of the vendor booths. It had feathers attached to it. Scratten was touched when he thought someone gave him a bird.

Guffaws of laughter broke out when he shoved it into his mouth then spit it out when he found it was a stuffed toy. He hacked it up in the direction of the one who gave it to him. "Hey."

Scratten gave a hissing cackle in response.

They took a step forward. Scratten arched his back, hissed and unsheathed his claws. It made him stop looking like an overgrown tabby-cat. His would-be tormentor realized Scratten was a man-sized cat with muscles and claws to match.

"Security!"

* * *

The felines and humans disputed the events. The security team had to use security cam footage to show everything. Bunny and Brutus groaned. "Look at that harassment. That's a lawsuit waiting to happen," Brutus muttered.

The ones who teased the felines were escorted out while the felines were led to a quiet room for a talk. Bunny and a man dressed as a beagle went into the room with them as well. "You two can stay in this safe room until you feel you can face the public again," Bunny told the felines.

Purra's ears perked up at this. "Is this going to be our room all semester?"

"Huh?"

"We were looking for student housing for our first year at Luni Uni."

Bunny glanced at the adviser that served as their legal counsel. Beasley was dressed up as a legal beagle. "Would you be willing to settle with the Anthropomorph Alliance? We can find and pay for student housing for you."

Scratten sniffed, "That depends on the quality of the housing you find for us."

"Of course," Beasley said.

* * *

Beasley escorted the felines to dormitories on Luni Uni's campus. He'd narrowed it down to the top three student unions.

The campus had its own bio-dome with air and artificial gravity. Most of Luni Uni's students and faculty stayed inside the artificial environment. The first choice of the felines differed and there was one house they agreed to.

It would've been best to choose the last option. However, there was no way Scratten would pass up the Astro Fraternity house. "It says it's 'the best place to go tomcatting.'"

Beasley sighed.

"Well, if you're going to a place that's good for tomcatting, I want to go to the sorority that caters to Queen Bs," Purra sniffed. Yet her disapproval didn't faze Scratten. However, the fraternity's bulldog mascot did. It took one sniff of Scratten. A bunch of drunken fraternity brothers laughed and cheered at it chased him around.

Beasley took a video of it with his mobile.

Scratten growled. "That better not get posted to social media."

"It's so you can file a claim against the Astro Fraternity with the student council."

"I'll want money to put against my apartment's rent," Scratten said.

* * *

"Oh!" Lisa, the head of the Selene Sorority, cooed as soon as she saw Purra. Purra demanded the Anthropomorph Alliance pay for her professional grooming. She wanted to look extra fluffy for the interview.

Purra with her white fur and electric blue eyes looked like the perfect accessory. "We'd love to have you." Purra purred at this.

The sorority had a greenhouse full of flowers. They gave Purra a rose as pink as her nose to show their acceptance of her. Purra licked the petals. She found them so buttery soft they slipped down her throat before she knew it.

Lisa looked at her in disbelief.

"That was good. Can I have another one?"

Lisa sniffed. "Come back when you're housebroken."

Purra's ears flattened against her skull, and she hissed.

* * *

The Lunar Benevolent Society was Beasley's last hope for the felines. There was an atrium at the dorm's entrance reminiscent of lawns back on Terra.

They were greeted by a girl called Sophie Templeton. She pleased the eye, alhough she wasn't as pretty as those who came from selectively bred Imperial stock. *Mutts are more friendly than thoroughbreds.* Her eyes were bright and alert. Beasley found that reassuring at the moment.

The felines took off their shoes and investigated the lawn with all their paws. Beasley groaned when they munched on the grass but Sophie laughed at the sight. "You'll have to grow catgrass for them."

"They're not my pets. They're transfer students from the Core," Beasley said.

"Hm. I didn't expect the aliens to be so cuddly," she murmured.

Then she laughed, "Though I better keep my opinions to myself if I don't want to offend them. Since they're sentient beings, they're allowed to grow container gardens in their rooms. They can eat what is harvested from the communal garden, but it is carefully pruned and picked. They can't just grab and eat anything."

"Of course, I'll inform them of that. We need to see the rooms…"

Which turned out to be modest but adequate. They had all the necessary amenities and features. The felines would have to pay for their own luxuries but the felines deemed the lawn the biggest luxury of all.

* * *

The Anthropomorph Alliance planned to create housing for furries by the end of the semester. There were still snide remarks on social media. They claimed this advocacy was just an excuse for geeks to cosplay in furry costumes. However, the Imperials were happy to let them take over the job of catering to the most spoiled species in the Core.

He and She have not been out of their polished rooms for ages. For eons. But the rooms have started to blink. They know that if they do not fix the source of those blinks, that they would end in darkness and cold and starvation and suffocation.

And so they venture out to where the mold awaits.

Back Then

by Frank LeRenard

The rooms blinked.

It happened just after dawn. First came the automated white electric sunrise, then breakfast, then brushing off of dead scales, then to the garden to check the misters for leaks with palms trailing the thin hoses. But as he finished these tasks and made for his den to rest, the rooms blinked. So he stopped and he stood, thin clawed fingers stretched toward the garden's glass door, jeweled slitted eyes on the mercury gas tubes, waiting for it to happen again.

It didn't. Not for a while. Not for many more dawns of many more new days, and so eventually he managed to put it out of his mind. The young plants bloomed in clouds of chemically enriched droplets. Three times the others dropped their empty boxes by the elevator doors, and three times he filled them with the trimmings from these plants. One week passed, then two, and every evening he would crack open the valves to the universe's radio static, lay on his back on a bed of soft sand, and listen for the spirits of voices to sneak in from somewhere, from someone out there, and then to sprout in his mind and then to die.

Then, on another day far from the first, as he began to sort spare resistors, they blinked again. Not a bulb, but all bulbs at once, and other things as well that stole electrons from the deep, deep well of them at the center of all this.

He unearthed his multimeter, and he stuck its metal prongs into the outlets, across the diodes of lamps, of lights, anything positive and negative that needed juice. That time, he found nothing. The next time, nothing more. A few at a time, a few at every blink. He cleaned every dash of corrosion, polished all the copper and gold conduits, touched up the solder in circuits and tested the contacts of worn chips. But as the days passed, the rooms blinked, and blinked, and blinked again, until finally they struck off the end of his comfort by blinking at him directly in the universe's static, a silent word that meant that yes, it was breaking. After all this time, it was on its way out again. And so he knew that if he did not make the trip first to fetch the manual from her, and then to the hub of their small world to find and fix the source of those blinks, that they would end in darkness and cold and starvation and suffocation. And knowing that broke through the last of his mind's fortifications.

The door stood firm, settled into its edges. Orange lights and straight lines made a painting of the single glass pane. But when, after a long period of staring, that painting blinked too, with one delayed exhalation he pressed his palm to the flat switch and stepped outside into the tangy oil-spill lobby air.

She still wanted to see the sky sometimes. He slipped toward the chrome double elevator doors under buzzing rows of white lights, but at the last moment turned and entered the stairwell just beside. Someone's chemical glazed it, not old. Not hers, either. Someone mammalian. But stairs would not blink.

His body curled up the sets of mirrored flights past repeating windowed portals. Eyes watched him through that window on level three, unblinking, disklike, then vanished. On level two, the light was out, and on level one, it didn't blink but it fluttered. He pushed through into the hallway, to the entrance to her abode, and again he stopped, hand poised for a knock. Another short flight— a last short flight— was visible inside. If one climbed it and looked out, one would see through to a pressure-locked corridor, and from there to a sometimes pink tepid sky over rocks and a distant, drooping flag, too heavy for the whisp of an atmosphere, dusted ochre with all the sand that had stuck to it in the years since the old bosses had filled the books with red ink and left this all to them.

A form slid through the hall, one side to the other. He raised his hand again, realizing then he'd put it down, and he watched, waited for her to reappear. His heartbeats seemed to match the flickering lights at his back. Even out there, her scent stole into him.

Innumerable flickers. Innumerable blinks, at this point, probably, and so he closed his eyes and tapped his knuckles on the window. He tapped subsequently harder, and for longer, and then the window disappeared and he was tapping on nothing.

She stood before him with her body tilted to the side, watching him with one eye set over a deep burning red circle on her cheek. He stepped back, stiffening his jaw, and raised one hand into the air. Stock still. Both of them.

Then she turned her back, and he followed her inside.

It was where his faded memory told him it should be, in a room near the entrance occupied only by green filing cabinets. A brick of printer-paper pages in between rough-cut cardboard covers, stuffed into an oily plastic bag in the top drawer of the cabinet nearest the door: this she removed, pulled from the bag, and for a time she stood with it, eyes on the cover, flitting from one feature to another. Her long claws picked at a paper marker, stuck somewhere near the end, and then she handed the book his way.

Immediately he settled it under an armpit and walked back into the flickering hallway, gaze far from her. But, just as he stepped through the door, her claws lit upon his shoulder.

Head offset, one eye watching. Her other hand hung at her side, a rolled paper tube balanced on loosely curled fingers. He glanced at it and then at her, at that solid frozen pupil. His jaw began to lose its tension. His rocky lips parted. His mouth cracked.

Hers sprang to a gleaming pink cavern.

Map still in hand, she strode past him. Only when she reached the door to the stairwell did he follow.

On their way back down, then, together, to the floor of the complex, by all of the doors he passed on his way up to her and then by doors below. Doors he hadn't laid eyes on in years. Decades. He could scarcely recall the time that had gone by, and this, he assumed, was why he also did not recall that the final door, at level fourteen, would be padlocked and dead-bolted. The sight of it knocked loose mud that slipped from some lost place in his mind down into his stomach, where it formed a hard lump.

She was watching him. When he saw, she nodded, and he stepped forward. A small key hung from a chain on a nail by the door, and with this he undid the locks.

He waited. Despite her agitation, a pause here was necessary. This door had no window. The only view either of them had behind it was old and worn and grey. He breathed out. She turned her back.

He pressed down on the lever latch.

Behind this final door lay the connecting tunnels, and inside those were the railways. The start of them was visible from the door, at the end of a concrete platform. Tracks below, cables above, and a car resting in between, ringed in broad windows in which swam the ghosts of the red emergency lights embedded in the walls on either side. The sound of the door closing behind them shot out into the darkness ahead. Already she crouched and unrolled the map, placed it as flat as two arms and a knee would allow under one of those emergency lights. Printed at the top left was an overall picture of the complex, with the details of each piece underneath. Here, at this vertex: a schematic of their place, because down below one room was called 'Greenhouse'. The remaining space was cluttered with a dozen or so more like it, organized in no special way, with an inconspicuous marking at what might be called the middle.

He waited for her a moment, and when her eyes wouldn't stop he leaned down and tapped that one lightly with a claw. It was a symbol that marked every fuse box and electric closet. In searching the whole face of it, he found no traceable path between where they were and that place. Only a three-digit number, as every other place was also marked, and one which differed by only one digit from those immediately around it, like it was only a label. But he looked between that number and the car on the tracks, the number and the car, and some deep thing in the mud surfaced and whispered to him that yes, remember, the number was all they needed if they used the car. So he showed her this, and she rolled up the map, and they walked aboard. Maybe it too would blink. The thought churned. But the tunnels were measured in miles.

Splitting polyurethane leather covered the seats inside. At the head was a control panel, with a key pad, a lever, and a rounded steel switch, which when moved from one side to the other illuminated a small screen with a smiling noseless ASCII face. Its mouth scrolled through three repeating frames of animation, and as he stared upon it, not comprehending, not remembering precisely this, it flashed and turned blue and told them in white text, "Critical software error. Contact system administrator. In an emergency situation, use lever for manual control."

A breeze touched his face. Oil and gas and steel, ozone, dirty crusty fog settled on the concrete surfaces, white powder condensates. And mold. Mold atop everything else. They had no other map. There was no other map. Security reasons, it was said, not to make available the whole thing. Watching, staring into the dark straight ahead, she nodded and grabbed the lever and pressed it forward.

They sat at opposite ends of the car. Emergency lights slung by, low in frequency. Sometimes these would illuminate an alcove housing a gray-green box and featureless concrete ridges above. The wheels whispered on the tracks, and in time they came to a curled fork, a capital upsilon, with two numbers scrawled in red spray paint. Here she pulled back on the lever and again consulted her guide, but it was neither number. It was none of the numbers. Those were for someone else, who took their meaning with them.

A place so far from those they knew, symmetric, long, and still. But with the car stopped, every subtle break in the stillness had become brave. Taps and clicks and crumbling metal ringing from the deep.

Right or left. She stood at the head, hand on the lever. He closed his eyes, projecting himself back then, back to those early days, to those times they took him over there to teach, they said when he was on their minds, but mostly just to see, to put those things before him and let his long nails fumble their way into them. One would always uncross his arms and go put coins in a machine and come back with small steaming styrofoam cups with little plastic sticks poking out the tops, and they'd watch some more, sipping at the cups while he pried apart boxes, taught himself tools, broke and repaired whatever things they were interested in seeing broken and repaired, until he might grow tired and look up into that blinking red light by the curved dark glass full of distorted shapes, and his hands and eyes and face would stop long enough they would declare that it was time to go back home, declare this to each other because they never did come to know he understood their words.

But right or left. That part was gone. So he stepped out and pushed the stick that moved the track right, because the deep sounds, when they came, came mostly from the left.

Another fork, later on, and then one more. Both instances she simply chose to stay the course, to stay in the car, and with time the walls opened up into a ceramic-tiled chamber, lit in white. There they slowed to a stop, at a platform that served as the mouth of three other tracks. An open stairwell rose from the opposite end, and on the wall just left of this stair hung a metal sign with black print, and that print spurred her to unroll the map one more time. This one, here. Optics Clean Rooms, Data Center, Robotics Testing. She tapped her claw again, to another name: Servers.

The other tracks were empty. Servers. There were some places he had never been, even back then. But maybe, yes. Certainly, yes. Otherwise it was guessing and walking, and they hadn't brought any food or water. The map went back under her arm and they climbed the staircase.

Walls, floors, doors, and long lights hanging in sequence down the center of these, all white. Clean enough and deep enough that with the electricity on it could and would remain as a photograph of what it had likely always been. They passed room after room, coming on-beat on the left and off-beat on the right. Some were silent, some ticked, some whirred and buzzed. Only one was open, and inside they saw some color, some thin bright blue drawers embedded in the rows of tables and cabinets, and a wheeled red multi-leveled cart full of machine bits and the tools to manipulate them. At the back was an area shrouded by thick murky plastic straps. A dark shape stood behind it. Inside, a servo motor clicked into action, and when that dark shape changed into something thin and crooked she reached past him and closed that one open door, and they moved on, hunched more into themselves.

All the monitor screens were black in the server rooms. Many sat with bases wrapped in blue cables, pins exposed, discarded textbooks and comic books at their sides; others stood sentry over quiet towers crammed against the table legs beneath. It was never his place, but while he had been swapping from the backup generators to the full reactor, she had been here, running the remaining machines from the handful of UPSs the old bosses had left behind. And while the UPSs were still there, batteries degrade and capacitors wear out and fans break, so all the monitor screens were black in the server rooms.

They walked into a room with a green sofa. Tape stuck to plastic, just under the display. Below that, face-up on the desk, lay a yellow square paper sprinkled with writing that read: "UN: gEnERic, PW: 438*Bd^&2". She dropped to a knee and pushed in a narrow switch with her forefinger claw.

It clicked on. She exhaled.

Boot up, UN, PW. White text on black, rapidly scrolling, blanking out, then reborn and stopped at a dollar sign. Her hands spilled over the keys, and she began to click them down with the tips of her claws. This was her thing. Back then, they would always bring them in together, because they were siblings, he supposed, and though their smells would always push them to opposite ends of the room, still he would watch her, watch her fingers tap dance across the keyboards of the laptops they would bring her, watch her eyes narrow and twitch, widen, the keys go silent, her mentors lean in and curve their lips up and wrinkle their eyes and rest hands on her shoulders and say things to her to which she would never react. He would watch her, and he knew that sometimes she would watch him, too, out over that deep red circle.

Like she was watching him now. Her hand was out, palm up.

The pages of the manual spilled open when he gave it over. Diagrams sped by, of coolant tanks, turbines, pipework, solenoids, outlines of magnetic field lines and fluid flow, chemical equations and decay rates and step functions and circuit diagrams. But it had been hers that whole time, in her dry place, in a filing cabinet without a key, so when she took it from him, she slid a claw into the place where she had laid the paper marker and opened it there. The grain here was different, and so was the handwriting, and so was the content.

Eventually, yes, there. In a few dozen keystrokes, a graphical program sprouted on the screen, a way to track the cars through the facility. This was their car, here were others, here were the tracks between them and among them. Along the side were numbered buttons. Their car was the wrong car; its tracks never connected to the central hub. Without coming here, it would have been guessing and walking, and mostly walking. Click the button that corresponded to the right car, open the new window, click where it said "Move to", type in the building code, press the Enter key. Simple. The software told them the car was moving from where it had been to the set of tracks down below.

She closed the manual and returned it. His eyes, too, then, searched the cover, examined the thin teardrop gap where the bookmark broke the pages' flow. They went to meet the car downstairs.

Another breeze was blowing. It seemed wrong, that it would happen on its own in these dead spaces. The surface above was sealed off, and while the air here surely must circulate, he strained to recall if ever, standing still in the deepest parts of the complex, he felt the stroke of such a damp wind across his scaly flesh. He turned his eye to her, and her throat and her chest were passing air quickly back and forth.

They stood at the tracks, gazing down the dark tubes, until the car came rolling to a stop before them. Though it was losing a battle with rust in places, it accepted her three-digit code and began to take them through the tunnels, and one of its wheels was noisier than the others.

The car approached the entrance to the plant. No stairwells, no layers. Here it was just a smooth platform lined with chain-link fencing enclosing flat gray buildings and whatever lay buried underneath. Immediately before them was the security booth, standing empty beside the parted gate. They stepped through, and he examined the complex, and though each image struck a new spark in his mind, the whole wouldn't light. It was the mold smell, maybe. Because here it was always present, stronger, and there was no reason for it that he could recall.

A squat box, in the center of it all, and in the center of that was a gray door with a round knob, and to either side of this door were two windows, one of them cracked and missing a pointed chunk. Screwed into the wall above the door was a sign proclaiming, "Viewing Room", and while that was the reason they approached this place, when they first took in the air leaking through the broken glass they slowed and began to approach for another.

From here, then, it seemed. She stood to the side, and he placed his hand on the knob. She nodded. He pulled open the door.

Damp spores exploded out with the change in pressure. Both of them began to wheeze into the crooks of their arms. He gave it a moment to pass, a moment to catch his breath. Inside, then, with muzzle buried in elbow, searching out the islands of floor that were not covered in white fuzzy fungus. It was on the monitors, crawling up the walls, reaching fingers across glass, hanging from the lights. It wasn't that the air here was humid, or that there was anything to decompose, or any other thing, but here it was, growing everywhere nonetheless.

Some residual of the old bosses, surely. They had been doing many things here, after all, before they left.

When he picked his way to the viewing window, he saw that it was in there too: clouds of it condensed onto the hundreds of protrusions emitting from the metal doughnut of the reactor down below. With slitted eyes, he fled to the platform and shut the door and lay back against the wall, heart pounding to the beat of his thoughts.

At the end of his final rounds of testing and touching up, he had left all of his tools in the cabinets throughout the facility where he'd found them, save those small things he wanted in a home. But it was all for mechanical and electrical work. He had little to remove organisms from metal and glass. Layers of organisms. He thought of the tanks used to store the deuterium, those that supplied the reactor for decades, and he pictured them full of acids or ammonia or bleach, and still it looked insufficient.

She touched his shoulder again. Her finger pointed to the door, which had cracked back open. Another breeze blew, stung their eyes, hurt their throats, and the door began to move. Stopped.

Moved again, but without a breeze.

He scrambled to his feet and backed away, and only in between other thoughts did he recognize that he was holding her hand. Something rustled behind them, behind the glass of the unbroken window, and he turned to it, his eye flicking from one place to another. It all seemed still. But no, there. One finger of it, touching its friend where they met on the glass. As he watched, these two friends bid farewell, and began to walk back to join their separate families again.

She pulled at him, pulled him away, backed them toward the gate and the security booth. The tendrils of mold continued to recede from the center of the window. From the edges of it. Gone. All clean. Behind, some other shape grew, bulbous and dark, and this swayed back and forth, heavier and slower at each pass. The doorknob rattled, jerked, slipped, and the door shoved open and hit the wall behind it, and the noise of it shot them both into the security booth to the floor under the desk, chests and throats heaving and eyes flicking in every direction.

All it did was rustle. The sound of his claws stroking the leaves of his tomato plants. They listened and waited.

Minutes went by. Twice, a new breeze passed over them and trickled down into the booth. Then nothing.

She set the map down and pushed herself upright. She put a knee on the stool, anchored herself against the desk, lifted her head, and peered outside. Eventually, he echoed.

The mold had spilled onto the platform. Again, for the moment, it was still. But far along the trail it had made there was a shadow growing across the concrete, and he followed this shadow across the moldy stream, behind a drab wall, up, up to its source, a slight shape protruding out into the air. As they watched, it grew longer and became more defined. And they saw that it was a face.

Ideas blossomed, died. Made soil for new ideas to blossom and die. Too much darkness for them to grow, too few nutrients. It moved. It had a face. It breathed sometimes. That was all.

That face was turned now to them. Both met its blind white gaze, frozen.

It moved toward them. It changed, rearranged. Protrusions formed under its eyes, jagged, mirrored rows of fungal spikes like an inverse mouth.

It accelerated.

It charged.

He reached out a numb fist and slammed it down onto the control panel, and just as they dropped and ducked back under the desk the gate slid shut and stalled. But she was only there to fetch the map, and so he trailed after her, at the tip of her whipping tail, and jumped into the car just as she began to hammer in a three-digit code. As it sparked on and gained momentum, the mold creature was squeezing through the holes between the chain links and plopping onto the ground outside, and there these were beginning to coalesce.

A spring pushed into his back, near his kidney, but he lay still. She stood rigid at the control panel. Sometimes she would turn her head and look and smell behind them. The tension in her body never altered, said nothing new.

They drew to a halt, somewhere. She ventured off at once, and when he found courage he dashed out after her onto an unfamiliar platform.

Behind a latched door. She once again spilled open the map to find the number she had somehow brought them to. There. One digit off from what she had intended, from the number last in her memory. Pathogen research, animal testing. It mattered little. He crouched just under the door's thin reinforced window, watching, listening, smelling, knowing they would discover soon how quickly the monster could move, and thinking, thinking. How.

He saw it then.

The stairwell doors would not lock, so again they fled, in the only direction available. Up past pathogen research, up past animal testing, cell cultures, the neuroscience lab, up toward the dry daylight above where they would be forced to stop because there would be no more up. And he thought, and he realized that it was a solution if the piece of it chasing them was the most important piece for the survival of the rest, and so when she once tried to change direction to find a room with a lockable door, he stopped her, and he shook his head, and he pointed up.

One time back then they had taken them to such a place. They'd called it a field trip. Above the power plant sector was an old shuttered loading bay, a garage with a long and wide airlock and a hole in the floor into which they would feed bulky, partly assembled metal pieces carried in on trucks with cabins sealed against the dry poison air outside. Until that day he had thought little about how the facility had come to be, and he found himself gazing into the deep darkness and imagining the crane lowering piece after piece into the reactor chamber, where men and machines with hammers and diamond saws and blue focused torches and laser-guided measuring tools would assemble it all perfectly into the facility's forever pulsing heart. But she hadn't been interested in the down or the around. Her eyes always drew toward that chamber, the fat corridor and the heavy steel and glass portal at the end of it. While he was looking down, she had walked over there and put her head to the glass and looked out.

This one was smaller, suitable for vehicles to make deposits and no more. Pink light from the outside splashed on the floor of the airlock, competing with and losing to that from the mercury bulbs on the inside. One chamber and the main room. A mobile platform in the center, a truck still parked just beside, and a service elevator on the right.

He eyed the airlock, but such things were built with safety in mind.

He eyed the truck. She eyed him, and he met her gaze, and they nodded.

Time passed to the beat of the idling engine. She watched, invisible, from the service elevator. He stood, bait, by the open truck door. Outside, the dim sun crawled across the sky by arcseconds, minutely tilting the long sides of the pink slab on the airlock floor.

The handle of the stairwell door tilted, and he placed a foot on the running board. By a ghost's touch, the stairwell door slid open. Tendrils followed, spilled onto the floor and rolled in trailing droplets.

There, again: its face. Its cloudy eyes.

He pulled himself inside and slammed the door before it made contact, hit the vacuum seal on the cabin. Reverse, crank the steering wheel. It engulfed the grill, splayed itself out across the windshield, up to the roof. Casual, almost. Use the side-view mirrors to angle into the lock. Lumps of it began to tear away, form a ball, slam back down. He hit the external port, stopped. The balls turned into spikes. Hit harder. Its white eyes watched him, and they gave him nothing to watch back, but he felt its hunger, its single mind fed by its one devotion.

The airlock sealed shut and began to depressurize.

In all its fury, the creature made of mold seemed not to perceive the slowing and solidifying of its appendages. As the air in the chamber swapped from warm and wet and oxygenated to sparse and cold and CO_2, he saw the fungal coating grow rigid and crystalline, saw the extant water in its body turn it slow, slower, stop. First to ice, and then the ice turned to steam. And in that steam its lifeblood went invisible and drifted away, off through the vents and out into the arid sky.

And then it was completely still.

She waited a long time before reversing the process. Mummy chunks of the thing cracked off as he steered the truck back into the loading bay, and when he stopped and exited she began to tear off the rest and carry them back to the ashen pile in the airlock chamber. When every piece of it was accounted for, she once again sealed the door and opened the chamber to the outside, and this was how they would leave it, just in case.

Exhausted, they looked one more time to each other. Looked each other over, closely, until their hearts had slowed to a normal pace. And then they made the journey back to their original destinations.

It was not so long, this time. Most of the mold had come with, as it turned out, and the remainder of the damage was simple to repair if one was diligent. The fuel tanks still held plenty— such was the nature of energy gleaned one atom at a time— and the reactions in the chamber had not been interrupted. While he worked, she came twice to bring him trimmings from the garden and fresh water, and then she would disappear, and he would not watch where she went, and she never did bother to let him know.

Sometimes he thought about the creature and why it had chosen to reside here, at the facility's core. He didn't know where it had come from or why it would have left that place, but the reactor complex had little for it. Much against it, in fact. Heat, heavy water, sparks, sodium. It must have been starving. Insane with thirst and hunger, if it had had such feelings. He didn't know. And he did know that no matter how much thought he might give the matter he would not come to know more, and he considered whether or not this was for the best. Then he finished his repairs.

When he finally returned to their abode, he found the padlock missing and the stairwell door open. He pushed it shut, stared at its windowless backside. The bolts were still available. Back then, it had been just them and the padlock, that whole time. He flipped one forward, saw its one flat end welcomed by its house on the other side.

He flipped it back.

Resting all the way at the top was the one final thing. The stairwell light on level one still fluttered. Tomorrow, perhaps, he would try to fix it. For now, he strode again through the short hall to her door, and he raised his hand, poised for a knock. And he knocked, and she came to the door, and he followed her inside.

She held the bag open for him. He dropped the manual into it. She took it from him and placed it into the top drawer of the filing cabinet nearest the door, and she shut it away.

Then, he turned and walked out, walked until he was once again laying on a soft bed of sand under a buzzing heat lamp, listening to the open valves of the universe's radio static through a pair of headphones. And though he listened for a long time, the spirits of those distant voices never did come again.

Shreddy the cat catches Rosie the mouse by the banks of a small creek. But before he can do anything to her, a strange tortoise materializes...

(For six other Shreddy stories, see the collection The Necromouser and Other Magical Cats *by Mary E. Lowd, available from FurPlanet Productions.)*

Tortoise Who

by Mary E. Lowd

By the concrete steps up to the footbridge over Dixon Creek, a tortoise shell phased in and out of existence, accompanied by a strangely cheerful wheezing sound.

Rosie the mouse was too busy running away from a cat to notice. The cat, a gray tabby named Shreddy, was having too much fun to care.

Rosie scurried around the steps and under the bridge. The babbling rush of Dixon Creek blocked her way. Shreddy caught up and swatted Rosie with a clawful paw. The air was knocked out of her lungs as the paw smashed into her, knocking her into the wet dirt beside the creek.

Shreddy drew back his paw to look at his handiwork, a satisfied smirk under his whiskers.

Rosie got her legs under her and took off toward the concrete steps. She thought she'd cross the creek on the footbridge, but the mottled green dome of a tortoise shell—now solid—gave her a different idea. Perhaps, she thought, she could hide inside it. Rosie skittered around the edge of the dome until she came to a crack between the top and the bottom. Before she could climb inside, an ancient face with wrinkled skin and two scaly legs emerged from the opening.

Rosie watched amazed as the ancient face, nearly as large as her whole body, rose above her on a gently curved neck. Toothlessly, the tortoise smiled down. "Hello," he said. "I'm The Tortoise."

"The tortoise?" Rosie squeaked

In her surprise, Rosie forgot all about the cat that now crouched behind her, wiggling his haunches and preparing to pounce.

"Yes," the tortoise said. "Just *The Tortoise*." He turned his slow, steady gaze from Rosie to Shreddy and then back again. "You look like you could use some help running away from this cat."

Rosie nodded solemnly, her entire body shaking.

Shreddy flattened his ears and stopped wiggling. He was a house cat and didn't need to catch mice for food. He'd only been hunting for fun. And suddenly, this eccentric tortoise seemed much more amusing than an ordinary, frightened mouse.

Shreddy flopped onto his side and made himself comfortable, stretched out on the sidewalk. He began, nonchalantly, to wash his paws. Meanwhile, the tortoise lifted one of his scaly feet and took a single step toward placing himself between the cat and the mouse.

Shreddy looked up from licking his paw and meowed, "How are you going to help a mouse run? You're the slowest thing I've ever seen."

"It's true," the tortoise said, lifting his other foot. "I walk slowly."

"If you think you can block my way," Shreddy meowed, "you're wrong. I'll go around you."

"Of course," the tortoise said. "I'm much faster when I fly."

Shreddy didn't expect that response. Neither did Rosie, but she liked it. She squeaked happily and scrabbled at the side of the tortoise's shell, trying to climb on top. Shreddy's heart jumped at the sudden rodential motion; he nearly decided to pounce.

The moment passed. Shreddy was a lazy cat. And he was more interested in seeing a tortoise fly than eating a mouse. Mice were fun to chase, but they tasted icky. He never knew quite what to do when he caught one. Sometimes, he brought them as gifts to his human, but she didn't properly appreciate them.

"Please, Madam Mouse," the tortoise said. "I'm not a flying carpet. Kindly give me a moment to prepare."

Rosie stopped scrabbling, but she scurried quickly behind the tortoise, placing the green dome of his shell between her and Shreddy.

"Thank you," the tortoise said. Then he leaned back, placing his weight on his back feet and reared up, revealing the smooth, pale green of the belly of his shell. Right in the center of his shell's belly, a tiny blue door gleamed with a brightly polished tiny brass doorknob and knocker.

Rosie squeaked and jumped for the blue door, but it was out of her reach.

Shreddy blinked in surprise.

With a flourish, the tortoise put his scaly front feet to his belly, took hold of the door, and removed it—white-washed frame, brass hinges, and all—as easily as if it had been held on merely with static cling. His belly underneath was as smooth and unblemished as if a door had never been there.

The tortoise moved the tiny door through the air, down to the side of one of the concrete steps that led up to the footbridge. As the door moved, it seemed to change size, growing smaller and larger almost at the same time. On the side of the concrete step, it coalesced into the perfect size for a mouse.

Rosie wasted no time in scurrying to the blue door. The brass doorknob turned in her paw, and she didn't wait to look before disappearing inside.

Shreddy, who had been lying on his side, sat up suddenly. "My mouse!" he yowled. "Where did you hide her?"

The tortoise's ancient face transformed into an enigmatic smile, but he did not answer.

The tortoise reached for the tiny door. Shreddy sprang for it as well, but his paws struck empty concrete as the tortoise affixed the blue door once again to his belly. Shreddy raised his paw to strike the tortoise's wrinkled face, but the long green neck and legs withdrew into their shell. The tortoise's enigmatic smile receded into the darkness within.

Shreddy clawed at the hard dome of the tortoise's shell, uselessly dulling his claws, until the shell itself phased out of existence with a cheerful wheeze, leaving an angry cat yowling at nothing.

* * *

Beyond the blue door, Rosie found herself in a long oval room, the perfect size for a mouse. The cat would never fit in here, but his paw would fit through the blue door. Rosie slammed the blue door and bolted it shut. Then safe from the cat and his long paws, she looked around.

In the center of the room, a beam of light shimmered like sunlight on a lake. The light didn't seem to be coming from anywhere, simply shimmering improbably in the middle of the room like an optical illusion. Rosie didn't understand it, but she decided to give it a wide berth.

All around the edges of the oval room, doors and windows in wildly varying architectural styles alternated with each other. The windows framed all manner of different vistas. One window with white shutters and lacy curtains looked out on rolling hills covered with golden grass under a deep blue sky. The view couldn't be a painting, because the golden grasses rippled in the wind and the clouds drifted.

Another window, round and reinforced like a porthole on a sailing ship, looked out on the blackness of a star-studded night. Rosie saw no ground beneath the sky, but a ringed planet in partial eclipse, beautiful and impossible, outshone the stars like a diamond does sand.

Another window looked out on a forest, except the trees swayed their branches with a springy quality like they were dancing, and the color of their leaves shifted like the rainbows on an oily puddle. These places couldn't all be real. They were nothing like the world Rosie knew, but she could see them with her own eyes, through these impossible windows.

Finally Rosie's gaze came to a window wider and taller than the rest on the opposite end of the oval room from the blue door where she'd entered. This window's glass was a single, large, unbroken pane. On the other side, she saw the world she'd just come from—the street she'd run down toward Dixon Creek and the cat she'd run away from. Shreddy, magnified to even larger and more terrifying proportions than he'd had before, stared at the window, his green eyes burning angrily in his gray-striped face. He lifted a paw and reached, claws out, for the window.

Rosie cowered, clamping her paws over her head, flattening her ears to her skull and squeezing shut her eyes. She shivered and whimpered until a gentle touch to her shoulder made her jump.

"Don't fear, Madam Mouse," said the voice of the tortoise.

Rosie looked up to see his wizened face, much smaller than before—nearly the size of her own face, in fact—staring down at her. His scaly hand rested on her shoulder. He was strangely thin, wearing a dark, floor-length robe embroidered with the spirals of tiny galaxies instead of his bulky shell.

"Where's your shell?" Rosie asked.

"You're inside it," the tortoise said.

"I don't understand."

"I'm a Time Tortoise from Galapagofrey. We're both larger and smaller than we seem."

Rosie looked out the largest window again. Shreddy continued to claw at it, but his paw moved in a strange, slow motion.

"Why is the cat moving slowly?" Rosie asked.

The tortoise smiled, reshaping all the wrinkles on his face. "We're also faster and slower than we seem. Come, you're safe; no need to cower anymore." The tortoise helped Rosie to her hind feet. When he moved, the tiny galaxies on his robe shimmered. "Now I believe I promised to help you run away, Madam Mouse. Where would you like to run away to?" He gestured around the room, at all the many windows, with his scaly hand.

"These are places we can go?"

"I'm a Time Tortoise. We can go anywhere."

"Somewhere without cats," Rosie squeaked. She turned around, looking at every window in the room. There were too many to choose.

"Or maybe," the tortoise said softly, "somewhere cats and mice get along?"

Rosie finished turning around the room and blinked at the tortoise in surprise. She almost laughed, but instead she asked, "Is there such a place?"

The tortoise didn't answer, but his smile grew enigmatic. He walked toward the large window that looked out on Shreddy's threatening paw. Instead of a sill, under the window was a control panel covered in knobs, switches, flickering lights, and all manner of buttons. The tortoise flipped a switch, pressed a button, pressed several more—his scaly hands moved with an uncanny speed.

The view of Shreddy's paw distorted, disappeared, and was replaced by a swirling vortex of colors. Rosie noticed the scenes began changing erratically in the other windows around the room. Rolling fields were replaced by yawning blackness and stars only to be succeeded by crashing oceans, barren deserts, bustling metropolises, one after the other. All the windows changed rapidly. It was dizzying, and Rosie crouched back down, four paws on the floor. She stared at the smooth, dull floor to steady herself.

When Rosie looked up again, she saw a mouse-sized mansion through the window. She knew it was mouse-sized because a group of mice dressed in three-piece suits and bouffant ruffled dresses stood on one of the balconies. One of them, wearing a top hat and monocle, seemed to see the tortoise's shell. He pointed at the window in great excitement, but before anything else could happen the whole scene disappeared in a vortex of colors like before.

"Too early," the tortoise muttered, still working the control panel with his scaly hands.

The vortex on the front window didn't last as long this time. It gave way to a view of a gleaming silver structure built from hexagons and triangles. Beside the silver building stood several rocket ships, classically designed. Rosie couldn't be sure of the scale, but the silver building seemed larger than the mansion had been.

"Here we are!" The tortoise clapped his hands, then looked at Rosie critically. "We'll need to find you something to wear." He went to one of the numerous doors around the perimeter of the room—a simple wooden one with a round doorknob. He opened it. Inside hung a collection of clothes.

The tortoise looked through the clothes and selected a garment—a simple red vest and darker red pantaloons—on a wireframe hanger.

"This should be suitable," he said, holding the clothing out to Rosie. She took them, tentatively.

"I've never worn clothes before," she said, fumbling with the hanger. The pantaloons were attached to little metal clasps, and the vest had been buttoned in place.

"Let me help you," the tortoise offered. He removed the clothes from their hanger deftly and helped Rosie step into them. The cloth felt strange against her fur, but Rosie liked the pearly buttons on her vest.

"Now wait a minute while I get the door ready," the tortoise said. He took off his robe and hung it on an otherwise empty coat tree near the middle of the room, right beside the shimmering beam of light like sunlight dancing on water. Then he stepped into the beam and disappeared. The large window that looked out on the gleaming silver building went dark.

A moment later, the view returned to the window but now there was a rectangular blue door at the base of one of the trees. The tortoise reappeared in the center of the oval room, bathed in the shimmering beam of light. He took his robe from the coat tree and wrapped it around his wrinkled, green body. Then he led Rosie to the blue door in the back of the room, the one she'd entered his shell by. This time, they stepped through it together.

* * *

Outside the light was strange and bright, almost blue although the sky was a washed out shade of white smeared with cotton-candy pink clouds. Trees on the horizon sported autumn colors, but something about their briskness made Rosie suspect they always looked that way here. When she turned to look at the blue door, it was set in the trunk of one of the trees, just how it had looked through the giant window inside. The tortoise's empty shell loomed beside it—much too large for the skinny, be-robed creature standing beside her now. Although the shell seemed oddly smaller than she'd remembered it being when she first saw it beside Dixon Creek...

"You're still the same size as me," Rosie said.

"I'm the right size for the door," the tortoise replied, gesturing at the handsome blue door with its brass hinges, still ajar. Through the door, Rosie could still see the interior of his shell with all its windows, strangely displaced from the outside of the shell. "When we walked through the door to my shell, our sizes relative to it stayed preserved."

Rosie remembered how the tortoise had stretched the door to be the perfect size for her before she'd first entered his shell. "So... You can use that door to change to any size?" She thought that must be useful for escaping cats. She liked the idea of being larger than a cat.

"Any size I can stretch the door into, yes. The door is very stretchy, but there are limits to its elasticity," the tortoise said.

"It's still a useful trick," Rosie observed.

"Indeed," the tortoise agreed. "So, when visiting the mice of Mouselandia, I choose to be the size of a mouse. Like you." His eyes twinkled with a smile. "Although, actually, you're twice as tall as your usual self right now."

Rosie could hardly believe the tortoise. She didn't feel any larger. Though his shell did look smaller. She looked back uncertainly at the green dome abandoned under the tree. Then she looked forward at the silver building made from triangles and hexagons.

"Mouselandia... Is that where we are?" Rosie asked. None of the mice she'd ever known lived in buildings like this silver monstrosity, but then, none of the mice she'd known wore vests and pantaloons—or top hats and monocles—or clothes at all. Rosie felt the smooth, pearly buttons on her vest. She decided that she liked this adventure. "Let's go meet these mice who get along with cats." Excitement filled her voice, and the tortoise smiled like he approved.

Two mice dressed in clothes much like Rosie's greeted them at the entrance of the silver building. The mice were delighted to see the tortoise and seemed to have met him before or at least to have heard of him. The Mouselandian mice agreed to give Rosie a tour of their facilities and invited her and the tortoise to a banquet that evening to celebrate a rocket launch scheduled for the morrow.

On the tour, Rosie was startled to see several mouse-sized cats—or very catlike mice—working side by side with the normal mice. She asked her tour guides about them, and one of them explained that the Mouselandia Space Administration engaged in a cultural exchange program with New Catta.

"But... They look like cats," Rosie said.

"They are cats," the tour guide mouse replied.

"But... They're so small."

The tortoise leaned close to Rosie and whispered, "You're forgetting, Madam Mouse: you're twice as tall as usual."

Rosie thought about that. "Even so, they're very small for cats."

"Demographic statistics show that mice have been getting larger and cats smaller for centuries," the tour guide explained. "In fact, the fossil record suggests that there were once cats even larger than this building! Imagine that!"

Rosie didn't have to imagine. She'd seen such a cat only minutes ago. (Centuries ago?) She remembered Shreddy's clawful paw, swiping through the air, coming for her—*waiting* for her—back on her own world, in her own time. She shuddered. She couldn't believe her good luck, being swept away by the tortoise from her horrible fate.

Mouselandia seemed to be a much more civilized world for mice than her own. The banquet before the ball was held in a room with three long tables set with fine plates, silverware, and dishes—like the gigantic human dining tables that Rosie had glimpsed through windows back home. She'd heard tales of mice brave enough to break into the warm human homes and steal from their richly laden pantries, but she'd also known mice who'd dared such endeavors and never returned. Rosie had chosen to stay safely outside, stealing only from gardens and sleeping in her drafty hole under the wood pile.

Here though, she dined on bread, preserves, and sweetened fruits. All the foods she'd only dreamed of before. The tiny cats had their own food—it smelled like fish. She sat at the table and listened to mice—free from fear—discuss politics, technology, and religion. Ideas she'd never dreamed of.

After dinner, a quartet of mice played music on stringed instruments, and everyone else danced. Even the tortoise. Rosie had never danced before, but the tortoise held her in his scaly arms and whirled her about the floor. It was magical. It was heavenly. A mouse asked if he could cut in, and Rosie danced with one mouse after another until...

A cat stepped in.

The cat wrapped his paws around her, his arms no larger than her own, but his eyes were green, his face gray striped, and his ears pointed. She squeaked, and her heart raced. But the twirling pattern of the dance and the brisk tempo of the music carried her along.

She stared into the cat's green eyes. They twinkled with good will and mirth. His face was so close, his whiskers brushed against her own. His paws were light and gentle against her back. No claws. He moved with her, easily gliding across the floor.

Only moments later, she traded partners again, and suddenly the cat was gone, lost from her sight, mixed in among all the other dancers on the floor.

Later that night Rosie and the tortoise returned through the blue door with brass hinges into the tortoise's shell. Inside he took her to a simple brown door set between a window looking out at a spiral galaxy and one showing a stark skyline of snow-crested mountains. Behind the brown door, there was a simple room with a four poster bed, and a dresser filled with clothes just Rosie's size. She didn't know how the room fit where it was, squeezed so tightly between those windows, but she didn't understand how each window looked out on a different vista, each more marvelous than the last, either.

"You can stay here tonight," the tortoise said.

"Only tonight?" Rosie asked, barely daring to hope that the tortoise might keep her, might take her with him to see more of the wide universe he seemed to know so well but that she hadn't known anything of before today.

The tortoise's wrinkled face showed only mystery, but he said, "You're inside a Time Tortoise's shell. Time passes both more quickly and more slowly here." He winked. "Tonight can be as long as you like."

"I think I'd like it to be very long," Rosie said. "Very long indeed."

"Good." The wrinkles in the tortoise's face contorted around a wide, contented smile. "I'm glad. You should get some rest, for we have a lot of places to explore."

* * *

Shreddy stared at the empty place beside the footbridge over Dixon Creek where the tortoise's shell had been. He'd lost mice before. He knew he wasn't much of a hunter. But he'd never before lost a mouse in such a strange way.

Minutes passed. He twisted his ears, listening to the running water, children playing in the distance, and a bird singing in a nearby maple tree. He decided to go home and claw up a couch cushion to express his frustration, but then the cheerful wheezing sound began again. The green dome of the tortoise's shell faded in and out, and finally back *in* to existence in front of him.

Shreddy watched dumbfounded as the tortoise's head and legs emerged from his shell. The tortoise pulled the blue door off of his belly and placed it on one of the concrete steps to the footbridge.

A mouse dressed up in fancy clothes like a human's doll stepped out of the door. Shreddy snickered.

The mouse looked up at him, resignation and determination in her eyes, and said, "I've come back to face my fate. I've traveled the universe,

331

seen a world where camellia bushes are at war with rhododendrons, flown on spaceships developed by *mice* and cats working together, watched stars explode—and through it all, your paw has hung over me. So I've come back to you."

Shreddy sniffed the mouse in front of him. "You're not my mouse," he said. "You're old."

The tortoise spoke: "Rosie has been my traveling companion, exploring the universe with me for many years, but I guarantee she is the same mouse you were tormenting when I arrived."

Shreddy looked more closely at the mouse and sniffed her again. Through the scent of age, he smelled other scents—subtle and expansive, foreign—but beneath those, he recognized the smell of the mouse he'd been chasing only minutes ago. "You are the same mouse," Shreddy said with surprise.

Rosie stared at Shreddy with a confidence unknown to the young mouse who'd run from cats. She'd fought in the war against the rhododendrons; she'd repaired a spaceship as it spiraled, lifelessly into the gravity well of a singularity; she'd shared tea and biscuits with a time-travelling bear; she would not run from a cat, no matter its size.

She stared him down.

Shreddy looked away. He wasn't used to mice standing up to him. He didn't want to eat her, and she wouldn't run. "I don't want you anymore. Go home to your hole."

A weight lifted from Rosie's shoulders. Her dreams had been haunted by Shreddy's raised paw for years as she lived inside the tortoise's shell. Now she was free. She said goodbye to the tortoise and went home, a different mouse than she'd been when she left it.

"You owe me, Tortoise," Shreddy said. "You stole my mouse from me."

The tortoise winked and said, "Maybe some day, I'll come back and take you on adventures as well."

The batlike Awraa have never ventured into the vast Vinja desert that marks the end of their territory. To try and cross it is to die. Finally their michee *(elders) organize an expedition—in experimental land-vehicles. What will Te-ron and his companions find there?*

I Am the Jaguar

by Cairyn

The Past

Awraa rarely left the jungle, so it was pure chance that Ge-fin and Sal-ree discovered the broken form of the survivor while fluttering over the vast grassland south of the Vinja. They were cartographing the edge of the desert, looking for permanent landmarks to use in their maps. It was a difficult task in an area of rolling hills and drying grass where the steppe slowly gave way to dust, stones, and sand. A dry wind blew from the north, making flight a challenge and irritating their eyes.

"We're not getting any reasonable distance estimations," Ge-fin noted.

"Can leave that for the next team," Sal-ree replied wearily. "Look, I need a break. We should turn to the south and get some food and water, at least. The Vinja is too close, nothing around..." She looped around in surprise. "What's that?"

Ge-fin followed her nodding head. A small black form lay outstretched in the grass, not moving. "It looks... like an Awraa?"

They glided slowly closer, wary of any predators that may stalk the steppe. What was little more than a blotch before resolved as a bat-shaped being: two wings spread, a canine-like head; yes, definitely an Awraa, or the remains of one.

Ge-fin and Sal-ree landed close by and inspected the stranger without touching. The body was emaciated, ribs showing, bones defining the skin; dehydrated as well. No ankle belt, no sign of identification, no ear mark. Ge-fin bent down over the Awraa and sniffed. "Can't be dead long, he doesn't smell of rot."

"Dunno, it reeks from *over here*." Sal-ree walked around the find, keeping her distance. "Perhaps he died of some disease; I'd not touch him if I were you."

"Don't worry. No, I think he came from the desert. The north wind carried him in."

"The Vinja? Come on. What would he have *done* there?"

"I suppose he got lost, maybe caught in a high altitude gale. Remember, we had a strong southener until a week ago. Let's report…"

A wing shot up, two fingers clawing at Ge-fin. The Awraa jumped back, beating his wings frantically. "*What the…*" Two eyes opened in a face of parched skin.

"He's alive," Sal-ree murmured. "Looks pretty dead but somehow he survived. Got some water left?"

Ge-fin didn't need to check the small waterskin on his ankle belt. "Nothing.—We need to get him to a healer."

"How? Can't carry him."

"We build a stretcher. But first, water." He handed his waterskin to Sal-ree. "Fly back to the last brook we crossed and fill up both. I'll tend to him until you're back."

Sal-ree wrinkled her nose. "You are crazy. We can't carry him in flight. We'd need to go by foot, and it's at least four days of *flying* to the next settlement. Provided we go straight, which I can't see with all the wonky distance estimations."

"We must do something," Ge-fin insisted.

The stranger opened his muzzle, murmuring something.

"Record his last words, I suppose," Sal-ree suggested. Which was kind of cruel, but also true. Ge-fin frowned but bent his head down to listen.

"… we drank…"

"Can you hear me? What's your name?"

"… we drank…"

Sal-ree reluctantly edged closer. "I think he wants to tell us there's some water nearby. He drank. Let me have a look, it might be closer than that brook back there." She took flight and spiraled upward.

Ge-fin shook his head. If the desert's victim—provided his evaluation was correct—had encountered a stream, why should he have left it again before recovering? Searching for food? Goodness, this guy was so haggard he probably couldn't even walk, much less fly, except perhaps when the wind blew him up.

"… we drank…" The stranger's voice got softer, his eyes closed again.

"I do not understand what you're trying to say. Tell me your name, so we can…" *Inform your next of kin?* That was probably not a nice thing to say to a dying person.

Sal-ree landed again. "Nothing as far as I can see. I wish I had eagle eyes." Awraa vision had developed for the jungle canopy, not for long distance viewing—one thing to envy birds for.

"Doesn't matter. I think he's dead anyway." Ge-fin searched for a pulse and found none.

"He must've been in the desert for a week, or so. Lost all his stuff, and then stranded here. Pity, a few more kilometers and he'd have made it to the jungle."

Ge-fin felt saddened at the stranger's passing. "I wonder… what did he want to tell us? What could be more important to him than his name?"

"Look at him," Sal-ree pointed out. "His brain was probably fried already. Perhaps he meant 'Give me something to drink', and didn't get it right."

"Maybe. 'We drank', who's *we*? Are there others around?"

"I think I would have noticed. If there were others with him, they most likely all perished in the desert. No, I'm not going to look."

"Perhaps…" Ge-fin tried to reason. "Perhaps they found a stream in the desert. Kept them alive until the south wind turned, and they could attempt to fly back."

Sal-ree made a disdainful sound. "The Vinja is dry as death itself, as far as anyone ever flew."

"Which is not very far," Ge-fin stated. "There may be all kinds of things in the desert, just waiting for us to discover them. Maybe… maybe there is something on the other side."

"It's not as if we are going to look. You know—if we're going to end like that, flying the desert winds."

"Help me pile up some stones. We need to send back a search and rescue team, to identify this guy and look for more bodies around. I don't want predators to get to the corpse." They went to work, covering the pitiful body with boulders. It would not help against large animals, but with a little luck the search and rescue team would be able to collect the remains mostly intact.

After finishing the task, the two Awraa took flight again, using the northern wind efficiently to cross the grassland. Ge-fin flew higher than usual, every now and then spiraling back to look at the distant edge of the Vinja. *We drank.* There was water out there, maybe in the desert, maybe beyond. And that information had been important enough for a dying Awraa to convey.

The Vinja was hiding some fabulous new land. Some day, an Awraa would venture out to find it.

The Present

Te-ron noticed the Jaguar travel group while flying barely above tree height. He could smell the fires, smoke rising through the branches, covering up even the sweetish scent of night blossoms. The Jaguars had set up camp quite close to the Awraa settlement, bold as always. Te-ron wasn't sure whether they had come to trade or were just passing through, but seeing Jaguars gave him a tingly feeling in the stomach every time. He added a bit of height to his trajectory and glided in a curve around the camp. No time to stop and ask; he was late for the meetup as it was, and he didn't recognize the pennants anyway. The sun had set already, turning the jungle below into a darkened world only lit here and there by scarce artificial lights.

The *ut-an* was built in the upper branches, an airy construct made from ornate wooden beams carrying a roof of interlocking palm leaves. There was no floor below the roof, nor were there any walls except the low-strung leaves, just a maze of bars to hang from, and a few platforms to deposit things. Te-ron aimed at the nearest bar, turned in flight, and took hold, shaking his wings until the muscles relaxed. It had been a long journey.

The closest Awraa rustled their wings in acknowledgement of his presence, but didn't offer talk. About forty Awraa were already present, hanging comfortably upside down, waiting for the *michee* to open the talks. Some were engaged in conversation. Two Awraa on the opposite side kept their wings open, cooling off in the slight breeze. Deep below the *ut-an*, lights revealed the presence of other *uts*; quite a few built since Te-ron had last visited.

"Te-ron? Te-ron, is that you?" Another Awraa climbed closer, foot over foot, not bothering to fly. "It's been a while!"

"Ka-lin, good to see you." Te-ron made the customary wing gesture. "Didn't know you became a scout."

"The meetup is for scouts *and* leaders. Why do you assume I'm not a leader?" Ka-lin grinned mischieviously, his long snout twitching.

"Leader. Yeah, sure. Next time I see you, you'll be anointed *michee*, right?"

"Stranger things have happened.—Hey, do you know what all this is about? I've been called off from Sinuee River patrol, and you know how that is at this time of the year, with snakes and all. Jaguars on the prowl, and the *danmei* pigs all riled up."

"I saw Jaguars when I flew in. But really, we are at peace with them, aren't we? Nobody made a mess while I was at Orofenn?" Te-ron sniffed. There was always the possibility that someone's blunder created a diplomatic incident, and tempers flew high, and there was another skirmish. Jaguar pride was such a precarious thing.

"Nah. If anything, I'd say they are more occupied with their own stuff these days, some of them have even moved... Sk! There they come!"

The *michee*, the seven eldest and most respectable of the Awraa, came fluttering, took their place in the middle of the assembly, and folded their wings. The only sign of their rank was the little golden ring in each of their ears, as any elaborate clothing—like the Jaguars preferred—would hamper their flight. But even without this outward symbol, Te-ron knew them all: Ras-ennet, first among the *michee*; Lor-end, who was the leading scientist; Sur-kaa the scoutmaster; as well as the others.

"Welcome to the convention, friends," Ras-ennet began. "I am sure you wonder why I have called upon you out of turn. Be assured that it is not a grave reason, although time is of the essence."

"Jaguars?" someone hanging on the higher bars offered.

"No, we are not expecting trouble with the Jaguars. I have heard some rumors going around, indeed; it was not my intent to foment these. The Jaguars are our trusted allies, I am tempted to say our worthy friends. Let's not spread baseless speculation as if it were facts."

"Nevertheless," Lor-end began, just to be hushed by Ras-ennet.

"No, no, don't speak as if we were challenged. It's still our decision, our plan, our... may I say *destiny*? We are the Awraa, the keepers of the treetops, the dwellers of the sky."

Te-ron found the *michee's* manner of speaking quite tedious, and judging from Ka-lin's bored face, the scout shared his sentiment. However, Ras-ennet's voice displayed a certain quiver, and the urgency with which the convention was called in belied the appeasing words. And didn't Lor-end show quite a bit of impatience in his ear movements?

He noticed that he had missed some of Ras-ennet's speech, and forced himself to pay attention, although what was not said seemed to be more important than what was proffered.

"... with hope and confidence into the future. Now, Lor-end, would you present the project?"

The scientist cleared his throat and pricked up his ears towards the ground. "Yes, yes. I will make it short, as some of our guests had a long flight"—some of the audience sighed audibly at that—"and get to the core of the matter. We have constructed a new type of ground vessel meant to cross the Vinja desert."

Vinja? Te-ron shook his wings a little. That was the northern border; a wasteland treeless and hostile to all Awraa. Crossing it seemed as impossible as climbing the freezing mountains, or flying over the boundless seas.

"The intent is to send out a scouting expedition to the lands beyond, to discover their possibilities and to make contact with whoever inhabits them. We are confident that the Vinja is not endless, and that such land exists; nevertheless, we are aware that this is a dangerous endeavor. So we are asking for volunteers among our most experienced scouts."

"Can we hear a bit more?" an Awraa on the lowest bars asked. "Like, those vessels, what are they? We're not going to fly?"

"If you are interested, please join us tomorrow for a tour." Lor-end gestured towards the lower *uts*. "Rest a bit; with sunrise we will show you everything, and share the details."

Little waves of commotion rippled through the audience when Lor-end finished. Ka-lin bent over to Te-ron. "Vinja, break a wing. I have heard the last expedition ended up all dead."

"There was an expedition? I thought those were only a few Awraa who got caught in an unlucky wind and starved in the desert."

"That's the story they keep telling. Ask Lor-end, he probably knows." Ka-lin clicked his claws, but it was clear that he hadn't any definitive information. Typical of him, always spreading rumors. But he was right in one thing: Lor-end probably knew. The question was, would he tell everyone, or would he try to keep the stories under wrap, afraid of scaring away volunteers?

In fact, some Awraa had already taken flight towards the trees, not bothering to visit the *uts*. The forty scouts and leaders dwindled to twenty-five within minutes, some silent and disaffected, some chattering away while they left. The support for this project wasn't so enthusiastic, after all.

And who could hold it against them? The Vinja; what an idea.

* * *

Despite being tired, Te-ron couldn't sleep. He took up a space in one of the highest *uts*, insects buzzing in the dark, but the sounds of the night didn't calm him. Was something amiss, or was his natural distrust playing tricks on him? Closing his eyes, his wings wrapped tightly around him, he decided to rest.

Sleep didn't come. Jaguars, the Vinja, a lost expedition? Lor-end should know.

Te-ron loosened his foot claws, dropping like a stone. He spread his wings only after passing three lower *uts*, filled with Awraa fast asleep. Downward still in an effortless glide, to the single *ut* that was home to the scientists, a peculiar construction that had walls and a floor and was altogether upside down.

He couldn't enter directly, so he landed on a platform before the *ut's* door and knocked.

It didn't take Lor-end long to answer the rap. The scientist didn't even seem surprised to see him.

"Te-ron, be welcome. Come in, I almost could tell you would drop by."

"You know me?" Te-ron entered the *ut*, which was filled with containers and vials and platforms with instruments and shelves with raw materials. There were no bars to rest, and being under a roof but unable to hang head down gave Te-ron a dizzy feeling. Naturally, the laboratories needed to be set up this way, considering the many things and fluids the scientists were working with, subject to gravity.

"Surely, I rarely forget a promising student. A pity you chose the scouts. But it will be a huge benefit if you join the expedition."

"The expedition, yes…"

"You were always a little impatient."

"I know. I should probably wait until tomorrow, but I'm not sure what to make of Ras-ennet's speech here. Is it true that the Jaguars have nothing to do with this? I saw a whole camp of them quite close."

Lor-end folded his ears. "The Jaguars, yes. Well, they are not the direct cause, at least. I wouldn't go so far to claim they have nothing to do with the expedition, but it's not as if they were forcing us."

"So?"

"It's their progress. Centuries back, they were a wild bunch, fairly primitive. And it happened indeed that they killed and ate Awraa. Can't blame them for being hungry, but that time is still deeply rooted in our lore. We were sophisticated and knowledgeable; they were savages. We had skills in plant handling and woodwork; they had sticks and stones. When we made a treaty with them, we were the proud tamers of the beasts. When we shared our knowledge and culture, we groomed the ferals. Ever since, we rule the treetops, they rule the ground. It is a reasonable arrangement, and they never killed an Awraa after that. There were a few conflicts and a few fights, because they are a proud people, but, you know, there is also respect."

"But they have caught up. And they are developing their own science. Their metalwork is remarkable; they have progressed from bronze to iron, and some of their art is splendid. They have boats now to sail the rivers, and no one would be surprised if they start venturing the seas, even. And they can settle the mountains, where no Awraa would prosper. I once asked them how they make their fur grow to keep the cold at bay, but they just laughed."

"It's growing denser by itself when it gets cold," Te-ron explained. "They don't do it deliberately."

"Oh. Yes, of course. You know them; you were our contact over at Orofenn. I suppose your fur didn't start growing? No, of course not. Fur on the wings would be an unfortunate thing."

"Orofenn is just at the foot of the mountain. The Jaguars live even farther up these days, mining for ore."

"See? That is what all of the *michee* notice. They don't need us any more. We have next to nothing to offer, to swap, to trade. There will come a day when they have surpassed us in everything, even in botany. We have become complacent and slow."

Te-ron wrinkled his snout. "So, you think the Jaguars are becoming a threat? Although they haven't violated the treaty in centuries? I doubt they would ever go back to killing Awraa; they're too sophisticated for that."

"They do eat *danmei* pigs. Some Awraa find that disconcerting."

"*Danmei* are animals."

"Fairly close to sentience, as some scientists claim. They may not have tools or fire yet, but with a little time… It's not the direct threat, though. It's the change they are bringing." Lor-end leaned heavily against the wall. "The change will engulf the jungle. The Jaguars will leave us behind—the *future* will leave us behind. We need to do something bold to catch up. Find new knowledge. Awraa can't cross the mountains, and it would be fairly difficult to voyage the ocean, so the lands beyond the Vinja are what we seek."

"The Jaguars will always have an advantage. Five fingers, where ours are mostly wings." Te-ron wriggled the two digits and the thumb that had not grown into supports for the wing membrane. "Dense fur where we have little. Strong bodies that can carry great weights. The ability to eat meat, which they can dry and carry around on longer journeys."

"Actually, we could digest meat," Lor-end interjected, falling into teacher mode. "Not the dried stuff, our teeth can't chew that, but fruit is still more a choice than a necessity. The sugars, of course, they help us fly. But our close cousins the bats—they have many varied diets among them, depending on the species. Ever tried to eat insects?"

"Not on purpose.—So, Ras-ennet suddenly wants to find a new land beyond the Vinja because he doesn't feel *superior* enough?"

Lor-end shook his wings. "That is a fairly unfriendly way to phrase it. He's not wrong, you know. A culture must grow and change to stay alive. We are well adapted to the environment, as are the Jaguars. But the Jaguars *change* the environment, while we still try to fit in. Soon, we will live in their world. Ras-ennet is not unreasonable, asking for our advance.—And we've been very careful in our planning. It's not like we'll send you on a suicide mission. You'll see."

Te-ron nodded. He could see the point, even if he didn't agree completely.

Only after returning to the sleeping *ut*, he noticed that he had forgotten to ask about the lost expedition.

* * *

The "tour" Lor-end had mentioned turned out to be exactly that, a long flight north towards the edge of the Vinja. Four more Awraa had left in the morning, so their remaining swarm consisted of twenty-three people: eighteen scouts (Te-ron and Ka-lin among them), three leaders, Lor-end himself, and Sur-kaa supervising the flight. Ras-ennet and the other *michee* did not follow; well enough, none of the swarm felt any great need for more pompous speeches.

In fact, no one talked much during the flight. It was difficult enough to keep up with Sur-kaa who maintained a demanding pace. She was the youngest of the *michee* and in good shape, but Lor-end surprised everyone by following with ease, despite his advanced age.

They traveled sometimes above, sometimes below the canopy, depending on the wind. Te-ron watched bats and birds fluttering around in the branches, hunting for beetles and bugs who feasted on overripe fruit. He remembered Lor-end's remark about eating meat or insects. It didn't seem very attractive. Jaguars knew a few insect recipes and even had an appetite for certain fat grubs, but this was a kind of feast in which Te-ron never partook. Really, what better to eat than fruit, refreshing, juicy and sweet?

The Awraa had to stop often for food. Flying long distance required frequent meals to replenish their energy. Twenty-three was a sizeable swarm; when they fell upon a tree, they picked almost all of the ripe fruit and left only the green ones. Certainly, an advantage for the Jaguars:

they could carry much of their food when traveling; Awraa had to take whatever could be harvested along the way. Flying with an additional load of food and water was difficult.

Te-ron shook his head. Food seemed to be on his mind all the time. Strange, it wasn't as if they were lacking in sources. The jungle provided for its inhabitants, other than the mountains or the steppe where pickings were slim and dependent on the season.

Te-ron plucked a ripe mango and sniffed it. Yes, very ripe. He didn't even bother biting into the peel, instead, he stuck out his tongue and drilled a hole into the fruit with the sharp raspy tip, then started to suck. Oh, mushy pulp. Perhaps even a bit overripe, with a hint of fermentation.

Quite a hint. When Te-ron took off again, he already felt a bit squiffy. Fortunately, queue flying didn't require too much concentration and focus, and his quick metabolism burned through the alcohol pretty fast.

Birds crossed overhead, their flight easy and effortless. Sometimes, Te-ron envied them for their specialization. Awraa weren't built for the long distance, but for quick changes in direction and agile flight in dense branches. They could glide, use the thermal lift, and ride the wind, but the birds were so much better at all of this. Naturally, they paid for it by having no fingers or thumbs at all, yet they were undisputed masters of their domain, the high skies.

Some species even migrated regularly to the cooler south and back, year after year, across the jungle and the steppes. Amazing feat, that. Te-ron wanted to talk to Ka-lin about migration, then noticed that he had lost the swarm in his reverie. The other Awraa were far ahead. Cursing overripe mangos, he hastened to catch up with them.

* * *

Three days to the Vinja, and his wings hurt a little when they arrived. All of the scouts had followed through, driven by curiosity, so they were still twenty-three. On the last kilometers, Sur-kaa had told them to use any food source that they could find, and indeed, the rim of the desert was bad land for fruit trees. The jungle thinned out, gave way to vast stretches of green, brown, and then gray grass. Bushes dominated the hilly terrain rather than trees, and even the animals were different. Huge hoppy antelopes and fat bluish beasts roamed the open landscape.

Their target consisted only of three *uts*, built between a trio of trees that formed a lone copse by itself. One of the trees was pretty much dead, only a few branches still desperately tried to push leaves. The *uts* were stacked. Close to the ground was a tooling *ut* that featured a floor and a retractable ramp to the ground, but no walls; higher up hung a laboratory *ut* equipped with outer platforms and an inner wall; the *ut* on top, slightly to the side and tightly anchored in the dead tree, provided sleeping and convention bars.

The thing that caught Te-ron's eye was not the small settlement, though. It was a group of four vehicles, down on the ground next to the tooling *ut*. Each resembled a simple pointy triangular frame, a wheel at each corner, with the front wheel embedded in a movable frame for steering. The center of the vessels was taken up by a mast with a single triangular sail—currently folded up—on a movable boom, and some permanently installed boxes.

On flying closer, Te-ron noticed that the foundational framework for the things was actually T-shaped, the center beam being the most massive. The back cross-beam carried the wheels; the outer framework which formed the longer sides of the triangle providing stability. Ropes connected the mast and the framework and apparently controlled the angle of the boom, as well as providing a means to haul up the sail and reef it again. The back of the vehicle showed a divided cube of bars which offered a resting place for the crew, but apart from that the vessels did not arrange for comfort or ease. They were constructed in a bare-bones, almost frugal way, and even the usual adornments of the wood were missing.

"The progress in research allowed us to design tires made of rubber filled with air," Lor-end explained later after a much-needed rest, demonstrating the features of the craft. "In addition, the wheels are mounted in a spring suspension that absorbs shocks and allows the crew to sail the vessel on uneven terrain. Nevertheless, you should not drive it across boulders or clefts; it's constructed for flat stretches of sand."

"Doesn't look like much sand around," one of the scouts remarked, who apparently had never been to the Vinja before.

Lor-end pointed farther north. "This location has been chosen as our base because it still provides food. The land around here is a nice grass plain, with not many obstacles to avoid. Farther north, you'll have all the sand you wish. Not all of the Vinja is suitable for the sand-sailers. Once you leave the area that we already scouted, you will need to find the best path yourself."

Another scout—heavyset for an Awraa, and with a mien of boredom—fluttered up to the top of the mast, where a lookout crossbar allowed resting. "Now why all the hurry? These things... sand-sailers... seem to be ready to go, so you've been working on them for quite a while already."

"Indeed." Lor-end and one of his local assistants took up a seat on the resting bars of the vehicle. "Here's the reason why we are on a schedule. The winds change with the season. At the moment, a strong current hails from the south, which seems ideal for crossing the Vinja in this direction. We will have a few weeks to train you on the sand-sailers, then conduct the expedition, before the winds change and blow in the opposite direction. There is no exact date, of course, but we gather that the reversal will happen while you are scouting the lands beyond, so you can catch the south current and return home easily. Once the rainy season is upon us, the winds will become erratic and unpredictable, and the journey will become a lot harder."

The assistant showed a notebook around with data about wind currents for several years. The scouts just nodded politely; this stuff was meant for scientists to figure out. Te-ron noticed that the reversal of the wind was not quite as predictable as Lor-end suggested; it happened somewhen over the period of three weeks. Well, maybe more predictable than the start of the rainy season, at least.

"You will learn all the details during the next days," Lor-end continued. "Sur-kaa will schedule the training for the sand-sailers."

"Two scouts and one scientist per vessel," Sur-kaa announced. "Four sand-sailers, so we need eight scouts. Everyone is going to train, though; we'll select the members of the expedition depending on how well you do. Questions?"

Wings went up, and the debate continued well into the night.

* * *

The sand-sailer howled across the grassland. This was actually exciting, Te-ron thought. Faster than flying, sometimes. That was not the recommended speed—for best operation, one Awraa was supposed to fly ahead and look out for obstacles—but it was thrilling. Close to the grass, the sand-sailer's frame sped with the wind, terrorizing the sleek antelopes and rousing the fat four-horned buffalos.

Te-ron knew the basics of sailing from meetings with Jaguars whose river-boats featured a similar sail arrangement, but he had never operated a boat himself, nor had any of the other scouts. Despite their inexperience, they made progress, each scout trying to surpass the others. The scientists were not so happy about all the recklessness and wild abandon the scouts showed in sailing, but it was still friendly competition: everybody was well aware that they would not be able to display the same kind of bravado during the actual expedition, when their lives would depend on sober minds and careful action.

The crew for this sailer currently consisted of Te-ron, Ka-lin, and a female scout named Jin-kee. Sleek wide wings, a gently sloped muzzle, and impressive ears: that was someone to seek out during mating season, definitely. But for the moment, she was a competitor for a space on the expedition, and Te-ron was determined to be part of this endeavor.

The three leaders had returned to their usual duties after two days, and five scouts had left as well, not so enamored with the prospect of crossing the desert. One had injured himself, that left twelve scouts for the eight spots on the sand-sailers. Good prospects but no guarantee. All of the remaining scouts were able-bodied, experienced, smart, and skillful. And this venture was unusual enough, enthralling enough to capture the minds of everyone. A new land, far from the familiar jungle, with new people to meet, and a sand-sailer to whip across the endless reaches. What red-blooded scout could resist?

After some hours of maneuvering, they reefed the sail and applied the brakes, and stopped for a simple lunch. Ka-lin quickly circled the area for predators and larger animals that might take exception to their presence, while Te-ron unpacked the glass jars with the conserved food.

Glass, a metal cover, and a rubber ring to seal it: simple enough, but a testament to the long treaty between Awraa and Jaguars. The glass and the rubber were Awraa inventions; the metal was all Jaguar. The Awraa still traded them for metals; if not for the mines the Jaguars dug back in the mountains, Awraa might never have learned about the benefits of these materials. Same for the waterskins; these were made from *danmei* pig hide. Only meat-eaters could have come up with that.

Te-ron turned an unmarked jar between his fingers. Cooperation had advanced both species, so was a pure Jaguar world really likely, as Ras-ennet feared? Was there nothing Awraa could add to their joint civilization, except for imagined riches in a hearsay land across the desert?

Jaguars had eaten Awraa, back then. Were those ancient events so deeply embedded in the Awraa subconscious that they still evoked fear? Te-ron had to acknowledge that tingly feeling in his stomach that was present whenever he was close to Jaguars; an instinctual if residual dread of predators. It might have helped their ancestors to survive, but these days it struck Te-ron as… impolite sentiment.

Ka-lin landed with a shrug, not finding any dangers around, and the three of them opened their food jars. The cooked stuff within was supposed to serve as their rations on the expedition as well—sugary, concentrated fruit prepared as a tasty jelly, so eating it for days on end was an experiment in itself.

"So," Ka-lin began, "you never told me what Lor-end said about the lost expedition."

Oh, right, that one. "I think I never got around to ask."

"Come on! We've been here for a week!" Ka-lin stuck out his tongue in annoyance.

"Sorry, it just didn't seem so important."

"Lost expedition?" Jin-kee asked. "There was an expedition to the Vinja already?"

"Rumors and stuff about some people." Ka-lin put his jar down to emphasize the tale with wing gestures. "All dead, though. Scattered by the wind and starved, died of thirst. Probably most of them were eaten by snakes."

Te-ron was sure Ka-lin had just made that up.

"That group of wanderers, about eighty years back?" Jin-kee waved the idea aside. "Not an expedition, and not scouts either."

Ka-lin leaned forward. "So, you know about that?"

"Not much to know. Yes, I talked about it with one of the scientists, He-sii. Some travelers were blown out into the Vinja by ill winds. Heh, probably the same winds we want to use to cross. No one actually learned how many they were, or what their original destination was. One of them was found at the edge of the desert, almost dead. He could only say 'We drank', over and over, before he died. Starved, they say."

"We drank?"

"Yeah, he probably wanted to indicate that there is a river beyond the Vinja. He-sii said the incident was investigated. This poor guy traveled with at least five others, maybe more, none of whom was ever seen again. We know about it only from the tales of Awraa who met them before the mishap. They may all have perished in the Vinja, either on the way to the other side, or on the way back. The victim said '*we* drank', so there was at least one other who reached the land beyond."

"And then died."

"Somewhere, yes. Or maybe that other Awraa survived and got back and just decided never to tell anybody." Jin-kee pursed her lips in jest.

"Doesn't sound likely," Te-ron remarked. "Though, that's not much to go by. Anything might have happened."

"He-sii said he had no notes on him, so the scientists are only speculating. In fact, his mutterings are the only indication that there even is land beyond the Vinja. Who knows; without that hapless guy we might still believe the desert goes on forever."

"'We drank' is not really a great expedition report."

Jin-kee shrugged. "The scientists extrapolate any kind of stuff. They think the guy used the wind reversal to get back—he was sort of lucky to get lost exactly at this time of the year. So, the land on the other side is even within flying distance, if you catch a gale or two."

"Flying distance?" Ka-lin muttered. "Now let's not forget about the *dying* part. It's far enough to die of hunger and thirst in the middle of the desert."

"Scaredy-bat," Jin-kee scolded. "We are scouts, we have sand-sailers, we have provisions. And we *chose* the best time of the year to make the trip."

Te-ron raised a wing. "What if the river they drank from is only temporary? Some *wadi* in the desert that only fills up at a special time of the year? So they got there, and then the wind reversed, and they tried to fly back, and there is not really another land but just that lonely brook among a pile of desert stones?"

"Is there really such a kind of river?" Ka-lin asked.

"Down at the mountains, there are clefts that are dry most of the year, but sometimes fill with water from the summer melt. Yes."

Jin-kee frowned, getting back to the point. "In that case, we'd just wait for the reversal and head back. It's just a first expedition, with many more to come, it's not as if the life of all Awraa depends on it. Land or no land, we will have conquered the desert!"

The remark, as casually and mirthfully as it was offered, sent a shiver down Te-ron's spine. The life of all Awraa? Ras-ennet's thinking, again. Did Ras-ennet know what scant information his idea was really based on? How much might go wrong?

No. Thinking about failure before the deed did not become a scout. One wing beat after another, the goal firmly in mind; that was the way to go.

That was the way to reach the faraway lands.

* * *

When they returned, it was Te-ron's turn to take the flying lead. The sand-sailer had to beat to windward and made only slow progress. Twice, higher patches of grass rustled in a suspicious way so all three of them took flight and waited until they were sure no predators were hiding there. Neither of the Awraa wanted to test the speed of the sand-sailer against hungry fangs.

Something was different at the scientists' settlement. Colorful blotches dotted the vicinity. Getting closer, Te-ron recognized tents, some already erected, some flat on the ground. Jaguars? Only they were using tents, unafraid of any danger that might lurk on the ground. But what were they doing here?

The clan pennants erected between the tents seemed familiar. Of course, these banners belonged to the Jaguars that had camped near the *ut-an* almost two weeks ago.

When the sand-sailer had arrived, Te-ron landed and observed several Jaguars milling about. Lor-end was talking to one of them, so Te-ron went over and tried to barge in.

"... quite impressive setup, I would say," the Jaguar was complimenting. "You may want to pack a smaller alternative sail, just in case the wind gets too strong. With that mast height, the sailer would probably topple."

The Jaguar, bipedal and wingless, was more than twice the height of Lor-end, so the scientist had to look up. It occurred to Te-ron that it might help the conversation if the Awraa sat on the floor of the tooling *ut* instead.

"Friendly winds and slow prey," Te-ron greeted the Jaguar. "I am quite surprised we have guests today."

Lor-end cleared his throat. "Te-ron, this is Ciaquex Hitzla, an engineer of the Fulnea clan. He originally helped with the sailing idea. Ciaquex, this is Te-ron, one of our most able scouts. He has had dealings with Jaguar tribes before, down at Orofenn."

The towering Jaguar nodded. "I believe we haven't met before. Sweet harvest and safe flight, scout Te-ron." Out here in the grassland, the orange and black pattern of his fur that disguised him in the shifting sunlight of the jungle stood out aggressively. He smelled of cat, of predator.

Te-ron fluttered up to the tooling *ut*. "I was not aware the sand-sailers were Jaguar work."

Ciaquex grinned toothily. "Oh, the sails have always been a joint venture of Jaguars and Awraa. The Awraa have a unique understanding of wind and flight, a sense of air currents, if you want. That is lacking in Jaguars. On the other paw, Jaguars are fairly comfortable on the water, while Awraa are not even good swimmers. Discovering the nature and possibilities of sails together was, if I may say so, obvious.—Naturally, the rivers are the only opportunity to use sails as a means of propulsion; the jungle just doesn't provide the even grounds and open areas that such a ground-sailer requires."

"Other than out here," Lor-end interjected.

"Yes, yes, when your scientists asked us about the concept, I was wondering how you would put it to practical use. We were curious and came to have a look at the finished vessels. From what I have seen, most impressive. Neat mechanics to support the wheels."

Te-ron was unsure what Ras-ennet would say about the involvement of the Jaguars. Did he even know? Did the *michee* agree to the Jaguars knowing about the expedition? It would be very impolite, to say the least, to send the big cats away, but Te-ron wasn't sure whether the venture was supposed to be a secret if it really gave the Awraa some advance over the Jaguars. Well, it was not his place to speculate about politics.

Ciaquex Hitzla strolled towards a sand-sailer and admiringly stroked its wooden frame. Lor-end followed on the ground, while Te-ron fluttered over and hung from the mast's lookout crossbar.

"I wonder whether a Jaguar could drive a sand-sailer," the cat mused. "Not this model, naturally, but if we enlarged it a bit, add a bench here, get rid of this framework... I'd really like to try. It's so much faster than a boat, or top running speed."

"It might be dangerous, too," warned Te-ron. "If something goes wrong, we can just spread our wings and let the wind carry us. A Jaguar might get injured when he needs to jump off."

Ciaquex nodded. "I see the issue. We'd start slow, then."

Lor-end gestured placatingly. "It will certainly be a worthy project. But I am afraid we are on a schedule, so we'd need to delay that idea a bit." He started a lecture on sails that might be meant to distract Ciaquex, or maybe not. Te-ron didn't want to get involved any longer and flew back to Ka-lin and Jin-kee.

* * *

Three days later, Te-ron's words proved almost prophetic when a sand-sailer crashed when one of its hind wheels got caught in a ditch. The wheel exploded, the frame broke, and the mast came crashing down. None of the crew was injured, but it proved to be a close call; evacuating a sand-sailer in an emergency was not as simple as jumping in the air.

After that, the scouts drove more carefully, and always had a crew member in the air to look for obstacles. Losing a sailer did not bother Lor-end much, though. He took it as an opportunity to study the wreckage—the behavior of a sand-sailer in case of catastrophic failure.

Ciaquex Hitzla suggested a different way of fastening the ropes that stabilized the mast. The engineer team also added one more box to the sailers' decks, holding a kit to repair wheels and a full replacement wheel, as well as some all-purpose ropes.

"It's getting too heavy," one of the scientists warned. "All that wood. A sailer needs to carry those provisions already, food and water, first aid kit, tests for common poisons and other basic stuff. The more we load, the less predictable it will behave on the way."

To compensate, the scouts started training on fully loaded sailers, which was indeed a bit of a difference. Slowly, they adapted, each day getting them closer to the scheduled departure, each day making them more aware that this was no longer just careless fun, but training for a dangerous journey to an unknown destination.

Nevertheless Te-ron was confident about the mission. The thing that really bothered him was something else.

On the day the sailer crashed, his first thought had been whether the Jaguars had done something... sabotaged the vehicle, perhaps. It was profoundly untrue, of course. The Jaguars had never been anything else but helpful, and indeed their strength and abilities were very welcome among the scientists. It was Te-ron's own attitude that fomented suspicion, however unwarranted. That tingle in his stomach. Ras-ennet's fear of the future. The instinct that kept Awraa wary of predators.

The hidden distrust that poisoned a potential friendship.

* * *

And then, like a dream suddenly bursting into wakefulness, the day of departure arrived. The wind was still steadily blowing from the south, and was supposed to continue for at least two more weeks. The scientists had finished their lists, and the crews were assigned.

Te-ron and Ka-lin were on the team, assigned to one sailer together with He-sii the scientist. Jin-kee had also made the roster and rode the second sailer with a stocky, well-muscled Awraa called Pen-dor and a reclusive, taciturn scientist by name of Yon-fia. For a while Te-ron thought that Sur-kaa the scoutmaster and Lor-end would actually accompany them on the third sailer, but then a different team was selected.

The disappointed rest of the scouts stayed behind, together with scientists already eager for the findings, and the small group of Jaguars who would doubtlessly pester Lor-end for building a cat-friendly sand-sailer. Well, this would be Lor-end's worry now.

The three sailers used the smaller sail to cross the grassland; the wind had actually gained force and showed no sign of relenting. The grass parted under the vehicles, then it got shorter, harder, and went all brown, then there was no more grass.

The Vinja stretched before them.

They were not the first Awraa to get here; scouts had checked out this part of the desert before them to find an optimal route. A day of sailing or so would take them out of this safe area, however, and lead them into the unknown.

Surprisingly, the desert was not as hot as they had expected. It was an arid waste, but the temperatures did not rise much above what the Awraa knew from the jungle. Nevertheless, it was a good feeling to anchor the feet on the sailer, spread the wings, and let the wind cool them down that also filled their sails. Flying ahead, which was now invaluable practice, was not difficult as the wind carried them steadily. In fact, when gales caught them and propelled them ahead, it was more difficult to fly back to the vehicles than to stay ahead. Sometimes the flying scouts just landed and waited for the sand-sailers to catch up.

At the end of the first day, they went through the routine of securing the vessels for the night. Reefing the sails, putting in the pegs to anchor the sand-sailer, and erecting a marker from stones was only half the work. They also had to bury a part of the provisions and a filled waterskin. Should any catastrophe happen—like the total loss of all three sailers— they could still fly back after the wind's reversal, from marker to marker, resting and feeding. The status of the provisions was also a measure of how long they could go on. Once the stock of food jars or waterskins dwindled, they would need to turn around, whether they had found the remote lands or not.

"Did we dig deep enough?" Jin-kee asked. "I don't want the waterskin to dry out."

"If we take too long, the water will spoil anyway," He-sii answered. "It's been boiled and cleaned and sealed, but if we need more than three weeks, it might become unpleasant to drink."

"One week out, we'll need to reconsider the trip altogether," Yon-fia interjected. "Our assumption is that we will find fresh water beyond the Vinja, where we can replenish the supply. If there is no sign of a *land beyond* within a week, we will need to decide what to do. Either we stop, wait for the reversal of the wind, and then turn back. Or we turn back immediately and beat against the wind." She looked at the sky. "Which may be difficult if these gales don't abate."

Te-ron wasn't sure why the scientists liked to debate eventualities that Lor-end had already laid out, repeatedly. The crews were familiar with all the contingencies of the journey; turning around without result was something they didn't look forward to. But they knew that the provisions were limited, and there were risks. The distance between the rest points they created were meant for a regular return with the north wind. As long as the wind came from the south—moreso with its current strength—it would take them far more than a day to travel from one to the next, maybe two or three days even. And if calamity befell the sand-sailers, flying back against the wind would be impossible, so waiting out for the reversal was imperative.

The farther they got, the higher the risks piled up. But they were scouts; they knew the odds.

* * *

The stars were beautiful out here, stretching from one horizon to the other, with no treetop to get in the way. Te-ron had seen such a sight before, but only when flying up and above the jungle at nighttime. In the Vinja, he could relax and peacefully hang from the mast lookout, watching the slow dance of the stars beyond his feet. It was almost as if gravity lost its meaning and reversed like the wind, and if he just let go of the bar, he would endlessly fall footward into the sky and be lost among the stars forever.

No animals, no Jaguars, not even a rustling of plants; no humming of beetles or tweeting of birds. No weird thoughts about instinct and enmity and spoiled friendships. Nothing but the soft, soft rustle of sand moving under the wind.

And someone of the third crew snoring loudly. Te-ron folded his ears inward and tried to ignore it. Sleep, sleep until the next day would carry them on to the unknown shore.

* * *

The Vinja was not pure sand, even if there were stretches of rolling dunes where the sand-sailers made good speed. Most of it was baked, scorched earth covered in stones. The unknown region began with rough terrain and didn't get much better until noon.

That was when they lost the second sailer.

What seemed to be firm ground suddenly gave way and revealed a hidden hole, the edges crumbling and disintegrating. The sand-sailer's front wheel caught the edge, and the impact damaged the steering mechanism. The sail ripped forward, the boom almost killing one of the crew in the process, and the boxes tore out of their mounting.

No one was seriously injured, having practiced the emergency exit many times, although the scientist of the vehicle suffered a small but painful hole in the wing membrane from some splinter.

"At this rate," Ka-lin grumbled, "we'll not even reach the point of no return. We'll run out of sailers long before."

They discussed the options. With a crash so early on the journey, it made no sense to transfer the load from the destroyed sailer to the others and split the crew among the remaining vessels, as Te-ron mused at first. That would overburden the vehicles and make the next accident more likely... unless they broke off the expedition altogether and returned home. Not even the crew of the damaged sand-sailer wanted that.

The three unlucky Awraa could dig in and wait for the expected reversal of the wind. Although some food jars were broken, despite the careful packaging, and a few of the waterskins were ripped, the remaining provisions should last them long enough to wait out the time, and then use the northern wind to fly back to the base, abandoning the vessel.

Returning right now without a vehicle was too dangerous; the wind forcefully blew in the wrong direction and made southward flights almost impossible. By sand-sailer, they were only half a day away from the last waypoint, but on wing, the journey might take several days. They would only be able to fly during the rare calms—going on foot was not an option, as the short Awraa legs didn't support extended marches. The night wind seemed more benevolent than the day gales, but any flying with even a few waterskins and food jars would be painful.

The final option offered itself when the scientists thoroughly investigated the damage.

"It is repairable," Yon-fia claimed. She outlined the way to fix the steering with rope and splints and some rubber glue. "Will take some hours to set, and it won't be as good as before. But if you don't go too fast, it should hold. I won't recommend continuing, though."

"So, we're turning around and beat to windward," a crew member stated, "until we're back home. We won't need to hit the waypoint, I guess, so navigation is not an issue."

Te-ron nodded. "You keep the provisions so if the steering breaks again, or the sailer gets damaged by something else, you can still wait out the reversal. Or use the calms if you're close enough to the steppe to fly."

"I wish we could see the land on the other side." The scout sighed. "Perhaps the next time."

"The next time," Te-ron nodded.

The crew went to work on the repairs. The other two sailers didn't wait for their results, though; they continued their journey as a pair. Six

Awraa now, and six days until they would need to make a decision of their own.

Unless Ka-lin was right, and they would run out of sailers. The next damaged vehicle would mean the end of the expedition; it would force them to turn around and slink home in the last sand-sailer to get everyone to safety. And the undiscovered land would stay undiscovered for a while longer.

* * *

"We should change crews every now and then," He-sii offered. "Give everybody a chance to work with everybody else."

They had sailed for another day, slower now and more careful, avoiding suspicious ground. By now, even a high-flying Awraa could see only the desert around, seemingly endless in all directions. Just the compass pointed back to the jungle and promised home.

Te-ron accepted He-sii's idea, although he had to admit that perhaps he just wanted to spend time with Jin-kee. Throughout the next days, which passed ominously without notable events, they switched crews and vessels, so Te-ron sometimes sailed with Jin-kee and sometimes with Pen-dor and then with Ka-lin again. He-sii and Yon-fia expanded their knowledge of sailing, and everyone did their stretch of scouting with the wind.

The two surviving sand-sailers behaved slightly differently, but when the last day came, everybody knew every maneuver and every trick imaginable. They talked, and they laughed, and they tried not to think about the arid wastes around them that would carelessly devour them if they weren't careful.

And then the week was over, and the Vinja didn't end.

They anchored the sailers and ate some jam, a dark mood spreading. There was no river or brook or even foul waterhole around. *We drank*, no, not here, and nowhere near. Perhaps they had missed the spot. Perhaps there was no land on the other side of the Vinja. Perhaps the desert was really endless.

The sun was setting quickly. Temperatures, strangely, had fallen during their journey, day after day, until the daytime was cool and the night was cold enough for them to huddle together for warmth. The air still had no hint of moisture in it. The desert was still a desert, with little plant life and sparse animal activity, as if the steady wind was sucking every drop of water out of the ground.

"The climate is changing," He-sii stated. "We are definitely close to *something*."

"*Something* that may be a week from here, or more, and which may turn out to be another desert made of ice," Yon-fia complained. "We just don't know. I say we stick to the plan. Either we stay here now until the wind reverses, or we try sailing back tomorrow."

Te-ron looked at the horizon, which showed no hint of change. "That was a long journey for us, and we have nothing to show for it."

"We gained a lot of experience," He-sii insisted. "The next expedition will use larger sailers, more provisions, and a bigger crew. Then they can set out for a two-week journey. And if that doesn't suffice, a three-week journey the year after."

"And then four, and then…" Ka-lin grumbled. "What if the desert really is endless, and we could sail on for a lifetime without reaching some *other side*?"

"The Vinja is certainly not endless," He-sii corrected. "The world is shaped like a ball, so some day you would have gone all the way around."

"Do we know for sure?"

"We fly. Have you ever watched a bug crawling on a mango?"

Pen-dor interrupted her. "We must have gone farther than those lost wanderers ever went, so now we're out of hints. That dead guy must have meant *We drank the rest of our water and then returned with the wind*, or something like that. There is no water here that he could have spoken of. There is *nothing* here. I say we start our journey back tomorrow."

Ka-lin wrinkled his muzzle. "I hate failure."

"Well," He-sii started. "If these wanderers had been caught in a high gale, and didn't land immediately…"

"Which they should have done…" Ka-lin pointed out.

"They might have been confused, and when instinct kicks in, an Awraa goes *up*," Yon-fia asserted. "Because of the ground predators."

He-sii sighed. "*If* they didn't land, a storm might have carried them far out into the desert.—Now they sit there, knowing they can't go against the wind, knowing they can't walk home. What would they do? Flying with the wind might be the best option."

Jin-kee lifted her head, incredulous. "Going across the desert on purpose? With not a single scout among them? And no experience with this terrain? That's crazy!"

"Any hope is better than dying," Pen-dor declared.

"At the current wind speed, flying would be twice as fast as the sand-sailers. We were holding back a lot because of bad ground. Remember when you flew out yesterday, and we needed two hours to pick you up again?" He-sii was visibly impatient to finish her thought. "So, in four days you could make it here, maybe even a bit farther. Assuming they still had water, they would not have starved yet."

"Jaguars don't starve that easily," Te-ron noted. He didn't even know why he had to bring Jaguars into play again.

"Jaguars don't fly."

"Just a bit farther, then?"

"I still don't believe…"

"Carrying how much water?"

"… debatable speed…"

"… crazy I say, and that's not even counting…"

Te-ron listened to the crew arguing back and forth, and finally he came to a decision. "Listen." He fluttered up to the sailer's lookout. "Tomorrow first thing, I will fly up and get a look at what's ahead. Really high up, I mean. Bird high."

"The wind's gonna carry you off."

"You will follow my position and pick me up. We won't lose much time. If I can see something else but desert, we'll assume that the wanderers got there, and we have a look."

"That's not what the plan said," Yon-fia disputed.

"I know. It's not much of a risk. If I see nothing, we'll turn around." Slink home with the wings in front of your face. Admit defeat. Leave the discovery to others.

Ka-lin nodded. "I agree. If Lor-end isn't happy, we'll at least know we have done everything and then some."

The rest of the crew approved, overriding Yon-fia's concern. They went to sleep with a sense of determination, if not achievement.

At early dawn Te-ron ate some jam to replenish his energy, then took off while the others prepared the sand-sailers. He tried to rise straight, but the wind got him immediately and hurled him northward. Te-ron attempted an upward spiral but soon the resting place lay far behind.

Up, and farther up. The wind got colder, the sky shone blue and cloudless above. Higher than the trees back home, higher than the common travel height. There were no birds around to match with, but this had to be their domain.

The horizon shimmered where the merciless blue met the beige, gray and light brown of the desert. It seemed to dance. Was that the dust and the sand carried on the wind? Te-ron couldn't see as far as he had hoped although the air was crisp and clear at this altitude. Awraa eyes, not bird eyes.

But wasn't that a dark green line far, far in the north? A hint of... grass? Trees? Or perhaps the ocean? Hills covered in plants. Maybe.

Without getting closer, he couldn't tell for sure. But something was waiting for them over there, something that was not desert and stone and baked ground.

He began the descent, gliding and falling and catching himself again, with the wind, against the wind—no, it was just an illusion, his wings were just not strong enough to beat the mighty current—and finally dropped to the ground. The sand sailers approached quite a while later, almost missing him.

"It's there," he panted, breathless not from the effort but from excitement. "The land beyond is over there."

North.

* * *

It took them all day to get there, although they sometimes got careless and sailed at higher speed than their experience told them. Pen-dor was the one who admonished them and held them back, or else they might just have left the sand-sailers in the desert, flying the rest of the way on their own wings and on the wind, so helpful and friendly.

"There" was a forest. And what a forest it was, with trees piercing the skies, grey and brown and dark green, so much more forbidding and austere than the colorful jungle. The tallest trees might have grown beyond a hundred meters in height, and their conical shape spread out twenty meters wide.

The jungle did not touch the desert. The steppe separated them and provided a gradual transition between trees and grass and sand, many kilometers wide. Not so this forest; its trees formed a legion standing tall against the Vinja. Where the desert began, hardy dark grass and saplings pierced the ground; smaller trees were behind them, and then already the first wooden giants towered. This growth zone was barely a few hundred meters wide: the forest sending out conquering troops that took root and anchored the dominion of the woods over the Vinja. And the Vinja, as incredible as it seemed, appeared to retreat.

"That is not what I expected," Te-ron murmured, facing the alien forest.

"How's that even possible?" Ka-lin demanded to know. Both He-sii and Yon-fia started to answer but then just shook their heads.

They reefed the sails and anchored the sailers on desert ground, hesitant to destroy the valiant saplings. Then they flew across the growth zone, into the shadow of the trees.

From beneath the canopy, the trees looked even larger. The sunlight filtering through the long, hard leaves was scarce, barely enough to feed the undergrowth and more of the defiant grass. Here and there, a tree had fallen, leaving a glade where other plants eagerly spread. Large insects populated these clearings, lazily buzzing by. They left a strange smell in their wake.

And there was even a brook, a tiny rivulet of water, fresh and clean, on its way to drain into the Vinja, perhaps feeding the saplings. The crew landed, inspecting the miraculous stream.

Despite better knowledge—they should have boiled the water first, as every scientist had told them—Te-ron bent down, his muzzle touching the water. He took a sip, then another. Sweet, sweet water, so much tastier and better than the stale stuff from the skins. Ka-lin and Jin-kee did the same, barely hesitating longer.

Water beyond the Vinja.

"We drank," Te-ron coughed, cold fluid running down his throat. "We drank."

The Land Beyond

They spent the night out at the sand-sailers, not trusting the new environment altogether. The crew was exhilarated, but they had allowed the agitation to carry them away, making mistakes against their good judgment. Sailing too fast despite losing two sailers just a week ago— going farther than originally planned—entering the forest without leaving a guard at the sand-sailers—drinking water without boiling it— that was quite enough. Nothing had happened, but discipline should be maintained.

Yet they couldn't help but talk and giggle and laugh aloud.

In the morning, they started their regular investigations. Lor-end hadn't given them many specific tasks, as the nature of the land beyond was unknown, but the scientists wanted to carry back a wealth of observations, samples, and notes.

"This is wood," Te-ron noted when He-sii carried a piece of root towards the sand-sailers. "Do we need to take it?"

"*Very* interesting structure and color," the scientist apologized.

"Don't overload the thing." Of course, there was room enough, since the provisions were dwindling. Te-ron would have liked to stack them up with fresh fruit, perhaps some juicy berries, but they hadn't found any fruit yet.

Or anything that an Awraa would like to eat.

There was water enough. Pen-dor was boiling it, replacing the stale fluids from the waterskins. But the forest didn't yield nourishment easily.

Not an issue yet; their provisions were calculated for enough days to allow for an easy journey back. If the wind reversed, the travel would take them eight days, with six waypoints to hit where they would find buried jars. They hadn't left a hoard at their last resting place, but that didn't matter. The only question was *when* the wind would turn into a northern current—no one doubted that it would, as the reversal had happened for decades in the past, ever since the Awraa started taking notes, and probably well earlier.

One week, no problem. They wouldn't even need to bother finding local food.

Two weeks, they would have to ration the provisions a little.

Three weeks, and the Awraa would definitely need to replenish their stock with something the forest offered. Fruit would be most welcome. Fruit that didn't exist here.

Annoyingly, they didn't know the wind's schedule. Either they started rationing right away, or they spent more time searching for edibles, or they prepared for a longer journey, leaving before the reversal, beating to windward on the travel back.

Who would have thought that the land beyond was so stubborn in yielding its treasures?

Te-ron fluttered to the other sailer where Yon-fia performed some tests on dark scaly cones.

"This is what the trees bear instead of fruit," she explained. "I had hoped we could cook it. But it's not just hard and brittle, it's also poisonous." A sharp reek emanated from her experiment, reminding Te-ron of the insect smell. "Inedible, most likely deadly for us."

"The beetles too? The big blue ones?"

"I haven't tested them, but if they feed on this stuff, it may very well be. I hope you don't really want to eat them."

Ever tried to eat insects? Te-ron looked over at the forest line. "Are the trees toxic all over? We have already touched them. Would it rub off?"

"Not the bark, at least. But if you smell something like this here—it might be best not to touch it, or if you can't avoid that, don't lick your fingers afterwards."

Great, so much for food. They couldn't eat the grass, or the leaves of the bushes, or… well, there was not much to find in the forest that even looked edible.

"Tomorrow, we start rationing," Te-ron decided. "And we won't stay for more than a week. That way, we'll have some extra jars for the journey back, just in case the reversal comes late."

Yon-fia nodded, already distracted again by her findings.

It was a good plan, Te-ron told himself. A reasonably good plan.

* * *

The next day, Te-ron and Jin-kee ventured farther into the forest, looking for different kinds of plants. While they found some new trees and bushes, none of them bore fruit, however, and some even had that smell that hinted at poison.

"Maybe it's the wrong season," Jin-kee tried.

"Maybe this land is just not meant for Awraa," Te-ron returned. What would Ras-ennet say? The expedition was a success and a failure at the same time. There was a land beyond the Vinja, but with no proper food Awraa couldn't survive here. A permanent settlement was unthinkable. Perhaps the forest held some interesting plants to harvest and carry back, at least. Something, anything of scientific value.

If Ras-ennet desired to barter the bounties of the new land for something the Jaguars produced, he might be disappointed.

There was a noise in the air, a snuffle and wheeze and a rustle of vegetation. Silently, the Awraa took off and positioned themselves some branches higher up, where they could observe the cause of the sound.

Below them, a procession of creatures broke out of some dense underbrush and occupied the space around the tree trunk. They were walking upright; fat brown beings with coarse, sparse, black fur and short trunks that ended in two protrusions. Some of them fell to their knees and started to sniff the ground.

"*Danmei* pigs?" Jin-kee was as surprised as Te-ron.

"Not… quite?" The pigs back in the jungle walked on all fours, and they did not carry tools and weapons. The ones below held small axes, shovels, and spears. *Danmei* at home could not speak; these here apparently had a language, conversing in soft grunts and coughs.

One of the pigs pointed its trunk at the ground. Did it track the Awraa who had been sitting on the ground only a short time ago? No. Another *danmei* took its shovel and started to dig, finally pulling an ugly rock-shaped thing out of the earth. The pigs danced ecstatically, then cut the find into pieces. Each one of them got a small sliver, which they devoured with obvious pleasure. The largest part went into a bag.

Te-ron wondered if that plant was edible for Awraa. It didn't look appetizing but was better than nothing.

"Shall we contact them?" Jin-kee whispered.

Te-ron shook his head. Not yet, they needed to observe first and find out whether the *danmei* were potential allies or...

Well, they certainly weren't predators. As advanced as they seemed, they were still brethren of the animals in the jungle, and back home *danmei* did not eat meat. They also weren't any larger, which meant they were a bit smaller than an Awraa on average.

The *danmei* group continued on their way, soon to disappear in the forest again. The Awraa stared after them, questions in their minds.

* * *

"I need to see them myself," He-sii demanded. "Perhaps they originally come from the jungle, and migrated here, long in the past."

"Through the Vinja?"

"*Danmei* are a hardy lot. They can survive without food or water much longer than us."

"They walk on two legs."

"Very long in the past, then. Remember, Jaguars were wild animals once, too, and ate Awraa. Perhaps these *danmei* tried to escape Jaguars, got lost in the desert, and ended up here."

"And didn't starve," Pen-dor remarked, wistfully considering a jam jar.

"They can probably eat the grass, and much of the other vegetation. They might even have become immune to the poison over time."

Yon-fia nodded. "Their knowledge of the forest may be invaluable for us. We should contact them as fast as possible. Try to learn their language, and everything. Do you know where they went?"

"We can track them," Te-ron confirmed. "I'm not sure we should impose us upon them so early, though."

"Time is of the essence," the scientist dissented. "Provisions are limited, and once the reversal happens, we need to head back. We should at least establish a first contact, even if we can't learn the language in that time."

"Signals may suffice," He-sii added. "Maybe even body language. Don't stand too straight, keep the head down, show the fingers, fold ears down. Don't move too fast, make no threatening gestures."

"I worked with Jaguars," Te-ron reminded her, somewhat offended.

"I'm sure your being nonthreatening helps a lot with Jaguars?" He-sii remarked mildly.

Pen-dor chuckled. "Well, we are no Jaguars ourselves, so we probably won't make them run in panic."

"Don't assume," Yon-fia admonished.

Te-ron nodded. "Good, so we will make contact. I'll go first; He-sii and Ka-lin hide and observe. The others stay here as backup."

It was not too difficult to find the tracks of the pigs again; they didn't bother hiding them. Not far from the tree where the *danmei* had dug out the root, or whatever it was, the footprints joined a regular trail, and the trail opened into a larger path. It was early afternoon when the three Awraa arrived at a settlement, flying only slightly lower as the lowest branches required.

The village consisted of huts constructed from branches and hardened mud. Grids of dried red leaves covered the buildings. It was artlessly done, but efficient. Te-ron saw no hides from animals around. Either the *danmei* were the only beasts apart from insects, or they just didn't hunt. There were ropes, though, and nets, knotted and woven from a fiber that the Awraa hadn't discovered yet.

A dozen *danmei* were milling about, working and talking and eating. A bored guard patrolled around the settlement, clumsily holding a spear, but there was no wall around the huts, no visible defenses. No Jaguars around this forest, probably.

"Go farther up," Te-ron commanded. "They don't need to see you yet."

Ka-lin and He-sii didn't object and obtained position several meters above. Te-ron breathed deeply, and glided to the ground. He stood motionless for a minute, then approached the guard, stopping some meters away.

He didn't even need to say something. As soon as the guard spotted him, his tiny eyes widened, he fumbled with the spear and pointed it at Te-ron. His body tensed, and he wheezed a few times before screeching something that sounded like "I-jaa! Hi-feee!"

Te-ron lifted his wings and showed his fingers. "Hello? We are coming in peace." Naturally, the *danmei* didn't recognize the words, but he should understand the calm voice.

Other pigs looked into their direction and panicked, running off or disappearing into the huts. The guard raised his spear aggressively. "He-maiaiai! Siiii wa!"

This was not going well. Te-ron made a step back, then another. "We are looking for food," he attempted.

The guard hurled his spear at him. Te-ron evaded—the guard was not very good at spear-throwing—and took flight. This encounter turned out to be a disaster. Behind him, Ka-lin and He-sii left their perch, hopefully unseen, and followed through the denser canopy.

* * *

"We should bring them gifts," Jin-kee suggested. "A jar of jam. It's sweet fruit, I am sure the *danmei* would like it."

"They didn't even listen." Te-ron shook his head. "They saw me and just started to scream."

"I suppose they are the only animals in the forest," He-sii stated. "Except for beetles. There aren't even any birds around."

Pen-dor grunted unhappily. "The beetles eat the poisoned cones; the birds eat the beetles; the birds drop dead. Let's eat and forget about those *danmei*."

"No, no." He-sii was remorseless. "Jin-kee is right, a gift would be a great opener. Tomorrow we'll try again with some jam. Now that we have shown ourselves, we must proceed. Alleviate that instinctual fear of strangers; become friends."

Te-ron felt an ear itch coming up. "I am not so sure I want to get another spear thrown at me."

"They have poor aim," He-sii claimed. "That guard would not even have hit you if you had stayed still. He just wasn't good with a weapon. I doubt they get much practice."

"He still *had* a weapon. Spear or not, they want to defend themselves against something, and I bet that something is not large beetles."

"Well, what would you do?"

The question left Te-ron at a loss. The obvious answer was: take the sand-sailers and return home, even if the wind was still coming up from the south. Leave this first contact stuff to the next expedition, which could properly prepare and come back next year with better gifts than a jar of jam.

But that would leave the *danmei* in a state of disarray and insecurity, and they might prepare for hostilities later on. They had no reason to trust this sudden stranger.

The crew just couldn't let the tender fruit of the first contact fester and rot. He-sii told the truth, they needed to continue. Perhaps it would have been better not to face the pigs, but it was too late now for second thoughts.

"We'll do the following," Te-ron began. "I will return to the *danmei* settlement with the gift, Ka-lin and He-sii come with me. Jin-kee and Yon-fia will scout the vicinity of the village. I'd like to know whether there are others close by. Pen-dor stays with the sand-sailers just in case."

"I'm not complaining," Pen-dor murmured.

"We'll see whether a gift will make them any less suspicious. We can only hope."

* * *

The morning sun filtered lazily through the strange leaves and gave the green a golden rim. Dust flecks danced in the light. A plethora of insects marched up and down a tree.

Te-ron carried two jars in his feet, fluttering cautiously towards the village. Ka-lin and He-sii followed at different heights. The air was cool under their wings; it smelled of moisture and moss.

The commotion in the village had abated; the *danmei* had returned to their usual business. A different guard was on duty—Te-ron saw brown hair and a scar on the snout that the previous guard didn't have. Good, maybe this pig was not as easily scared.

The Awraa landed on the far side of a tree, picked up the jars with his fingers, and walked towards the front of the village. "Hello," he called out even before the guard had taken notice of him. It might be more polite to announce himself instead of sneaking up to the *danmei*.

The guard snapped to attention, pointing the spear. "I-jaa! Hi-feee!" His voice was not quite as shrill as yesterday's guard's, but just as agitated. Te-ron bowed down, putting the jars on the ground. Should he open them, for the *danmei* to smell? Before he could come to a decision, the spear whistled past his right ear.

"Ri-ri-ri-ri!" the guard shrieked. Beyond, pigs came running out of the huts—not the peasants the Awraa had already seen, but some kind of warriors, all armed, all adorned with a scarf around their necks, dyed red and yellow.

So much for the gift. The newcomers had spears as well, so it was time to leave. Te-ron spread his wings and jumped into the air.

From above, Ka-lin and He-sii dropped, stretched, then hurled themselves forward only a meter aboveground. *Stop*, Te-ron wanted to yell, but it was much too late to break off the move. The two Awraa headed towards the guard, passed him, continued a short distance to the village, then veered off—Ka-lin to the right, He-sii to the left. Although He-sii was a scientist and not a scout, the maneuver worked perfectly. The onrushing warriors scattered, but only for a moment.

The Awraa tried to join flight and get upward, out of range of the *danmei's* weapons. They had passed the lowest branches, when a hail of spears hissed in their direction, thrown with more power and precision than Te-ron had expected from the pigs. Most clattered against the branches; some fell short.

One spear pierced He-sii's wing.

The Awraa screamed, lost control, and dropped groundward, her muscle injured. Te-ron wanted to loop back down and catch her, but gravity was faster to embrace her. With a muffled thump she hit the forest floor. The warriors that hadn't thrown their spears raised their weapons and stabbed.

Horrified, Te-ron fluttered upward, almost losing his balance in shock. They were bringing gifts! They wanted friendship! He circled among higher branches, trying to get a glimpse of what the pigs were doing.

They dragged He-sii away, her body motionless and limp. Some of the *danmei* warriors shook their spears at him. Others collected the weapons that had fallen back to the ground.

Te-ron's heart beat rapidly while he followed Ka-lin out of the area. He didn't know what to say. The *danmei* weren't just refusing the Awraa's advances, they were deadly hostile. Those warriors, none of them had been there the day before. The pigs must have had assembled them overnight from other places.

Trembling, they perched in the high canopy, letting their bodies hang down. Te-ron discovered that he had suffered a small cut in the ear, not serious, but it started to hurt. He-sii was dead though; this loss hurt much more.

After a while, Jin-kee and Yon-fia returned from their reconnaissance flight, immediately worried at the sight of the shaken scouts.

"He-sii was killed," Ka-lin explained. "They were waiting for us."

"What!" Jin-kee shook her wings. "An ambush? How…"

"Warriors, hidden in the huts. We tried to deflect their attention from Te-ron, but when we turned to flee, they hit her."

Te-ron was content to let Ka-lin speak. This was a disastrous development. Whatever had evoked the pigs' hostility? The Awraa had barely arrived at this land. They hadn't done anything.

Was it something the lost wanderers had caused, eighty years back? That equaled ten generations of *danmei*, if their lifespan was still similar to their jungle ancestors. And those wanderers couldn't have lingered long enough in the land beyond to create such an unspeakable evil that would still echo after all those years, could they? They had been without provisions by then, all things considered, and the land didn't offer food to Awraa, so they must have turned back immediately after obtaining some water. If not for the lucky reversal, they would have died.

They *had* died.

Lucky reversal or not, they had probably starved or died from exhaustion. It was a miracle that this one survivor—if that was the right word—had even arrived at the steppe. Crossing the Vinja twice, even with the wind, should have killed him much earlier.

Except...

"They ate them," he murmured.

"Who?" Yon-fia looked straight at him.

"Those lost ones. When they came here, they ate the *danmei*. They didn't have anything else. So they slaughtered the pigs. That's why they are so hostile now."

Yon-fia whistled disapprovingly. "*Danmei* meat, at least back home, is quite indigestible. Tough and leathery, like the beasts themselves. We don't eat meat, and even if we would, we would not eat *that* meat."

"Lor-end said we can digest meat." Te-ron remembered the dialog clearly. "Just our teeth..."

"That's pure theory," the scientist scolded. "We have lived on fruit since the beginning of the world. We are not Jaguars to devour other animals. The old fool Lor-end has a lot of weird ideas when the sun is hot and the fruit ferments nicely."

Te-ron sighed. He couldn't verify that, and he couldn't ask the pigs either. "Whatever. Let's go back, We will sail home right now. Awraa lives are too high a price to pay for a poisoned land."

Sadness made his bones weary, but they set out to return to the sand-sailers. Not a single night more, even if it meant hard work on the journey back.

He-sii's demise had ripped a hole into their team. But it wasn't their fault; they had tried to be friendly. And even with the shadow of death hanging over their heads, they needed to complete the mission, for their own sake and for all the others back home who must never journey to the land beyond again. Let the pigs have it. Whatever Ras-ennet might think about it, this forest should be taboo forever.

There was smoke on the horizon, darkening the sky.

* * *

They never found out how the *danmei* had managed to surprise Pendor. The Awraa should have seen them coming across the growth zone of the forest. Did they hide their spears? Did they feign friendship? Did they turn to attack all of a sudden so the unsuspecting Awraa wasn't even able to fly up? Or did he turn to flee, and the pigs hit him with thrown spears?

The blaze had consumed everything when the Awraa arrived at the camp; firewood stacked on the sand-sailers had made sure of that. Pendor's charred remains were unrecognizeable. The food jars were broken, melted even. Their gear was either stolen or destroyed, it was impossible to say. Nothing useful was left.

Te-ron felt as if he couldn't breathe. All of their expedition, lost, except for the little things they were carrying on their ankle belts.

Their means to get home, gone.

Perhaps the tracks surrounding the former camp would have meant something to the scouts, but they didn't stay around—they turned to flee and took up a perch in the high branches of a tree where no *danmei* could reach them. The full extent of the disaster just started to dawn on them.

* * *

"What did we do to them!" Yon-fia wailed. She had been fine at first, coping with the loss of two crewmates well enough, but by the time night fell, she was drenched in tears. All of her scientist demeanor was gone.

Jin-kee was more practical. "We won't last without the pigs' knowledge. Nothing we found was edible. Either it's poisoned, or indigestible."

"There may not be anything." Te-ron stared at the stars that now seemed ominous and cold. "This is not the jungle where fruit waits everywhere."

"We should kill them," Ka-lin spit out. "Slaughter them like they slaughtered us, and feed on them."

"That won't do us much good," Yon-fia murmured, barely containing herself. "Perhaps the organs. I don't know much about that. The only way to make their meat digestible may be to cook it for some time. Maybe. And they are already hunting us. We don't know how many of them are around, how many villages. If we build fires, we'll give ourselves away."

Te-ron couldn't believe the things the other Awraa were considering. Killing, like Jaguars? "It's a misunderstanding. There must be a way to clear this up. Leave them messages, maybe. Pictures that they can understand."

"Too late for that," Ka-lin brooded.

"We must try! They must see that we are not hostile!"

"Waterskins."

"We don't have any left. What about them?"

"If they have searched the sand-sailers before burning them, they have found the waterskins."

"So?"

"Made from *danmei* hide."

Right. It was animal *danmei* back from the jungle, but the pigs here might still recognize hide of their own kin. Damning proof that the strangers that had come to the forest killed *danmei*. Te-ron groaned.

The wind was blowing from the south, strong and steady, carrying fine dust.

* * *

For two days they managed to evade the *danmei*. Sleeping in turns by day, foraging by night—Awraa eyes didn't see far but had good night vision—the four survivors had avoided any conflict with the pigs below. On occasion, they had spotted patrols of these red-scarfed warriors. None of the *danmei* had been seen climbing a tree so far, which was comforting.

Foraging was an optimistic way of expressing it, though. They hadn't found anything. With much luck, Yon-fia had managed to dig out one of the stone-like roots that the *danmei* liked to sniff for. But it stank and was hard and tough. Ka-lin dared to eat a piece and was rewarded with an aching stomach.

Even getting water became an endeavor. Three of them needed to stand guard while the fourth was drinking. With no waterskin, they couldn't gather a reserve; they weren't even able to boil it but had to drink from the source.

On the third day, Te-ron seriously considered crossing the Vinja against the wind. But any practical attempt to best the current ended in exhaustion. They had spent so much time creating the waypoints on the journey here, but even the closest one was now out of reach.

"We could continue northward," Yon-fia suggested. "Cross the forest. Try to find some other land." But they didn't know the extent of the forest, and there was no guarantee that this other land was less hostile. The forest might end in mountains, or border the sea.

At night, Te-ron dreamt of circling the globe. The world was a sphere, so if they just went on and on, they would get back where they came from. Approaching the jungle from the south, carried by an endless southern gale.

And he was drifting on the storm, and the storm was soothing and comfortable; he felt like a leaf on the wind. Across the forest and the sea, across the mountains and fields of yellow grass, across lands that he could barely describe full of strange beings that took no notice of him. Then he died flying, and—wings still outstretched—he continued his travels, the flesh melting from his bones, his skin a dried sheet keeping a skeleton together. From unseeing eyes he stared at the ground below, a mummified Awraa caught in the neverending current.

Huge pigs were roaming the ground, scratching at roots and shrubs, chewing on bark. Scratching, scratching…

He opened his eyes.

There were *danmei* in the tree. Their skin disguised them against the bark somewhat, and they wore wooden climbing gear. Warriors, most likely, although they didn't wear the red scarf. Te-ron emitted a piercing shriek.

The other Awraa woke immediately from their own dreams. Without thinking, they just dropped from their perch, unfolding their wings only after their bodies had gathered speed already.

Noticing that their quarry escaped, the *danmei* nestled their spears from the slings on their back and threw them at the Awraa. None hit its target, until a *danmei* just jumped and sailed through the air like a fat wingless bird. He hadn't thrown his spear but held it with both hands, ramming it in one brutal movement through Yon-fia's body mid-flight. The scientist was too surprised to act; she barely was able to turn and attempt to change course when the pig collided with her.

They fell. At a height of fifty meters at least, the *danmei* could not hope to survive, but he had attacked anyway. With all spears thrown and the Awraa out of reach for the remaining four or five *danmei* in the tree, Te-ron just fluttered on the spot, his eyes trapped by the falling bodies until they hit the ground.

There was another dead *danmei* close by; apparently he had fallen earlier off the tree while trying to reach the Awraa. Te-ron didn't remember hearing a scream through his dreams—this warrior had just dropped, apparently, without making a sound, dying on his mission of murder.

How much hate must these pigs feel to perform such a deed?

* * *

There were proper rites for when an Awraa died. They had not performed them for He-sii, they had not performed them for Pen-dor, and they were not able to perform them for Yon-fia either. The three scouts just dashed through the forest canopy, following the edge of the desert, until they believed that they were out of reach of the *danmei* warriors, and then even farther until they were too tired to care.

Half of their crew was dead; all of their scientists. They had no gear left and no way to return home.

"The wind must reverse," Ka-lin demanded, "before they kill us all." He did not mention killing *danmei* in retaliation again; these warriors were more than a match for them. Even if they had weapons, which they didn't. Even if they were strong enough, which they weren't.

But the wind did not reverse, it just blew with no change in direction at all, hour after hour. Dimly Te-ron remembered the weather charts and the degree of uncertainty.

Their hunger grew unbearable over the next three days. Awraa didn't have much reserve, as carrying fat around was not convenient for flying. Other than with Jaguars, who could get plump at times, although they didn't like to be reminded of that. Te-ron's stomach hurt, and he felt weak and emaciated. Soon, he would not have the strength to fly.

Were they meant to die in the land beyond? Awraa did not put much belief into concepts of fate and destiny, as some Jaguars did, but right now, it seemed as if every step they had made led towards death.

They swallowed some insects which did not smell of poison, but they were small and fast and difficult to catch. Neither did they satiate their hunger. It was not a meal, it was desperation.

Ever tried to eat insects?—Not on purpose.

Now, Te-ron wished he had one of the fat grubs at hand that the Jaguars liked. He would eat it raw. He would bite into it and let its fluids run down his chin. He would savor it from head to tail, in all its disgusting greasiness.

What is happening to me?

Jin-kee seemed the weakest of them by now. She looked at the sky as if frantic wishing could just summon the reversal.

"We're dead," she finally said.

"We cannot be dead. We must at least bring the message home." Te-ron wasn't quite ready to give up. He had made notes and tucked them safely away in his ankle belt. But their options were nonexistent. Even continuing the journey further north was no longer imaginable; they didn't have the energy left. He pulled at his downy body fur. Strands of hair came undone and floated down. His gaze followed them, half expecting to spot *danmei* climbing up the tree. But there were none, only the silence of the shadowy depth.

"I need water," Ka-lin complained.

Jin-kee nodded. "I'm not thirsty, but it makes one forget the hunger."

They dropped off the tree and glided towards a brook that they had used twice before without being spotted. It was dusk already, when the *danmei* normally didn't range the forest. The warriors didn't seem to be active around here either. But they kept their guarding routine nevertheless, Jin-kee and Te-ron on the lookout while Ka-lin bent down and drank.

The undergrowth was denser than Te-ron liked. Ideal for an ambush. Perhaps they should not use a watering hole more than once. Not that it mattered anymore; they didn't have that much time left.

Looking down, Te-ron noticed a long branch with a splintered tip. Not quite a spear but an adequate weapon. Then again, it was mostly useless for him; his hands were part of the wings, he couldn't properly hold a spear and thrust, as *danmei* or Jaguars could. Worse; in flight he could only clumsily hold a spear in his feet as his wings needed to move, and even that was limited as his wing membrane was attached to his legs.

With all their specialization towards flight, the Awraa had lost a number of abilities that might have been useful in so many other situations. Perhaps the future really belonged to the Jaguars. Te-ron picked up the branch and straightened his body, and then he stared right into the face of a *danmei* who had obliviously advanced through the undergrowth.

The pig squealed, its eyes widening. Apparently it was not a warrior, and meeting the Awraa filled it with utter terror. Nevertheless, Te-ron lifted the branch and thrust at the *danmei* instinctively, without thinking. Ka-lin jumped up from the brook; Jin-kee whirled around.

Good luck or bad, the splintered tip caught the pig's neck and penetrated its hide. Blood poured over the wood. Te-ron lost his grip when the *danmei* turned to flee. The tip broke off, stuck in the injured pig's wound, while the rest clattered to the ground. Apparently the wood was rotten already and made quite a bad spear.

The Awraa lifted off, trying to flee as well. But the pig didn't notice that its adversaries did not follow. The beating of black wings behind it was enough to chase it along. Then it stumbled on the uneven ground, staggered, lost control over his body, and fell.

It did not get up again.

The Awraa saw that it struggled and wanted to rise, but the unlucky fall had driven the splintered tip even deeper into its body, and something was mortally broken.

"I didn't mean to," Te-ron gasped.

They landed again and assembled around the *danmei* who was still trembling and twitching, so much blood coming from the wound. For a second, Te-ron thought of helping the pig, but they didn't have the equipment. And they didn't have the equipment because the *danmei* had burned it. And they had killed half of their crew.

"Why bother?" Te-ron answered the question that no one had asked. "Let it die." It was the wrong thing to say, the wrong thing to think even, but bitterness and hunger burned within.

And there was something about this pig that triggered an instinct in him, buried deeply before, a knowledge and a craving that he had never been aware of. Blood, so gross and red and disgusting. Blood, so foul and nauseating and loathsome. Blood, so...

... *delicious.*

He knelt down, bent over the quivering, dying pig, and touched the wound with his tongue. It tasted metallic and a bit salty, and the texture was unpleasant at first, but there was the hunger that told him it was okay, it was not poisoned, it was nourishment. Te-ron sucked, hesitatingly, then eagerly.

Beside him, Jin-kee and Ka-lin gave in to the instinct and Te-ron's example, and together they feasted.

... *We drank....* .

And they knew why this was the last thing the lost wanderer had said, the last thing important enough to convey before he perished. Be it as a confession or a warning, that final report he had never been able to finish.

We drank their blood.

* * *

"I really didn't mean to," Te-ron repeated after they had fled the scene, leaving the pig behind who had long since breathed its last.

And it was true; this branch that was not even a proper weapon had just been lying there, waiting for someone to pick it up. Destiny? Had it not been there, would Te-ron have attacked the *danmei* with his bare hands? That instinct, would it have changed him into a predator lest he starved?

None of them could answer that. They were only scouts; their scientists all dead. They might muse where the instinct came from: some ancient time when Awraa did not just eat fruit?

"We must be careful," Ka-lin nodded, ignoring Te-ron's words. "They will hunt us even more fervently now. They'll set up ambushes and traps. We will need to change our hunting grounds often."

Hunting grounds? That sounded like something a Jaguar would say, and it was slightly unsettling that Ka-lin used the phrase so effortlessly.

"We don't have to kill them, you know. We could take only so much blood that they survive."

Ka-lin frowned. "We would need to hunt more of them, then, to feed us."

"It's still the better way. We—the Awraa—started it all. We must not allow the situation to become even worse."

The hunger, the desperation, the instinct. The lost wanderers must have made the same experience, drinking of the *danmei's* blood, and whether they had killed or managed to avoid it, this had started the feud with the pigs. Over generations, they had kept the memory alive and trained warriors against the Awraa, should they ever return.

If only they had listened. It was an unnecessary conflict, with lives lost to no cause. Would they voluntarily have given blood (only some… only a little…) to save the lives of their guests? Too late now; this was far beyond distrust, and Te-ron could not imagine how to repair this relationship.

* * *

The wind blew from the south. Dusk wiped the sunlight from the forest floor, dipping the bottom world in tones of blue and shady uncertainty.

They hunted.

The village out here had not been touched before, and the peasants were only vaguely aware of the threat. No traps, and the single guard was not too attentive. *Danmei* went about their own business. One of them left the collective, wandered down a path, looking for a herb or a treat.

Jin-kee whistled.

Te-ron and Ka-lin dove in, following the pig soundlessly, hidden by the branches.

The *danmei* stopped not too far away from the village and began to scratch bark from a tree.

The Awraa dropped down, grabbing the pig by the arms and throwing it to the ground. Te-ron got its right side, Ka-lin the left. Jin-kee swooped down, pinning the pig's body with her added weight, and bit its neck. Opening a vein with her raspy tongue, she started to drink hastily. The *danmei* squealed and struggled. It was fairly strong, and by itself a good deal heavier than an Awraa, but it had no chance against three of them.

Only a few seconds, and other *danmei* would come running. Jin-kee hurried to finish her meal. When she pulled her muzzle away from the pig's neck, the Awraa took off immediately. No need to kill. The *danmei* stayed behind, terrified and bleeding. Others of her species would tend to her.

Villagers saw the Awraa disappearing in the canopy, black silhouettes among the shadows.

* * *

I am the Jaguar.

Te-ron stared across the forest, a sea of trees that hid the life below. The parallels were unavoidable. Once, Jaguars had hunted and eaten Awraa. The memories of that time had become instinct; the instinct manifesting as leeriness towards the big cats. This tingle in his stomach, it was real, even if it might be no longer relevant. This worry about the future that Ras-ennet displayed, it grew from a past when force dominated the rapport among the people.

In generations, the Jaguars hadn't been able to undo this damage. A song of violence whose echo never had abated.

And now, even knowing all of this, Awraa had become the hunters, instilling fear and terror in the *danmei*. Of course, they had done so in mortal peril and desperation—twice. But the harm was done, and done again, and perhaps it would have been better if the Vinja just had swallowed all of them instead of letting them pass to the land beyond. That poisoned land, as poisoned as their relationship to the pigs now was.

What did the *danmei* see when they watched an Awraa passing? A shadow in the sky, a robber in the branches, a hideous monster that wanted to suck their blood. And wasn't it true?

All that desecration, all that shame.

And they couldn't stop, except maybe in one way, a way that Te-ron wasn't willing to go. *Come, you warriors with the red scarves. You killed us before.*

But no. He had a message to convey, for the sake of the future. More enlightened generations might be able to work it all out, start anew, bring hope.

Who would wash away the blood and bury the dead? Te-ron didn't know. Those yet unborn had tasks piled up before them. Sins of the elders.

* * *

The wind would reverse soon, carrying them home. They would be able to follow the string of waypoints, crossing the Vinja to find home.

The wind would reverse soon.

The wind would reverse soon.

The wind would reverse soon.

The wind would reverse soon.

The entire population of the idyllic planet Heffe VIII is evacuated just before its sun goes nova. Jeaunia, then a child, and her family end up on the human artificial satellite of Crossroads Station.

The refugees from Heffe are promised a new idyllic planet—a New Heffe—as soon as one is found.

A generation later, when Jeaunia is an adult, the government announces that a New Heffe has finally been found. But is it really a paradise? After so long on Crossroads Station, many of the refugees now have roots there and are wary about being uprooted again. Will Jeaunia choose to stay or go?

(This story, with permission, is a sequel to "Rekindle the Sun" by Mary E. Lowd, in the Australian anthology Belong: Interstellar Immigration Stories *edited by Russell B. Farr; available from Ticonderoga Publications, which can be ordered from Amazon.com.au)*

The Promise of New Heffe

by Kary M. Jomb

The evacuation of Heffe VIII occurred when Jeaunia was only a pup. Her memories of waiting in the long lines on the hot spaceport tarmac were dim. She did remember playing games with her cousins on the crowded flight to Crossroads Station afterward, and she thought she could remember the view of the swollen Heffen sun through the spaceship's rear windows. She couldn't be sure, though. The bloody smear of red giant sunlight in her memories could have been a fabrication. She had been very young.

Jeaunia's entire body felt light when she saw the news flashing across the vid screens above the embassy offices—*Expansionist Government Grants Deed for Type 1 Planet to the Confederacy of Heffen Refugees!* Her paw pads rested firmly on the cool floor of Crossroads Station's refugee district, but she couldn't feel them anymore. Her people had lived in borrowed, rented corners of human space stations for Jeaunia's entire adult life. Finally, they would have a world of their own. A new world. With a young, yellow sun.

Jeaunia padded the rest of her way to work in a daze. She wrapped her arms tight around herself, as if she could hold on tight to the feeling inside: her people would have a planet again. Forests. Savannahs. Real homes.

The glass-paneled door to the daycare where Jeaunia worked required a key-badge to open. It kept the pups inside from getting out, and it kept unauthorized adults from getting in. Jeaunia looked through the glass of the door. The wriggly Heffen pups ran wild on the other side, and her co-worker Aga looked back at her. Aga waved and started speaking to Jeaunia before the door even finished sliding shut behind her.

"So…" Aga said. "Will you move there?" Her flop-tipped ears kept twitching on the top of her head, catching the sounds of pups rough-housing and playing throughout the room. It was hard to have a coherent conversation while working, but it made the workers crazy when they didn't even try.

"Well… yeah," Jeaunia said. She grabbed a smock to throw over her clothes and fur. It wouldn't entirely stop the pups from getting food and paint in the long fur of her white ruff and orange mane, but it would limit the damage.

Aga always had an easier time with the pups that way—her fur was short. She was ethnically Golan instead of Petriezski, meaning her muzzle was flatter and her fur much shorter than Jeaunia's. Apparently, back before the exodus of Heffe VIII, Golan had been underprivileged minorities. That hadn't remained true among the refugees on Crossroads Station. Losing their planet had been a great equalizer.

"Really?" Aga said, wrinkling her already flat nose. "You'll be… like a pioneer." A pup crawled on Aga's lap and grabbed one of her ears. "Living in the wilderness."

Jeaunia barked a laugh. "It won't be that bad," she said. "The government's been planning this for years. Since practically before we moved away from Heffe. I'm sure, they'll have the infrastructure in place in no time."

Aga nodded solemnly, considering that. Well, as solemnly as she could with the pup on her lap pulling her ears, mimicking her nod, and whining, "*I want to paint, I want to paint*" at her. Aga stood up and walked the pup over to an easel. "I've been following the news reports all day," she said. "Well, whenever I can."

Aga might have been following the reports all day, but Jeaunia had been listening to her family plan and scheme about their future lives on a hypothetical New Heffe for most of her life. Several of her littermates would probably join the building teams that would be the first to set out. She'd have to say goodbye to them soon.

"I still don't see what the big deal is," Aga said. "Trees? Land?" She shrugged. They'd had this argument before. Many times. Jeaunia had always kind of thought that if Aga hadn't known she was planning to move away to New Heffe some day, the Golan woman would have asked her out. As it was, there was no future for them together, so instead Aga just flirtingly teased her. "If you want trees, there's always the arboretum."

"Speaking of which…" Jeaunia tilted her head toward the corner of the nursery closest to the arboretum, wordlessly asking if they should take the pups there.

"Oh, right. But, no, we'll just go to the playground today. The arboretum's too hard on a day this busy." Aga looked around the room, tallying the pups up. "We're still four short. We'll go when they get here."

Jeaunia nodded, absently gathering up a few stray robo-toys the pups had left whirring away on the floor. She was standing in a small, enclosed room on a giant, rotating space station, surrounded by the vast emptiness of dark, black space. In her heart, however, she remembered a forest, green with trees and shrubs, ripe with juicy berries ready for the picking, and echoing with the happy shrieks of her littermates and cousins playing chase among the towering tree trunks.

How could she explain that? Aga had been a city pup before the exodus. Gleaming metal walls that partitioned off the limited domesticated patches of wilderness, keeping all the trees trapped inside tiny bubbles of arboretum—that was normal to her. Maybe Aga didn't belong on New Heffe. But Jeaunia's heart had been reaching ineffectually toward it—not knowing the exact shape or look of what it reached for, except that it would stand in for the world she'd lost—since she'd first set paw on Crossroads Station. What was the possibility of one romantic relationship compared to a whole homeworld?

"Yeah," Jeaunia said. "I'm definitely going." She placed a paw lightly on Aga's shoulder, twitching her claws just enough to catch her friends' attention. "Will you visit?"

Aga looked uncertain. Of course, her expression might have had more to do with trying to fend off a pup wielding a paintbrush full of chameleo-paint. "Interstellar flights are expensive…" she said. And relationships stretched across solar systems untenable.

Before Aga could say anything more, a harried Heffen mother showed up at the glass door, four pups clinging to her. One held each paw, another was clinging to her knees, and the final one had hold of her bushy tail. Jeaunia helped the woman divest herself of her litter. She was a nanny herself, so she'd be spending the day watching a different child. A privileged child in the human quarter. A single human child watched by a single Heffen nanny, as opposed to the entire roomful of bouncing Heffen pups, crowded together under the watchful but overworked eyes of Jeaunia and Aga.

As soon as the mother was gone, Aga handed around wristlets. The youngest pups needed help snapping them on, but the older litters were used to the routine. Within minutes, Jeaunia and Aga were out the sliding door and walking down the hallways of Crossroads Station with a whirlwind of pups skittering around them. The wristlets exerted a gentle electro-magnetic force toward the master-wristlets Jeaunia and Aga wore, keeping the pups from straying far, but the entire walk was still an exercise in controlled chaos.

At the playground, Jeaunia adjusted the settings on her wristlet, expanding the field so the pups had the full run of the colorful jungle gyms and artificial gravity pockets. She sat down beside Aga on a bench at the perimeter of the wide, bubble-ceilinged room, and suddenly her pendant computer began to buzz. She flipped open the faux-locket case and looked at the messages streaming across the glowing screen, all of them from members of her big, messy family.

"What's wrong?" Aga asked.

Jeaunia's eyes must have betrayed her concern. "I'm not sure," she said, glancing rapidly between the locket screen and the gaggle of pups she was responsible for watching. The pups were more important—several of them looked like they would be whimpering for help with a particularly erratic grav-pocket momentarily—but the messages definitely had her worried.

Jeaunia shut the locket case and silenced the still-buzzing computer. "Some of my cousins are angry," she said. "Something about houses on New Heffe? I don't have time to read it now…"

As she spoke, both she and Aga saw one of the littlest pups get stuck in a gravity whirl. Aga ran to help him. Soon, Jeaunia found herself sucked into helping the pups in their play as well. The afternoon passed quickly and slowly at once. There was no time for anything but pups' concerns: who was playing the bouncy mount first; who pushed whom into the grav-pocket; who wanted to go home; and who missed their mums and dads.

Jeaunia was exhausted, as always, by the time she tightened the electro-magnetic field flowing from her wristlet. She watched the pups follow their wrists, reluctantly at first but more willingly as the pull grew stronger, toward her and Aga. She noticed something odd: there was a human, sitting on a bench at the far side of the park. A male with his arms crossed and his body leaned back. He looked harmless, but it was strange to see a human in the Heffen section of Crossroads Station, at least, one who wasn't buying food at one of the Golan booths. Spicy Golan confections had proved quite popular among the dominant species on Crossroads Station and was one of the main sources of Heffen income there.

After the playground, the pups were tired. Jeaunia and Aga put the littlest ones down for a nap, and the older ones read interactive stories on their own until snack time. Then they all played singing games together until, litter by litter, their parents came to pick them up.

All the while, Jeaunia worried over the messages in her locket. The pendant buzzed until she had to turn it off. When the final litter of pups were gone, she reopened the pendant computer. Messages streamed across the screen, all loading at once, all jumbled and out of order, too many and too fast to make sense.

"Your cousins are still angry?" Aga asked.

"I'd better get to my mom's quarters," Jeaunia said. "Besker is threatening never to speak to... someone?... again. I think there's some sort of family meeting happening. Or maybe it already happened..."

Jeaunia looked helplessly at the mess of a nursery, robo-toys strewn everywhere, carpet covered in crumbs.

"Go on," Aga said. "I'll clean up. But you better make it up to me tomorrow."

Jeaunia swished her tail, dipped her ears, and said, "Thanks!" Then she was out the doors, rushing through the alleyways of merchant stands in the main ring of Crossroads Station toward the inner ring filled with individual living quarters. From the messages, she wasn't completely sure whether she should head to her mother's quarters or her aunt's... They were at different ends of the Heffen section, twenty minutes apart by tramavator. She decided to start with her mother's quarters. Those were close enough to walk to. If no one was there, she could still catch a tramavator car to Aunt Kally's.

Outside the door to her mother's quarters, Jeaunia heard muffled yelling. A male voice—probably her cousin Besker—and her mother's voice barked at each other. Reluctantly, Jeaunia reached her paw to the door and opened it. The yelling stopped. She peeked in.

Besker's long black fur was rumpled and wild. His eyes glared. He stood over Jeaunia's mother who sat in a chair, looking determinedly at a holo-painting of the old family estate hanging on the wall—blue-leafed trees surrounded a red-stone building. She was studiously avoiding Besker's glare.

"You're ruining all of our lives," Besker barked.

Jeaunia's mother hunched her shoulders a little more. Her ears were already flat. She still wouldn't look at him, and she didn't say anything.

Finally, Besker huffed and turned away from his aunt. He looked Jeaunia up and down before speaking to her. His tone was eerily different when he did, much softer. "We're having a big celebration in Ma's quarters. You're welcome to join us." He looked back at Jeaunia's mother, and his tone turned cold again: "You're not."

Besker stomped out of the quarters. The rumpled black fur of his mane and tail made him look like a storm cloud. A moment after the front door slammed behind Besker, another door opened. Jeaunia's littermate Bala peeked her muzzle out of their mother's bedroom and said, "He's gone?" She looked around to be sure and then came out. Her fur was a pale gold, and her mane much shorter than Besker's. "Thank heaven. He's such a brute. I won't miss him at all."

Bala continued talking about how much she'd always disliked Besker. Their mother continued staring at the holo-painting on the wall. The blue leaves in the painting shimmered, moving gently as if in a wind. Mother's shoulders began shaking, and Jeaunia realized that she was silently sobbing, tears matting the fur under her eyes.

Jeaunia's head was spinning. "What is going on?"

"It's my money," their mother said, still looking at the painting. Her gaze moved over the scene of trees and paths around the central red-stone building. She was actually looking at the painting now instead of merely staring at it. It seemed to give her strength. She turned to look at her daughters, half of her litter. "When you were newborn pups, my parents divided their estate. They gave the land and the home I'd grown up in to my sister. It broke my heart for them to give it away—I loved it so much. But I was alone with a litter to raise. I couldn't care for a place like that."

When Jeaunia and her littermates were pups, they'd lived in an apartment in the city. They'd visited their cousins on the family estate, but they hadn't lived there. Jeaunia remembered their apartment, but her heart had been at their cousins' home. She understood how her mother felt.

Her mother continued, "But I needed the money. They gave her the land; they gave me and Peff the equivalent money. Peff spent hers on buying another piece of land. I kept ours in the bank."

Jeaunia realized that she knew where this was going. "Wait, are you saying that you still have that money? Money equivalent to the value of the entire property that the family estate was on?" All kinds of emotions screamed inside Jeaunia's chest. But one question rang out above the others: "Why have we been so poor if you have that much money?!"

Her mother looked her steadily in the eye. Her ears stood tall. "It's Heffen money, Nia. It's no good on Crossroads Station."

"But it'll be worth a whole lot on New Heffe, I bet," Bala said. Her muzzle split into a grin, and her ears flicked.

"Yes," their mother said. She didn't look happy, just determined.

"That's why Besker's mad?" Jeaunia asked, still figuring it all out. "Does he... I mean..." She couldn't figure it out. "Why would that make him mad?"

Mother shrugged.

Bala said, "He wants the money."

That incited their mother to speak. "No, he wants his old life on Heffe VIII back. He doesn't see why anything should change."

Jeaunia could understand that. Even though it had been years ago, she still wanted that life back too. She'd been looking forward to reconstructing it on New Heffe. She wasn't sure why extra money in the family should be a problem. She wasn't sure why they weren't all celebrating at Aunt Kally's right now.

"But everything has changed," Mother continued. "And it's not my responsibility to coddle my sisters' grown-up pups. If Besker wants a large estate in a prime location on New Heffe, he can work for it. Just like I worked to care for you two and your brothers when I was younger. Now, I'm getting the reward." Mother's head tilted up, pointing her muzzle into the air. She looked proud. More than proud—haughty.

Jeaunia could see how Besker would find such an attitude hard to take. Her mother was always irritating when she got this way. "What do you mean, 'large estate in a prime location'?" Jeaunia asked.

Bala's brushy tail began swishing wildly behind her, and their mother got up. She went over to the computer console and called up a rotating hologram of New Heffe—blue oceans and gold continents, frosted with white swirls of cloud—in place of the painting of the old family estate on Heffe VIII. It was the same image Jeaunia had seen on every holo-screen today.

Mother zoomed the image in, and one of the gold continents grew and expanded until it took over the entire scene. As the golden continent grew closer, blue snakes of river appeared. Greener and ruddier patches appeared. The gold took on the mottled texture of forests seen from above. Angular gray shapes appeared amidst the trees. Finally, the image was magnified enough to see that the angular gray shapes were streets and buildings. Whole networks of cities.

"Is this from a photograph?" Jeaunia asked. "They can't have built these cities already."

"This is an artists' rendition," Mother said. "But it's from blueprints that have been under development for years." She sounded really excited. She held out a paw and pointed a single dull claw at a corner of the hologram. "That's my estate."

Jeaunia peered at the angular splotch of gray surrounded by blotchy gold. It was near a spider's web of gray intersections. But not too near. It looked like it was a comfortable distance from a very big city.

It didn't look anything like the memory of space and air beneath the branches of the trees on Old Heffe that Jeaunia carried inside her heart. But, then, a zoomed-out artists' rendition of her old home might not look much like *home* to Jeaunia either. She tried to feel excited. She mostly felt confused and conflicted. "You've already picked where to live? Isn't that what everyone else is doing at Aunt Kally's right now?"

Mother shrugged again, nose still held high.

"Aren't we all going to live near each other?" Jeaunia asked.

"I can't help what choices others make," Mother said. She turned the hologram off. The screen went dark. No rendition of New Heffe; no painting of Heffe VIII.

Jeaunia stared at the dark screen, trying not to feel the same blank darkness inside. This wasn't going how she'd expected. Or how she'd planned.

"Mom's giving me an advance on my inheritance," Bala said. "So, Mekal and I are going to buy a place in the city near her estate. That way we can take our pups out to visit all the time. Like we used to visit Aunt Kally's when we were pups."

"I'd give you an advance as well, Nia," Mother said, tilting her head to the side, looking at her daughter closely. "I'm giving advances to both of your brothers and their families. Or, since you're still alone, you could live with me, help me care for my estate. I'd pay you."

The holo-screen was still dark, but Jeaunia pointed to where the spider's web of city lines had been. "Would I need an advance to afford to live in that city?"

"The capital?" Mother asked. "Probably."

Now it all made sense. Jeaunia didn't feel dark inside anymore. Just cold. "What about Aunt Kally and our cousins? Where will they live?"

"Wherever they want," Mother said. Then she revised her statement, "Wherever they can afford. They're welcome to visit." Suddenly, she looked small and sad. She looked away from Jeaunia. "Somehow, I don't think they'll want to."

The coldness in Jeaunia's chest clenched and tightened. She felt angry with her mother but also angry at her aunt and cousins. They should all be discussing this together. They should all be celebrating! Jeaunia clenched her paw into a fist and slammed it into the wall beside the dark, empty holo-screen.

Bala's muzzle gaped open. She stared at Jeaunia, stunned. "What's wrong with you? You just found out that you're rich, and we have a new world to live on. My pups don't have to grow up on this station. They'll get to run free in Mother's estate. You can even live on her estate. We're all better off than we were this morning."

"Not all of us," Jeaunia muttered, turning away. She stomped to the door, claws clicking angrily against the floor. "I'm going to Aunt Kally's," she shouted without turning back to look at them. She flattened her ears, refusing to listen to anything her mother or sister said as she stormed through the door.

Except Jeaunia didn't go to Aunt Kally's. She walked to the tramavator, even waited for a tram car to come. But she didn't take it. She watched the tram car fill with other Heffens and a few avian and reptilian aliens, but she didn't get on. She watched the doors slide shut, and the tram car pulled away.

Jeaunia walked the corridors of the station, seeing the shadow of her orange-furred body reflected dully in the metal walls. Her blurry reflection followed her as she wandered aimlessly, unwilling to go back to her mother and sister; yet unable to go be with her aunt and cousins instead.

She knew that if she went to be with her cousins, she'd get swept away in their plans. They were surely voting and negotiating and arguing over where to buy homesteads on New Heffe. Except it wouldn't be near the homesteads of her own mother and litter. She didn't want to choose which part of her family to be near. She liked it here—everyone was close. Why did that have to change?

But then she imagined trees and open air instead of metal corridors, closing her in. To hell with them all! Jeaunia wished that the swollen red giant of a sun that had scorched Aunt Kally's land had burned her mother's money as well.

She hadn't been rich this morning; she didn't want to be rich now. She wanted to be surrounded by her family. But she didn't want to hear Besker say that Mother should split the money between them all, that Mother was being selfish, that Mother was ruining the family. And she knew he'd say those things. Aunt Kally would agree, and her other cousins too.

They were the ones being selfish. It was Mother's money. Except why wouldn't Mother just give it to them? Money was nothing next to family.

Except… Why should she have to?

Did they all value money more than each other?

Jeaunia's wandering paws brought her back to the playground where she and Aga had brought the nursery pups earlier. She sat on the same bench where her locket computer had buzzed incessantly at her all afternoon, and she stared at the empty play equipment—brightly colored climbing structures and shimmers in the air, giving the tell-tale sign of grav-fluctuations.

The empty playground made her think of Old Heffe. The planet was still there, baked and broiled by a swollen sun. No one on it.

After a while, Jeaunia noticed that the human man was still sitting on the far side of the playground, staring at the empty equipment much as she had been. When he noticed her staring at him, he smiled, a weak turn of his primate lips. He looked sad and tired, like she felt. Jeaunia smiled back, and the human man gestured at the space on the bench beside him, inviting her to come over and sit beside him.

Jeaunia's ears flicked back, uncertain, but then the human man shrugged in such an unguarded, innocuous way that she decided she could use the company. Her tail swished behind her as she crossed the playground to sit beside him. When she sat with a comfortable amount of empty space between them, her tail curled around her side primly.

"What do you think of the images of New Heffe?" the human man asked.

Jeaunia narrowed her eyes at the human, trying to figure out why he cared. "It's beautiful," she said.

He nodded, but his lower lip pouted out. He still didn't look happy. "I lived on Heffe for, oh, about seven or eight years," he said. Then he looked at her, like he was sizing her up. "You must have been a puppy when…"

"Yes," she agreed. Neither of them wanted to refer directly to the evacuation of Heffe VIII. "I guess you lived there about as long as I did." She laughed at the realization. "What do you think? Does it look as beautiful as the Heffe you remember?"

Together, they stared at the image of a blue, gold, and green world, slowly turning on the vid screens.

"No," he said. "But memory does funny things to a place. Makes it glow."

Jeaunia turned her gaze back to the human man and tilted her head to the side. He looked old; he had the wrinkles on his face that naked-skinned species got when they aged. His head fur was thin, wispy, and gray. He'd have been an adult when he lived on Heffe. He'd seen it through an adult's eyes. "What brought you to Heffe VIII?" she asked.

"My understanding is that there weren't a lot of out-worlders who lived there…" It was strange to talk to an alien man who might know as much—or more—about her homeworld as she did. And he had the knowledge from a different angle than all the stories she'd heard from her mother and aunt.

The human frowned now and titled his head down, like he didn't want to answer the question. Eventually, he reluctantly said, "I was a solar physicist at Wespirtech, young and arrogant. The Petriezski government hired me as a consultant."

Jeaunia looked away from the human. Tears threatened to well up in her eyes. She looked upward and held her eyes wide, trying to stop them. But she couldn't stop her ears from flattening atop her head. "You're one of the scientists who accelerated the sun's expansion."

"I was part of the team, yes." He stuck a hand out. "My name's Alan."

Jeaunia didn't take the human's hand in her paw, and he let it fall back into his lap. She intended to glare at him. He shouldn't take his role in the past so lightly. He shouldn't dodge his responsibility for how things had unfolded. Their sun, a red giant, had been dying, but they'd have had another hundred years or so. Or maybe it was a thousand? Jeaunia wasn't actually sure. She hadn't studied the science. But she knew their sun's death had been slow, and after the Wespirtech scientists had tried their experiments, the expansion happened much faster.

Yet, as she watched the human's face, she could see he wasn't dodging responsibility. He was simply having a conversation, years after the fact. A conversation that he didn't have to have. Honestly, she was surprised he still cared about Heffe at all. Still, she couldn't stop herself from asking, "Have you blown any other suns up since then?"

"I don't do physics anymore," the human said. "I stopped after… that."

Jeaunia nodded curtly, but she kept sitting beside Alan.

"I was trying to help…" Alan said weakly. "It wasn't supposed to…"

"I don't care," Jeaunia cut him off. She didn't want to listen to his guilt. Still, it intrigued her that he looked so consumed by it. The more she thought about it, she realized she'd seen Alan around the Heffen sections of Crossroads Station before, buying Golan food, attending plays put on by the Heffen Actors' Guild, and watching the pups on the playgrounds.

"Are you planning to go to New Heffe?" she asked him suddenly.

"Oh, no, no," Alan said, clearly uncomfortable with the question. He probably thought he wouldn't be welcome there. And he might not be. Even so, Jeaunia wasn't sure how welcome he felt here.

"Are you sure?" she asked. "I feel like I've seen you around the Heffen parts of the station a lot."

Alan didn't have anything to say to that, and their conversation awkwardly petered out. Eventually, he excused himself and hurried away from the playground, heading in the direction of the more human parts of the station.

Jeaunia watched him go, and she wondered how old he'd been when he came to Heffe VIII as an arrogant, young scientist. Possibly the age that she was now. And yet, his life seemed to be as consumed by the destruction of her homeworld—her species' cradle in the universe and her own personal childhood—as her own life.

Jeaunia's pendant computer buzzed again, and she opened the locket to see more messages from her cousins. "*Where are you?*" "*Are you coming?*" "*We don't want to start making choices without you...*" Except, of course, they would.

And they should.

"Go ahead," Jeaunia messaged back. "I'll be there shortly, but you don't have to wait."

In response, she was barraged with messages asking, "*Are you sure???*" But she'd already told them what to expect from her.

Jeaunia took her time strolling through the metal corridors of Crossroads Station. By the time she arrived at Aunt Kally's quarters, the small front room was packed full of her relatives—everyone except her own mother and sister—and they were all arguing heatedly, passionately, but civilly about several different cities planned for the northern end of one of the gold-green continents of New Heffe. One was closer to an ocean. Another was cheaper. Yet a third sounded like it was likely to have a powerful art scene—many actors, musicians, and writers were already planning to buy lots there.

Jeaunia sat cross-legged on the floor, like one of the pups she'd watched all afternoon, and listened to the animated arguments rage back and forth. These were the people who'd be on New Heffe—adults with their own lives, not the young cousins she remembered playing with among the trees.

One of her cousin's pups, a boy named Ojo, came peeking out from Aunt Kally's bedroom where the rest of his litter was probably playing games. He scurried into the middle of the room and crawled into Jeaunia's lap.

The little boy turned his muzzle up close enough that she could feel the breath from his nose on her ear. He whispered, "Are we really all leaving? This is my home. I don't want to leave Crossroads Station."

Jeaunia squeezed Ojo around his fuzzy middle. "Don't you want a new home? Don't you want to live surrounded by trees and grassy plains? With a big blue sky above you?" she whispered back.

Ojo shook his head fiercely. "There are trees in the arboretum. And I don't want some stupid blue sky blocking out the stars. Or for the gravity to be *the same everywhere*. So boring!"

Jeaunia wanted to laugh, but instead she nodded solemnly. This was where he'd grown up. For Ojo, leaving Crossroads Station because his parents decided to move away wasn't all that different from when she'd had to leave Old Heffe.

"Tell you what," she whispered back. "What if I stay here, and you can come visit me when you're older?"

Ojo didn't answer right away, and Jeaunia realized the room had fallen silent around them. All of her cousins and her Aunt Kally were watching her. They'd heard what she'd said to the pup.

Besker asked, "You're not moving to New Heffe?"

Jeaunia tried to speak, but all her words got tangled up. She hadn't really thought this through yet, but she already had a whole room full of family looking at her expectantly, waiting for her to sort her life out to their liking. It might not be so bad to have some distance from them. Her friend Aga had been telling her that for years, but she'd been too afraid to listen. This was her family.

"Of course she's moving to New Heffe," Aunt Kally said to all the others. Her tone superior. "She's just trying to make Ojo feel better."

The presumptuousness of Aunt Kally's statement made Jeaunia angry, but she felt too tired to argue. She didn't want to explain herself or her uncertainty to everyone here. None of them would understand—they were worried about big things like where to raise their pups and long-standing feuds over inheritances. Jeaunia didn't want to pick sides. She simply wanted to spend time with all of them.

But that wasn't going to happen—here or on New Heffe. They'd all been too busy for her for a long time now.

She thought about Alan, still consumed by a disaster that had happened to someone else's world, trapped in the past. She didn't want her life to be defined by a disaster in the past. And truly, it hadn't been. She was happy here. The promise of New Heffe had always been tantalizing, but it hadn't stopped her from enjoying her life. It hadn't stopped her from spending time with Aga while they worked.

Then she thought about Ojo—and all the pups she watched at the daycare with Aga every day—and how they'd never lived on a planet.

Only here. On Crossroads Station. To them, a space station was enough. It was home. And it was beautiful.

Maybe Jeaunia hadn't been looking forward to the promise of a new world so much as she'd been looking back, missing her childhood. But her childhood was over, and a new planet wouldn't bring it back. A new planet wouldn't make her cousins young again; wouldn't erase their arguments and differing priorities; wouldn't make life easy.

"I can't make you and Mama get along with each other," Jeaunia told her aunt. "And I can't make her give you her money. But I do know that I don't want to be in the middle of it. I have a life here. Maybe when you're all settled, I'll come visit. Maybe I'll even want to stay. But for now? No, I'm not moving to New Heffe. And maybe not ever."

Jeaunia gave Ojo another squeeze and then eased him off of her lap. She left Aunt Kally's quarters before any of them could figure out what to say.

Jeaunia walked back through the halls of Crossroads Station to her own quarters. Her quarters might not be filled with trees or surrounded by grasslands. But they were her own small rooms, filled with the pieces of her own life. And she was looking forward to waking up in the morning and telling Aga she was going to stay. They hadn't talked about it earlier, because Jeaunia knew it would have been too hard. Maybe tomorrow, Jeaunia would finally ask her out. Maybe she'd take her some flowers, too.

And maybe when Jeaunia did go visit her family on New Heffe, Aga would come along, and they could visit their people's new homeworld together. For now, though, it was time to get serious about her life on Crossroads Station, instead of waiting for an imaginary future.

About the Authors

M. R. Anglin

M.R. Anglin is an imaginative author who explores tons of new worlds and cultures throughout her various novels and stories. When her writing's done she returns to her home in Florida where she draws, crafts, and sews—sometimes well.

The first book in her ongoing *Silver Foxes* series (also entitled *Silver Foxes*) underwent a severe revision/update and was re-released early 2018 in order to better flow with the remainder of the books: *Winds of Change, Prelude to War, Into Expermia, Interlude: a Series of Shorts,* and *Celebrity Dish.* Her other works include *Lucas, Guardian of Truth* (LampPost 2012) and *Prince of the Sun, Princess of the Moon* (CleanReads 2018) as well as short stories included in the anthologies *Gods with Fur* (FurPlanet 2016), *Dogs of War Vol. 2* (FurPlanet 2017), and *Extinct* (WolfSinger 2017).

Adam Baker

Adam Baker is a dedicated screenwriter currently residing in Texas. He was born in 1985. Inspired by whiskey and influenced by the likes of H.P. Lovecraft and Stephen King, Adam loves all things horror. Since the debut of his found footage short film *Angler,* he continues to work on his comedy web series *Swatters.* Check it out on YouTube!

In his spare time he enjoys writing, watching and creating films. Contact him at adam.baker214@gmail.com

Cairyn

Ronald W. Klemp, a.k.a Cairyn, was born in 1964 in Northern Germany and became acquainted early on with science fiction and fantasy literature. Despite these leanings, he chose computer science as his professional career; the starving poet firmly in mind. As one of the first German furries, Cairyn has been actively (not to say obsessively) involved with anthropomorphic characters since the early '90s. He is one of the founding members and main staffers of Eurofurence, the European furry convention held in Germany.

As an author, he has been writing several short stories and the novel *Khiray of the River*, serialized online during the 1990s and published in both German and English since then. He is currently working on a new novel and a too-slowly growing array of CGI character designs.

Amy Fontaine

Amy Fontaine has studied hyenas, wolves, and other creatures as a wildlife biologist since earning her bachelor's degree from Humboldt State University in 2015. Her work has taken her to beautiful places, including Yellowstone National Park, the Sierra Nevada, the Gila National Forest, and the Maasai Mara National Reserve in Kenya. Exploring new places is one of her favorite things to do. Amy's experiences with animals in the wilderness influence much of her fiction and poetry. Since she loves to daydream, fantasy and science fiction are her preferred genres. She enjoys imagining what the world could be and hopes to inspire a sense of wonder in her readers. In addition to writing, traveling, and conducting research on wild animals, Amy likes to play guitar and draw. Her fiction has been nominated for two Leo Literary Awards and one Cóyotl Award. You can find more of her published work at https://amyfontaine.wordpress.com.

Vixyy Fox

I have been writing as Vixyy Fox from somewhere around the year 2000. Oddly enough, or not so oddly, it was the finding of Dark Natasha's artwork that solidified who I am as the funny little Fennec who is everyone's grandmother. Vixyy is my totem, and when we found her image, she told me, 'That's me… that's who I am.' It's times like this where one might question their sanity, but personal things like this touch the soul. I asked Dark if I could use the image and she agreed.

Since that time I have never stopped writing. After several books and countless short stories, I can now look back and say with certainty, 'You don't have to be crazy to be a writer, but it certainly does help.'

Geoff Galt

Geoff Galt started creating at a young age with the Newgrounds animation community. While working at *Cyanide & Happiness*, he partnered up with two of his friends to collaborate on the Umbra's Legion saga. Galt is no longer at *Cyanide & Happiness*, but the trio still hope to share more exciting adventures with interested readers in this expansive universe they've created.

Pepper Hume

Pepper Hume is an artist who deals in pictures and words, just never trust her with numbers! Being a refugee from the gypsy life of professional theatre design, she tends to think in four dimensions, often in reverse. Add compulsive people-watching and an addiction to reading, and that's why she writes. She is also addicted to the conversational dynamics of classical music and plans to write a story someday that exactly matches the dynamics of Ravel's *Concerto for the Left Hand*. Nonetheless, the only Pepper Hume on Facebook is a nice little old widow lady whose cat, a notoriously picky eater, recently gifted her with a headless dead squirrel on her birthday.

Dan Leinir Turthra Jensen

Dan, or Leinir as they are more commonly known, hails from the tiny country of Denmark, but resides in England, where they live with their partner of many years writing science fiction and making food that some people have described with a variety of superlatives. Since leaving university, they have worked for several companies as a software developer, working primarily on free and open source software. They have also been known to dress up as a fluffy cat type thing, and a blue bird type thing, and enjoys spending a relaxing time and a bottle of wine shared with friends.

Kary M. Jomb

Kary M. Jomb is a shadow mage who accidentally summoned a wormhole and fell into a twisted, sideways dimension where the animals talk, robots walk among us, and fairies hide in the flowers. She loves daffodils, sparkling water, and dark chocolate. She spends her time writing in coffee shops but doesn't drink coffee. Kary lives on the side of a hill in a liberal college town in the Pacific Northwest. She wants to thank Mary E. Lowd for the opportunity to write in her universe.

Frank LeRenard

Frank LeRenard is the pen name of someone who, at the time of this publication, lives and works as an astronomer in Finland.

Alan Loewen

Born in late 1954 in Easthampton, New York, in his early years, Alan Loewen became an avid reader, devouring fantasy and science fiction as fast as he could read. His favorite novels to this day will always be H. G. Wells' *War of the Worlds* along with Jules Verne's *Journey to the Center of the Earth*. Loewen knows that his writing did not originate in a vacuum and acknowledges he stands on the shoulders of giants who have inspired him over the years: C. S. Lewis, H. P. Lovecraft, Alan Garner, Robert Holdstock, and many others.

Loewen's stories come from a plethora of experience he has gathered over the years in working as a factory worker, inner-city security guard, park ranger, youth worker, radio personality, stage actor, stage and parlor magician, an ordained member of the clergy, computer salesman, counselor for mood disorders, life coach, and a host of other vocations.

A lover of cinema, cats, neolithic survivals, oriental cuisine, gardening, used bookstores, old houses, and sacred architecture, Loewen presently lives in Pennsylvania. Married and with three sons, he shares his home with a Sheltie named Socrates and way too many cats. You can follow him at alanloewen.blogspot.com

Mary E. Lowd

Mary E. Lowd writes stories and collects creatures. She's had more than one hundred short stories published, and her novels include the *Otters In Space* trilogy, *In a Dog's World*, and *The Snake's Song: A Labyrinth of Souls Novel*. Her fiction has won an Ursa Major Award and two Cóyotl Awards. Meanwhile, she's collected a husband, daughter, son, bevy of cats and dogs, and the occasional fish. The stories, creatures, and Mary live together in a crashed spaceship disguised as a house, hidden inside a fairy's garden in Oregon. Learn more at marylowd.com.

MikasiWolf

MikasiWolf travels through yet another world as told by him, braving angry lizards and suspicious Mercfolk. Like Keeshod, he'd been finding purpose in life through his Writer's Pilgrimage, also known as "experimenting and submitting". Sometimes, the enemy comes from within, none other than the ancient demons Writersblock and Lethargy. Inspiration and Enthusiasm works are the only known counter-spells to exist. When he's not pilgrimaging, Mikasi masquerades as a Design Engineer to fund his pilgrimaging. Things always come full circle, for balance must be maintained.

Mikasi hopes to someday experience the Novel Publication, one of many end destinations of his pilgrimage. For the WordFolk, the journey never ends. Several completed pilgrimages includes Furplanet Productions' *The Furry Future* (2015), *Gods With Fur* (2016), *Dogs of War* (2017), and *Dogs of War II* (2017), Jaffa Books' *Claw the Way to Victory* (2016), Thurston Howl Publications' *What the Fox?!* (2018), and the upcoming *Furry Trash*, *BREEDS: Foxes*, and *SLASHERS* anthologies. He currently hides in the follow lairs:

https://twitter.com/MikasiWolf
http://www.furaffinity.net/user/mikasiwolf

He doesn't mind the occasional message posted to his lair. After all, his tomahawk and spear-throwing skills have only a 70% chance of success.

Michael H. Payne

Michael H. Payne's stories about Cluny the sorceress squirrel have appeared in 11 volumes of the *Sword and Sorceress* anthology, and his novels *The Blood Jaguar* and *Rat's Reputation* are currently available from Sofawolf Press. His webcomics *Daily Grind* and *Terebinth* appear six times a week at pandora.xepher.net, and he hosts *The Darkling Eclectica*, a weekly radio program full of music and stories, every Sunday afternoon from 4 till 6 over KUCI in Irvine, California. He writes and curates *My Little Pony* fanfiction for the websites of Equestria Daily and the Royal Canterlot Library, and he'd like to give extra special thanks to the writing community at writeoff.me without whom his story in this volume simply wouldn't exist.

Cathy Smith

Cathy Smith is an aboriginal writer who lives on an Indian Reservation within Canada. Her people have a long tradition of animal tales. Plus her cats' antics inspire more stories. She always seems to get the goofy ones when she adopts a kitty. Modern day cats are less mythic than the animals in her people's folktales, although they are a lot funnier. It's like having a comedian in the house.

She has nine publication credits. She has also won an honorable mention from the L. Ron Hubbard's Writers of the Future contest and is a co-winner of the 2016 Imagining Indigenous Futurism Contest. You can follow her latest projects at:

Mailing List: http://eepurl.com/cfyngI
Wordpress: bit.ly/2e41qWT
Facebook: bit.ly/2dP3rXd
Twitter: @khiatons
Instagram: @cathy2891

Thomas "Faux" Steele

Thomas "Faux" Steele began writing fiction after being inspired by a 9th grade writing assignment. He's an Arctic Fox whose works have been published in multiple conbooks and anthologies, most recently *Dogs of War Volume II*. He enjoys fast cars and travel when not studying foreign affairs and politics. In his free time, he enjoys reading fantasy, furry literature, and science fiction; coin collecting; and playing clarinet in his university's band.

Harwich Wolcott

Harwich Wolcott is a pen name because seriously, who would name their kid that?* The guy behind the pseudonym has been involved in this furry business since about 1993, mostly as a spectator, but increasingly as a contributor. Better late than never. He lives in Houston, Texas and does something with computers for a living. He's new to this "being published" thing, but hopes to do more of it in the future. If you run into him someplace, be sure to remind him that novels don't write themselves.

*Outerbridge Horsey III is my favorite funny name. He was a U.S. Senator from 1810 to 1821.—FP

About the Artist

Demicoeur

Demicoeur is a freelance artist from Toronto, currently living in the U.K. Demi started out in the furry fandom during her college days, taking on commissions to help pay her tuition. She attended Sheridan College and received her Bachelors in Animation, but by then animating wasn't floating her boat, so she continued freelancing and drawing comics on the side. Her current comic titles include *Cinderfrost*, *Tidal Wave*, and *The Silk Sash*. She enjoys a thoroughly boring lifestyle of drawing, writing, gardening (succulents are her favorite plants), and gaming. She hopes there will be more comics and novel writing in her future, and possibly a golden retriever puppy!

About the Editor

Fred Patten

Fred Patten (1940-current) joined the Los Angeles Science Fantasy Society in 1960 while in college, and has been an active s-f & fantasy fan ever since. He began writing for and publishing fanzines in 1961 (see http://www.zinewiki.com/Salamander), and has written over a thousand reviews of anthropomorphic literature since 1962, irregularly for s-f fanzines in the 1960s, 1970s, and 1980s; for *Yarf!* from 1990 to 2003, for *Claw & Quill* in 2004-2005, for *Anthro* from 2005 to 2008, for *Renard's Menagerie* in 2008, for *Flayrah* from 2011 to 2014, and for *Dogpatch Press* since 2014. He has written three non-fiction books and edited fourteen anthologies of furry fiction. He founded the Ursa Major Awards and has been on its administrative Anthropomorphic Literature and Arts Association since 2001. He is a member of the Furry Writers' Guild and the Furry Hall of Fame. He co-founded Japanese anime fandom in 1977, and was awarded the Comic-Con's Inkpot Award in 1980 for helping to introduce anime to America. He wrote a weekly column on animation, *Funny Animals and More*, for Jerry Beck's Cartoon Research from 2013 to 2017. A stroke in 2005 has left him hospitalized, from which he carries on his fanac.